SINS
OF
THE
FATHER

A Nathan Parker Detective Novel

SINS OF THE FATHER

A Nathan Parker Detective Novel

James L'Etoile

LEVEL
BEST BOOKS

First edition

ISBN: 978-1-68512-992-7

Cover art by Level Best Designs

This book was professionally typeset on Reedsy.
Find out more at reedsy.com

Chapter One

Death to a ten-year-old is a pause in a video game. It's temporary. A momentary setback until you're back into the game again. At their age, the boys of Boy Scout Troop 116 thought they were immortal. Or they did until they got their first glimpse of human remains.

Ken Dryden stood on the brakes, sending the fifteen-passenger van into a skid on the hard-packed desert road. A flock of eight turkey vultures pecked and tore hunks of flesh from their prey. The enormous birds didn't budge at the approach of the speeding white passenger van. Only one bothered to look up with a flap of meat hanging from its curved beak.

The birds ignored a loud burst from the van's horn. Dryden unbuckled and turned to the eight boys in the back. "Stay here."

Dryden and the assistant scoutmaster, Bill Cope, stepped from the van and approached the circle of birds.

"Must've found themselves a coyote or something," Cope said. "Why'd you insist we take this road? It's in the middle of—"

"This can't be..." Dryden trailed off and crept toward the flock of scavengers.

"Whatever they found, they sure don't want to give it up," Dryden said as he waved his arms trying to chase the birds off the road."

"Don't blame them. Pickings are probably a bit thin out here."

From behind, a high-pitched voice called out. "Oh, cool. What did they kill?"

Dryden turned, and three ten-year-old boys stood a few feet away, gawking at the feeding frenzy on the hardscrabble dirt road.

"I told you guys to wait in the van."

"What did they find?" The tallest boy asked.

"Probably a coyote or something run over on the road, Chase."

"There's no tracks in the dirt but ours," Chase said.

The birds fought and squawked at one another, tearing bits of flesh out from the beaks of weaker birds in the flock. Wings flared and cupped over the remains, claiming them.

"Mr. Dryden? What's that?" Chase asked.

"What?"

"That," the boy said with a trembling finger, pointing toward the largest vulture with a torn hunk of flesh hanging from its red beak.

Dryden followed the boy's line of sight, and under the bird's talons were the remains. He felt sick when he saw it. A brown work boot. Coyotes didn't wear boots.

"Oh my God."

"Is it a dead person? Chase said.

"Back to the van boys," Cope said.

"But—"

"Now!" Dryden barked the order, and the three scouts scurried back to the van.

"Why did you take us on this back road to begin with? What do we do now?" Cope asked Dryden. The two adult supervisors of this scout troop stood at the desert crossroads.

Cope pulled out his cell phone. "No signal out here. We need to call 911."

Dryden looked back to the van and all eight boys pressed up against the windows, gawking at the human remains as the carrion birds devoured their treasure.

"We gotta get them outta here," Dryden said.

He charged the birds, and most of them backed away. Dryden got a good look at what lay in the desert crossroads—a man, twisted, mangled, and broken, with huge swaths of flesh torn away by the feeding birds. Dryden's shoulders drooped at the sight—a dead man left in the crossroads.

"I'll try and keep them away. Drive the boys back out to Quartzite. Call

911. I'll wait."

"You wanna stay out here? In this heat?" Cope said.

"It's early, the heat won't top out for a couple of hours. I'll take my pack and all the water we can spare. I'll be fine. There's a little shade over there under that Palo Verde."

Tall, dry creosote brush, gangly green Palo Verde trees, and Saguaro cactus lined the crossroads.

"You sure? It's not like you can help that guy?"

"Whoever he is, he doesn't deserve to get eaten by these feathered desert rats either. How would you feel if it was someone you knew?"

Dryden retrieved his day pack and two canteens from the van.

"Guys, Mr. Cope is going to take you out. He'll stop in Quartzite for a pee break."

"I'll stay with you, Mr. Dryden," Chase said.

"Everyone's going with Mr. Cope."

A sigh of disappointment filled the back of the van. Dryden knew Chase's mother was going to melt down over her precious offspring's exposure to the dark fringes of life. He figured the Scottsdale socialite would spirit her son away to a resort in Sedona for a crystal bath and chakra realignment.

Dryden hefted his pack and slung the canteens over his shoulder while the van cut a three-point turn and returned in the direction they came.

Once the dust and engine noise died down, all that remained was the breeze cutting through the dried brush and the cackling of the vultures fighting over their prize.

Setting his pack down, Dryden broke off a creosote branch and swung it in front of him, forcing the birds away from the remains. Reluctantly, the birds gave up and hopped to the other side of the crossroads.

Dryden closed in on the dead man and grimaced at the mess the vultures made. Unrecognizable. Legs twisted and folded under the body, with a boot sticking out at an impossible angle. No way Chase would earn his first aid merit badge here.

The arms were flayed out over his broken head.

"Oh God."

Dryden noted the wrists bound with zip ties. This wasn't a lost hiker. This was a murder victim.

He snatched his cell phone and tried calling Cope to warn him, but the screen reminded him there was no cell signal out here. He shot a series of photos of the dead man, figuring the police would want to see what they found before the vultures could finish it off.

Dryden backed off into the shade and moved out when the vultures grew brave enough to advance. Back and forth for an hour until Dryden spotted a dust trail.

It was too soon for Cope to have summoned help. Quartzite was more than an hour away, and the authorities would need time to respond after Cope called them. And this dust plume was coming from the other direction and building fast.

A dead man. Murdered. Alone in the desert. Only a twinge of relief, it wasn't someone he knew. He knew what that kind of loss felt like and felt guilty about feeling thankful. The dust plume was coming in fast and there was the faint whine of an ATV engine—high pitched and loud.

Dryden snatched his pack and blended into the brush along a game trail, hoping he didn't encounter an unfriendly javelina. Fifty feet from the road, he hunched down as a green ATV tore into the crossroads and skidded to a stop a few feet away from the body.

Two men stepped from the six-wheel ATV, and one used a bulky satellite phone. After a quick call, the two men donned gloves and picked up the remains, tossing them into the rear cargo compartment of the ATV. They weren't gentle about it—they were hurried. They needed several trips to gather the bits and pieces.

Once they finished loading the dead man, they sped off in the direction they came from.

Dryden waited until the dust plume died down before he stepped out from his hiding place. He approached the spot in the center of the crossroads where the body had been. There was little to prove a life ended there. The red dirt was marked by a dark circle—what Dryden believed was blood. A single human finger was left behind by the men on the ATV.

A second trail of dust appeared on the horizon in the direction Cope and the boys used on their way out.

Dryden sank back into the brush again until the Black and Yellow Maricopa County Sheriff's Office SUV pulled to a stop near the intersection.

He couldn't stop thinking about the finger. Had they left the finger by mistake, or was it a message?

Chapter Two

Sergeant Nathan Parker, the detective leading the Maricopa County Major Crimes unit, pulled his county-issued SUV to a stop at the dirt crossroads.

"You sure this is the spot?"

Cope, the assistant scoutmaster, had ridden along with him to make sure Parker found the exact location. One of the parents met Cope in Quartzite and drove the van of excited boys back to Scottsdale while Cope waited for someone from the sheriff's office.

"I'm certain. I mean, I think I am. The dead man was right in the center of the intersection." He pointed ahead. "There. See the dark spot in the dirt?"

Parker opened his door and stepped from the SUV.

"Didn't you say your friend was supposed to be here watching over the remains? They didn't both walk off, did they?"

Parker thought he'd been brought out on a desert snipe hunt of sorts if it weren't for Cope's dead serious demeanor. The man definitely believed he saw a body out here in the remote section of the desert south of the Hummingbird Wilderness Area.

Walking toward the spot Cope pointed out, Parker figured the man panicked when he came across the scavenged remains of a road kill animal. It wasn't unusual for deer, coyotes, or javelina to wander down from the wilderness.

Cope got out of the SUV when Parker reached the spot. It was blood-soaked. But there wasn't anything to point to a human origin. What was odd was a set of narrow tracks, tracks with deep, aggressive off-road tread, circling near the blood spill. Two sets of footprints ran from the tire tracks to the dark dirt patch.

"Where'd it go?" Cope asked a few paces behind Parker.

A rustle and snap in the brush to their left caught their attention. It sounded too large for the small game that thrived in the creosote brush. Seconds later, a man emerged from behind a tangle of Palo Verde branches.

"Ken! You all right?" Cope called out to his friend.

Dryden was red-faced and breathing fast when he stepped onto the road surface.

"Deputy. Two men. Took him," Dryden said in between ragged breaths.

"Ken? Where's your pack? Your water?" Cope asked.

Dryden shot a finger to the brush where he'd emerged. "Dropped them."

Parker noted the man wasn't sweating in the hundred-degree heat and showed signs of heat stroke.

"Let's load him in the SUV. Get him some water and let him cool off."

Cope helped his weak friend back to the passenger side of the SUV while Parker looked at the dried, darkened dirt patch for a moment. Something bled out here, but there wasn't anything to tell the story of what might have been.

Parker joined the two men at the SUV. Cope had gotten his friend into the passenger seat and found the case of bottled water Parker kept in the backseat. Heat-related sickness was a deadly threat in the desert. Last year, six hundred forty-five people died in Maricopa County from heat stroke and exposure.

Cope handed Parker a cell phone. "It's Ken's. He captured these."

The small phone screen displayed a disturbing image of a man, freshly disfigured and broken.

"You saw this?"

Cope shook his head. "Yeah, and so did the kids. What happened to him? I mean. He's—did the vultures do the damage?"

Parker slid his thumb to the next photo. The one showing the man's hands bound.

"Definitely not." Parker couldn't explain the severity of the crushing and bone-breaking trauma. It was the worst he'd seen in nearly fifteen years on the job. He'd discovered migrants left in shipping containers, Cartel assassinations, beheadings, and vehicular homicides. Nothing came close to the injuries in the photos.

"These remains were here when you left your partner behind?" Parker asked.

"They were right there, I swear. Ken wanted to stay behind and—how do you say it? Preserve the evidence. Those damn vultures were picking him apart. It didn't seem right, you know?"

"Think he can tell us what happened to them?"

Cope looked back to the passenger seat. Dryden had his head back sipping on a bottle of water. The man was thin to begin with; an L.L. Bean shirt and day-old beard growth didn't make him an outdoorsman.

"I don't think he did anything with them, if that's what you're getting at," Cope said.

"No. I don't think he did. They disappeared somewhere, and your friend was in the best place to see what happened."

Parker stepped around Cope and opened the driver's door. A waft of cool air-conditioned breeze hit him in the face. He gestured for Cope to hop in the back seat and out of the heat.

"How you feeling, Mr. Dryden?"

"Better. Thanks." He held up the water bottle."

"Mr. Cope here tells me when he left you behind, there was a full set of remains out there on the road. What happened to them?"

"Two men. They rode in on one of those six-wheel ATVs from that direction." He pointed to the road heading east. "They took him—the body—they grabbed up the pieces and tossed them in the back of the ATV. Then they ran back to wherever they came from."

"They took him?"

"And they didn't have an easy time of it. They needed a bunch of trips to get..."

"You get a look at the two guys?"

"Oh, I found this after they left." Dryden pulled a handkerchief from his shirt pocket and handed it to Parker.

As Parker unwrapped it, Dryden said, "I couldn't risk the vultures flying off with it."

Parker had a bad feeling about unwrapping the package. The last fold stuck to the torn skin and tissue clinging to a human finger. He wrapped it back up carefully. He pulled a small paper evidence bag from the center console and dropped the body part in the brown paper container.

"Who could do that to a human being? Animals. Why'd they leave that behind?" Dryden said.

"Couldn't say. Maybe they were in a hurry," Parker said.

"They were moving pretty fast when they left."

Dryden's eyes held back something. Parker figured it was shock from the discovery or heat stroke. The guy was going to need years of therapy to get past this moment.

"I'm going to need these photos. I've called in our people to go over the scene. They can give you guys a ride back to civilization."

As Parker pulled his cell phone out, Cope said, "No signal out here."

Parker glanced at his screen and confirmed as much. Reluctantly, he reached for the SUV's radio. Transmitting a request for crime scene technical support would alert the media hounds who monitored the channel. At least he wouldn't be asking for a coroner to respond, which would inevitably attract news crews like bees to honey.

He made the radio call and snapped a series of photographs of the scene with his cell phone. The warm breeze coming from the south marked the potential for monsoon weather. Any evidence out here would be washed away. The deep ruts worn in the soil crossing the roadway testified flash flooding was a possibility in the remote desert drainage.

Parker caught photos of the quickly drying bloodstained soil at the center of the crossroads. The size of the stain had shrunk by half since he'd arrived at the location. The desert had a way of reclaiming any sign of life. It was the way of nature. It was the way of life in the harsh environment where man was simply another source of sustenance.

The ATV tracks leading east were disappearing in the wind-blown topsoil.

9

The fine dust returning to its natural state. A section of tracks, sheltered by a wall of thick creosote brush, maintained the deep V pattern left by the off-road tread. Hundreds of weekend hobby riders ran their motorcycles and ATVs out in the desert on the weekends, and Parker hoped the photo would show some anomaly on the tread pattern to single out a particular vehicle. He knew it was a long shot, but he needed to cover the bases.

Finished taking photos of the area, Parker noticed a plume of smoke to the east, a dark and boiling column of smoke. He couldn't shake the connection of the missing body and the sudden appearance of the smoke rising in the east.

Parker trotted back to the SUV, made a quick radio call reporting the smoke and possible woodland fire near the wilderness border. He tossed a traffic cone out on the desert track near the blood-soaked dirt. Maybe the crime scene analysts could find something to hint at why the body was dumped there—and why it vanished.

"How you doing, Mr. Dryden?"

"Better, thanks."

"I want to go check this out up ahead—don't think it's far, maybe a couple of miles. You up for it?"

"I guess."

"I want to get you checked out by medical, they're on their way and they'll meet us up the road."

"What about the guys who moved that body? Won't they be up there, too?"

"If they were in as much of a hurry as you said they were, probably not."

Parker pulled the SUV into drive and swung hard around the bloodstained soil—not so much for destroying any evidence left behind, but out of reverence. A life might have ended there on the patch of dust.

Parker shot up the heavy, rutted road to the east, bouncing along the trail as the dark smoke plume beckoned in the distance.

Two miles from the crossroad, Parker turned a slight corner to the right and found a small shack in flames. It was likely an abandoned, decades-old silver mining camp. No sign of an ATV or the two men who Dryden watched. But Parker had a bad feeling about what lay inside the burning shack.

"Stay put," Parker said, as he pulled the SUV to a stop at a distance from the burning shack.

He grabbed a fire extinguisher from the rear of the SUV and trotted toward the structure. Most of the flames were coming from the inside of the wooden structure. They had burned up and through what remained of the wooden roof.

He shot a burst of white powder from the extinguisher at the doorframe, and the tendrils diminished for a moment. Enough for him to spot human remains on the floor in the center of the blaze.

Chapter Three

Parker emptied the extinguisher at the base of the flames near the body. The powder sputtered out, and the blaze temporarily weakened before it rebuilt again, consuming the tinder-dry wooden siding on the exterior of the building.

Nathan fell back to the SUV and tossed the empty extinguisher in the dirt, watching the flames consume the corpse. Someone was being careful about leaving evidence behind.

By the time the first Maricopa County units pulled to the scene, the shack had collapsed around the body, and the smoke dissipated.

A black SUV pulled next to Parker. Detectives Pete Tully and Barry Johns joined him.

"Nice day for a barbecue, boss," Tully said. He'd left his usual tweed sports coat behind, and his sleeves were rolled up, messing with his professorial image.

"Not so good for the guy inside."

"Yeah, makes for a bad day."

Barry Johns, six-and-a-half feet tall, muscular former college football standout, glanced in Parker's SUV at the two men inside.

"What's their tie to the dead guy?"

Parker turned and saw both men staring at the burning embers. "Dryden in the front seat caught these." He handed Barry the cell phone he'd taken from the man. "Came upon the body back at the crossroads. Two men on an ATV scraped the dead guy up and apparently gave him an impromptu cremation."

Barry leaned to Tully and shared the images. "Damn. This dude was messed up. Your witness see what happened to him?"

"No. They were driving a van full of Boy Scouts and found him in the middle of the road."

"Now, there's a merit badge for you," Pete said.

"The injuries. They're—extreme," Johns said.

"Those photos might be the best we have to work with. With the body incinerated, the medical examiner will need to put the puzzle pieces back together to figure out how this guy died."

The rumble of a lime green U.S. Forest Service fire engine sounded as the bulky vehicle pulled into the clearing.

Two firefighters exited the crew cab, and one pulled a black hose from a reel mounted behind the cab. The other firefighter came to Parker and the detectives. Black stitched letters on his yellow Nomex said his name was Tiller, the crew engineer.

"You call this in?" Tiller asked.

"I did," Parker said. "We've got a body in there. Try and preserve as much of the scene as possible." Parker had seen what a straight stream of water from a fire hose could do to a body.

"I'll let 'em know and we'll do what we can."

"Leave it in place. We'll have our crime scene people and the medical examiner take it from there."

"No worries there. I don't wanna mess with it."

The engineer returned to his crew, and they attacked the flames from the outside, directing the hose on the remnants of the burning shack that had tumbled in on itself. Within five minutes, only wisps of steam came from the ruins.

The crime scene unit pulled into the clearing, followed by the medical examiner's van. Parker turned to Johns and Tully.

"I didn't call the M.E. No signal and hadn't found a body."

"I don't think they're psychic—yet," Tully said.

Parker met the M.E.'s van and met Dr. Kelly Sherman as she stepped from the dark blue vehicle. Sherman was the county's chief medicolegal forensic pathologist.

"Doctor, how'd you find out about our little get together? I was about to contact you."

"It seems mom picked up her son from a hike, and the boys were worked up over a dead body their scoutmaster found. Mom is connected with the Scottsdale social scene, she got to chatting with the other moms expressing outrage at what their poor offspring were exposed to. One of the other moms is the ex-wife of Tony Oliveira."

"Oliveira, as in County Board of Supervisors?"

"As in the county budget chairman who holds the purse strings for my office."

"So here you are."

"What can you tell me? Is our body in there?" she said, glancing at the glowing embers of what was left of the mining shack.

"'Fraid so. The guys in my truck found him back at the crossroads you passed." He handed the cell phone with the photographs to Dr. Sherman.

"The one sitting in my front seat stayed behind while his buddy drove the kids back to town. Claims two guys scooped up what was left of the guy and—well, I think you've figured out what happened next."

"Did they run this guy over? All kinds of crush trauma and symmetrical long bone injuries from what I can see on this small photo."

"They claim they found him that way. I'll look their van over. Might be some trace left on the undercarriage if they ran him down."

She handed the phone back to Parker. Hard to tell from those photos, but he died hours ago-I don't think they hit him with their vehicle either. One of those photos showed injuries just above the ankles. If they hit him with a van, those injuries would be femur height."

"They did find one finger when the body was moved. It's in the SUV."

"I'll need that."

Dr. Sherman stepped to the edge of the smoldering remains. It was kicking off heat to her outstretched palm. "We need to extricate our remains before this heat ruins any forensic trace."

Parker gestured to the fire crew, and they began using McClouds and

Fire Rakes to peel away layers of debris. The hot, dried, charred lumber was pockmarked with glowing red embers as the firefighters pulled them off the pile.

A few minutes of labor and the first peek at the remains revealed themselves pinned under a thick roof rafter. Dr. Sherman directed a slim young man dressed in blue coveralls to take photos of the body in situ before the rafter was removed. It was going to be a painstaking process to determine which injuries occurred as a result of the fire, and even more so for the cause of death.

Slow, deliberate work cleared the debris from the body. It was clear whoever dumped the body was in a hurry. It was tossed in a heap, probably in pieces, as they unloaded the ATV.

Parker glanced around the clearing, and the ATV wasn't hidden away in the brush lining the dirt roads in and out of the area. Slight indentations on the road surface leading away from the shack trailed off to the east.

"Pete, I need you to debrief our witnesses and collect their statements before we lose them to the EMTs. Cope's probably going to ride in with his buddy Dryden."

"I'll take care of it."

"Tell Dryden to forward these crime scene photos to you. They're the best we've got, showing the condition of the body before it was torched."

Parker handed him the cell phone and had no trouble finding Barry Johns among the fire crew, medical examiner's technicians, and crime scene analysts now combing through the scene. He was the tallest person in the area and loomed over Dr. Sherman as she directed the excavation and preliminary examination of the body.

Johns caught Parker looking in his direction. He held up two fingers. Dr. Sherman stepped back from the charred tangle of remains.

Sherman pulled her mask down and found Parker.

"Detective, you've got a second victim in there."

Chapter Four

Parker leaned and looked over Dr. Sherman's shoulder. "Two bodies?"

"It's kind of what I do, detective. We have multiple victims here."

The heat was dissipating from the blaze, so Parker could approach the victims, careful to sidestep darkened piles of ash which might hide bone fragments. He used Dr. Sherman's footprints as a guide.

Unless the victim from the crossroads had sprouted another leg, a second victim lay amongst the charred wood and tangled body parts.

The sudden roof collapse prevented the fire from consuming more of the remains. The lower portion was saved from severe heat, and the pair of legs closest to him were intact and looked different from the body in Dryden's photo at the crossroads. The dead man wore heavy green canvas work pants—worn, but in serviceable shape. The lower portion of a gray t-shirt poked from under a heavy roof timber.

"Doc, any chance you can tell me time of death—on either of them?"

"The fire is going to complicate things. Though the unburned tissue on this one," she gestured to the body with green pants on the top of the pile, "There's not as much decomposition visible—much less than the body you showed me in the photo. I'm not going to be able to pinpoint time of death without lab work, but I'm certain he died long after John Doe number one."

From the side of the shed, one of Dr. Sherman's techs called out. "We're ready to lift the timber." The technician recruited a deputy, two firefighters, and a crime scene analyst to heft the large beam off the victims.

Parker moved a few steps back to give them space to work.

"Carefully, now. Conner, I want you in here with a camera as they lift. On three gentlemen."

The team lifted the heavy six-inch timber from the shed floor and sidestepped toward the rear of the shed in unison. Once clear of the structure, they dropped the beam to the desert soil.

Dr. Sherman crouched over the bodies and directed her technician to shoot more photographs of the scene. The crime scene analyst lined up another series of photos. This paparazzi display focused on the dead rather than a B-list celebrity, without the pop and whine of flashbulbs.

"Got your cause of death right here," Sherman said.

She pointed to John Doe number two's skull. He was face down, and his burned, sandy blonde hair was matted with blood. Blood which had flowed from a large wound in the back of his head.

"Gunshot wound?" Parker asked.

"Looks like it. The damned fire got this end of his body, and we have bone chipping from the heat. I'll be able to confirm when I get him back to the ranch."

Dr. Sherman and the crime scene techs continued their painstaking, methodical processing. They would only get one chance at the crime scene. Once the bodies were removed and the responders left the area, the desert would reclaim what was hers.

Parker joined Johns, who was making a hand-drawn sketch of the clearing, the shed, and the locations of the two victims in the burned structure.

"We didn't miss them by much. They torched this and split," Parker said.

"There's not much out this way. Wilderness, folks out on recreational vehicles, a meth lab or two. We're miles from any settlement, or town."

"You got this for a minute? Stay with Dr. Sherman and her people. I want to check out something."

"Sure. What you thinking?" Johns said.

"The ATV tracks. I want to follow them for a bit."

"We could call in for air support," Johns said.

Parker grinned. "Good idea. I know you think I'm old and stuck in my rocking chair, but even I can admit when you kids with your technology

17

come in handy."

"Boss—I didn't mean."

"Easy, Barry. I know."

Parker plodded to his SUV for the radio as the two witnesses, Dryden and Cope, shuffled to an ambulance for a ride back to Banner Memorial for an evaluation.

"Excuse me, Mr. Dryden. You didn't take any photos of the two men who removed the body from the crossroads?"

"No. No, I didn't. I didn't want to risk getting spotted. Figured if they were moving a body, I didn't want to make their acquaintance."

"You're probably right. You remember what they looked like?"

"I told Detective Tully."

"What were they wearing?"

"Wearing? I—I wasn't paying attention. No—wait. One of them—the guy doing most of the work—he was maybe six feet tall and had light brown hair."

The skin on the back of Parker's neck began to tingle.

"Recall what he wore?"

"What he wore—what he wore? Oh, I do remember. He had a red and green ball cap and tossed it in the ATV when they started—you know. But he wore green pants—like the national park service people do?"

"Got it. Yeah, I think I know the kind you mean. Take care of yourself, Mr. Dryden, and thanks for your help today."

Dryden half waved, and an EMT guided him to the rear of the ambulance for the ride to the hospital.

Tully joined Parker and watched as the EMT set up an IV to start rehydrating Dryden.

"He's got quite a story to tell back home."

"That he does."

"Too bad I don't believe a word of it," Tully said.

Parker stepped back and eyed his detective. Tully had nearly two decades on the force, and Parker had always relied on his instincts—what did he see that Parker missed?

"You think he lied about what he saw?"

"I believe he did find a body at the crossroads. After that, I have a gut feeling everything else is a lie."

"What makes you say that?"

"Nothing specific. It was the whole thing—what were they doing out here when the trailhead was back in the other direction? You only come out here if you're looking for something. What was he looking for? And, maybe I'm jaded by seeing too many shadows, but why was he here? He didn't even have a kid in the scout troop."

"What about his story about the men on the ATV?"

"The guy went all *CSI-Miami* on the body, taking photographs, making sure he—and we—saw what we needed to see. A body—badly beaten, in restraints, and dropped in the middle of the desert. Why didn't he take one photo—not a single one—of the guys in the ATV as they stole the remains away? I don't buy it."

Said he was afraid of getting spotted," Parker said.

"Even as the ATV headed down the road? No. Something's not right here."

"You think he's involved?"

"He's something. Mind if I run him down? See what he's about?"

"Can't hurt. If he's tied up in this, it puts a whole different spin on what happened out here. Let's see if he's got prints in the system, which I doubt, or a firearm registered to him—might link him to the second victim."

"I'm on it. I'm going to follow the ambulance in and show our 'witnesses' how concerned we are for their welfare. Can you give Barry a ride back?"

"Sounds like a plan."

Parker located a small rise some fifty feet from the activity at the shed. It was nothing more than spoils from the mine, and they had remained piled in this spot for over fifty years. It was only ten feet tall, but from the top, it gave Parker a view above the creosote brush and cactus covering this patch of desert. To the north, the foothills gave way to the Hummingbird Wilderness.

Parker swung around and gazed back toward the crossroads. He couldn't see the dirt road intersection to the west. He looked back to the Wilderness boundary.

If Dryden was driving his boys to or from the trailhead to the Hummingbird Wilderness, he wouldn't have been out here in this stretch of remote dirt track.

Maybe Pete Tully was onto something. Dryden wasn't telling the truth.

Chapter Five

Once the Medical Examiner had separated the remains, laid them out on plastic tarps, Dr. Sherman confirmed John Doe number 2, the man in the green work pants, was killed after the first John Doe.

Parker kneeled near the remains still in the work pants. "Doc, mind if I search his pockets? Looks like a wallet in his left hip pocket."

"He's yours. I can't do much more with him until he's on my table. Looks like GSW with no exit wound. Hopefully, I'll be able to retrieve a slug for you. I'm going to see what I can make out of his messed-up friend over here."

Parker put on a set of nitrile gloves and patted the victim's pockets. The body was warm to the touch—a sensation which felt off to a detective used to a cold corpse. A key fob in his front left pocket. Parker noted two silver keys, padlocks, maybe. They weren't house or auto keys.

Barry Johns held an open evidence bag for Parker, and he dropped the key fob in the paper container.

Parker pulled a thick leather wallet from the dead man's left rear pocket. "Let's see who we have here."

The first thing he saw when he opened the wallet was a badge. The identification card beneath the badge said Jeffery Clark. A Special Agent with the U.S. Department of Justice.

"DOJ? What's a fed doing out here?" Johns asked.

"What's he got to do with what's behind door number one?" Parker gestured to the flattened remains Dr. Sherman was documenting.

"Witness protection gone wrong?"

"Wit Sec is a Marshal's Service thing. DOJ wouldn't usually move a protectee."

Parker stood and dropped the wallet into the evidence bag.

Dr. Sherman kneeled near the broken, flattened skull of the first victim. She traced a finger along a visible fracture. The long bones were curved and broken.

"Detective, this one is going to be a puzzle. The heat from the fire damaged the bones and left us with warping and microfractures, or craquelle. The exposed bone is ashy gray with what appears to be lime deposits, meaning it was exposed to high temperatures, above five hundred degrees, perhaps as high as eleven hundred. I'll run a series of panels to be certain."

"Accelerant?"

"That's a question for the arson investigator, or your crime scene people. I wouldn't rule it out."

"You said he wasn't run down by a vehicle. How can you explain these injuries?"

Dr. Sherman leaned on her haunches. Her brow furrowed. "The only time I've seen similar injuries was a suicide we worked a few years back. A tax attorney jumped from Phoenix City Hall. Even his trauma wasn't this significant."

"The tallest thing around here is a ten-foot-tall saguaro. Wouldn't even sprain an ankle."

"I'm telling you what it looks like. I'll be able to narrow it down after some X-rays. If he's got compression fractures, then we'll know for sure."

Where would our victim fall from? No cliffs or waterfalls around here." Barry said.

Parker drew a deep breath. Trauma. More significant than leaping from a twenty-story skyscraper. He tossed his head back and exhaled. From the corner of his vision, a small private plane cruised through the blue sky.

"He was tossed from an airplane," Parker said.

Dr. Sherman nodded. "It's a possibility."

"Damn, what a way to go out," Johns said.

Parker followed the small airplane, and it seemed to descend on a slow path to the east.

"Barry, you know if there's an airport nearby?"

He shrugged.

One of the firefighters chimed in. "There's a small airfield about five miles out. No commercial operations. Mostly private, from what I know. We do run helitack and fire-retardant planes out of there during wildfire operations."

"I've done all I can do with these remains on site. Oh, the finger bone you turned over would seem to belong to our first victim. He's missing his right index finger. I'll confirm with tissue typing. That's what I can tell you now, Nathan."

"Thanks, Doc."

After the bodies were wrapped and sealed in body bags, the activity level diminished. The fire crews left, and the crime scene analysts were ready to bug out.

Parker called to a young CSI he recognized as William, who didn't like being called Willie, who was proving to have an eye for detail.

"William, on your way back out, I need you to take a look at something."

Parker explained the crossroads location where the body was first said to be found. He asked William to find any evidence of how the body ended up there. "Look for any trace evidence, or more missing pieces like the finger Dryden recovered."

He didn't tell the CSI the body was likely tossed from a plane. Parker wanted the young investigator to come to his own conclusions. If there was evidence of a fall and a sudden stop, William would find it.

Parker motioned Johns to the SUV.

"Got everything we need from here?" Parker asked.

Johns scanned the clearing. Only the burned patch of wooden debris and tire tracks remained.

"Dr. Sherman's people sifted through the ash for any human tissue left behind. They recovered a few sections of collapsed roofing with charred tissue from victim number 1. Victim 2 was fully intact, and Dr. Sherman got him out without much fanfare. I shot a hundred or so photos of the scene, the shed, the clearing, and the ATV tracks heading in and out of the area.

"Pete said you have him following up on our initial witnesses, Dryden and Cope? You think they'll give us more?" Johns said.

"Pete had a feeling Dryden wasn't telling us the truth. If he was coming back from a camping trip with his little minions, he was driving in the wrong direction. How and why was he out here in the middle of this empty patch of desert? The fact Dryden didn't take any photos of the two men in the ATV who moved the body seems fishy too."

"Pete's got an internal lie detector. I swear the man can sense when a suspect even thinks about spinning a tale."

"Which leaves us with the ATV trail to the east," Parker said.

The detectives climbed in, and the air conditioning hit them when Parker turned the ignition.

Parker pulled the gear shift and headed down the narrow dirt path. Barely wide enough for their SUV, the trail didn't show evidence of frequent use. A pair of ruts ran down the surface, narrower than Parker's SUV.

Dried tendrils of rush scraped and snapped off the driver's side of the SUV as Parker drove on.

"Sergeant Chen in the motor pool won't like this," Johns said.

"It'll buff out."

A mile and a half down the trail, Parker came to a chain-link fence with a padlocked gate. Beyond the barrier, waves of heat rose from the black tarmac of an airstrip. A line of metal buildings sat on the north side of the runway. Five single-engine airplanes were moored to their tie-down anchors on the opposite side.

An engine whined from the far end of the runway as a Cessna 172 rolled down the runway and climbed up over the desert.

"Can't turn around. I'll grab the bolt cutters," Johns said as he unbuckled his seat belt.

"You got the evidence bag with the key fob we found on the dead guy back there?"

Johns twisted and snagged the paper evidence bag from the back seat. Parker unsealed the bag and removed the key fob.

He slid from the driver's seat and tried one of the keys on the padlock. It didn't fit. The second one did and unlocked the gate. It slid back on rollers, allowing Parker to drive through the opening.

After closing the gate behind them, Parker piloted the SUV to the side of the runway where the metal buildings—hangars, he saw they were now, where one door stood ajar.

Inside the wide hangar was a green ATV and a stack of boxes in the process of going onto a small twin-engine plane. A rattle from inside the plane drew their attention.

Parker sent Johns to the right, covering the far side of the plane, while he circled to the other.

An open door to the airplane loomed ahead. A shadow moved beyond the opening.

"Sheriff's Office. Come out," Parker called, his voice echoing in the metal-skinned hangar.

A face peered out from the door.

"Detective Parker?"

Billie Carson stood in the open doorway.

Chapter Six

"Billie? What are you doing here?"

Billie Carson was a riddle. She and Parker first came together on a case where the Cartel set up a fentanyl manufacturing plant in the desert near Cave Creek. She was an isolated desert dweller who lived off the radar, partially because she left witness protection after testifying against the Sinaloa Cartel. She preferred the isolation because she didn't feel comfortable around other people who treated her as a bum, a hobo, or a desert scavenger making a living scrapping what she could find along the isolated roadways in the north county.

She came into money—a lot of it—when the former president of the Immigrant Coalition died and left her the non-governmental organization. The coalition served the undocumented migrant population once they got to Phoenix, providing food, medical services, and connected them with immigration attorneys. She also made regular runs over the border to Hermosillo, where makeshift camps filled with migrants waiting to make the crossing. While they waited, they fell prey to cartels, criminal gangs, and disease.

A millionaire on paper, Billie only recently moved out of her fifteen-foot dilapidated travel trailer—reluctantly, because it burned to a cinder. She and her seventeen-year-old son, Armando, lived in a home she built near Coyote Wash.

Barry Johns circled around the aircraft and spotted Billie from the tail section of the plane.

"Billie?"

"Oh, hey, Detective."

"Billie, anyone in there with you?"

"In here? Nah, ain't nobody but me."

Parker holstered his weapon. "Billie, what are you doing here?"

She squinted her blue eyes at the question and readjusted her frayed Arizona Diamondbacks cap on her shaggy blond hair.

"Whatdayamean? I'm loading up relief supplies."

"By plane? You haven't done that before. You always drive them down," Parker said.

Billie stepped down from the plane's door. Johns slipped behind her and ducked inside, confirming it wasn't hiding anyone else.

"What's goin' on, Nathan? Why you care what I'm shippin' to folks down south?"

Parker pointed to the green ATV tucked in along the opposite side of the hangar.

"You know anything about that RV?" he asked.

"Some guy drove it in an hour or so ago, why?"

"An hour ago? You get a look at him?"

Parker strolled over to the ATV. It was covered with a thin coating of dust from recent use in the desert. Blood and bits of tissue clung to the ATV's cargo bed.

"I didn't pay much attention to him. White guy, average build." Billie closed her eyes, trying to recall the details. "Sorry, Nathan. I don't much remember. I was kinda busy with my own stuff."

"How long you been flying supplies down south?" Parker asked.

"This will be my third trip. I mean, I don't fly them down. I just load them up. Ends up being cheaper than drivin' my rig down there. And less chance of hassles with local cops on the take."

"Your people on the other end meet the plane?"

"Yep. They meet the plane, pay the necessary bribes, and deliver the supplies to the network."

"You're not exactly going through official channels, are you? No customs inspections…"

"Don't nobody care what's going down south. They only pay attention to what's coming north."

"And what is coming north on the return flights?" Parker envisioned Billie returning to her coyote days and smuggling migrants back to the U.S."

She narrowed her eyes at Parker. "These ain't my planes. I only pay them to ship my stuff down to Hermosillo. Don't know what they do after that."

Parker believed her. Billie's work with the Immigrant Coalition focused on helping the undocumented once they arrived here. She hadn't been involved in arranging passage for the hundreds who waited to come north.

"You ever see the guy with the ATV on your other visits?"

"I seen the vehicle, but today was the first time I seen someone use it. Nathan, what's goin' on?"

"I'm trying to nail that down. But the guy you saw looks to be connected to two bodies we found."

"Bodies? Dumped out here?"

Nathan nodded.

"Damn, wish I'd paid more attention now. You know how come they were killed?" she said.

Parker glanced at the blood-stained ATV. A lot of effort to destroy the evidence—the first body—scraping it off the road and incinerating the remains. Almost. They'd nearly gotten away with it—except for one of the ATV crew ending up on the funeral pyre.

Someone was getting rid of loose ends.

Parker scanned the interior of the airplane hangar. No visible security cameras mounted along the walls. Maybe the ATV driver knew.

"Billie, who owns the plane?"

"Miller. J. T. Miller. You don't think he had anything to do with this do you?"

"I need to find out. He might know who drove the ATV."

"I know that weren't J.T. I've met him and the guy today weren't him."

"I'll need to talk to him. This is his building, right? The hangar?"

"It is. Nathan, J.T.'s is doing me a solid by running these supply trips. If he thinks—he could stop makin' these runs."

"You have Miller's contact information?"

Billie dug out her cell phone from her back pocket, scrolled, and couldn't find it. "Lemme call Miguel. He's at the office after his classes."

Parker couldn't help but grin. Miguel was his foster son. He and Billie had encountered him in Mexico when the young man was making his way north after MS-13 gang violence had claimed his family in El Salvador. Alone in the world, Miguel had left everything he knew and traveled by himself to start a new life. His start was cut short when he was taken by the Sinaloa Cartel.

Despite everything he'd suffered, Parker was amazed at the kid's resilience. Truth was, Miguel came into his life at a time when Parker needed him— still reeling after his partner's murder by a ruthless coyote on a human smuggling run.

Billie hit a speed dial button and tapped the speakerphone.

After a single ring, Miguel answered. "Hey Billie. Done already?"

"Not quite. Hey, I got Nathan, here—"

"Dad? Everything okay?" the boy's voice turned sharp.

"All good. We're trying to track a guy's contact information. Billie said you'd have it."

"On my desk. Check the roll-a-dex thing for J. T. Miller," Billie said.

"When are you going to use the contacts on your phone? Hang on." Miguel put the phone down. He came back on the line a few seconds later. "Okay, I've got your artifact from the 1950s. Who were you looking for again?"

"J. T. Miller," Billie said.

"The plane guy. Sure."

Parker jotted down Miller's address and phone number as Miguel recited them over the phone.

"Thanks, Miguel," Parker said.

"Any problem with Miller and the plane?"

"Too early to tell. You gonna be home for dinner? I can pick something up."

"It's Tuesday. Class tonight.

"Oh, right. I'll see you later then."

"That's the plan. Oh, could you let Linda know I'm good this weekend for the big move."

"Great. I'll let her know." Parker shot an eye to Billie, who gave him a sideways glance.

Miguel hung up, and Billie pocketed her phone.

"The big move, huh?" Billie said.

"Yeah, we're finally doing it. Linda and Leon are moving in."

"Bout time. Miguel and I had a bet when you were finally gonna do it."

"Time seems right."

"Linda's good people. Miguel and Leon seem to get along—with their shared experience of being lost at the border with no one to turn to. Lucky for them, you and Linda came along. You need help this weekend? I got my truck."

"Thanks, I don't want to put you out."

"You aren't. I don't mind. If you don't mind me hangin' around."

"You're family, Billie. You're welcome anytime. And the truck might be a good idea. Linda's got stuff…"

An electric vehicle pulled to a stop at the hangar door. A portly security man unfolded from the compact sedan, emblazoned with security on the doors.

"Everything okay, Billie?" the man asked, hiking up his belt loaded down with a flashlight, radio, and two pairs of handcuffs.

Billie waved. "I'm good, Paulie."

"I saw the SUV pull up and block the hangar. Wanted to make sure you're not in trouble. Don't get many visitors here."

"Paulie, this here is Detective Parker."

"What's the problem, officer?" Paulie asked.

Parker pointed to the ATV. "You know anything about who owns it?"

"Don't keep inventory on what folks keep in their hangers."

"Happen to see anyone drive this today?"

"No. Why you asking?"

"The detective thinks it was involved in a couple murders," Billie said.

Parker narrowed his eyes, and Billie cut her eyes to the asphalt. She'd said too much.

"Murders? Here? I gotta call this in."

"We're following a few leads. Nothing happened here, and I'd appreciate you keeping this between us for now." Parker didn't want a crowd gathering to trample over any potential evidence pointing at who drove the ATV and parked it in the hangar.

Paulie pocketed his cell phone and stood a little straighter, feeling he was on the inside of something important. "What do you need me to do?"

Chapter Seven

Parker followed the flatbed tow truck out of the Yavapai Dunes Airfield, the name he learned only after leaving the front gates of the small private strip. Barry Johns remained behind with the crime scene technicians going through the hangar and getting copies of the lease agreements from Paulie.

The green ATV was covered with a tarp and was headed to the lab for the forensic specialists to swab, sweep, and scrape. He knew the chances were slim the blood and tissue in the cargo area would pop on any DNA database, contrary to the public's television cop-drama perception. If there's no DNA in the system to compare against, there won't be a hit in the database. It's what kept serial killers like The Golden State Killer from being unveiled for decades.

His cell phone chirped in his pocket. Fishing it out, she saw the caller ID was Captain Morris, Parker's no-nonsense boss who booked nearly thirty years on the street and who, in his younger years, would wade into a biker bar fight with nothing more than a baton. Parker heard he'd mellowed over the years—but only by degrees.

"Parker, here."

"You wouldn't be heading back this way already, would you?"

"Why? Should I turn around and head to San Diego?"

"You might want to after you hear what I gotta tell you. Just a heads up. The Feds are waiting for you in your office."

"Which branch of that poisonous tree? FBI, DEA, Homeland?"

"Joint Terrorism Taskforce."

"What's the JTTF want with me? None of our active cases should cross streams with them."

"They wouldn't say, which frankly pissed me off."

"What's with the need for cloak and dagger?"

"I don't know. But the thing that really got stuck in my craw was they came in with a federal court order for your personnel file."

Parker let off the gas. "They did what? I'm not getting a warm and fuzzy feeling about the reception I'm walking into."

"I'll be there, too. No one comes into our house and tries to intimidate my people. The head Fed is a guy named Thompson. You ever run into him?"

"Not that I remember."

"Well, we're about to make his acquaintance. Wanted to give you a heads up on what you have waiting for you. Like I told you, I'll be there."

Parker disconnected the call. What would a high-powered task force want with him, and what was the necessity of getting a court order for his personnel file?

His recent dealings with the criminal gangs operating near the border—could one of them have painted him as playing both sides? That would make the feebs angry. It would be on brand for the remnants of Los Muertos to set him up. The Sinaloa cartel? They were possible, too. Although they were saved from a savage attack because he warned them.

What was the source of the JTTF interest? His contact with the head of the cartel?

A half dozen similar scenarios flipped through his mind as he parked in the garage at the sheriff's office headquarters off of West Jefferson.

He got out of his SUV and sent off a quick text message to Tully and Johns to stay away from the office until he gave them the all clear. The only explanation Parker offered was "palace drama."

Parker stopped in the parking garage behind six matching black Ford Explorer SUVs with government plates. The number of vehicles the feds needed to bring was troubling.

Parker pulled out his cell again and hit the speed dial button for Lynnette

Finch, the Senior Special Agent in Charge of the Phoenix FBI office. Lynne and Parker were once in a relationship, one which turned sour after Parker's partner was murdered. He withdrew, threw himself into the job, and spent nearly every waking minute searching for a path to avenge his partner's death. That put his relationship with Lynne on the back burner, and it never recovered.

They'd worked together on a few cases since, and the ice was beginning to thaw—but she'd never quite forgiven him for shutting down and leaving their relationship in the dust.

"SSA Finch's office. How may I help you?" The chain-smoking, gravelly voice on the other end of the connection was as soothing as fingernails on a chalkboard. Lynne's guardian, Delores, protected her boss, and she took her responsibility to heart when it came to keeping him away from Lynne.

Parker grimaced. "Delores, it's Nathan Parker. May I have a word with Lynne? It's urgent."

"Urgent for you, or Ms. Finch?"

"It involves the JTTF and some agent named Thompson."

"I'll put you through."

Parker expected to wrestle with Delores over the phone before she let him speak with her boss. Mentioning the task force and agent Thompson shook something loose, and he wasn't sure he liked the response.

"Nathan. What's going on? Delores mentioned JTTF—"

"And a special agent named Thompson."

"Where did you run across that name?"

"He's in my office right now and has apparently demanded my presence. Wanted to see if you had any idea what I'm heading into—another fed and all."

"Thompson's here? In Phoenix?"

"Apparently. And he's brought backup. I'm looking at six government-issued SUVs in the sheriff's office parking lot."

"I didn't know he was here. Thompson is out of D.C. And runs an operation focused on the ISIS offshoots we're seeing spring up over the last couple of years. The same group that claimed responsibility for the mass shooting attack in Moscow and the bombing of the checkpoint in Afghanistan, where thirteen of our people were killed."

"What's he doing here?"

"I—I don't know. And it pisses me off. He should've given our office a heads-up. The protocol is the field office serves as backup to the JTTF as needed. If he's got an operation going…"

"What's it got to do with me?"

"You come across anything with Middle East connections, or terrorist implications?"

"Nothing like that. Just came back from a fresh crime scene out near the Hummingbird Wilderness. Haven't nailed down what's behind it yet, but it looks like one of our victims was tossed from a plane."

"Was your victim of Middle Eastern origin?"

"Hard to tell, but I don't think so based on what we had to work with. What can you tell me about this Thompson guy?"

Lynne let out a deep breath.

"Thompson has a reputation of being a shoot first and ask questions later guy. Quick to make a snap decision—not always the right one—but in his mind, the ends justify the means. His task force even has a name—JTTF Black Bag. Most of the task force members are former HRT types."

"I take it he's had enough success the FBI brass give him a free rein?"

"He does get results. Why he's interested in you—I'd suggest you play it straight and don't deliberately push his buttons."

"When have I ever pushed buttons?"

"Do I really need to answer?"

"No. Maybe not. Thanks, Lynne, and I'll let you know what Thompson is up to."

Parker pocketed his cell. He'd kept the identity of the dead DOJ Agent under wraps until he could pin down the connection. He didn't need more federal agents bigfooting his case. He turned in his seat, and two tall men with short clipped hair, both wearing black utility pants, black polo shirts with some dark embossed logo, and a Glock 21—the large .45 caliber model strapped on a drop rig holster mounting the firearm on their thighs, appeared at his door.

"You need to come with us, Parker," the one on the right said.

"Yeah? Who's us?"

"Agent Thompson is waiting for you."

"I should care, why? I don't work for Thompson."

"Come with us now."

"And if I don't?"

"You're coming with us—one way or another."

"I guess we'll see, won't we?" Parker said. So much for not pushing buttons.

The two men stepped toward him when a voice called from the parking lot. "Parker!"

Captain Morris stood near the entrance.

"Excuse me, my boss is calling."

Parker stepped around the two men and headed toward the Captain. He didn't need to look over his shoulder to know his two fed shadows were escorting him.

"Captain. I might be getting older, but you didn't need to send anyone to make sure I remembered where I work."

Morris glanced at the two men, and his expression was tight. "Glad you could make it."

Parker followed the captain, and the two black-clad operators were a pace behind.

Morris took the hallway to the left toward his office, and one of the feds called out. "Agent Thompson is this way. Waiting in Parker's office."

"Then he can keep waiting," Morris said.

"Our orders are—"

Morris wheeled around and got within inches of the taller fed. "I don't give a damned what your orders are. In this house, I'm the one giving orders. I'm going to get a briefing from my Sergeant on a crime scene, and then if I'm in a charitable mood, we'll come down to chat with your boss."

"Sir, I insist—"

"And I insist you back the hell off or I'll toss you from the building. We outnumber you here."

Three deputies who heard the loud voices gathered behind the two feds.

One fed touched an earpiece and listened for a moment before responding. "We'll expect you in Parker's office shortly."

"That's Detective Sergeant Parker, and we'll be there when I'm damned ready, got that?" Morris's face was mottled red.

Morris continued to his office with Parker while the two JTTF operators remained in the hall.

Once in the Captain's office, Morris slammed the door. "What the hell is this about?"

"I hoped you had some idea. I called Lynette Finch to see what she could tell us about this Thompson guy."

"What's her take?"

"Never met him. Knows him only by reputation and that rep is a hard ass out of D.C. who doesn't always play by the rules but gets results."

Morris sighed and paced his office. "Great. Any idea why he's here?"

"None."

"Today's crime scene have anything to do with it?"

Parker filled him in on the two victims and how they were discovered by a roving band of Boy Scouts and their leaders.

"We have no idea what got Agent Thompson and his crew fired up? Or if it has anything to do with this new case?"

Parker shrugged. "If it is, it's because one victim was a DOJ Special Agent. I'm not firm on the connection yet."

Morris stopped pacing the track across his office carpet.

"They know who the dead guys are. Or one of them anyway."

Parker nodded. "It's the only thing I can think of."

"Well, it's time to find out what Thompson knows."

Parker and Morris strode out of the Captain's office and past the two black-clad feds who had waited in the hallway.

"Don't worry, we didn't try and escape," Parker said, as they moved past the two men.

Parker pushed into the Major Crimes Unit. A handful of detectives were parked at their desks, but they were monitoring four other men dressed in the black tactical gear gathered at Parker's office door.

The group gave off an angry vibe. Parker couldn't tell if he was the target for their heat because of making them wait, or something else lurked beneath.

"Which one of you is Thompson?" Parker asked as he reached his office.

From behind the group, a voice called out. "I'm Agent Thompson," and a woman with dark eyes stepped out from the others. "We need to talk."

Chapter Eight

Agent Thompson turned on her heel and entered Parker's office. She was slim, athletic, and the black tactical boots pushed her to five-seven. Thompson sported the same black polo shirt her team wore, and her belt pinched in on her small waist. The Glock strapped to her thigh looked somehow more lethal.

Her dark brown hair was pulled tight into a ponytail, and it swung around when she turned to face Parker and Captain Morris.

"Shut the door," she ordered.

One of her men complied, closing the three of them inside Parker's space.

"What brings Club Fed all the way from D.C.?" Parker asked.

Thompson's eyes narrowed at the mention of the District of Columbia FBI headquarters. She knew Parker had done some homework.

"You. You're the reason we're here, detective."

"I'm flattered. But I'm taken."

A sly grin appeared on Thompson's face. "Detective, you have been on our radar for a while now. Your relationship with Esteban Castaneda—"

"There's no relationship there. The bastard murdered my partner, and now he's rotting away where he belongs in the Supermax prison in Colorado."

"Even after he managed to survive a prison stabbing by a pair of inmates who were also in his protective custody unit."

"Sleepers—they were just waiting for a command," he said.

"Did you give them that command, detective?"

Morris huffed and said, "You can't be serious."

"Someone ordered the hit. We know Parker had a personal ax to grind. Castaneda took that foster kid of yours, right? You wanted revenge. I get it."

"You don't get to talk about Miguel," Parker said through a clenched jaw. He knew she was baiting him. But why?"

"We also know you've had direct communication with the Sinaloa Cartel."

"That's no secret. When one of your Homeland Security friends tried to use military resources to pit Cartels against one another."

"My point is—"

"I do wish you'd get there," Parker said.

"You're a man who gets things done and can think out of the box. My guys out there," Thompson tipped her chin to the office door. "They're great at what they do, but they are rigid when it comes to unconventional problem solving."

Parker didn't respond and waited her out.

"I need you on my team. We're working an unusual case, and your unique skill set will make a difference."

Thompson put her hands on her hips. Her expression gave away her belief she had bestowed a great honor on Parker.

"I already have a job. And a new double murder. My dance card is full."

"You'll find you have some free time. The case you mentioned. It's been reassigned to my team. As we speak, my people have taken custody of the two bodies you found in the desert earlier today. The confiscated off-road vehicle is at the FBI field office. This investigation is no longer your concern."

"You've bigfooted my case?"

"The circumstances around the deaths are a matter of—"

"National security. Yeah, I've heard it before."

Thompson's eyes clouded for a moment. She was clearly not used to being ignored.

Parker's cell buzzed in his pocket.

It was Pete Tully. Parker hit the accept button and had a bad feeling of what was to come.

"Pete, what's up?"

"What's up is a gang of fed ninjas swooped in and took Dryden into custody. Right from his hospital bed into a black van. Had a federal court order as a material witness."

"Is that right?" Parker said.

"Got some interesting info on Dryden before the body snatchers came. I kept it to myself. They'll uncover it too—he invited himself along on this scout day trip. Claimed knowledge of the area—used to take his kid out there. Having trouble getting much background on the guy. I'll fill you in. Barry should be heading back, too. Another crew of Feds chased him out of the crime scene. They confiscated his cell phone—claimed they wanted the photos of the bodies."

"Thanks, Pete. Hang on until—"

"One more thing. Barry had to borrow a phone to call. Tried to reach you. The feds grabbed Billie. He said they snatched her at the airport. No warrant or anything."

"Thanks, Pete," Parker said as he disconnected the call.

"You people snatch a witness from a hospital? And a woman at the airport who has nothing to do with this?"

"You mean Billie Carson? Yes, we know who she is. Her cross-border entanglements are well known. I'll decide if she has anything to do with these murders."

"Bullshit. If you know about Billie Carson, then you know she's about getting relief supplies down to the migrants stuck in places like Hermosillo before the cartels suck them into their misery."

Thompson pulled a cell phone from her pocket and brought up a series of photos. He recognized the airplane hangar. A dozen cardboard boxes were arranged on the cement floor. They'd been unsealed and opened. Most looked like the medical supplies he'd seen in other shipments going south. Three of the boxes in the center were different, packed with cash. Bundles of U.S. currency, tightly banded together.

"Did you know Miss Carson was sending money out of the country, detective?"

"No. What is this?"

"What this is, is evidence of providing material support to a terrorist organization."

Parker had no reason to doubt the authenticity of the photographs. What was Billie doing with boxes of cash—thousands of dollars stuffed in boxes for shipment to Mexico?

"There's no evidence of a tie to criminal organizations. Billie runs a network of relief groups down there, getting medical supplies, food, and clothing to people in need. You know that. What are you hoping to accomplish?"

"Sending the amounts of cash out of the country, Miss Carson is likely in violation of several federal statutes like the Bank Secrecy Act, which requires notification and a tax on transfers in excess of ten thousand dollars. Which she failed to do."

"Tax evasion? That's your big takeaway here?"

Parker shoved his hands in his pockets to hide the balled fists.

"It was enough for Al Capone."

"Billie Carson is no Chicago mobster. What's your end game here? Locking down some Boy Scout troop leader and Billie isn't going to magically make the world safer. What are you after?"

Thompson leaned back and rested against Parker's desk. Her face carried no outward expression—Parker couldn't read her.

"We need to get to the bottom of where Carson's money was going. If you agree and join my team, we'll see to it she's released and free to go about her charitable endeavors."

"You're using her as leverage—to get to me? That's—"

"What's your answer? You in or out?" She pulled her cell phone out and tapped in a number. "What do I tell my team? Do they release Miss Carson or not?"

Parker turned to Captain Morris, whose face was bright red. He was fuming over the arrogance of this FBI agent.

"This is extortion," Parker said.

"Think of it more as your duty to serve this country."

"Fine. What do you need me to do?"

"I need you as bait."

Chapter Nine

"Bait? What the hell are you talking about?" Parker asked.

Thompson ignored him and spoke into her cell phone. "Release the Carson woman to the sheriff's deputy on scene."

She cut off the call and slid the phone into a tight pants pocket. She strode past Parker and Morris, opened the door, and called for one of her team. One of the thugs who tried to corral Parker in the parking garage handed Thompson a file folder.

Thompson placed the folder on Parker's desk and laid out official-looking forms with a Department of Justice logo on the top of the page.

"These are non-disclosure agreements and an acknowledgment of the Official Secrets Act under 18 U.S.C. § 798—which states disclosure of said secrets is punishable by imprisonment. There's a set for you, Captain, if you want to be read in on this case as well."

Parker's cell buzzed with a text from Barry Johns. Billie was released by the feds. They confiscated the entire shipment, the cash, and medical supplies.

"Satisfied? I kept my end of the deal." Thompson said.

Parker signed the two forms, and Captain Morris followed suit, saying he needed to be aware of what his detective was being recruited into.

She collected the forms and perched on the corner of Parker's desk.

"Welcome to Taskforce Black Bag. You might want to sit while I get you up to speed."

Parker sat stiffly in a chair, one of his deputies usually parked in when he was giving out case assignments. He felt the tension building in his shoulders.

"Are you familiar with Red Dawn?"

"The movie?" Parker said.

"No. A multi-national criminal organization going by that name."

Parker shook his head.

"There's been a spike in cartel violence in recent months. At first we tagged it as the usual territorial expansion. These groups do enjoy throwing their weight around. But what we found was much different. The cartels were fighting off incursions, but not from one another."

"Red Dawn," Parker said.

"Exactly. We've intercepted chatter the cartels are joining forces to fight off the attacks against their manufacturing and distribution facilities in Mexico."

"Red Dawn is taking on the cartels? They must be a significant force—and well-funded to go to war with multiple cartel organizations."

"They do appear well financed, and their organization seems to show some sophistication in the tactics they use during their raids. We suspect the group uses expertly trained PMCs."

"Private military corporations? Mercenaries?"

Thompson nodded. "With ties to Eastern Europe, Southeast Asia, and the Middle East. They've left a few bodies behind."

"What's the connection to my crime scene this morning?

Thompson's jaw tightened. "Red Dawn is pushing the Cartel out and starting their own network to distribute heroin and fentanyl. We found out about a run recently, and we managed to place people on the inside. We were finally getting some valuable intel on the structure, command, and reach of the organization."

"One of the victims we found out there?"

She nodded. "The bastards tossed Peter out of a plane, making the delivery. They shot Jeff in the back of the head."

"Both of them were your people?"

"I don't know how they found out. Our operational security was tight. We have a leak and I don't know where it is."

Parker saw the first crack in Thompson's facade of strength. She was protective and guarded over her team. She felt their deaths personally. Parker knew what it felt like after his partner was murdered.

"How long had your people been undercover?"

"A month. They'd reported on two shipments and were finally in position to be on both ends of the one today."

"Someone blew their cover. Was there anything you've picked up about being compromised, or someone within Red Dawn figuring out who they were?"

"I've been over and over the situation. They were both too good to slip and give away their cover. This could only come from two sources—and neither of those is something I want to think about. A leak inside DOJ, above my team, or from one of my team themselves. The chance it was the latter makes me sick to my stomach."

Parker grew silent. He'd been where agent Thompson was—second guessing every decision made which put her people in jeopardy. What could she have done differently?

"What did your people tell you about today's drop? Agent Carter, Jeff—had his badge on him. Not standard for an undercover op." Parker asked.

"No. He shouldn't have risked getting discovered. I don't know what he was thinking. Red Dawn uses small commercial aircraft and picks up the cargo at a location known only to the pilot. They fly in at low altitude with a flight plan taking them over the border and landing at Tucson, Phoenix, or San Diego. They shut off transponders and divert to a secondary location once they clear the border. By the time air traffic controllers notice, the plane has landed at the secondary location, the cargo offloaded, and the plane is abandoned."

"The plane they came in on was left at Yavapai Dunes Airfield?"

"It was and we're going through it now. It's been expertly wiped down and cleaned. Registration comes back to William Johnson, who kept the plane there at Yavapai. He's not home."

"Why do you need me? Looks like you have a grip on what's going on," Parker said.

Thompson sighed, crossed her arms, and pushed away from the desk. "My team. We got hit today, and we lost two people. I can't risk another loss. Until we know where the leak came from, my team is compromised. Red Dawn doesn't know about you. Parker, you're in a position to get closer to the organization than we can."

"Here's where you get around to using me as bait."

Thompson shrugged. "The way I figure it, Red Dawn is onto us. They have inside information on the task force, and they are probably watching our movement. You are a wildcard. They won't be onto you."

"Unless they followed your team here. You aren't exactly subtle."

"They'd be too busy watching the team at the airfield to see what we discovered."

Parker had to admit she had a point. If a smuggler was making a drop, they'd want to make sure the transaction was secure and the material was delivered as planned. If Red Dawn had someone watching the pickup at the airfield, they would have seen him on the trail of the ATV and in the hangar where Billie was preparing for her relief flight.

The task force swooped in, confiscated the evidence, and found the airplane used to make the delivery. Red Dawn would focus on the risk the discovery posed.

"What do you need me to do?"

Thompson pulled a folded slip of paper from the folder with the non-disclosure agreements. She handed it to Parker.

"We know when the next delivery will happen. I want you on the inside."

Chapter Ten

"**N**o way! Parker, you're not doing this," Captain Morris said.

"We'll have eyes on him the entire time," Thompson said.

"Like you did your two guys today? How'd that work out for you?"

Parker strode around to his desk and picked up a photo of him with McMillan, the partner he'd lost to cartel violence. Murdered and left to bleed out on a remote north country road. If Thompson was right, the Red Dawn posed more of a threat than the cartels. Two federal officers were dead—like his partner—he couldn't stand on the sidelines and watch the violence and intimidation creep into his city.

"What do you know about this next drop?" Parker said, putting the photo back on his desk and sitting in his chair.

Thompson put both hands on the desktop, leaned in, and closed her eyes. "Thank you."

"I haven't agreed to anything yet. Tell me what you know about the upcoming drop."

"Carter was working the airfield to unload the delivery and was supposed to drive it out. I don't know what went wrong. They had someone else drive the cargo out. We were following Agent Carter to the distribution center and ready to take it down."

"They knew and they killed him."

She nodded. "I don't know how, but yes. He got word to us about another shipment coming out of Sinaloa to the Phoenix area. He narrowed it down to three locations. Red Dawn makes the decision in flight. It's supposed to occur two days from now."

"Which three airfields?" Parker asked.

Thompson turned to the map of the county mounted on the office wall. "Carter believed it would be Scottsdale, Chandler, Buckeye, or maybe back to Yavapai. So four, I guess." Her finger tapped each of the locations on the map.

"Yavapai is blown. They wouldn't use it again, would they?" Parker asked.

"Probably not. They know we were onto the location. Scottsdale is too commercial and too busy. I'd think they'd avoid that one."

"Chandler has a National Guard unit using their facility, if I recall."

"So, Buckeye?"

"If those are the options your intel gave you, that would be my pick. But, they might have fed him that information after they knew he was your undercover."

"We're back to square one on the location."

"Even if we knew the place, how would I get access?"

"We tracked a couple of mercenary types to a biker bar in Surprise. They aren't known to be Red Dawn members, but they would be the kind of people they would recruit from. Those types like to brag. They share war stories. We've tried to get a task force man inside, but they smelled fed before we got in the door."

"You want me to go and find out what I can hear?"

"Yes. We'll have you wired—"

"No, you won't. If these people are as cautious as you say they are, they'll be looking for a stranger coming in wearing a wire."

"We need to listen in to what's being said."

"I can't wear a wire. I might be able to slip in a listening device to get you what you want."

"That might work," she said.

"Parker, can I talk to you for a moment?" Captain Morris said.

He pulled Parker to a corner and leaned in close. "You aren't thinking of going along with this, are you? She's a loose cannon and already lost two of her team. Now she wants to put your ass on the line."

"Two cops down. If a new criminal organization is trying to establish a foothold here, there's going to be more violence, more of our people in the line of fire. We need to try to prevent it from spreading up here. You know what happens when a cartel, or a group like Los Muertos, moves in—innocent people are squeezed."

"I'm not going to talk you out of this, am I?"

"It's more like, why shouldn't we?"

Morris turned to Thompson. "If, and that's a big if—we allow Detective Parker to work this investigation, he's not going in alone. He gets to pick his team. If yours has been compromised, it won't be one of them."

"Agreed."

"I'm not done. "We need your intel—the raw info—from the source so Parker and his team can operate with full situational awareness."

"I don't think that's good operational security."

"You don't have your intel locked down. Two of your team were murdered because someone broke their cover. You should be busting ass to find the leak. You don't know what intel is compromised. Red Dawn could be feeding you deliberate misinformation to lure the rest of the team into an ambush. We need the raw, source-level intel to make decisions that will leave my people safe," Morris said.

"Fine."

Parker knew she wasn't fine with it. From this first interaction with Thompson, it was clear she thrived on control, demanded loyalty from her team, and trusted no one. A shadow crossed her eye momentarily, and Parker saw it for what it was. The task force leader was desperate. Scared. Despite her bluster, she knew her team was compromised, and she'd failed to keep them safe. It was never a guarantee. Staying safe. It was a dangerous business, especially for the officer who went deep undercover.

He'd known quite a few deputies and a few DEA agents who accepted these assignments. It was challenging and dangerous. All of them were changed by it. The lies, relationships, and the depravity witnessed from a dark swirling vortex tugging you closer to its heart. When you're pulled to the center of darkness, you can't help when it seeps its way inside. How you deal with that stain on your soul—that is what separates the survivors from the damaged.

"Agent Thompson, I get it. I've been right where you are. You want answers. You want someone to blame. Until you do, you're going to second-guess every action you took leading to your two agents being murdered."

"I'm not—"

"Yeah, you are. We have a chance to find the people responsible for their deaths, and that's the only way you're ever going to get through this. You'll never put it behind you or get over it. You need a way through. I think we can help one another."

"I'm listening. But if you think I'm turning this over to you and walking away—"

"I'm not suggesting you walk away—I think you need to run straight at them."

Chapter Eleven

For the next hour, Parker and Thompson replayed what they knew about the botched operation to infiltrate Red Dawn. The more they talked, the more Thompson seemed to accept the thought the leak came from within the task force. Deliberate or not, someone ran their mouth, and two agents paid the price.

The death of the two agents changed everything.

"We have to assume Red Dawn knows everything about the task force operation. The need for covert operation is over. You've been outed. It's time to use that against them."

"We have a chance to infiltrate their operations," Thompson said.

Parker shook his head and glanced at his half-empty coffee cup parked on a corner of his desk. He pulled it to the center of the desk between them.

"This is the task force. You know what's in it—I know what's in it—Red Dawn knows what's in it. They know where you are, what your next move is, and what your resources are. There's no sneaking up, or infiltration. They found it before, and they will be extra vigilant now."

"I'm supposed to give up? Let them win?"

"Not at all." Parker moved the coffee cup toward her. "Go at them. Directly. They won't see it coming and you'll catch them off guard, because they expect you to keep doing the same thing, trying to get a man on the inside."

"We don't know who runs the organization at the highest levels."

"You have some intel on who the local connections might be, right? You mentioned tracing back the soldiers they left behind in East Turdistan, or somewhere, but they need a local connection to make these drops and pickups."

"If we can trust any of our intel."

"We can run down the local targets. Red Dawn won't know my people. They'll be looking for you."

"We'll be a diversion?"

"If they focus on you, they won't be expecting me."

"If I put the task force at the expected drop location, they'll abort."

"Yes, and they won't risk returning to the border, they'll divert to a secondary airstrip en route. You said they make the call while they are in the air, right?"

"That's what Carter could tell us before they killed him. He gave us the possible next locations. If we can believe what he gave us," Thompson said.

"At the point he passed that onto his handler, we had no reason to believe he was compromised. No way to tell for sure…"

"How many people were in the communication pipeline with Carter and—"

"Salazar and White. They were the point of contact for each of them."

"Where are they now?"

"Salazar is at the airfield where Carter was supposed to meet the shipment—and. White is at the medical examiner's offices with Peter—Agent Rivers."

"Both in a position to destroy evidence which might lead back to Red Dawn," Parker said.

"I can't believe they would."

"The team you have here—how did you select them? If we're going to pull off a run at Red Dawn, they could leak the fact we've talked."

"They won't know what we talked about. They knew I wanted to bring you on and try to convince you to meet the next shipment."

"Let them keep thinking you tried, and I told you to pound sand. If we try to make an end run on Red Dawn, they can't suspect what we're up to."

"I don't like lying to my team."

"Until you can find out where the leak came from, no one outside this room knows what we're going after. You'll catch Red Dawn off guard, and we might force them out into the open."

"Where we can take them out."

Parker nodded.

"Who are you going to pull in to work with?" Thompson asked.

"Better you don't know. People I can trust—who've had my back when it got ugly."

"I thought I could trust my people, too, remember?"

"We'll go to the bar in Surprise and start some misinformation. About the task force watching the Yavapai airfield for a second drop. If it gets picked up in chatter coming back from Red Dawn, you'll have your leak."

Agent Thompson pulled up from the chair and nodded. "All right. Let's make this look good."

She strode for the door and threw it open. "That's the last warning I'm gonna give you, Detective. Keep your local ass out of my investigation."

Heads popped up in the detective bureau, peeking over cubicle walls.

"You can't swoop in here and push your way into our case," Parker said from his office door.

"I can and I did. The U.S. Attorney has given the JTTF complete authority in this matter because it's a matter of—"

"Don't say it. All you feds know how to do is repeat the words, 'National Security'."

"If you even think about interfering with my investigation, you'll find yourself in front of a federal grand jury."

Thompson gestured to her team, and they stormed out of the detective bureau. Parker felt the other detectives in the unit turn in his direction, and one of the gang investigators piped up. "Way to go, Parker. Put those feds in their place."

Morris joined Parker at his doorway. "She sounded convincing."

"Let's hope it's enough of a distraction. I gotta pull my team together."

"Keep it small—a tight circle on this one."

"I hear you. Probably best if we don't meet here—at least not today."

"Watch your ass on this, Nathan. Sounds like these Red Dawn characters play for keeps."

Parker returned to his office and made a show of slamming his door. He made a series of text messages. Meet at his home tonight at six.

With the feds compromised, he needed a team of people he could trust to keep a lid on the investigation and watch one another's backs. Pete Tully and Barry Johns were a given. The others were a bit unorthodox.

Chapter Twelve

On the way home to his place in Litchberg Park from sheriff's headquarters, Parker called Miguel, who he figured would be getting out of his last class at Arizona State about now.

Miguel picked up on the first ring.

"Hey, Dad, what's up?" The background noise made it sound like he was in his car.

"You on your way back home? I'm gonna stop and pick up some stuff for dinner. We have people coming over."

"People? When do you do people?"

"Pete, Barry, and a few others you already know."

"What's going on?"

"Just work stuff."

"The last time you had people over, you were about ready to go after Los Muertos. So what gives?"

Parker had to admit the kid was perceptive. If he could call the eighteen-year-old a kid anymore. Miguel's keen perception was fine-tuned from years of fending off threats from criminal gangs in his home country of El Salvador, and it kept him from harm.

"There is something kicking up. Are you connected with Billie's network down in Hermosillo?"

"Yeah, I work them on almost a daily basis. It's Immigrant Coalition stuff. After her son, Armando, moved up here, there is more coordination down south. We are getting some of the routes taken over by the Sinaloa Cartel. We keep the migrants away from them."

"Ever hear about a group called Red Dawn?" Parker asked. As connected as Miguel was, he was in a good position to hear gossip and talk about any organization making a move into the region.

"Red Dawn? Haven't heard anything about that one."

Maybe Agent Thompson had it wrong.

"Any special requests for dinner—and it won't be pizza."

Before Miguel could respond, Parker's cell vibrated. The caller ID was Linda.

"Oh, hey, Linda's on the other line."

"Oh, good, if she's coming over, ask her to cook."

"What are you saying about my cooking?"

"You're great as long as it's microwaved, or barbecued."

"Goodbye." Parker hung up on him and connected with Linda.

Parker met Linda Hunt at a foster parent group. They'd both recently fostered migrant kids, and she was a deputy with the sheriff's office. She'd picked up Miguel after an immigration protest blocking freeway access. She called Parker, and they slowly hit it off. They'd been dating for about a year, and it seemed pretty serious. At least Parker thought so. He did ask her to move in with him about three months ago, and she said she wasn't ready for that kind of commitment.

Parker wondered if it was more her not being ready for a commitment with him.

"Hey Linda, get my message?"

"That's what I was calling about? What's going on?"

"We're getting the band back together?"

"Huh?"

"We need to bring you, Pete, Barry, and a couple others up to speed on a new case."

"Me? I'm not in investigations anymore, remember? I'm in the court liaison unit where I listen to attorney-speak all day long, and nothing gets done."

"How would you like a little break from monitoring consent decree compliance?"

"Don't tease me. You know how much I want out."

Captain Morris is letting me pull a team together for a special investigation. Bring Leon over and we'll have dinner and brief everyone on what we know."

"Dinner? You're not going to try and cook, are you? Let me take care of it. You want these people to agree to work on the case, right?"

"You and Miguel teaming up on me again?"

"Well, if the burnt casserole fits."

"One time. And I followed your recipe."

"Apparently not. What time tonight? How many people?"

"Six. Maybe eight or nine people. Wouldn't pizza be easier? Just grab a slice and go?"

"I'll see you at six."

They ended the call, and Parker glanced at his watch. It was early enough to catch Lynnette Finch at the FBI offices north of the 101 off of Deer Valley Drive. The crosstown traffic was mercifully light, and he pulled into the parking lot next to the brown concrete structure.

After getting a visitor's badge, he found Lynne's outer office empty. No, Delores, which boded well for him. Until she stepped out of Lynne's office.

Her flinty glare cut at Parker. "You don't have an appointment."

"No, something urgent came up and I need a word with Lynne."

"She doesn't have time."

"Tell her it's regarding Agent Thompson."

Delores stiffened at the name.

"You know Thompson?"

"Only by reputation." She picked up her phone and turned away from Parker while she whispered to her boss over the connection.

She hung up the phone. "She has a minute for you. And Detective, don't drag her into any of your mess. Trouble seems to have a way of finding you."

"It's not my intent."

Parker rapped a knuckle on Lynne's door and entered.

Lynnette Finch sat behind her desk. Blonde hair pulled back tightly. She pulled a pair of reading glasses off as he entered. They were a new addition, and he knew she must hate having to use them. Her blue eyes narrowed as she closed a file.

"Agent Thompson let you walk free?"

"Not exactly. Would it surprise you to find out Agent Thompson is a woman?"

"Huh. A little. Most JTTF types are former military, you know, special forces, or our people with HRT experience. There are analyst types who support task force missions, but Task Force Black Bag is more the tip of the spear, if you get what I'm saying."

"I think I do," Parker said as he parked in a chair opposite Lynne. "She lost two of her operatives today. Both killed—looks like their cover was blown."

"The one you mentioned this morning—thrown from an airplane?"

"He was one of them."

"Thompson didn't let us know they were working an operation in Phoenix. Two were killed?"

"And she doesn't know how they were compromised."

"What did Thompson want from you?"

"She wanted me to join the task force and act as bait to draw out their target."

"I hope you told her to head back to D.C. and don't look back. I don't understand why the task force was here in the first place. We've had no indication of cross-border terrorist activity—nothing unusual on the homegrown front either. Just your garden variety neo-Nazi torch lighting parties."

"Ever hear of a group called Red Dawn? That's who Thompson is going after."

"Red Dawn? No. That's a new one."

Lynne had hidden the truth from Parker on more than one occasion, but he got the sense she was playing straight this time. An operation running out of the D.C. Office in her backyard was clearly discomforting.

She swiveled her chair to the computer and snagged her reading glasses from the desk. "Not a word about the glasses," she said while tapping commands on a keyboard.

"Huh, there are files related to Red Dawn, but they are restricted. I can't access them."

"Is that unusual? One arm of the FBI keeping secrets from another?"

"No, that I get. What's different here is the contact number isn't from the D.C. Field Office. This is my number. What the hell is she doing?"

Chapter Thirteen

I t didn't take any arm-twisting to have Lynne to agree to meet at his place tonight with the rest of the team. He was almost home when a black SUV cut him off in traffic on the westbound lanes of I-10. One angry driver wasn't unusual, but a second SUV pulled in behind him and closed in within a few feet of his rear bumper.

The SUV in front slowed down and flicked on flashing blue and red emergency lights. The trail vehicle followed suit, and Parker edged his SUV to the shoulder.

"A door opened on the lead car, and he recognized one of Thompson's task force goons as he stepped from the passenger side. Tall, muscled, and thick-necked. The black BDUs gave him a sinister vibe. The man strode to Parker's window and knocked on the glass.

In the rear-view mirror, Parker got a glimpse of another task force operative out of his vehicle. This one held a stubby black MP5 rifle close across his chest.

Parker lowered the window. "Whatever you're selling, I'm not interested."

"I don't like you," the task force man said, loud enough for his partner to hear. "Another local po-dunk cop with his head up his own ass. The boss says you refused to get on board, and it leaves me wondering why?"

"Hey, like you said, I'm just a local cop. I don't have any involvement in JTTF action."

"Agent Thompson hopes you have a change of heart." The thug handed a USB drive through the window."

"The man's eyes flicked to the rear vehicle. Then, in a low voice, he said,

"The Red Dawn intel is on this. The boss said you'd know what to do with it. We lost two good men today, and we're no closer to finding out where we went wrong. If it was an inside job, they'll wish they were the ones thrown from a plane."

The thick-necked man straightened from the window and returned to his vehicle. The rifleman in Parker's rearview slipped back into his SUV. The two black SUVs slid into the traffic and sped away.

Parker let his pulse rate back down before he was ready to move. The slim chrome USB drive in his palm was Agent Thompson's intel on the criminal group and the potential next drop location. He closed his hand around it and hoped he hadn't made a mistake offering to intercept this airport delivery.

Parker merged back into the westbound traffic and made it home to his Litchfield Park home, as Miguel was pulling in the drive.

The eighteen-year-old hefted his backpack from the back seat and smiled when he saw Parker unburdened with grocery bags.

"You call Oregano's for pizza? I can go pick it up?"

"No pizza. Linda's coming over and she's doing the chefing tonight."

"That'll be safe."

"What do you mean?"

"Oh, nothing. My system might not handle anything not related to microwaved Hot Pockets, instant noodles, or frozen burritos."

Parker laughed, and he knew the kid was right. Their schedules were tied up in long days and longer nights. Parker with his investigation work which meant he was on call, or on the job twenty-four seven, and Miguel with his full course load at ASU, holding down a job as Billie's second in command at the Immigrant Coalition, and his blooming relationship with Sarah, a graduate teaching assistant he met while at Glendale Community College.

Once inside, Parker stowed his duty weapon in his fingerprint-activated safe and stood under an air-conditioning vent in the living room. It wasn't even summer yet, and the heat was getting uncomfortable.

"Leon's coming over with Linda. I need a favor from you two."

"I know—stay out of the way while the adults talk business."

"No. I need your help."

"Really?" Miguel's face brightened.

Parker came to realize Miguel was plugged into the migrant community over the border. It was part of what he and Billie did for the Coalition. They knew where migrants gathered, when they would attempt to make a crossing, and what resources they would need once they arrived north of the border.

Billie had been careful not to arrange for the border crossings, but would advise the migrants where to avoid cartel, or other criminal elements who would prey upon them.

"I need you to find out if migrants are running into a group called Red Dawn. I'm hearing they are moving against the cartels and taking over the crossings. I don't know much more about them—other than they seem to be bad news.

"Leon is a whiz with computer stuff, right? I have this USB drive and I need him to check it out—before we open it."

"Like it might be a virus or something?"

"Or tracking software—I don't trust where this came from?"

Miguel wrinkled his forehead.

"The FBI."

His eyes widened. "Whoa. Okay. When he gets here, we'll both dive in. He knows how to scan a drive, and I can use an encrypted browser to see if we're hearing anything about Red Dawn."

"Be careful. Don't do anything that can trace back to you. These guys don't like people snooping at whatever it is they're involved in."

A knock at the door, and it was pushed open. Linda bumped it open with her hip while she clutched grocery bags in both arms.

"Let me," Miguel said, taking the bags from her.

She blew a strand of blonde hair out of her face. "Sorry, I'm late. The unit decided to have a last-minute staff meeting on the Melendres Consent Decree status."

"You're never late," Parker said, as he gave her a hug.

"What's got you so tense?" she asked, looking up at him.

"I'm not tense."

"You can't hide it from me, mister. This investigation? It's big?"

He shrugged. "Where's Leon?"

"He's on his way."

"Hey, where's the food?" Miguel called from the kitchen.

Linda pushed away from Parker. "I thought I'd try something new."

Parker and Linda joined Miguel in the kitchen where he'd unpacked the groceries. Flimsy plastic bags with vegetables lay on the granite countertop.

"Have you ever tried Eggplant Parmesan?" Linda said.

"Not on purpose."

"It's good and it's better for you than the diet of pizza and fast food you two exist on."

"Eggplant?" Parker asked.

"Don't turn your nose up. You will like it."

"Yes, ma'am."

Another knock at the door, and Parker trotted over to find Pete Tully, Barry Johns, and Billie.

Billie glanced up at Parker and waited until Pete and Barry stepped inside. "Nathan, I didn't mean to cause no trouble. Them federals—they said I was supportin' terrorist groups, or some such. I ain't never…"

"I know, Billie. We'll sort it out. You're gonna be okay." Parker knew they leveraged her to get to him. It was a crappy stunt to pull, and told him what he was dealing with when working with Thompson and the task force. "We do need a better way to fund the Coalition operations down south. Sending bundles of cash is a problem."

"I need to buy food and medicine from local suppliers, and they don't do no bitcoin or nothin'."

"We'll figure it out."

Before Parker closed the door, Lynne Finch parked at the curb, and behind her, a lifted Ford pickup truck came to a stop. Dion Espinoza, Special Agent with the Drug Enforcement Agency. Espi and Parker were sheriff's deputies together before Espi went off to the dark side and started working with the feds.

Espi was well connected with the intel around the border, the cartels, and where the balance of power between the criminal organizations tilted at any given point. Recently, there had been a truce of sorts between the Sinaloa and Juarez cartels. The activity Agent Thompson described with Red Dawn threatened to upend the peace.

Lynne waited for Espi at the front door.

Lynne leaned to Parker and whispered, "I'm glad you called, Nathan. Turns out Agent Thompson isn't exactly what she says she is."

Chapter Fourteen

Parker called everyone to the dining room where he stood, too anxious to sit at the table.

"Thanks for coming, everyone. Where's Leon? He and Miguel need to work on something."

"He'll be here. He has an internal early warning system when it comes to dinner," Linda said.

Parker quickly got everyone up to speed on Thompson's demand he join her team, the murder of the two task force members, and Red Dawn's planned drop at a local airstrip.

"The intel is on the USB drive?" Lynne asked.

"It is. I want Miguel and Leon to take a look. Leon's an IT genius, and I want to find out if our friend Agent Thompson has tracking software, or some other little jewel on the drive before we jump in and act on the intel."

"Which brings me to what I discovered about Agent Thompson," Lynne said. "The D.C. Field Office wouldn't let loose with a whole lot about the Black Bag task force. What they are focused on. Where they are deployed—which I think we know the answer. But what I could pull from D.C. was the fact Agent Thompson is on admin leave and pending reassignment."

"She's supposed to be on the beach? For someone on mandatory leave, she was pretty active today. They tell you why she was pulled from the field?" Parker asked.

"My contact was kinda vague on that point. Other than an operation didn't go as planned. The task force might have been compromised."

"We know that's true. Two of her task force members were killed today. She was supposed to have been sidelined because the task force was compromised—and she knew and put her people at risk, knowing they were exposed. Why would she do that?"

"Thompson has a rep—she's been able to ask for forgiveness instead of permission because she got results. Until now. Her level of arrogance cost the lives of two agents."

"Any clue what made her press forward, knowing the task force was compromised?" Tully asked.

"Nothing. She should have pulled her team back. Full stop," Lynne said.

"She's convinced this group, Red Dawn, is pushing out the cartels to control distribution channels to the north," Parker said.

Espi nodded. "She's onto something there. The DEA has picked up intel the Sinaloa, Juarez, and Los Zetas cartels have joined in their own version of NATO—a joint defense pact. They must feel the threat to agree to do anything together."

"Ever hear Red Dawn, specifically?"

"Not by name, no. What our people have been able to learn is there is an outside organization—a multi-national group hitting cartel-run manufacturing and distribution facilities."

"Tracks with what Agent Thompson said. They are supposed to be using private military contractors for their muscle. There's a bar out in Surprise where PMC types gather and get a line on employment opportunities."

"If the agency has Thompson on leave, why is she running field ops? I can connect with D.C. and ask them to pull the task force out," Linda said.

"How much pressure can they put on an agent who's already supposed to be on admin leave. With two of hers down, I think she's doubling down on Red Dawn. I think we can use that."

"You aren't thinking of joining up with her, are you?" Linda asked.

"No, and I don't think that's what she really wants either. Thompson and the task force are going to serve as a distraction. She knows they're compromised. While the task force is making a show in one location, we have a chance to catch Red Dawn making an exchange here."

The oven timer sounded, and the front door opened. Leon dropped his backpack and ambled over, looking a little surprised at the gathering at the kitchen table.

Linda placed the hot casserole dish on the table. "Get washed up, Leon, you're right on time."

She leaned to Parker and whispered, "It's like he has a sixth sense about when dinner is ready."

"This smells amazing," Lynne said.

"Thank you. It's something new I'm trying. Eggplant Parm."

Barry Johns took a plate from the stack Linda had placed on the table. "Count me in."

"It's not too late to order pizza," Miguel said with a grin.

Linda pointed a spatula at him. "You will eat it and you will like it."

"Yes, ma'am."

Linda dished out portions for everyone. She placed a platter of toasted garlic bread in the center of the table before she sat.

While everyone tucked into the eggplant, Billie paused before she spoke. "I know I ain't got no say on nothin', but don't it sound like gettin' the cartels to stop killin' each other is a good thing? I mean even if some new group comes in, they can't be no worse than what we got now."

"We don't know what Red Dawn has planned. So far, they don't seem too hesitant to take out anyone in their way. What are your people in Hermosillo saying? They have to be seeing some change in what's going on there?" Parker said.

"Din't say specific like. But the migrant camps outside the city been takin' more hits than usual. Pressure to pull up stakes and move. Like they got somewhere to move. It ain't the cartel been makin' the play. Could be your new group, the Red Dawn."

"What's in it for Red Dawn? Why would they want the migrants to move?" Espi asked.

"Don't know for sure. The message they been gettin' is they ain't gonna be making a crossing, so leave."

"Red Dawn won't be using the migrants to smuggle their product? That's one small ray of sunshine," Parker said.

"Unless they are the product," Lynne said. "Billie, were the migrants down south told where they needed to move to? Like a place Red Dawn controls?"

Billie shook her head. "I don't know. I can put some feelers out and see what they bein' told."

Espi pushed his plate aside and dropped a folder on the tabletop. "When Nathan called and filled me in on Red Dawn's PMC connection, I pulled up these three yahoos. They're connected with private military companies and post up in our area. The bar out in Surprise is a known hang for these three."

Espi fanned the three photos out on the table. They looked like men you'd pick from a lineup of outlaw bikers.

"These three have prior military experience. Haskins and Watson," he tapped a finger on their images. "They were both Army." He pointed at the remaining photo. A man with dark, close-set eyes, long black hair, and an attitude radiating off the page.

"Who's this winner?" Tully asked.

"Yeah, a booking photo. He was involved in some bullshit border militia activity last year. Threatened a border patrol officer. Name's Jack Talent. His real name. Former Air Force—dishonorable discharge after assaulting an officer. Requested the details. If there is some cross-border action going on—I'd start with him."

"Barry, what say you and I take a drive by at the bar in Surprise later?"

"Fine by me."

"Need me to tag along?" Espi asked."

"I think we can handle a little listening tour. I wouldn't want to out you to these types, Espi. And Pete, I'm sorry, they won't buy you as a man looking for a job."

"I'm hurt," Pete Tully said.

After they cleared the table, Leon and Miguel disappeared with the USB drive and told Parker they'd give him a report on their progress within the hour.

"What can I do?" Linda asked. "I can play the biker chick." She put her hands on her hips and cocked her head to the side in an attempt to look hard.

Parker smiled. "Better let Barry and I take the first run at this place. Could you keep an eye on Miguel and Leon and make sure they don't try and do anything with the intel they might find on the drive?"

"I can do more than babysit those two."

"I know. I want to get the lay of this bar before a hot biker chick rides up."

"Hot?" Linda blushed.

"I didn't say that."

"Yes, you did."

"Whatever. Keep those two out of trouble and make sure they call me when they have anything."

Chapter Fifteen

The Kickstand was a well-known biker bar to the west of Surprise at the base of the White Tank Mountains. Well-known because of the frequent disturbance calls to the establishment. Two rival outlaw biker clubs took turns claiming the turf as theirs, and this month it was The Chain Slayers.

The Slayers were relatively new to the scene and had migrated east from Riverside, California, and their members had encounters with local law enforcement for dealing meth, trafficking in stolen motorcycle parts, and the occasional bloodletting.

When Parker and Barry pulled into the chipped asphalt parking lot, a row of motorcycles lined up near the front of the bar, each one backed into place. Two thick-necked thugs stood watch over the chrome and steel display.

After tucking Parker's off-duty Jeep into a space, he pulled the photo of Jack Talent, the mercenary Espi tagged as having the most likely connection to private military company activity in the Southwest.

"Six-three, Two-and-a-quarter. Should stand out in a crowd," Barry said.

Parker stole one last glance at Talent's image before tucking it away in the console.

They walked to the bar entrance, and the drone of heavy metal blasted through the open door. The two guardians cast a suspicious glare at the two strangers but made no move to stop them from entering.

The wooden bar top was a seedy affair and looked made from scrap lumber pilfered from construction sites. Two pool tables were shoved to the wall on the left side of the room, the legs broken and tables unplayable.

There were thirty bikers wearing a small, colorful collection of leathers. Most bore the emblems on the back of their black leather vests, testifying their allegiance to The Chain Slayers. There were a couple of other factions in the mix Parker couldn't identify. The Chain Slayers' emblem consisted of a broken motorcycle chain with blood dripping from the links.

A few of the men gathered at the bar clocked the detectives as they entered. After a whispered conversation, one man broke away and strode to Parker and Johns. The biker's vest was unadorned with a club patch except for a white lettered "Prospect" label on his chest. The guy was earning his way to membership, and the detectives were his to deal with.

"Think you made a wrong turn," the biker said. He focused on Barry.

"Is that right? And here I thought this place was a Michelin star gastronomic wonder," Barry said.

The biker's forehead wrinkled in confusion. "A what?"

"Never mind. I see a dude I need to have a word with." Barry tipped his head to the crowded bar.

Parker scanned the bar and found Jack Talent leaning with his back against the bar. As Barry predicted, the six-three Talent was easy to find in the crowd.

The detectives started toward the bar, and the prospect biker stepped in their path.

"I don't think you belong here." Again, the biker focused on Barry Johns.

"Listen, Junior, I'm not looking for membership in your all-white church of the blessed window lickers. I'm here on business. So step off," Barry said.

The biker pushed Barry in the chest as he pressed forward.

Barry grabbed the man's wrist with his right hand, shot his left out against the biker's elbow, and forced the prospect to his knees with pressure against the joint.

Parker stood nearby to make sure no one tried to pile on and make it an unfair fight. He didn't need to step in as the Chain Slayers were casually watching the events unfold. By their expressions, he knew the bikers were going to let this play out. The prospect needed to earn their support—and it wasn't looking good for his future membership.

The prospect cried out when he dropped to the floor, face down on the filthy, worn linoleum. "Okay, okay. Stop."

"You need to say you're sorry to the nice Black man," Parker said.

"I'm sorry. I'm sorry."

Barry released pressure on the man's elbow, and he crawled out from under the detective. A few of the Chain Slayers shook their heads and turned away from the prospect's display of weakness.

One member stepped over and ripped the prospect patch off the man's leathers as he slunk out of the bar.

The Chain Slayer member strode over to Barry and held the patch out to him. "Yours if you want it."

"Thanks, I'm good. Just here to talk business with Jack."

"He know you're coming?"

"Nah, friend of a friend kinda deal."

The Chain Slayer stepped aside, and the detectives strode to the bar through a small knot of bikers.

Talent eyed the detectives for a moment.

"We met before?" Talent said with a slight southern drawl.

Parker leaned back against the bar, mirroring Talent's position. It let him watch the crowd while Barry used the dirty mirror behind the bar to keep an eye on the bartender and the bikers.

"We hear you might be looking to put a team together," Parker said.

Talent hefted an amber beer bottle, drew a sip, then looked to Parker. "What kind of work you looking for?"

"Whatever you got. We got back from down south. Got tired of dealing with the cartels—you know—changing who they hold allegiance to one day to the next. Where's the honor?"

"I hear you, brother. I'm done working for them Mexican factions."

"Speaking of—I understand there might be some work around here with people who are pushing the cartels out of the way. We'd be down."

Talent put the beer bottle on the bar top and turned to Parker.

"I don't know you."

"That's fair. I'm not asking for an introduction or anything. We're looking for work—if it's work against the cartels, it's a plus."

Talent's expression tightened. He was considering it.

"Where you work before?"

"I don't kiss and tell," Parker said.

Talent seemed to appreciate the secrecy.

"Let me make a call. I'm not working for this organization. I have sent them some good field operators. Your friend can handle himself, and I think you can too."

"Much appreciated."

"I'm not promising they will take you on, but I do know they are a couple men short on an operation they have coming up. Like I said, I'll make a call."

"That's all I can ask." Parker motioned to the bartender. "Another beer for my friend."

"You aren't interested in what it is they're doing?" Talent asked.

"Nope. Work's work. I do my part, that's all."

"That's healthy. From what I hear, this organization is all about op sec."

"It's good for everyone," Parker said.

"Unless someone gets a little loose with their mouth. Then, adios."

"Like I said, operational security is good for everyone. If you can't hold your mud, you don't belong in the field."

"Amen to that. You got a number I can reach you?"

Parker smoothed a wrinkled bar napkin with the blade of his hand and jotted down a phone number and his first name. He slid it to Talent. "It's a burner. Whoever calls won't have to worry about the call getting caught up in some trap and trace nonsense."

Talent nodded as if Parker passed another test.

"I'll make the call, and if they're interested, you'll hear. If not—"

"Understood. Appreciate the referral."

"I take this seriously. If you flake out on them, or try to screw them, they'll kill you. But I'll burn what's left."

Chapter Sixteen

As Parker and Johns headed to their car, a shadow moved from behind the line of motorcycles. The former Chain Slayer Prospect waited for them and based on the stagger and the half-empty bottle of Jack in his hand, he'd been nursing his bruised ego with whiskey.

"I been waiting for you, asshole."

"Go home and sleep it off," Johns said.

"Don't tell me what to do, darkie."

"And here I thought we were friends…"

The biker stumbled over a concrete parking bumper, dropped his bottle, shattering the glass on the pavement.

"You're gonna pay for that." The biker's hand fumbled for a knife in a sheath on his belt.

Barry lashed out and struck the man in the throat with the web of his hand. The Biker gripped his throat and toppled backwards. He staggered and fell against the line of motorcycles, sending three of the polished chrome street bikes to the rough asphalt.

The two thugs who served as bouncers were able to grab the next bike to prevent it from taking out the entire club's garage.

Once they preserved the rest, they wrestled him up and hustled him back inside, where Parker knew he faced an unhappy reception.

As they got in Parker's Jeep, he asked, "You catch the last bit from Talent? The threat to burn what's left?" Parker asked.

"I did. You peg him for our arsonist?"

Parker started the Jeep and pulled away from the biker bar.

"Maybe. Seems to fit, doesn't it? Maybe our Boy Scout leader can ID him from a driver's license photo."

"Pete seemed to think something was off about our witness."

"We'll meet with Pete in the morning and figure out the best way to find Mr. Dryden. The feds scooped him up from the hospital."

Parker's cell phone chirped, and an unknown number registered on the display.

"Hello?"

Talent's voice sounded over the connection. "This more of your handiwork? Disrespecting a man's ride is a serious matter."

"Wasn't us. Your boy did that by himself."

"Figured as much. I made the call. Stay local and flexible. I think you might have a job offer."

"Much appreciated."

"Remember what I said. These boys play for keeps."

"Got it," Parker said to a dead connection.

"Talent did his part. Now we wait."

Parker returned to his place, and Johns got in his Audi, agreeing to meet up at the office in the morning.

When he returned, Linda was waiting for him. She looked relieved to see him back safe and sound.

"I wish you would have let me go with you," She said. "I can handle myself."

"I know you can. It worked out, and we made the connection with the guy Espi said was plugged into the PMC network around here."

"Did he tell you where Red Dawn is delivering next?"

"Not yet. I'm waiting for a call."

Parker glanced to the dining room table where Miguel and Leon huddled over a laptop computer.

"The boys working on the USB drive?"

"They haven't come up for air since you left."

Parker put his arm around Linda, and she melted into him.

"Got it!" Leon said, throwing his hands in the air, signaling victory.

Linda and Parker moved to the dining room and stood behind the two boys. The screen was a list of file names with long, indecipherable strings of letters and numbers.

"What are we looking at?" Parker asked.

"You were right about the tracking software."

"The USB drive had two programs embedded in the code."

"You didn't open it, did you?" Parker asked as a shiver of anxiety swept over him.

"No. I have a program I created to let me look at the drive without triggering the .exe file that would open the file directory. I'm able to take a snapshot."

"You sure you didn't tip anyone off?" Parker wasn't sure of most of what Leon said.

"No chance. This program scans and copies. Something I came up with."

"Two bugs in the drive? What would they do? Tell Agent Thompson where we are when we open the drive?"

"No way to know for sure. Could be malware of some kind, maybe a key logger, but the second thing I found was more telling."

Leon moved the laptop, and Parker's eye was drawn to the disassembled USB on the tabletop. The silver plastic housing was separated from the electronic guts of the small storage device. A hole had been drilled through the case, and a piece of circuitry filled the gap. Parker recognized it immediately. A bug. An electronic surveillance device. It wasn't big enough for a camera.

"Is it still active?"

Leon shook his head. "I disabled it. It only works when powered up, you know, plugged into a computer. No internal battery. Which means it could only listen when its plugged in."

"So they—whoever they are—didn't hear any of our dinner discussions, or you two messing with the thing?"

"I did plug it in to scan the device, but first off, I used an air-gapped computer, and secondly, for the few minutes I had it connected, I had it on an energy-restricted, non-load, circuit."

"I'll pretend to know what that means."

Leon smiled. "Let's say I could scan it without letting the drive access a power source to activate the bug. Besides, since it was air gapped and not connected to the network, it couldn't transmit the data."

"It would have sent the audio over the internet? No one needed to be nearby to pick up the signal?"

"That's what it looks like. There is no transmitter in here. Probably what the malware was coded for—to use whatever network the user has when the drive is plugged in. Kinda slick actually."

"Is there any way to see the drive's content without tripping the bells and whistles they had set up?" Parker asked.

"Done. I have it on the screen here and this clean USB drive, if you need it."

Leon handed a drive to Parker and slid the laptop to him.

"Thanks, Leon. This was great work. Thanks for being extra careful. I don't trust these people—and it seems I had good reason."

"Sure thing. I'm gonna run. Miguel said he could bring me my laptop tomorrow. I'm doing some work at the Coalition offices for Billie."

"One favor, before you go. Can you put this back together and make it operational again?"

"And let it transmit?"

"Yeah. I've got an idea."

Leon dove into the work, and Linda brought Parker a glass with a generous pour of bourbon with one large ice cube.

She held another in her hand.

He nodded at her drink. "This mean you're staying the night?"

"If you play your cards right, mister."

"You shouldn't drink and drive…"

"Yeah, that's what I was going for." She said, rolling her eyes.

Miguel nudged Leon. "Hey, let's get outta here, the old people want to be alone. Want to come hang with me and Sarah? There's a new place off of Baseline with live music. We've been wanting to check it out."

"You don't mind me tagging along."

"It's fine. Besides, Sarah might bring a friend."

"I-I don't know."

"Come on. Live a little. Besides, you need your nose out of the computer screen for a night."

Leon grinned. "Well, maybe."

"Good."

Linda cleared her throat. "The old people want to remind you it's a school night."

"I don't have a class until ten," Leon said.

Leon handed the reassembled USB drive back to Parker.

Parker thanked him as the two boys gathered their backpacks and readied to head out. Leon left his laptop behind for Parker.

Parker hefted the chrome USB drive in his hand, glanced at Linda, and asked, "How's your acting?"

Chapter Seventeen

Parker gathered his laptop from his home office and brought it to the kitchen table while Linda poured them another bourbon.

"What?" Linda said. "I'm a method actor."

Parker shook his head. "Speaking of actors, where'd Billie run off to?"

"She mentioned something about replacing the supplies these feds confiscated. Said she had a line on where she could make up for the stuff the feds stole."

Parker didn't like the feeling. It started with an itch between his shoulder blades. Billie had a knack for skirting the edges of conventional humanitarian-aid distributors. Which really meant she got them wherever she could, and "gray" if not completely "black" market sources were often where she found her supplies.

"Miguel, how long has Billie been shipping cash along with her supply boxes?"

"Cash? I don't know. She personally takes care of packing everything for each trip. Why?"

"I didn't know she was doing that, and it got her into a little hot water with some feds today. I have a feeling there's more going on that she's not telling us."

"She has been kind of weird lately, like she and her son, scheduling the runs with our connections in Hermosillo. I used to, but the last month or so, she took it over. Then, we have distributors here with some non-governmental organizations who donate medical equipment, clothing, and food vouchers—She's cut them out. Won't tell me why."

Parker could see Miguel was upset at being shut out of the day-to-day Immigrant Coalition operations. He felt it personally. Like he had let Billie down.

"You know how she gets sometimes. She forgets we're here to help her. Billie's afraid to open up and ask for help."

Linda cleared her throat. "Remind you of someone else we know?" Her eyes bore in on Parker.

"I'm a work in progress."

He turned to Miguel. "Have fun tonight and tell Sarah I said hi. Be safe."

"Yes, Dad..."

No matter how many times he heard Miguel call him that, Parker warmed at the change in the boy who made a solo crossing from El Salvador.

"Okay, let's do this," he said to Linda as he straightened the laptop.

"What do you want me to say?"

"Follow my lead. I have a suspicion Agent Thompson isn't the one listening."

Linda's eyes widened.

Parker booted up the old laptop, made sure it connected to his Wi-Fi network, and shoved the USB drive in the small slot on the side of the laptop case.

He half expected a splashy banner to pop onto the screen announcing he was accessing confidential documents, or a warning federal prosecution awaited for possession of the material. But nothing happened. It was a little anticlimactic.

"Okay, let's see what we have here."

Parker clicked on the file manager and the directory listing the unknown device. A single file folder appeared with the label Red Dawn. When he clicked on the icon, a subdirectory of files scrolled onto the screen.

Parker nodded at Linda. "I don't know what to make of the FBI's interest in our murder investigation."

Linda nodded at the cue to chime in. "It's a fed thing. Stepping over the locals and taking over our case."

"Because two of theirs are dead. My gut tells me we're dealing with a whole different level of cover-up."

"That explains the fire in the old shack. The lab able to tell you what was inside? I mean other than the bodies?"

"Not yet. Be a few days before we have anything. This isn't a priority case for them," Parker said.

Parker clicked on the file folder labeled Red Dawn, and as Agent Thompson promised, documents, surveillance reports, and transcripts of the last communiques from the two deceased operatives. But large swaths of redacted text, with black bars obscuring chunks of the reports.

An organizational chart was of limited value because most of the boxes were blank with labels identifying them as "unknown." Three minor players at the bottom of the pyramid were called out as area commanders in San Diego, El Paso, and Phoenix. Photos with each man were taken from a distance, but it was clear they were white and even in a snapshot carried themselves with a paramilitary swagger.

One image stood out to Parker. The Phoenix area Red Dawn Commander was Jack Talent, the biker he and Barry Johns met at the bar. He wasn't a recruiter; he was in the Red Dawn command structure.

"The feds didn't give us much to go on. Some new cartel is posturing down south. They don't give us anything connecting them to our murders. This is a waste of time."

Parker unplugged the USB drive from his laptop.

"If Agent Thompson wasn't listening, who is?" Linda asked.

"Her task force is compromised. We know that. I don't think she knew the files she gave me were redacted. Tells me someone on the inside, a person she thought she could trust, is covering Red Dawn's tracks."

"But those three area commanders were identified," Linda said.

"My guess is they were outed already. Espi knew to look for Jack Talent as the man who was involved in the paramilitary and militia scene in Southern Arizona. Low-hanging fruit. Red Dawn probably saw them as disposable."

"Where does it leave us?"

The answer came in a chime on Parker's cell phone. The caller ID read "unknown caller."

Parker hit the accept button. "Hello."

"You looking for work?"

"I might be. Who's this?"

"A friend of Jack's. You met him at The Kickstand. He said you and your sidekick seemed up to the job."

"Depending on the job," Parker said.

"You mean depending on how much we're paying."

"That too."

"Come out to the Buckeye airport at four tomorrow afternoon. We'll work out the details."

"How will I know you?"

"You won't. But I'll know you. You want the job—be there." The line fell silent.

"Well?"

Parker tapped the USB drive with a fingertip. "Someone was listening. They want Barry and me to go out to the airfield near Buckeye tomorrow afternoon."

"If they called after you went to the bar and heard us on the USB bug—"

"Yeah, they know we're cops. And we're heading into an ambush."

Chapter Eighteen

"Asetup?" Barry said.

Parker assembled the team in his office hours before sunrise the next morning. Barry Johns, Pete Tully, Linda, Espi, and Lynnette Finch gathered before the rest of the detectives began crowding the unit.

"Someone on Agent Thompson's team doctored the files on the USB drive to make sure we couldn't get anything useful out of it and picked up audio while Linda and I were checking out the files. Within a minute of using the drive, I get a call about a meet at the Buckeye airport. Too much of a coincidence to be anything else but a setup."

"What makes you believe Agent Thompson didn't know about the device?" Lynne asked.

"It was a thought. But she believed she was giving me the files on Red Dawn. She made a big show of acting like she was going to take us in for obstructing her investigation. She wanted us to find out because she knew her team had been compromised. I don't think she knows how deeply the compromise goes."

Pete Tully tightened his jaw and looked to mull over the new information. Parker recognized the look.

"Pete? What ya chewing on?"

"The witness I interviewed—the scout leader, Ken Dryden. He knew to be out there when the plane came in. Someone told him where to go. I need to lean on him. He knew, and there's some dirt he's not giving up."

"If the FBI will let you talk to him. It's not a bad thread to pull on."

"What do we do?" Barry asked. "Are we gonna show up at the Buckeye airfield like they expect us to?"

"No. And neither will they." Parker turned to Espi. "That's where I hope you and Lynne can help.

"How's that?" Espi asked.

"When's the last time you guys helped a joint training exercise?"

"Oh, I get it. If there's a visible presence of federal agencies at the airstrip, Red Dawn won't be able to do their thing," Espi said.

"That kind of exercise takes a lot of advance notice and interagency agreements. You don't know the bureaucracy it takes to approve something like that. Then there's the budget cost associated with training—"

"There wouldn't actually be any training," Parker said.

"Just a show of force," Espi said.

"I'm looking for a handful of feds in tactical gear, a vehicle or two.

"Maybe," Lynne said. "HRT owes me a favor."

"Perfect. I don't expect whoever Red Dawn has at the airport to go hot. I think it's a delivery crew like we had yesterday at the Yavapai Dunes Airfield."

"And we know how it ended up for Thompson's people," Barry said.

"If we bring in a visible presence, it will make them divert to a secondary location. Agent Thompson's intel—the final decision on the drop was made in flight. If we're able to lock down the Buckeye airfield—"

"Then the Red Dawn pickup crew can't sprint off to the new location," Espi said.

"At least those members can't. They'd cancel the drop—which means a loss in revenue, or they would pull a secondary crew in to make the pickup somewhere else," Parker said.

"And you want to be at the alternate location," Barry said.

"They'll be expecting us," Espi said.

"And they know where the new drop location will be," Lynne said.

"If we have their crew occupied at the Buckeye airfield, they will be forced to call in local manpower as backup," Parker said.

"Jack Talent," Barry said as he straightened up.

"Exactly. Talent and probably a crew of his misfit biker buddies."

"If Red Dawn knows we aren't who we're pretending to be, what makes you think Talent will reach out?" Barry said.

"Because of what they did, let us have on that USB drive. They gave Talent up as one of the local commanders. They've labeled him as disposable. I don't think he has a large merc pool to draw from with his Chain Slayer drinking pals. He'll have to call us."

"And if Red Dawn told him we were hot?"

"We'll be ready for it, but I don't think they did. The organization left him out in the cold. They would compartmentalize their intel. If they think that little of Talent, they wouldn't share anything with him."

"I dunno, man. That's a high-risk proposition there," Espi said.

"I agree with Espi," Lynne said.

"It's not without risk, I give you that. Listen, it might give us the best chance to get inside Red Dawn. Talent has a connection—sure it might not be the top dog, but it's a step closer than anyone's been able to find."

"Even if we grab Talent, you think he'll roll on whoever the next link of the chain might be? He seems pretty closed off when we had our face-to-face in the bar last night," Barry said.

"Once he realizes the organization has cut him loose, he'll want to throw them under the bus. He's a soldier for hire. They cut off his funding, he's not going to take it on the chin."

Espi rocked back and glanced at Lynne. "He has a point there. As long as we have some operational control over the secondary airfield—where Red Dawn is coming in—we can keep—"

The conversation stopped when one of Thompson's men strode into the main office.

Parker stiffened. "We expecting anyone? Pete? You or Barry have a play date?"

Pete shook his head. "Not with these robots."

Parker strode to the threshold of his office door. The tall and thick-necked man wasn't alone. His black-clad twin waited in the hall.

"What's out there, Nathan?" Linda asked in a whisper over his shoulder.

"FBI, Thompson's task force."

"What do those goons want?" Barry Johns asked.

Having the task force appear in his office didn't give Parker a warm and fuzzy feeling. The Operation Black Bag team was desperate to nail whoever was responsible for the deaths of their comrades. What would desperation bring this early in the morning? Had they listened to his and Linda's charade last night, through the listening device?

"Only one way to find out."

Parker recognized the task force operator from his encounter with the team at his office. The man dressed in the black utility uniform was one of the pair who pressed him in the hallway outside of Captain Morris's office.

The man's face was tight. He was hiding something behind a stone facade.

"Detective."

The task force man looked behind Parker at the group assembled in his office.

"Detective, is Agent Thompson with you?"

Parker pulled back at the question.

"Thompson. No, she's not. Why?"

"We can't locate her, sir. I—I think she's been taken."

Chapter Nineteen

"Taken?" Parker asked.

"She was supposed to meet the team this afternoon to go over our operational plan for the airport takedown. The diversion you and Agent Thompson talked about."

Parker bit the inside of his cheek. If this man knew about the JTTF being marshaled as a diversion, who else was aware of Thompson's deception?"

"Let's unwind this a little," Parker said. "What's your name for starters?"

"I'm Deputy Marshal Paul Compton. Assigned to the Joint Task Force from the Southern District of California Field Office."

"Marshals Service? You're not FBI? I thought Thompson's team was made up of former FBI HRT types."

"Most are. Rivers and Carter were from outside the FBI, too. I'm the only one left."

"More than a bit disconcerting," Lynne said.

"I was under the impression Agent Thompson kept our arrangement—the whole diversion bit—between her and me. How come you know?"

"Kira kept me in the loop. We had each other's backs more than once. She told me about her plan to have you to intercept the Red Dawn delivery while we ran interference. I told her I didn't like the approach."

"Why's that?" Parker asked.

"Because we knew the team had sprung a leak. Someone was giving our mission intel to Red Dawn. We have two team members down. If we posted our team at a bogus location, whoever is giving information out will sniff it out like a dirty gym sock. And, apparently, they did if they have Kira."

"What's the Marshals Service doing on a border task force anyway? Don't you guys usually pick up fugitives?"

"Yeah—yeah, one shitty movie and it's all anyone knows. The Marshals Service does the fugitive apprehension for sure, but we're the federal agency charged with cross-border fugitive work, where we leverage a network of investigative teams and organizations across the globe, prioritizing the location, apprehension, and removal of violent transnational fugitives. Well, that's what it says on the recruitment poster anyway.

"Red Dawn is a multinational criminal organization, and it fits with our charter."

"Makes sense. Come on and tell the team what you know about Agent Thompson—could help us figure out what happened to her."

Marshal Compton paused, and Parker sensed he wasn't comfortable.

"Listen, I can't stay because if they got to her then they might be watching me too. I had to come here on the remote chance she was meeting with you. I dropped by her hotel room, and the place had been turned out. Her stuff was there, Radio, Op files, and the reports from Rivers and Carter. All of it would be incredibly valuable to Red Dawn."

"They didn't take it?" Johns said.

"Which tells me they didn't need it—they already have it. But her gun and her backup piece were there too, and she'd never go anywhere without them. Someone took her."

"Someone from the team?" Parker asked.

Compton shrugged. "Could be. I'm trying to round them up now."

Lynne leaned on the desk and looked up at the deputy marshal. Parker had seen the look before—one she used when she was trying to assess the level of bullshit—one she usually reserved for him.

"You haven't alerted your chain of command yet?" Lynne asked.

He shook his head. "I can't trust anyone there. I don't know how deep this goes or who else is involved in taking her."

Lynne backed away from the table and snatched her cell phone. "I need to call this in."

"No. Please don't. Kira warned me. If something like this came up, I can't go to the FBI."

"That's absurd. She's one of ours, and we need to get her back."

"Please." The nervous energy spilled off of Compton. His breath was rapid, and a bead of sweat was building on his brow.

"What would you suggest we do? This group doesn't seem one to ask for ransom. The two agents you lost would seem to testify to that, don't you think?"

"Yes—No—I don't know what to think. She knew she was a high-value target for the group. She told me if something like this happened—if she was killed or captured—I was not to put anyone on the team at risk."

Parker put a cold bottle of water in front of the deputy marshal. "That was before she realized her team was compromised." Taking a step back and leaning on his desk, he had trouble getting over the taking of one team member and the outright murder of two others. It wasn't because they hoped to pull more information from Thompson. If what he believed was true, whoever nabbed her had the information because they were on the inside. Why not murder her in her hotel room? It didn't leave him with a good feeling.

"Are you certain she was taken?" Parker asked.

"What? Haven't you heard a word I've said? Yes, they have her."

"Could she have run off?"

Compton didn't even take a second to consider what Parker said. "No. Of course not. She would have told me. I can't find Dryden, our witness, either."

Linda and Parker came to the conclusion at the same moment. Compton and Thompson had something more than a task force relationship going on. It's happened before. People working in high-pressure situations grew close, and sometimes closeness led to intense personal relationships.

"How long have you and Kira been together?" Linda asked.

Compton's eyes widened. "It's not like that—it's—"

"Who else knew?" Parker said.

Compton's mouth gaped open. "We were careful. No one knew."

"Someone knew. Someone always knows," Linda said.

"She's right. One of the team knew and they are going to leverage your relationship to get what they want. Who have you told she's missing?"

"Leverage? No, they wouldn't."

"We're talking about the same person who killed two of your team. Yeah, they're capable of a little extortion."

Compton put his head in his hands. "I can't believe this."

"Who else knows?"

"Metzger, Williams, and Prokop. I told them when I started looking for her."

"Where are they now?"

"I told them to wait for me to check in with them."

"Do you have tracking software on your phones?" Lynne asked.

Compton nodded. "Kira insisted we install it. They team didn't know. But she left her phone in the hotel."

"What about the others?"

"What do you mean? They aren't missing. We know where they are."

"Do you?" Lynne asked.

Parker nodded. "Can you track them from your phone? If Agent Thompson trusted you enough to let you know what she and I discussed, then it stands to reason she'd let you track the team's location."

Compton struggled pulling his cell phone from his pocket. "I've never tried. I don't know how to do it."

"I can help," Linda said. Parker wondered why she knew about cell phone location software, but her foster son Leon installed it on his phone and Linda's after he was taken by a Los Muertos thug last year. Leon felt it was a compromise to let Linda know where he was, rather than the two dozen phone calls and texts every day to check on him.

Compton handed the phone to Linda. Parker thought the task force would have some highly encrypted black-box type cell phones. Instead, it was a standard iPhone, and not a new model.

Linda scrolled to the last page where the apps loaded on the device were displayed. There were only a handful of them on the government-issued cell. "I think it's this one."

Linda tapped on the icon, and a password screen popped up. She handed the phone back to Compton. "It needs your password."

He glanced at the screen. "I don't have a password. I've never used this before."

There was a prompt on the screen. "1x." The space only allowed three letters or numbers.

"One x?"

"Any idea what that means? Agent Thompson would have entered that, right?"

"I guess. One time? No, first time...like where we met."

Compton tapped NYC. "We met in New York when I was serving a fugitive warrant on a couple of Aryan Nation members. She was meeting with the U.S. Attorney. That's where she asked me to join the task force."

He pressed Enter, and the screen flickered to black.

"Oh, I guess it didn't work."

A second later, it blossomed with a map of the Phoenix area and a series of blue dots—eight of them clustered on the screen. All but one way off by itself. Compton tapped a fingertip on the lonely blue dot.

"Metzger."

"Where is he?" Parker asked.

Compton handed him the phone. "You tell me. I have no idea where any of these landmarks are."

Parker held the device, and a chill crept up his spine. The blue dot where Metzger blinked at a remote section of road he knew well.

The exact spot where Parker's partner, Deputy McMillan, was murdered over five years ago. How would a task force member know the location? There were only a few people who did, and most of them were in this room.

One lived in a Supermax prison cell. Esteban Castaneda murdered his partner and was responsible for more than a dozen other bodies dropped in the desert.

"We need to take a drive."

Chapter Twenty

The remote potholed road was well out of the path of traffic in the northern quarter of the valley. The towns of Cave Creek and Carefree were the closest developments. Billie Carson built her new place not far from the spot—largely because it was isolated. There was no reason Metzger would know about the place.

Parker, Johns, and Tully drove out to the location on the map. Lynne and Compton left for her FBI offices to find out what the official records held about Metzger.

Parker turned off his headlights as they approached the spot. The pre-dawn moonlight cast a pale blue light on the desert landscape. Perfect for spotting lingering ghosts of the past.

"See anything?" Johns asked from the passenger seat.

"Nothing," Parker said.

Mac's memorial was up ahead. A faint outline of the white wooden cross erected in the weeks after McMillan was killed morphed out of the darkness. Parker never figured out who put the memorial out here. Mac's wife never came to the spot—she couldn't bear to see where her husband bled out in the dirt. Billie was the one Parker suspected was responsible for the roughhewn wooden cross. It could have been her that night who died during an illegal smuggling run.

"Keep your eyes open," Parker said as he cruised to a stop on the red dirt shoulder.

"You sure this is the place? I mean, why would this fed come out here, of all places?" Johns said.

Parker tapped out a text message to Lynne asking if the blue dot on Compton's phone had moved location. She responded immediately, saying she had the phone in hand and the dot hadn't changed since they brought up the task force team members.

He pocketed the phone and opened his door.

"Where you going, boss?" Tully asked.

"Gonna go take a look."

Parker exited the driver's side, and Tully hopped from the back seat. The moonlight cast shadows on the hillside and turned the creosote brush along the roadway into an inky black mass.

Behind the wooden cross, Parker noticed a smooth surface, out of place in the rough rock and broken Palo Verde branches. As he drew close, he recognized it as a cell phone, tossed behind the white wooden cross.

When he was a step away from the device, it rang, sending a shrill electronic buzz into the desert night.

"Pete, they know we're here." Parker looked to the hill above the road and down the dark dirt game trails crossing the wash. No reflective surface in the distance to mark a watch post.

The phone kept ringing.

Parker bent to pick it up. The display read "unknown number." It looked like the same model of phone the deputy marshal used.

Parker hit connect and listened.

From the phone, an electronically scrambled voice sounded. "You are predictable, detective. I knew it wouldn't take you long."

"Who am I talking to?"

"A friend of a friend."

Parker felt it in his gut. The friend this caller was talking about was Castaneda.

"You got me out here, what do you want? Where's Agent Thompson?"

"Parker, you need to back away. My issues are with Thompson and her irritating task force."

"If you thought the task force was irritating, wait until you see what happens after taking a federal agent."

"They need to be taught a lesson. Apparently, I haven't been clear. The task force is to pack up and leave. The southern border is ours to control."

"Doesn't seem like someone in control. It seems like someone's afraid."

"The task force—I want to see them leaving."

"Agent Thompson—I want proof of life."

"I don't care what you want."

"Why should the task force do anything for you?"

"We won't tolerate interference in our operation."

"I need proof of life."

"Ah, detective. You are being troublesome. There is always a price. You want proof of life, are you prepared to pay the price?"

"Cut the crap. Proof of life or I'm hanging up."

"Very well. But remember, there is a cost."

A shuffling sound on the phone was followed by a few seconds of dead air.

Agent Thompson came on the line. She sounded sluggish, slurring her words as if she were drugged. "Parker. Leave this alone. Get my team out of here. I can't have more of them hurt."

"Can you tell me where you are?"

"I'm listening, detective," the scrambled voice said.

"You have nothing to gain by keeping Agent Thompson."

"If the task force isn't gone in twelve hours, Agent Thompson will find out if she can fly."

Parker seethed at the voice without a name.

"Now I told you there was a price, and you said you were prepared to pay it. Life for life as it were."

Abruptly, the phone connection died. Parker's mind spun at the threat leveled at him. His first thoughts were of Linda and Miguel. Would they be the next targets?

As he hit speed dial on his phone, a zip sounded in the dark, followed by a shallow pop.

"What?" Parker said.

Tully spun and dropped in the dirt near McMillan's memorial marker.

Parker ran to him and rolled him over to find a bullet wound to the chest. Blood poured from the wound.

"Barry! Pete's down. Bring the trauma kit."

Barry was already out of the SUV when the gunshot sounded from the hill to the right of the vehicle. He grabbed the kit from the rear hatch and ran to where Parker leaned over the fallen detective.

"Oh, God no," Barry said as he got on his knees next to Parker.

Johns froze at the sight of the blood oozing from his partner's chest. Parker tore open a package of Quick-Clot from the kit and poured the powder into the exposed wound.

The blood slowed but the desert underneath the detective bore a dark stain. Parker tilted Pete and spotted the exit wound.

"Dammit. Barry. Hand me another Quick-Clot."

Barry didn't move, transfixed at his partner bleeding out in front of him."

"Barry!"

That shook him out of his trance, and he dug another Quick-clot from the kit and prepared a pressure bandage for the wound, applying it after Parker emptied the bag of clotting agent into the gaping exit wound.

They carefully rolled him over again and applied a second pressure bandage to the entrance wound.

Parker put a finger to Tully's carotid artery. "Got a pulse. It's weak. We gotta get him outta here now.

They both lifted Tully, carrying him to the SUV, when two additional shots rang out from the hillside. Parker and Johns ducked, but the shots flattened the tires on the right side of the SUV. There wouldn't be any driving out.

Parker got Tully safely hidden behind the SUV. Barry glanced at his cell phone.

"Boss, we got a problem. No cell signal."

Parker had been on the phone. There was a signal out here. His cell showed nothing. The cell phone he found behind the memorial bore the same notification. No bars. The cell signal was being jammed. Whoever pinned them down wanted to make sure Tully wouldn't make it out alive.

Parker had agreed to pay the price—he didn't know the cost would be so steep.

Chapter Twenty-One

"Did you see where it came from?" Parker asked.

Barry kept down with his back against the front tire, gun drawn.

"I was busy keeping my head down. Didn't catch a muzzle flash."

There was a slight mechanical sound spilling on the wind toward them. It had the unsteady, rough cadence of a dirt bike.

"Hear that?" Parker said. "I think they're bugging out."

"Sounds like someone riding away from us."

Parker would find out soon enough. He stood, pulled the passenger door open, and reached in for the radio console in the SUV. They'd jammed the cell signal, but were they thinking about the VHF radio in the department vehicle?

He grabbed the handheld microphone and clicked it with his thumb. The sound of the static click over the radio sent him back to the night his partner died out here on this spot.

McMillan had spotted a van running in his direction. The road was a known corridor used by the coyotes to smuggle undocumented migrants through the valley to avoid the checkpoints. After Mac stopped the van, Parker tried reaching him by radio. All he received in response was a click on the radio in return. By the time Parker found him, McMillan had nearly bled out before dying in his arms.

Here he was again. He couldn't do it once more. Pete Tully couldn't die out here.

The radio signal from the sheriff's SUV wasn't going through. The VHF band was being jammed, too.

He switched to a UHF band reserved for local agencies. And put out a distress call.

"11-99. Officer down. Need immediate transport by Air 1." He gave the location and waited."

A static-ridden reply came back in return from an Arizona Fish and Wildlife officer east of Cave Creek. Parker repeated the distress call, and he thought he heard a positive response from the game warden.

There was nothing to do but wait.

Tully was gray from the blood loss. Parker had to check, because his respiration was slow and shallow.

He pulled a foil blanket from a pouch in the back of the SUV and unfolded it before placing it over Tully.

"Think they heard us?" Barry said.

Parker prayed the call went through. Tully didn't have much time left. He kneeled in the dirt next to him, cradling his head, just as he did with McMillan before.

"I'm sorry, Pete."

A breeze blew in from the south, and a faint whirring sound came and faded with the wind.

Barry perked up. "I heard it too."

He sprang up to the passenger door, reached in, and turned on the headlights and the flashing red and blue strobes. They cascaded off the brush around them and created a macabre display of dancing specters celebrating the evil that visited this place.

In the sky to the south, Parker saw it first. A red strobe heading directly at them. The whirring became more pronounced, and the rhythmic pulse of a helicopter came swooping at them.

Dust from the road began kicking up as the craft descended on the road behind their disabled SUV.

Within seconds of touching down, two paramedics ran from the helicopter door and kneeled over Tully.

One exchanged a grave look with his partner.

The paramedics quickly transferred Tully to a sturdy orange litter and, with Parker and Barry's help, got him to the open helicopter door.

The litter slid in on a track and secured Tully in place. One paramedic inserted an IV and grimaced as he assessed the entry wound. He quickly attached electronic leads with sticky adhesive patches.

Parker wasn't a medical expert, but even he knew the slow, irregular heart rate wasn't good. He started climbing in, and the paramedic held him back.

"No room."

"I can't leave him."

"You're not. We've got him now. We gotta go now," the second paramedic said as she shoved past Parker and climbed into the compartment with Tully.

"Where you taking him?" Parker asked.

"Scottsdale Osborne is the closest Level 1 trauma center. Ten minutes out, tops."

Parker thought he could wedge in behind the paramedics. He didn't want to abandon Tully. Seconds mattered, and every moment he delayed them from taking off put Pete at risk.

He backed away from the helicopter, and the door slid shut. Road dirt and small pebbles pelted Parker as the orange and white craft lifted from the desert floor. It spun around and tilted nose down as it rose and sped south toward Scottsdale.

Parker's gut turned to ice as he watched the rescue craft leave. He hoped Tully would survive. It didn't look good—so much blood loss. He couldn't bear another loss like McMillan. In this same location. It was too much.

The ball in his stomach tightened when it became clear the location wasn't by chance and only a handful of people knew its significance to him. It always came back to Esteban Castaneda. Even locked away in a Supermax prison in Colorado, the man continued to torment Parker and those close to him—like he had promised before his capture.

Parker believed it was behind them. Even though he was certain the electronically altered voice on the phone wasn't Castaneda, the thug had a hand in getting Tully drawn into the line of fire.

"Boss, we got headlights coming from the south," Barry Johns said.

They held positions behind the disabled SUV. The shooter on the hillside had vanished, but were these Red Dawn forces closing in to finish them off?

Through the dust plume kicked up from the approaching vehicle, Parker caught the dim red and blue strobe.

"I think it's the cavalry coming to the rescue," Parker said.

Barry stood and clocked the three incoming vehicles.

"I'm sorry," Barry said in a soft voice.

"For what?" Parker said.

"I—I froze up back there. My partner needed me, and I froze. If something happens to him because I waited too long…"

"You have nothing to apologize for. You came through when it mattered. Whatever happens to Pete—it's on them—not you. Trust me on that score."

Barry nodded, but Parker knew the young detective wasn't ready to write off the guilt yet. Parker knew from experience, the trauma Barry Johns experienced, seeing a partner and friend bleeding out in the desert, wasn't an event you could ignore, or pretend didn't bother you. Trauma like that wormed its way into your core. It poked out from the depths when you least expected it.

The lead vehicle skidded to a stop near their SUV. The familiar black and yellow Maricopa County Sheriff's Office logo on the side allowed Parker to let out a deep breath he didn't know he was holding back.

A deputy hopped from the vehicle and jogged to Parker, glanced at the flattened tires, and his eyes widened. "Damn. You guys okay?"

Parker had seen the young deputy before, but needed to glance at his name tag to place it. Valdez. Young, headstrong, but trainable.

"Valdez, I need you to get Detective Johns and me to Osborne Medical Center."

"You hurt?"

"Not us. Detective Tully is on his way there by chopper."

Three additional vehicles pulled to the roadside. One was a plain black SUV. Lynne and Espi jumped from the vehicle. Lynne ran to Parker and hugged him.

"I was—I thought you…"

"It's Pete. It's bad." Parker glanced at his blood-stained hands. He clenched his fists to hide the tremor.

"Come on, let's get you out of here," Espi said.

Parker had Valdez wait with the disabled vehicle until the motor pool tow truck came to take it back to the yard. The SUV would be picked apart by scavengers if left unattended.

Parker and Johns got into the rear seat, and they pulled around, heading back out toward Scottsdale. He checked his cell phone, and when they were less than a quarter mile away, his signal popped back on.

Whoever attacked them used electronic jammers to keep them from calling for help. They used a device with a limited range so it wouldn't draw attention. Sophisticated and it required planning.

Parker leaned forward. Any word on Pete? At the hospital, yet?"

Lynne turned in the seat and said, "Just before we got to you, we got word."

"And?"

"He didn't make it, Nathan…"

Chapter Twenty-Two

Parker's world fell black.

Pete was gone. He couldn't be. Yet the blood on Parker's hands told a different story. He was responsible for what happened out there. Out there at the same damned spot. Why did it have to be Pete?

Parker glanced over at Barry, and the big man wept. Streams of tears ran down his face.

Parker could hear Lynne talking, but the words were a buzzing sound fighting against the recriminations pounding against the walls of his skull. He knew he'd have to tell Pete's wife, Janet. She needed to hear it from him, not some anonymous department chaplain she'd never met.

He called Captain Morris and gave him the news as best as he could. The words clung to his throat, and when he hung up, he wasn't sure what he'd told the Captain.

"Nathan. Are you hearing me?" Lynne said.

He glanced at her. "Castaneda had a hand in this, Lynne."

"That's what I've been trying to tell you. When you mentioned his name, I called the Bureau of Prisons. Castaneda is in lockup and hasn't had a visitor."

"His handprints are all over this. He knew the location, more than anyone. He killed McMillan there and now…"

"I understand, but Castaneda is deep in the most secure prison in the country. He didn't have the chance to conspire with anyone to arrange this. The ambush out there tonight was related to Red Dawn and the JTTF."

"Listen to me, Lynne. Castaneda is involved."

"I know it seems that way, but—" Lynne was cut off by her phone buzzing.

"Lynne Finch," she said into the phone. Her blue eyes brightened, and she turned to face Parker in the back seat. "You're sure?"

She hung up the phone. "He's alive. Pete's alive."

The news hit Parker in the chest. Afraid to believe it and elation in equal measure.

Anticipating his question, Lynne told him Pete flatlined twice in the helicopter. He was gone. They revived him in the trauma center. It was a matter of minutes. If you hadn't stopped the bleeding and gotten him in the air ambulance..."

"Pete's a fighter," Parker said.

"He's in surgery now."

Parker knew any number of complications could change the outcome. Pete was alive, but could he survive?

He made another call to Captain Morris with the update, and the relief swept over him. The relief crystallized into something more. Anger. At Red Dawn. Castaneda. And the forces that brought them into their lives.

As they pulled into the Osborne Medical Center on Drinkwater Boulevard, Parker leaned forward and tapped Lynne on the shoulder.

"Thank you. For coming to get us, for getting that helicopter going. All of it."

"When I heard an officer was down, Nathan—I had this bad feeling in the pit of my stomach. I didn't want—"

Parker cut her off when he saw her eyes welling. There would be time for that later.

"I need you to call the ADX. Have someone search Castaneda's cell. There's something there to connect him to this—I know it."

"Nathan, I know you want everything bad that happens in the world to be on Castaneda's shoulders. The man is barely alive after surviving a stabbing assault at the prison six months ago. He's in no condition to run anything."

"Please, just ask the prison staff to search him."

She nodded. "All right. I will. But the helicopter—that was you guys. The radio call you made got picked up by the local fish and wildlife officer, and he called in the air ambulance on its way back from dropping off a stranded hiker who'd gotten stuck on The Flatiron summit on the Superstition Mountains to the east. That's why they got there so quickly."

Parker spotted the distinctive orange and white helicopter on the landing pad above the trauma center. They'd kept Pete alive long enough to give him a chance.

Parker hopped out the moment the SUV pulled to the emergency entrance. Barry Johns was on his heels as they ran inside and approached the ER reception desk. Parker tried to get someone's attention, but they were busy with patients, families, and the flow of ambulance traffic coming in from the retirement communities surrounding the Scottsdale facility.

"Parker, over here."

Captain Morris was already on site.

"Any news?" Parker asked.

"They got him in surgery. The in-flight ambulance crew started CPR and gave him a chance."

"What are the doctors saying?"

"Too early to tell. He's critical. The blood loss alone..."

"I need to get word to his wife. She should be here."

"I have a deputy bringing her in. I didn't think I could wait. He's bad, Nathan."

"Did they give you any idea—"

"Of his chances? They wouldn't say, other than he's lucky."

Barry turned at the entrance doors opening. Janet Tully entered, and Barry went to her and hugged the woman tight. Parker started to her, but the Captain held him back.

"Go clean up first," Morris whispered.

Parker glanced down at his blood-stained hands and shirt. Janet didn't need to see the visceral reminder of what her husband suffered.

"Thanks, cap."

Parker approached the nurse's station and explained what he needed. A young nurse guided him to a restroom and tossed a set of scrubs for him to change into.

When he came back out, he had his soiled shirt in a plastic bag and felt conspicuous in the light blue medical scrub top. The evidence was gone from his hands, but not from his soul.

Janet spotted him from across the waiting room. He approached him and held it together until she hugged him. Then he fell apart. Heavy sobs came from the slight fifty-year-old woman. She was a cop's wife and always had an event like this in the back of her mind. Always there, but carefully tucked away. Until today. And it all came out.

"Thank you for giving him a chance," she said, not letting loose of Parker.

Parker only felt guilt he put Pete in harm's way to begin with. Making a deal with the voice on the other end of the phone.

"They said if you hadn't used the radio and found a game warden—"

"Can I get you anything, Janet? Need me to call the kids, or some coffee?"

"I called them. Told them to wait until I have news. They both live on the East Coast."

A hospital worker dressed in a cheap suit found Janet and cleared his throat.

"Excuse me, Mrs. Tully?"

"Yes. What's happened?" Anxiety etched over her face.

"I have these forms we need you to take a look at."

"Forms? Oh, insurance. I have our cards here." She stared, searching her purse.

"No, no. These are forms asking if you know your husband's preferences. Did he want to be an organ donor?"

"What? What are you saying? Is he…"

Parker got between the hospital paper pusher and Janet. He got within inches of the man's face, close enough to smell the tuna salad the man had for dinner.

"Listen, pal, back the hell off."

"I'm only trying—"

"You don't walk away right now, you're gonna need those forms for yourself. You feel me?"

The man's face grew pale. He tried to respond, but nothing came out when he opened his mouth. He turned on his heel and strode off behind doors marked "staff only."

Parker turned back to Janet, who was hugging her purse. "I'm sorry."

"Thanks for shooing him off. I couldn't think about anything like that right now. When he came out—I assumed the worst."

A doctor in surgical garb came out from behind the doors and checked in at the nurse's station. The nurse pointed at Janet Tully.

Janet gripped Parker's hand.

"Mrs. Tully?"

"Yes…"

"I'm Dr. Berg, one of the surgical team. I wanted to let you know we're working on your husband. It's going to take a while. We've got to repair a lot of damage. If you want to go home, we'll call you when he gets out of surgery."

"I'm staying here."

"That's fine, of course. But it's going to be several hours."

"I understand. I'm staying here."

"Fine. I'll let the desk know. Oh, are you the one who used the Quick-Clot out there?"

Parker stiffened. Did he do something wrong and make Pete's condition worse? "Yes, I did."

"Good work. You saved his life. Gave him a fighting chance."

The doctor excused himself and disappeared behind the doors.

"Let's find a place to park. How about over there where Captain Morris is standing?"

"Okay. Thank you, Nathan. Thank you for giving me a chance at a tomorrow with my Pete."

Parker's lip quivered, and he gave her a hug instead of responding. He held her hand and found a sofa against a wall.

As word traveled about the injured detective, a constant flow of Maricopa deputies and officers from allied agencies passed through the waiting room. It was a show of support, respect, brotherhood, and recognition of the nature of the job.

Lynne found Parker sitting with Janet Tully.

"Nathan, can I see you for a minute?" Lynne asked.

Nathan shifted his gaze to her and was about to tell her no. He was where he needed to be when he caught a steely glint in her eye.

"Janet, will you excuse me for a bit? Barry. Stay with Janet."

As Barry settled in, Parker leaned in and whispered to him. "She needs us now. If anything changes with Pete, you call me immediately, understood?"

He nodded.

"Lynne have something?"

"I've seen that look before. She's on the hunt."

Chapter Twenty-Three

Parker didn't tell Barry the last time he saw that look, she was after him.

"Lynne, what do you have?" Parker asked as they strode from the medical center waiting room.

She stiffened her shoulders, her jaw tight. "The field office got a call."

"From?"

"They didn't say."

"Was it electronically altered? Because that's what we got out there at Coyote Wash."

"It was. They had a message for you. He said you have another choice to make."

"This guy and his fucking games. Your tech people able to track the call? Anything to uncover who's making these calls?"

"Nothing yet. They spouted something about internet phone call routing and a bounced the signal from four different routers in three different countries. They are trying to pinpoint it, but they didn't seem too optimistic."

"He say what this choice was?"

"No. He said he'd call you. In the morning, at my office."

"Your office? How come?"

"Beats me. I hoped you'd know why."

"Last time he wanted me in a specific location, someone was waiting to take a shot at Pete. This is another setup, Lynne. Castaneda. He's promised to go after people close to me—Pete this time. If he wants me at the FBI offices, means he wants you next."

"I think you're putting too much of this on Castaneda. He's out of the picture. This—whoever it is—is pulling the strings on this Red Dawn organization. This is someone new."

Parker fell silent. As much as he wanted to believe Lynne. A new player on the scene wouldn't be able to pick off undercover operatives infiltrating their organization, snatch the lead agent running the task force, or lure him out to the exact location of his greatest failure. If it wasn't Castaneda, it was someone who held intimate knowledge about him and his team.

"What time is the call expected?" Parker asked as he stepped aside to let an older couple into the emergency room entrance.

"Seven-thirty."

Parker bit his bottom lip for a moment. A spark of recognition lit.

"I know what he's doing. He wants us busy while he makes the next delivery. Jack Talent said it was going to be tomorrow morning. I don't know the exact time, but I'll bet it's within an hour of this phone call."

"Okay, I'm following. But, what's the choice he wants you to make? Go after the delivery, or take his phone call? Doesn't seem important enough to me," Lynne said.

"I think there are a couple of things in play here. The call is a way to keep us away from the intended drop and lure people close to me. I know you don't put much stock in Castaneda's threats, but he did promise to target those I cared about. You've seen what he can do."

"If Red Dawn is bringing in another shipment by air, we can task the JTTF to intercept."

"The task force is compromised. Not all of them, but enough to be fairly sure any operational plans or intel on an airport takedown will be a dry hole."

"If not the task force—then what?" Lynne was interrupted by the chirp of Parker's cell phone.

"Parker, here."

He listened for a moment before putting the call on speaker.

"Hey, doc, I have Lynne Finch here from the FBI, could you repeat that last bit?"

"Hello, Lynne, it's Elizabeth White at the ME's office. I was telling the detective I'll have an ID on one of the bodies—the one I was expecting to have trouble identifying because of the massive trauma."

"The one who may have been tossed from a plane?" Lynne said.

"That's the one. As you both know, the facial and dental markers were not going to help us in this case. But our victim did have an orthopedic plate attached to his left ulna to repair a fracture."

"You pulled a serial number?" Parker asked.

"We did. It wasn't an autopsy, really—we would have called you for that. We discovered the plate when we X-rayed the remains for an inventory."

"How difficult will it be to run the serial number down and find out who you have on your table?"

"If the medical facility properly documented the surgical procedure, I should know tomorrow. It's contacting the manufacturer, who leads us to the medical facility, who should be able to tell us the name of the patient who had this implanted device. It'll take some time, but it's the best I can do."

"No, that's great. It'll be faster than waiting for DNA. We need to confirm if the victim was one of the task force members. That's what Agent Thompson believed. Peter—Peter Rivers."

"Nathan, does your department have a Rapid DNA sequencer?" Dr. White said.

"I honestly don't know."

"They're expensive, upward of a hundred-thirty K. And the test kits are expensive too. There's been some push back on the accuracy in court, most labs end up doing the standard DNA profiles with thermal cyclers and electrophoresis units to amplify the sequences."

"Okay, I'll pretend to know what that means," Parker said.

"We have access to a Rapid DNA unit," Lynne said.

"If we're trying to confirm if the deceased is a task force member, we should be able to run it as a priority," Parker said.

"Great. Can you send someone? I'll prepare a tissue sample for you."

"I'll send someone—no, I'll do it. I'll be at your office in twenty minutes." Lynne said.

Parker disconnected the call after asking Dr. White to let him know the minute she had an ID from the serial number.

"What do we do about the call tomorrow morning?" Lynne asked.

"It's time we start calling the shots. Screw him and his call."

"What are you going to do?"

"Right now, I need to make sure Pete and Janet are all right."

Lynne nodded. I am glad you're okay, though." She parted with a hug before she stepped off the curb and into the parking lot.

Parker wasn't okay—not even close.

Chapter Twenty-Four

As Parker entered the waiting room, Espi motioned him over. He handed Parker his cell, where a series of photos displayed on the screen.

"What are these?"

"I had a team of detection specialists go out to the ambush site. The first one—a radio transmitter. I think your shooter might have dropped it when he fled on his motorcycle. The second is a multi-frequency jammer. That's the one that has me bothered."

"It tells me they knew I'd need to call for help. They planned to shoot one of us and cut off any means of calling for backup."

"It's more than that, Nathan. This jamming device. It's state-of-the-art. It's the same model our military special operations units use. One of our techs was a former operator and recognized the unit. Who are these people?"

"Well funded and connected. How difficult would it be to get one of those?"

"For the average Joe? Damn near impossible. Which tells me you're up against some heavy hitters."

"Would a PMC have access to them?"

Espi thought for a moment and nodded. "Private military contractors would want to have these. They have to find them on the illicit market. I don't know if I can find out where these came from because by design, they have absolutely zero identifying characteristics—no manufacturer ID, no language written on the case or the components inside, and of course no model number."

"So we're nowhere," Parker said.

"I wouldn't say that. These tell us we aren't dealing with some street thugs, or cartel sicarios. These people are well-trained and well-funded."

"Doesn't make me feel better, Espi."

Espi shrugged in response. "Forewarned is forearmed. The dropped transmitter is the wildcard. We might be able to use the device to pull a location."

"Let me know if it pans out. I have a feeling these guys are too careful to make a mistake."

After Espi left, Parker found his way back to the sofa, where Janet Tully and Barry waited.

Parker sat on the other side of Janet, and she reached for his hand.

They didn't move from the spot for three hours. The visiting officers and local law enforcement agency representatives filled half of the waiting room. The worried glances from one to another increased as time ticked on.

By the time the sun came up, Janet leaned on Parker's shoulder as they waited for word from behind the doors. Every time a hospital staffer pushed through, a dozen officers turned for the news.

Parker kept replaying the events out on the roadside preceding the shooting. He blamed his arrogance for what happened to Pete. If he hadn't antagonized the caller, or made a demand for proof Agent Thompson was alive, Pete would be home with his wife instead of fighting for his life. He kept glancing at his hands, which had been soaked in his partner's blood.

Why were people around him always at risk? McMillan, Miguel, Billie, and now Pete. None of them deserved the pull of the dark eddy, which seemed to swirl around him. Parker knew he was the source of so much pain.

The last time he felt this way, in the wake of his partner's murder, he poured himself into the job. So much so everything else—like personal relationships crumbled. He couldn't go down that path again.

He excused himself from the sofa and stretched his cramped legs. He stepped outside, where he could monitor the waiting room, and pulled his cell phone out. He hit the speed dial number for Linda and soaked up the warm sunshine as it crested the mountains to the east.

"How is he?" Linda said as she answered the call.

"Still in surgery. We haven't heard anything yet. You and Miguel all right?"

"We're fine. How about you? Can I bring you anything? Want me to come and wait with you?"

Parker's do it alone approach the last time was a big flaming crash and burn. Not only for him, but for those around him. He couldn't go down there again. Linda and Miguel didn't deserve that treatment.

"If you can come down, I'd like it."

"I'll be there as soon as I pull myself together and let Miguel know where I'm going."

"Thank you. I love you."

He hung up before he started blubbering.

A coffee later, Linda came through the doors and found them. She parked between Janet and Parker. She rubbed Janet's back while she spoke with her.

The air pressure in the room changed when the interior doors opened and a doctor wearing surgical scrubs stepped into the waiting room. Parker's breath froze.

It was the same doctor who came out before, and he searched the room with exhausted eyes until he found Janet.

"Mrs. Tully—"

Janet popped to her feet for the news. "Yes. How's Pete? Is he going to be okay?"

"It was a difficult surgery. He's stable, but in critical condition. The next twenty-four hours will be important."

"Can I see him?"

"He's in recovery now and will be for the next hour or so. He's going to be unconscious for a while because we have him intubated. He needs help to breathe, and we don't want to make him work hard. We needed to take part of his lung. He's going to take some time to recover."

Tears flowed down Janet's cheeks. She hugged the doctor. "Thank you."

"Why don't you go home for a while, rest, and then by the time we have your husband settled in the ICU, you'll be able to see him."

"I can't leave him. I'm staying put."

"I understand. He's going to be in good hands. You need to make sure you take care of yourself, too. He's going to need you in the weeks ahead," the doctor said.

Parker nodded. "He's right, Janet. Let Barry take you home for a while. You've been up all night, and you need to rest. They will take care of Pete and call if anything changes, right, Doc?"

"Absolutely, make sure we have your number. We'll call you if there is any change in condition."

Janet looked to Parker. "Are you sure it's all right? I don't want him to think I've left him alone."

"Pete's resting now. And look around. Pete's far from alone."

She glanced around at the faces of the men and women who had stood vigil with her during the long night.

Barry escorted her out and commandeered an SUV to drive her home.

"Hey doc, thanks for everything," Parker said after Janet left. "How bad is it?"

"He flatlined on the table. The blood loss was significant. We gave him eight units during the procedure. I told you about the lung. There's vascular damage—the bleeding, a shattered rib which sent fragments deeper into the wound track. He's not out of the woods. But he has a fighting chance."

The doctor removed a circular container from the pocket on his smock. "I thought you might need these. The bullet fragments we removed. I was an Army surgeon in Afghanistan. I've seen these before. A high-caliber round designed to fragment upon impact. Less penetrating trauma, but more tissue damage. We needed to pull those small fragments out to avoid complications like infection and abscess down the line."

"Thanks, Doc. From your experience in a combat zone, who would use these rounds?"

He thought for a moment. "Special ops types."

From behind, a young man dressed in a FedEx courier uniform said, "Is there a Nathan Parker here?"

"I'm Parker."

"Here you go." He handed the detective a small six-inch square box.

"What's this?"

"I don't know. I just deliver them...this was an overnight priority."

Parker examined the label for a return address, and the space was empty. A single strip of masking tape sealed the box. Parker tore it open and inside found a cheap cell phone and a photo of a bound and gagged Agent Thompson.

In small, crisp handwriting, a message on the border of the photo read, "You have a choice to make."

Chapter Twenty-Five

The screen on the phone lit up, and the cell vibrated in the box. "Caller Unknown" was displayed on the screen.

Parker searched for the delivery driver, and the man had disappeared out of the hospital entrance. The flash of a white van with the company logo swept past the windows.

The cell continued to vibrate. Parker knew it was the caller playing his sick games again. Lynne's message about making another choice again made him sick to his stomach. As much as he wanted to throw the box, the cell phone, all of it in the trash, the photo of Agent Thompson stopped him.

If he had a chance to find her, he couldn't turn away—the caller counted on it.

Parker removed the phone from the box and hit the small green accept call button on the cheap burner.

"Yeah?" he said.

"You have a choice to make. Someone will die, and you will decide." The voice was cloaked again by an electronic device to alter the tone and modulation. It sounded more robotic than human. It made Parker wonder what the caller was trying to hide.

The phone vibrated in his hand when a photo was sent to the device. Parker squinted at the small screen where a brown-skinned man and woman were on their knees, a cloth shoved in their mouths, and hands bound behind their backs.

"Detective, which is it to be? Save the not-so-innocent federal agent or the migrant family?"

"How do I know you haven't killed everyone already?"

"Careful, detective. Sounds like you want another proof of life example. You know the cost."

"What do you want?" Parker asked.

"That's more like it. You are to have the task force leave within four hours. Then I will direct you to either Agent Thompson, or the husband and wife who are helping us with the next delivery."

"I have nothing to do with the task force. I can't make them lift a pencil."

"You'd better use your power of persuasion. Someone's depending on it. Call me when the task force is gone home. Four hours starting now."

The phone call abruptly disconnected.

Linda came from behind. "I need to get you home. You're exhausted."

He knew she was right. The caller counted on keeping him on edge.

"I could use a shower and a change of clothes."

"And some sleep, Nathan."

"I need to—"

"You need to take care of yourself."

"I know. Maybe I can catch a few winks in the car."

Linda led him to where she'd parked, and while she maneuvered from the parking lot, he called Lynne and gave her the update on the call he'd received.

"I can't make the task force to pull up stakes. They don't report to the field office. They're run out of D.C."

"Can you make a call to whoever runs the show and ask them to pull the team back, temporarily?"

"They won't do it, Nathan. The bureau's position is they don't negotiate with terrorists. That's what we're dealing with here."

"They're gambling with people's lives here. One of them their own."

"I know what you're saying. Once you give in to these types, they never stop."

"Yeah, you're right, I know. We need something to bargain with—I think I know where to start."

"What are you thinking, Nathan?"

"Jack Talent. I think we can squeeze him."

"Red Dawn seems to have sacrificed him. The files Thompson gave you—he was identified as an area commander or some such thing.

"Exactly. He's not gonna be too happy once he finds out."

"I can go snatch him up. We have enough with Thompson's files to bring him in for questioning. I don't think we have enough to hold him, though."

"You might not have to."

Parker heard Lynne sigh over the connection. "I'm going to regret this, aren't I?"

"When have you ever—"

"I'll save the I told you so's for later. Call you when we have him."

He hung up.

Linda turned onto their street. "You're going to try convincing Talent to give up what he knows about the organization? From what you've said, he's not the informant type."

"I think you're right. I need Red Dawn to think he is."

She nodded, and she pulled into the driveway.

"You want to use him as bait to draw them out."

"Something like that."

Parker entered his place, and the weight of the past twelve hours finally hit. He absently made his way for the shower and got the water running. He rested on the edge of the bed while the water warmed up.

Next thing he knew, he was under a blanket, the water was off, and he smelled something cooking in the front of the house. He glanced at the bedside alarm clock, and he'd been out for almost two hours.

He got the shower running again and let the hot water beat on him until it ran cool.

Dressed in a fresh pair of black jeans and a Maricopa County polo shirt, he followed the delicious cinnamon smell wafting in from the kitchen.

"I thought you could use a little pick-me-up," Linda said while she slipped a hot cinnamon roll onto a plate.

He dipped his head toward the plate and inhaled the fresh baked aroma. "You thought right."

He stood next to her at the kitchen island and snuck an arm around her waist. "I've got everything I need right here," he said.

"I think it's the cinnamon roll talking."

Linda stepped away and poured a fresh cup of coffee for him.

Parker stopped in mid-bite. "What are you doing?"

"Whatever do you mean?" she said in a playful tone.

"You're plying me with fresh-baked treats and coffee. What gives?"

"Can't I do something nice for you—just because?"

Parker continued to stare at her while she tried to ignore him.

"Fine. All right. I want to go with you when you talk to Jack Talent."

"Linda, I—"

"I'm a damned good cop. I've assisted on dozens of investigations. You're down a man with Pete on the sidelines. And dammit, I want to be able to keep an eye on you."

She'd worked herself up into a huff and stood on the opposite side of the island with her hands on her hips and her green eyes flashing.

Parker slowly nibbled another bite of the cinnamon roll. And she slid the plate away, waiting for an answer. "Well?"

"What I was going to say was, I think it would be a good idea if you came along with me."

"You mean I baked for nothing?" Linda said.

"I wouldn't say it was for nothing."

He put down his sticky cinnamon roll and strolled to the other side of the island, pulling her into a hug.

"You mean it? You're gonna let me go with you to interview Talent when they bring him in?"

"I need to clear it with Captain Morris, getting you temporarily reassigned to us, but you might be able to get something from Talent we haven't been able to—with the cinnamon rolls, I mean."

She pressed away from him, shook her head, and gave an eye roll that would make a middle school girl jealous. "You're such an ass." She wiped a smidge of frosting from his chin.

Parker grabbed his coffee, took his phone, and stepped outside to his back patio. He was a little disappointed his oasis needed attention. He'd been busy, and the weeds were starting to creep over the brick walkway. The small garden fence in the rear surrounding a cactus garden had blown down in the wind during the last monsoon. The disconnected slats hung haphazardly, and only one wooden crossmember needed to be replaced. It had broken off and clung to the post like a cross.

The cross jolted Parker back to McMillan's roadside memorial. The memory triggered a tightness in his chest and flashbacks to the scene the night his partner died. And it nearly happened again. Tully lay in a hospital bed, clinging to life, and here he was drinking coffee in his backyard.

Survivor's guilt. He recognized the feeling. Linda must have sensed it too, because before he knew it, she was standing behind him with her hands over his shoulders, softly rubbing his chest.

Her touch roused him from dwelling in the past. He shook his head and patted one of Linda's hands. He couldn't risk their relationship by going down a dark, isolated path again.

He made the call to Captain Morris, and Linda's temporary reassignment to the Major Crimes Bureau was approved.

No sooner than he disconnected from the Captain, a text message buzzed through on his cell.

"Well, detective, time to see what you've got. The FBI have Jack Talent in custody," Parker said.

Chapter Twenty-Six

Linda had worked through the nerves on the way over to the FBI building. Her eyes widened when Parker explained she'd be conducting the interview with Jack Talent—alone.

"By myself?" she said as they maneuvered through the FBI lobby.

They clipped their visitors' badges on and met Lynne in the hallway outside of a small interview room.

"Talent give you any problem?" Parker asked.

"Not a bit. Although he thinks he's here to answer for a probation violation. He was under supervision for a conviction of Trespassing on a Military Base. We think it was part of a conspiracy to break into the base armory."

"Weapons for Red Dawn?" Parker asked.

Lynne shrugged. "That was before we knew Red Dawn existed. It's possible. But Talent and his crew were sloppy."

"And the probation violation?"

"Felon in possession of a firearm."

"That tracks. Linda is going to run point on this interview. Two reasons—one is he's seen me before when Barry and I approached him at the bar in Surprise. Even though his handlers might have broken cover, they may not have reached out to their boy there. Second, I think Talent may respond better to a less confrontational approach. Linda's interviewed hundreds of guys like him. She knows how to handle them."

"You might be right," Lynne said. "We can watch the interview next door through a video monitor. I'll set it up." Lynne strode off and opened an adjoining door.

"You sure you want me to do this, Nathan? If I blow the chance to find out where Agent Thompson is being held—or when the shipment is coming in…"

"You've got this, Linda. He's like every other macho dirtbag you've handled. He thinks he outsmarted the feds. This file should shake him up."

Parker handed her a manila folder. She opened it up, and it was a page from the files Agent Thompson gave him on the USB drive.

"Use this and make sure he knows his relationship with Red Dawn is one way. They've given him up."

"Okay. I can do this." She was convincing herself as much as telling Parker.

She entered the interview room, and Parker slid into the observation room next door.

In the adjoining room, Lynne turned up the volume on the monitor.

"Mr. Talent, I'm Deputy Hunt."

"I don't know why you guys dragged me down here for this bullshit." Talent shook his hair out of his eyes.

"I don't know if violating the conditions of your federal probation would be considered bullshit. I'm sure the judge doesn't think so," Linda said.

"In possession of a weapon? Ever hear of something called the Second Amendment? I have the right to bear arms."

"You lost that right when you were convicted of a felony, Mr. Talent."

"You're violating my rights, is what this is."

"Really? You think?"

"Damn straight."

Talent postured, leaning back in his chair, a grin starting to grow.

Parker turned to Lynne. "She's about to break him down. Watch."

In the interview room, Linda scooted her chair forward and shook her head. She looked like a disapproving school teacher ready to scold a disobedient student.

"I think you're mistaken, Mr. Talent. Enemy combatants don't have

124

rights."

"Enemy what?" The smug grin disappeared.

"You heard me. You are an enemy of the state. An enemy combatant is someone who participates in or supports terrorist activity against the United States. We can detain you indefinitely."

"Terrorist? For a probation violation?" Talent was showing his anxiety now, his knee bouncing under the table.

"Familiar with a group called Red Dawn?"

He looked away. "Never heard of 'em."

"Really? Because they've heard of you."

Linda opened the file and placed the document on the table between them. The organizational chart for lower levels of the organization faced him. She tapped a finger on his name.

"Red Dawn's regional commander must have been a good gig."

"I-I don't know what this is."

"What this is—is a ticket to Guantanamo."

"This is—"

"Bullshit? Afraid not. Red Dawn gave this information away. They consider you disposable. Or maybe even a liability to them. How do they respond, Jack?"

"I don't know anything about this."

"Jack, Jack, Jack. Come on now. It's too late. The FBI have you dead to rights on being part of a criminal conspiracy. You know it. Make the best of what you have."

"What is it I have?"

"Leverage."

"On what? You want me to drop a dime on Red Dawn?"

"They've already dropped one on you."

Talent rocked slightly in his chair. His eyes betrayed his fear.

"If I talk to you, you gotta promise me."

"Depends on what you have to say."

"Okay—listen. I don't know much about the organization above me. Everything was compartmentalized into cells. I communicated with the people in my cell. If I needed to contact someone above me, I had a number to call."

"What can you tell me about the missing FBI agent, Thompson?"

"I had nothing to do with that! If they're trying to lay it on me, bullshit."

"What do you know about it?"

"I know what I heard. The FBI lady was getting too close to busting up the operations Red Dawn had going on. She needed sidelined."

"Is she alive?" Linda asked?"

"I don't know. It's not like them to keep a hostage or nothing. They've been pretty clear on leaving no witnesses behind."

"Like the bodies found near the Yavapai Dunes airport?"

Talent fell silent.

Linda scraped up the org chart and closed the folder.

"Listen, I need a deal."

"Terrorists rarely get deals.'

"I ain't no damn terrorist. I'm just a contractor."

"Well, I'll listen to what you have to say, but it better be good if you hope the FBI will play ball with you."

He shook while he pondered his shrinking window of opportunity.

"I know when the next delivery is coming. I can tell you where they are coming in."

Linda slid a notepad over to him.

"Write it down. Place—time—how many Red Dawn people will be there."

He started scribbling on the yellow pad. "This end of the delivery is handled by my people. There will be two Red Dawn soldiers on the flight."

"What are they smuggling into the country? Fentanyl? Guns? What?

Talent squinted at Linda. He was surprised at the question.

"Wait. You don't know?"

"Know what?"

He sat back. "I'm done talking. Lawyer."

Surprised by the sudden change in Talent's demeanor, Linda glanced up at the camera lens, then regained control.

"Sure. You can have a lawyer. I hear they have one or two down at

CHAPTER TWENTY-SIX

Git-Mo."

Linda rose from her chair and turned for the door.

"Wait," Talent said. "I need an ironclad deal, then I'll tell you what I know."

Linda turned, crossed her arms, and glared back at the man.

"Talk, don't talk, I really don't care at this point. I already told you, if you have something the FBI can use…"

Talent fidgeted in his seat. He struggled with how much he was going to give up. Linda sat back down. She reached across and retrieved the notepad from him.

"Let's start with this. Red Mountain Airfield. Where's that?"

"North of Peoria, off the 17. A private, remote strip. Mostly closed down because the people in some of the new retirement communities up there complained about the noise. They shoulda known it was there when they moved in. Damn snow bunnies come in and think the world revolves around them."

"When is the delivery coming?"

"I need assurances. If I tell you, I get total immunity."

"I can't offer you that."

"Then I'm done."

"Have it your way." Linda got up again and made out the door.

"Fine-fine, but you gotta promise me the feds will do right by me. I'm going out on a limb here."

"They're bringing them in tonight at six."

"Them?"

"Yeah, them. You really don't know, do you? Red Dawn brings in people."

Chapter Twenty-Seven

Talent refused to say more until he had an attorney in the room with him. Linda left him in the interview room and met Parker out in the hallway.

"I guess I screwed that up. He shut down when I asked him about what Red Dawn was bringing in."

"And you got him to tell you. They are smuggling people over the border. Not the guns and drugs we thought they might be moving."

"Doesn't that seem like a lot of trouble to go through to bring undocumented migrants over the border. The numbers they could move in a small aircraft—It doesn't seem worth the risk."

"Depends on the people, I suppose," Parker said.

Lynne popped her head out of the observation room and waved them both over.

They joined her in the room. "Check this out," she said, pointing at the video screen.

Talent was carrying on a conversation with no one else in the room. Lynne turned up the volume, and his mouth was moving, but nothing was audible.

"Is he talking to himself?" Linda asked.

"He started this the second you left the room."

Parker pointed at the screen. "There. Right there. He looked straight at the camera."

"He knows it's there?"

"He's talking with someone—or to someone. Cut the feed."

Lynne shut off the camera from a switch near the monitor. The same switch she'd use if an attorney came in to interview a client. There would be privacy for privileged conversation.

"Who else has access to this feed?" Parker asked.

Lynne's forehead wrinkled. "I'm—I'm not sure. Could be anyone with access to our server. It could be any of the dozens of agents, staff, or attorneys in the building."

"He knew the feed was being monitored. Did we record this?"

"Yeah—why? You need me to wipe it from the drive?"

"Not yet. Can you get a copy to someone who can read lips?"

"I think I know someone, yeah," Lynne said. "I need to find out who he was talking to—here in my building."

"Could that have been the leak—the one that gave up the task force to Red Dawn?" Parker asked.

Lynne copied the interview to a private server and wiped the initial recording off the main drive.

"I don't know. I mean, we didn't know the task force was here until Thompson and her team materialized out of thin air. I don't know how the leak could have been here."

"He was talking to someone," Parker said.

Linda put her notepad down on the desk and tapped on the location Talent wrote.

"What if he was leaving a message. Like, warning someone they needed to change the drop location after he'd scribbled it down. He started getting really squirrelly when he started talking about Red Dawn and the fact they were bringing people over on the drops."

Parker nodded. "Good point. Lynne, can your techie people tell you who viewed this feed? Might give us the source of the task force leak."

She shrugged. "I have no idea. I can ask. It's off the server now. Whoever it is can't play it. But I can ask if the IT people can see if anyone tries to access the file."

"In the meantime, we don't have long to get out to the—"

Parker's cell phone chirped again. An unknown number message displayed on the screen.

"It's gotta be him again."

"He get Talent's message already?"

"One way to find out."

Parker hit the accept call and then the speaker button.

"Well, detective, what's your choice? Your FBI friend or the migrant family?"

"You gave me four hours—it hasn't been—"

"I grew tired of waiting. You haven't taken steps to remove the federal task force, so the time is now. Make your decision."

"How can I make a choice like that?'

"I'll make it easy for you—pick one or the other. I'm dropping you the locations now. The first is your FBI agent. The second is where you can find the poor migrant couple. You don't have to tell me which. I'll know where you go. I know exactly where you are, and if I'm not mistaken, you're standing next to Agent Finch.

"Make your choice—death awaits."

The line fell dead.

"What a creepy bastard," Linda said.

"How did he know you were here?" Lynne asked.

Parker chewed on his lip for a moment. It came to him like a bolt of lightning. Of course, he knew where he was. It was the same way Parker knew the location of the missing task force member, Metzger's phone, out at Coyote Wash. He laid the task force phone on the table.

He motioned Lynne and Linda out of the room.

"Tracking software. He's using the same tracking software the task force has on their phones. We have to assume he heard everything as well."

"He knows Talent gave them up," Linda said.

"We have to believe he did."

"Explains why he moved up the timetable," Lynne said.

"We need to act fast. I can't be in both places at the same time—it's what he's counting on."

"So, we divide and conquer. I'll get a tactical team and head to the first location where he said Agent Thompson was. Can you take the second location?" Lynne asked.

Parker agreed. He knew rescuing the FBI agent would be a bureau priority.

"Lynne, be careful with these people. We know what they'll do—like with Pete. Don't take any chances out there."

"You either."

They split up, and Parker made a call on his cell to Barry, gave him the update, and where to meet. A shopping center near the airstrip Talent mentioned. Five miles away from the drop point, Parker was given by the voice over the phone.

As they drove, Linda was unusually quiet. Her expression was something between grim and angry.

"Spill it. What's got you twisted up?' Parker said.

"Did Talent know they were listening in on the conversation? Did he purposely give us a bad location?"

"I don't know if they were listening through that damn cell phone. The phone wasn't with you in the interview room, but if it was picking up sound, then it heard us afterwards. He tried to tell someone the drop was compromised—you know, through the camera feed."

"I feel like I let him get one over on me. Maybe a bullshit drop location, and if I was wrong, someone's going to end up hurt because of it—Agent Thompson or that migrant family. Because I couldn't cut through—"

"No, no. Don't go there. None of this is on you. It's only because of you we finally have a crack in this Red Dawn mess. Talent was so locked up on getting a deal, he got spooked—I mean, really spooked, when you got him to admit they were bringing people over on these flights. Whatever we find—whatever happens to Agent Thompson or the family isn't on you. You got us the best chance to get them before Red Dawn does something."

"I'm glad to see Lynne start to thaw a little when it comes to working with you. When she told you to be careful—I think she really meant it."

"Is that a little jealousy peeking out, Detective Hunt?"

Linda smacked him with a backhand to the shoulder. " I have nothing to be jealous about."

"Really? I'm a catch, I'll have you know."

"Please, the only thing you can catch is a cold."

"Now I'm hurt."

"You can pout after you pull in at the strip mall ahead."

Parker turned in and spotted Barry's SUV tucked in a row near a coffee shop. Barry was easy to spot inside the shop's window. He was the tallest figure inside by six inches.

He came outside carrying a tray with three iced coffee drinks.

"I know I could use the caffeine boost; I figured you guys could too," Barry said as he held the tray at Linda's window.

"How's Janet?" Parker asked.

"She's putting up a strong front. I got her to go home and rest for a while. Pete's stable and there's nothing she can do for him as long as he's in ICU."

"Glad you could take care of her."

Barry nodded, eager to change the topic. "We staging here to meet up with the rest of the team?"

"This is the team," Parker said.

Barry straightened, stretched his neck, and sipped from his coffee cup. "Of course it is."

"The coordinates Talent gave puts us two miles east of the airfield."

"If you can believe that knuckle-dragging yahoo," Barry said.

"We have to go with it for now. Lynne should have her team closing in on the location where Agent Thompson is supposed to be—we need to find our spot before the Red Dawn team passes through."

"Why away from the airfield? I mean, if Talent's people are making a pickup, they'd be at the airstrip, not miles away from it," Barry asked.

"That's been nibbling away at my brain, too. I don't know if it's where Red Dawn makes the hand off to Talent's people, or what. The burned bodies we found last time. It was a mile or so from the airfield. Could be what this spot is—what they plan to do with the migrant couple..."

Barry downed the rest of his coffee. "I don't like walking into another location where these people could be waiting."

CHAPTER TWENTY-SEVEN

"Let's be the ones doing the waiting this time," Parker said.

They set out in two SUVs, and the marked location was a bare patch of desert where two off-road trails converged. The makeshift road was well traveled, judging by the ruts in the dirt, but wide enough for the SUV to pass easily.

The clearing ahead was the spot. Parker wouldn't need the map or the coordinates. He'd found the location—a fresh mound of red dirt. A grave.

Chapter Twenty-Eight

"We're too late," Linda said.

Parker pulled his SUV to a stop at the crossroads. The grave was off the road on the north side. Barry parked behind him.

When Parker stepped from his SUV, he searched for any glint or sign they were being watched. The flat terrain gave no lair for a sniper to pick them off.

Parker listened for crackling in the brush around the dirt path. Nothing indicating a human presence waiting.

"This isn't new," Barry said. "The soil on top is completely dry. Hours old."

Taking a shovel from the back of his SUV, Parker carefully began moving dirt from the mound. After the third shovel of soil, the toe of a worn tennis shoe appeared.

"Dammit. They had no intention of turning them over to us."

Parker got on his cell and called Lynne. She reported no one at the location. It looked like someone had been beaten and bloodied there, but they were long gone before her team arrived. No sign of Thompson.

Barry brushed the dirt away next to the exposed foot. "Got another one here. No. Wait. Two more."

Parker unearthed the bodies carefully. Had Red Dawn dumped Agent Thompson out here with the migrants?

He knew he should wait for a forensic team to unearth the bodies, but Parker needed to find out if the missing FBI agent lay beneath the layer of dirt.

On his knees, and using his hands, Parker scooped away the soft dirt. The third body was male. A tall white male. He leaned back on his heels and looked at the three exposed corpses. The two bodies to the right were the migrant husband and wife he had seen in the photograph sent by Red Dawn. The other was unknown.

"Linda, call in for the ME and crime scene units, would you? Use your cell—let's keep this off the radio for now."

She nodded and started calling.

Barry helped Parker to his feet. "What are we supposed to make of this?" Barry said.

"They've been dead for hours. He was never going to give them up. Talent must have known." Parker circled around the burial mound. "Looks like they were shot. A small diameter entry wound in either the forehead or the top of the skull."

"They were on their knees. They knew it was coming."

Linda strode over to where they stood. "Dr. White and company are on the way. A crime scene unit is finishing up in Chandler. They won't be far behind. Those are the people in the photo, aren't they? I recognize the pattern on her blouse."

Parker nodded. "They were already buried when we got the photo. This guy and his damned games."

"What if it wasn't a game?" Linda asked, unable to tear her eyes away from the partially exhumed bodies. "What if he needed us to come out here?"

"So we could witness what he's done? Mission accomplished," Parker said as he kicked a rock off the road.

"If we're here. We can't be—"

"Somewhere else. I need to warn Lynne."

He snagged the phone from his pocket and pressed the button for the last number dialed.

"Come on, Lynne, pick up."

After a half-dozen rings, it flipped to voicemail.

"Dammit. Something's going on with Lynne's team."

As he tried calling again, his phone chirped with an incoming call.

"Lynne, are you okay?"

"I had to shut my phone off. We found two explosive devices wired to cheap cell phones."

"Are you okay? The team?"

"Yeah, everyone's good. We had a canine go through and clear the rest of the place. You guys get anything?"

"They were dead and buried by the time we got out here. Hours old. The couple in the photo and one more—a white guy. All shot and quickly buried in a shallow grave."

"No sign of Agent Thompson?"

"None. I take it you didn't find anything out there?"

"It looks like the building—an old warehouse—had been a meeting place for Red Dawn. Empty ammo crates, the place reeks of gun oil, and there's a room. I think they used it as a torture chamber. Blood on the floor. Some empty water jugs like they water boarded someone."

"The explosives? How'd you find those?"

"We got lucky. When we entered, it was by the front door, like a claymore mine. Our team activated cell phone jammers before they breached. Otherwise…"

"We're waiting for the ME to come out and process the bodies here on scene."

"Can you send me a photo of what you found?" Lynne asked.

"Sure."

Parker snapped a series of quick photos of the bodies, the mound, and the surrounding area. He sent it off to Lynne and waited on line until she got them.

"Okay…hang on for a sec."

Parker heard background noise. It sounded like Lynne talking with someone else nearby.

"I'm back. One mystery solved. Your third body is Agent Metzger."

"Thompson's missing team member. Guess he wasn't our rogue agent. Which means the mole is still in play out there."

"Where's Thompson?" Lynne asked.

"She could be buried out here, too. There's hundreds of square miles of nothing out here."

"We're going to go through this building and see if they left anything behind to clue us in. They've been careful so far, so I'm not holding my breath."

"When the ME's done here, I think we'll head to the airfield. That's where the delivery was supposed to go down."

Parker disconnected and pocketed the phone.

Barry was examining the pockmarked trail leading to the east.

"What do you see?" Parker asked.

"It's hard to tell. I think the bodies were dropped, and then they circled back toward the airport. There's nothing out here. I pulled a map up on my phone, and these back roads go to the highway and an old copper mine up in the hills. But there's a recent track in the center of the dirt. Looks like a vehicle turned around here."

"Might be right. If Red Dawn was bringing in people, like Talent said."

Parker's phone vibrated once more. Dr. White's name appeared on his phone screen."

"Having trouble finding the spot, doc? It's kind of tucked away—"

"I'm here. Where are you?"

Parker turned on his heel. The medical examiner's van was nowhere in sight.

"I'm with the bodies."

"Bodies, plural? I'm with a single—at the airport. Isn't that where you called in from?"

"We're a mile or so from the airfield. Another body? There? Is it a woman?" Parker's mind clicked to Agent Thompson. Red Dawn was cutting off the loose ends.

"No. I'm looking at a young man."

"I'll be right there."

Parker asked Barry and Linda to watch over the gravesite while he met with Dr. White at the airfield.

He piloted the SUV back down the bumpy dirt track to the main road, turned right, and spotted a sign for the Red Mountain Airfield. The single runway ran parallel to the base of a small hill. It adjoined a recently constructed subdivision of large single-story homes wedged into the hillside. The homes at the base of the enclave had an extra-wide garage structure to accommodate their private planes. The streets were wide enough to serve as taxiways.

Several signs announced the private nature of the airfield and community. Private security was visible ahead at the entrance gate. A pair of golf carts with blinking orange lights were blocking the road.

Parker rolled down his window, and a security officer pointed back down the road. "The airfield's closed. Access for residents only."

"Sheriff's Office. The Medical Examiner is waiting for me. Can you tell me where she is?"

"Got any ID?"

Parker pulled his badge from his belt and held it to the window.

The security man nodded and waved for his partner to move one of the golf carts out of the path.

"Straight ahead to the airfield. Can't miss it."

Parker dropped the SUV into drive and pulled forward onto the airstrip property. Upscale for sure. Red brick outbuildings and immaculate blacktop surface streets ringed the outer perimeter of the complex.

Beyond the low-slung commercial coffeeshops, dry cleaners, and stores catering to the airpark, Parker spotted a row of small private planes, tied down neatly. Except for the last one at the far right. It had been parked at an angle. And it would have stood out among the neatly spaced aircraft even without the medical examiner's van pulled up alongside.

Parker found Dr. White standing at the door of a small aircraft. From where he parked, he could only see her back as she angled in the doorframe. The body wasn't visible. Red Dawn must have left someone behind.

Without turning away from her work, Dr. White said, "This wasn't the body you called me out for, detective?"

"Not at all. We have three partially buried—with gunshot wounds to the head. Not far from here. What's the story with this one?"

CHAPTER TWENTY-EIGHT

She stepped aside, and Parker edged in closer.

A younger white male sat behind the pilot's controls in the left-hand seat. Parker guessed he was in his twenties. Sandy blond hair, maybe six feet tall, and a thin, athletic build. Detracting from the preppy appearance was a knife wound to the right side of his neck.

The cabin, especially to the right of the dead man, was awash in arterial spray. The man's blood pumped out where he sat. His hands were covered in red from an instinctual act of reaching for his neck to stop the bleeding. There was no stopping this deep gash.

"Any identification on the man, yet, doc?"

"We haven't gotten that far. We're finishing up our initial workup."

She removed a liver probe from the victim's abdomen. She'd lifted his t-shirt to insert the probe. After jotting down the reading, she tapped in a quick calculation on a keypad attached to her tablet.

"The heat in the enclosed cabin might put us off a bit. But the liver temp put us at two to four hours."

"Fits with what we know about a smuggling run coming in from over the border. This could be the aircraft."

Parker glanced back at the six-seater passenger compartment. More than enough room for the two migrants and three more passengers— whoever they might have been. The whole arrangement, bringing over small numbers of people, and then tucking two of them in the dirt nearby, made little sense. Not from an economic standpoint, and that's what these cartels were usually about. Red Dawn was more of the same by a different name.

That's how he had to think of them—and there was only one place to get info on a cartel. From another cartel...

Chapter Twenty-Nine

The medical examiner finished up at the airfield, then moved to the dirt burial mounds. After three hours of processing, bagging, and tagging, the victims were loaded and transported off to the morgue.

Nothing left but a hole in the ground. Three souls evaporated in this spot, and no evidence they ever existed.

Parker told Barry to head home. He looked exhausted. Reluctantly, the detective said he would.

It was getting into the late afternoon, and the heat was making it miserable. Parker lugged his sweat-soaked body into the SUV and turned on the air. Linda tilted the vent to her and held her sticky shirt away from her body.

"We need to make a stop on the way back in," Parker said.

"Do I need to change first? I'm sweaty, dirty, and aggravated."

"I thought women didn't sweat? Don't you glow?"

"When some man drags us out into the middle of the Sonoran Desert, we're allowed to sweat."

"Noted. We're going to consider what we're dealing with—Red Dawn's like a cartel. We've been on the back foot, partially because we bought the private military contractor angle of the whole thing. They recruit from them, for sure, but what we're seeing—what we found out there today, is straight up cartel action."

"Okay, I'm following. Are we turning this over to the feds then?"

"Not at all. First off, we know the feds—the task force—is compromised. If we punt this to Homeland, or the FBI, it'll sit for months in a bureaucratic mess. We need a direct source."

"What do you have in mind?"

"The enemy of my enemy?"

"Did you get heatstroke out there?"

"Maybe, but we're going to ask a cartel what's going on. They have much to lose, with Red Dawn expanding their territory. We need to see what they have to say."

"You have the cartel on speed dial?"

"Sort of."

Linda got her answer when Parker pulled into the parking garage of Sutton, Wimmer, and Hudson, attorneys to the underworld, as Parker thought of them. Although Sutton played in the deep end of a very dark pool, he had served as a back-channel conduit to the Sinaloa Cartel when their interests and Parker's aligned.

"I remember this guy," she said. "Isn't an attorney bound by some ethical rules around talking about their client?"

"Ethics are a bit loose with this one."

"Aren't you worried he'll use it against you—the access to his clientele?"

"It hasn't come to that. He's about protecting his interests. Sometimes it means we're on the same side."

As they entered the law office waiting room, the dark red mahogany furnishings gave off a corporate Wall Street vibe as opposed to the fringes of criminal society.

A new receptionist parked behind the desk. Raven-haired, young, with dark blue eyes behind dark oversized frames, peered up at them.

"May I help you?" The tone carried a snap judgment that the two of them didn't belong here.

"I need to see Larry Sutton."

"I'm sorry, Mr. Sutton is fully booked today."

"You didn't even ask me my name. I might be his next appointment," Parker said.

"I doubt that."

"It's only common courtesy to ask."

She huffed. "Fine. Do you have any appointment?"

"No. I don't, but Larry will see me."

"And what makes you think he will?"

Parker slipped the badge off his belt and dropped it on the desk. The receptionist's eyes widened behind her glasses.

Linda leaned against the desk. "You might want to scurry back to your boss and tell him we're here."

The receptionist blinked, rose from her chair, and trod down the hall on three-inch heels.

Parker returned his badge to his belt. "Scurry? You told her to scurry?"

"She heard me..."

The receptionist returned, smoothed the front of her dress. "Mr. Sutton will see you. He has a few minutes in between appointments. If you'll follow me."

"We know the way, thank you," Parker said as he and Linda stepped around the desk and headed down the hall.

Sutton was standing behind his desk when the detectives entered.

"Will you need anything, Mr. Sutton?" the receptionist asked.

"No, Trina, we won't be long," he said as he shifted his eyes to Parker.

She backed out and closed the door.

"New?" Parker asked.

"Not my choice. Daughter of one of the partner's clients. In between modeling gigs, I hear. Anyway—this visit come with a warrant?"

"It does not," Parker said.

Sutton exhaled, reached for his bottom desk drawer, and withdrew a foil-lined bag. Parker recognized the Faraday Bag from prior visits with the attorney. Always cautious, to the point of paranoia. It came with the territory as counsel for the Sinaloa Cartel.

Parker dropped his cell in the bag, and Linda followed suit. Sutton dropped his inside the container, a move that got Parker's attention.

Sutton closed the bag and shoved it in his desk drawer.

"You worried about being overheard, Larry?"

"Things are a bit tense down south at the moment. They are being cautious."

"Exactly why I'm visiting—should we be talking here?"

Sutton pointed to a black box on the back credenza. "Signal jammer."

Parker stiffened. Whoever took a shot at them at Coyote Wash used a signal jammer.

"Not the first one I've run across this week. What can you tell me about a group called Red Dawn?"

"I'm not involved with them," Sutton said as he sat behind his polished desk.

"I didn't think you were. I asked you to tell me what you know about them."

Sutton remained silent for a moment. Parker thought he spotted a shadow behind the attorney's eyes.

"They are not a traditional criminal organization as we've come to know them. Not like a cartel. There's no territorial boundary. The cartels operate on a specific set of rules and geographic lines everyone agrees to accept. They don't piss in someone else's backyard. That's how they've lasted for years—Sinaloa, Juarez, Los Zetas—all of them. They know to stay within their own.

"Red Dawn doesn't seem to understand those rules. Or, if they do, they don't care. What we're seeing down there is—well, no one can make any sense of it. Red Dawn rolls into a territory, takes over a labor force, a distribution center, or a manufacturing facility, and destroys them. They don't take it over and call it their own. Red Dawn takes it off the board completely."

"They cut off the cartel's revenue, and don't try to use it? Doesn't make any sense."

Sutton shrugged. "No one understands what their long-term goal is. This—what they're doing—isn't sustainable. They are spending a lot of money and getting nothing out of it."

"They are getting something. We can't see it yet. There has to be a benefit for them," Parker said.

"They've managed one thing, though. Red Dawn has pushed the cartels together. Sinaloa, Juarez, and Baja have joined forces to defend themselves from further attacks."

"A NATO for drug dealers?"

"A mutual defense pact. No one is happy about it. But they see it as their only way to survive. Isolated cartels are easy to pick off."

"You hear anything about Red Dawn being involved in human trafficking?"

"No. I've heard they are into eradication. Dismantling any infrastructure that Sinaloa, or the others have in place."

"We believe they are bringing people over—small numbers. Some of them don't survive the journey—"

"I know someone who might know."

Sutton strode to a wall safe behind his desk, hidden behind a photo of the Supreme Court. He used his fingertips to unlock the safe and pulled out a bulky black satellite phone.

"In case of emergency. It's sounding like this qualifies."

Sutton extended the antenna and powered up the phone. He turned off the signal jammer at his desk.

"I need to speak with him," Sutton said into the phone.

"I have someone who needs to speak with you about the pressing problem to your south."

Sutton listened as his eyes shifted to Parker.

"You've spoken with him before—about the Los Muertos issue. Yes, Detective Parker."

Sutton handed the phone to Parker, and he knew who was on the other end of the connection. Joaquin Pimentel, the head of the Sinaloa drug cartel.

Chapter Thirty

The Sinaloa Cartel boss sounded angry as he barked out an order to someone in the room with him.

"Detective, I didn't think we'd speak again."

"Neither did I. I'll get to it, Red Dawn. They are starting to show their colors up here. I understand they have been making trouble for you and the other cartels."

Pimentel uttered a phrase Parker couldn't make out, but from the tone and the few words he recognized, the cartel ruler cursed them and their families.

"We have not seen anything like them before," he said. "These soldiers suddenly appeared and knew where to strike to hurt us. Our warehouses, fields, processing facilities—and they burned them. Millions of dollars of product—gone."

"That's what I understand. They didn't take it for themselves, they destroyed it. Why would they do that—destroy millions worth of product? Or at least take over the facilities where the stuff was made?"

"This is what is happening. Everywhere. The cartels are seeing the same types of attacks. We are fighting back. Red Dawn is better armed and trained. These are professionals. We are successful in repelling their advances, but they replace the ones we kill the next day. They have an unending supply, it seems."

Parker thought the account of the cartel chief was much in line with his experience with a well-armed adversary—the sniper, electronic jammers, and tactics.

"Have you had any communication with them? They making demands?"

"Nothing. They take. They destroy what we've built."

"Any thoughts on who is behind Red Dawn?"

"They are faceless. We are doing what we can to trace their money. Maintaining an army takes hard currency and lots of it. Most of it coming from Eastern Europe. They are buying everything they can't burn. Loyalty, services, and mordida in the right places."

Mordida, the bribes paid to public officials, was a common occurrence. Expected as part of doing business in some parts of Mexico. A criminal organization with a violent edge paying bribes didn't come together for Parker. It was something typically seen in the shadier side of government operations—paying off a city inspector, a town chief of police—mostly to get them to look the other way.

"What are they buying? Influence? Some official in their pocket?" Parker asked.

"There is some to be sure. They have been luring our people to join them. Not everyone; they are being specific on who they are looking for."

"Such as?"

"I cannot speak for other families. There are those who are used to deal with certain problems. Problems which oppose our business interest. These human problems sometimes need to be confronted. I believe you know of what I speak, Detective."

"People like Los Muertos." Parker knew the history of the group. Killers who would do the dirty work for a cartel. Always for a price. Pure mercenaries, all of them. Only loyal to the money.

"Los Muertos and others. Sicarios from other cartels have been bought off."

"They're joining the fight against their former bosses?"

"They are bought and disappear."

"Killed?"

"I don't believe so."

The hair on the back of Parker's neck tingled as it came into focus. The small number of transports over the border to Phoenix weren't undocumented migrants with the ability to pay. Red Dawn was smuggling in teams of assassins."

"What are they doing with them? This collection of killers?"

"I can't say. They haven't been turned against us."

"Sir, thanks for speaking with me."

"I owe it to you for warning us of the Los Muertos plan to attack us last year. Now, I consider us even. Do not underestimate these dogs. In some ways, they are much like Los Muertos."

The call disconnected. Parker looked at the satellite phone in his hand.

"Yeah, he's like that. Doesn't spend too much time with pleasantries," Sutton said as he replaced the sat-phone in his safe.

The electronic jammer switched back on.

"If you're seeing action on this side of the border, that's not a good sign. As much as you don't want to hear it, detective, my client and his associates are your only buffer right now."

"That doesn't give me a warm and fuzzy feeling, counselor."

"I'm not in the feel-good business."

"If you pick up anything related to Red Dawn, let me know, would you?"

Sutton flipped off the electronic jammer. "Detective, I have no idea what you're talking about."

Once Parker and Linda got into the parking garage, Linda whispered, "Was that really the Joaquin Pimentel? The FBI's most wanted Pimentel?"

"It was."

"How did you—he—you know him? Like know him, know him?" Linda asked.

"I've never met him. We've spoken before—you remember the Coyle Technology business and Los Muertos trying to take over the cartel? Our interests were temporarily aligned, I suppose."

"He sounded scared over the Red Dawn move into his territory," she said.

"Yeah, he did. And a Cartel boss doesn't spook easily. But he did give us something we haven't been looking at. The people Red Dawn is moving over the border might be the missing cartel hitmen, their sicarios. It explains the small numbers coming over in these drops, like we saw at the Red Mountain

Airfield. And it fits with the type of people Jack Talent would deal with."

"Talent would pick them up, but then what? Where do they go and what are they doing here?"

"That's the question. And I don't know the answer."

Chapter Thirty-One

Parker drove the SUV out of the parking garage and stifled a yawn when he pulled onto the main street.

"You need a break," Linda said.

"There's too much to do. We need—"

"You need to rest. Just like you told Barry. Let's go home, rest, and regroup. I'll call Leon, and he and Miguel can meet us for dinner somewhere."

"Linda, I can't walk away."

"I get it. But you need to eat, don't you?"

"Yeah, but—"

"No buts, mister." She dialed Leon on her phone. While it rang, she asked Parker what he wanted.

"Leon. You have any dinner plans? Nathan and I are on the way back in."

Linda listened, glanced at Parker, and smiled.

"I think we can figure it out. See you in a few minutes—at Nathan and Miguel's," she said before disconnecting the call.

"Let me guess, he wants pizza?"

"It's like he's making up for the time he didn't have it in El Salvador."

"Miguel's the same. Speaking of, let me call him and give him the heads up."

Parker hit the speed dial button and the speaker for hands-free calling. Miguel answered on the second ring.

"What's up?' Miguel said. There were voices in the background. Parker tried to place it. He wasn't at home. School maybe.

"Thought I'd bring dinner."

"Cool. We're about done here."

"Where's here?"

"At the coalition office. Billie is trying to figure out how to deliver the supplies down to Hermosillo. They need them, and she thinks she has a line on getting them there fast."

"She's not talking about sending cash over again, is she? That didn't sit well with the feds?'

"No, I think she learned her lesson."

"Tell her she's invited over too. Just you, me, Linda, and Leon."

"I'll tell her. Armando is here too."

"He's welcome to join."

"Pepperoni extra cheese."

Parker rolled his eyes.

"Pizza again?" Parker asked, trying to stifle the chuckle from Linda.

"It's—safe," Miguel said. "Oh, from Little Sicily?"

"How about if I grab a couple of frozen ones from Safeway?"

"Little Sicily and two of their family size should do it."

"Anything else?"

"If they have those garlic knots, that'd be cool."

"I'll meet you guys at home—maybe."

Parker stabbed the disconnect button.

"He's got your number," Linda said.

"Yeah, yeah. The pizza at Little Sicily is pretty good, I'll give him that."

* * *

Twenty-five minutes later, Parker pulled into his driveway behind Miguel's Camry. Billie's new Ford F-250 was parked on the street.

When he stepped inside, Miguel and Leon swept over, taking the pizza boxes from him and moving them to the table. They'd set a stack of paper plates, napkins, and a shaker of crushed red pepper on the table.

"Finally," Miguel said, peeling back the cardboard lid and taking a deep breath of the hot pepperoni pizza.

Billie waved from her spot, leaning on the kitchen counter. She was on the phone talking with someone, and she looked tense.

Armando came from down the hall. "Smells amazing."

The boys, Miguel, Leon, and Armando, swarmed the pizza, pulling cheesy slices to their plates.

Billie finished her call and joined Parker and Linda near the dining room table. "Got me a hook up to get them supplies to Hermosillo."

"You're not sending anything to make our federal friends upset, are you?" Parker asked.

"I don't see what's wrong with me sending what's mine wherever I want. It's supposed to be a free country, ain't it?"

"Some would take advantage. Please don't push them on this."

"Don't worry none. I ain't gonna do nothin' what'll get them fed knickers twisted up. Sending medical supplies, clothes, and blankets. Should be fine, less the FBI starts havin' issues with blankets."

"How you getting the supplies down there? Going back to the old way of doing things? You driving them down?" Parker asked.

"Nah, the border is a mess right now. The customs and border patrol have tightened up the crossings. Delays getting over—coming both ways. Then there's an uptick of militia at a few of the crossings. We got us the Mexican Federales settin' up checkpoints around, and then the Sinaloa cartel is pullin' the noose tight around Hermosillo."

"Seems the cartel is facing some competition down there," Parker said.

"Yeah, I've heard about the Sinaloa problems. Another reason I ain't sending no cash money down there for them to take off our people."

Parker gestured her and Linda to the pizza, handing each of them a paper plate.

"How are you getting your supplies down there?" Linda asked.

Billie tore off a bite of pizza and talked around the mouthful. "Miguel helped me. Found me a hookup."

Miguel nodded. "There's a club at ASU. They go down there all the time. To Hermosillo, Cabo, and Mexico City. They were willing to take Billie's supplies—"

"As long as they got paid," Billie added.

"A club? What kind of college club drives down there?"

Billie swallowed. "No driving. A club with planes. They fly down south on the regular."

"Fly? To Mexican airports?" An uneasy feeling hovered over Parker. Small private planes, like the one they found abandoned at the Red Mountain Airfield? The image of the dead man in the pilot's seat snapped into his mind.

"What do you know about these club members?"

Miguel tugged another slice onto his plate. "It's a legit club registered with the university. Really, it's a bunch of rich kids who have access to their family's airplanes. They arrange trips to Cabo and stuff. There's about a dozen members, from what I found."

"Yeah, they been kinda slow on the trips lately, they said. Spring break and summer vacations are their big deal. They do a few runs down there to drop off guys who want to go fishing in Baja and stuff."

"They had room to take your supplies along with their passengers?"

"Sounds like it. I haven't done a run with them yet. We're talking about arranging one this week. Maybe a small one. Sounded like a little plane— like a four-seater," Billie said.

Parker locked eyes with Linda.

"Could you hold off, Billie?" Parker asked.

"What? Why?"

"There might be a connection to a man we found killed at a local airport today."

"Was he connected to the ASU club?" Miguel asked.

"I don't know. We haven't IDed the guy yet. But it's connected to the smuggling operation were tracking with Red Dawn."

Billie put her paper plate down with nothing left but an orange grease smear. "I have been picking up some chatter about them. Like you asked. They been goin' after the cartels. Taking their drugs and guns. Kinda pushing them back. What my people are most afraid of is people are going missing."

CHAPTER THIRTY-ONE

"Missing? Cartel soldiers?" Parker said. The chill up his spine tingled.

"No. Regular types, you know? Like they's here one day and then poof, gone. Not big numbers. But enough to make people down in Hermosillo spooked. They's to the point of talkin' alien abduction."

"When did these people start to go missing?"

"About the time Red Dawn showed up at the camps. This group appears and starts bugging people in the camps, then people disappear. Ain't by chance."

"No, I don't think it is," Parker said.

Chapter Thirty-Two

Parker couldn't sleep. He caught an hour or two, then jolted awake with a flash of the sniper on the hillside and Pete Tully collapsing. In his nightmare, he saw muzzle flashes he didn't recall in real time. Everything else about the vision was an exact mirror of the events as they unfolded.

He found himself in a cold sweat, breathing hard like he'd climbed ten flights of stairs. The room was quiet except for the soft whoosh of the air-conditioning blowing through the register.

Linda had taken Leon home after their impromptu pizza party, and Billie left early with Armando to check out the medical supplies at the Immigrant Coalition offices to make sure they were ready for shipment.

The method of shipment stuck with Parker and made him uneasy. The connection, or similarity to the Red Dawn drops, if he was honest about it, was too much. The image of the kid in the airplane flashed through his brain.

He reached for his phone to call Billie. It was a little after four in the morning, so he thought better of it.

A quick, hot shower improved his disposition, and a cup of coffee on the back patio let him chase the flashbacks of Pete's shooting back into the shadows momentarily. He recognized what he was doing. He'd seen the pattern before. Ignoring the aftermath of his partner's murder six years ago was like shaking a Coke bottle. Do it long enough, and that bottle cap was going to blow. When it did, the fallout collected a price on everything around him. Relationships left in the rubble. Throwing himself into the job was not a cure last time, and it wouldn't be this time either. He wouldn't be doing any favor to Pete. And Linda certainly didn't deserve to be on the blunt end of the deal.

He rummaged through his desk drawer. His filing system wasn't exactly high tech. Business cards were tossed in the drawer, and depending on how long ago the contact was, determined how deep to dig around. The one he was looking for was four years old, so he fished around near the bottom of the drawer.

The third pull from the drawer got him the card he was searching for. The card was bent and ragged around the top edge, after living in his wallet for months. Eleanor Ells, Psychologist, Trauma Specialist.

He'd found Eleanor after hitting rock bottom and blowing up his relationship with Lynnette Finch. He thought throwing himself into the job was going to be enough—keep him occupied and away from the creeping dread following McMillan's murder. Everything suffered, including his job.

There's a culture in law enforcement, one rooted in the culture today, you can't show any sign of weakness. Going to a counselor was one of those signs. The old guard believed if you weren't the one shot or stabbed, then get on with it. The concept of Post Traumatic Stress Disorder, or PTSD, wasn't whispered openly. If you were weak, you couldn't be counted on when it mattered to back up your partner. The rates of divorce, alcohol abuse, and suicide were symptoms of a much larger problem.

It was more acceptable now for officers to seek counseling sessions, and some departments mandated them after a traumatic event. Parker knew the signs. He tucked the card in his shirt pocket and would call Eleanor to make an appointment.

Getting up for a second cup of coffee, Parker replayed the conversation from last night. Billie using rich college kids to ferry her supplies down south. Leave it to Billie to find a way around the government's red tape.

Rich college kids. Parker's suspicious edge wondered what the kids were getting out of it. Sure, there might be a few who would take on a humanitarian effort because it was a good thing to do. They were the exception.

Parker wriggled the mouse at his office computer and sipped the dark brew as the aging machine needed a moment to get going.

You and me both, Parker thought.

The university webpage listed a few of the clubs, fraternities, and sororities with official ties to the school—over three hundred of them. None specifically linked with flying, aviation, or the junior Air Force Reserve. Miguel mentioned a club. It had to be one with no official link to the school, except for the fact the kids involved attended ASU.

"You're up early." Miguel leaned on the office door with a cup in hand.

"Hope I didn't make too much noise."

"No. I did smell this, though," Miguel said, followed by another sip.

"Sorry."

"I was going to have to get up soon anyway."

Parker checked his watch, and he'd lost over an hour. It was nearly six.

"Guess I lost track of time. I was trying to follow up on the club you brought up last night—the one helping Billie. You remember what they were called?"

Miguel closed his eyes. "What was it? A take on the Mile High Club. Mile something. Fly High. Something like that. Oh, wait." Miguel put down his coffee and plucked his cell phone from his pocket.

He pulled up a text from Billie.

"Here it is, Sun Devil High Flyers."

"Sounds like a circus act," Parker said as he entered the name into a search engine.

There were a few pages of groups, or associations with similar names. One linked to a page featuring a group of college-age guys posing in front of their small private planes. The aircraft were in a semicircle behind the kids in their designer jeans and hundred-dollar haircuts. The smug looks on a couple of them reeked of entitlement.

Miguel stood behind Parker. "Yes. That's them."

Parker scrolled through a few pages of photo highlights from trips to Cabo and Mazatlán. Partying, accompanied by pretty young girls and scenes including bars, the beach, and a few shots of the group unloading their passengers at small, remote airstrips.

Parker recognized the low-slung red brick buildings from the Red Mountain Airfield. Parker leaned forward, and standing near the blue and white Cessna were two young men.

The caption beneath the photo read, "Gearing up for Black's Beach. It's gonna be epic."

"You know either of these guys?" Parker asked.

Miguel leaned closer.

"Don't think so. The guy Billie talked to had dark hair. His name was River, or something all new agey sounding."

Parker had seen one of the men in the photo before. The kid on the right. Tall, blonde, and tanned. He looked much different from when Parker saw him with his throat cut in the front seat of the same blue and white plane.

Chapter Thirty-Three

Parker finished getting ready for work, and Miguel left for school with a mission. Connect with River "what's-his-name" and Parker could identify the dead kid in the airplane. Miguel wasn't about to leak the fact the young pilot was no longer among the living—find out who the other kid in the photo was.

It wasn't on the way to the office, but Parker swung by the Osborne Medical Center. Pete's wife was asleep in a stiff-backed ICU waiting room chair. He let her rest and approached the nurse's station.

One of the nurses recognized Parker after Tully came out of surgery. Her face softened as he approached the counter.

"Anything you can tell me about Pete's condition?" he asked.

He expected her to tell him she couldn't release patient information.

"Mrs. Tully added you to the release of medical information list. Your friend is stable. He's no longer on a vent. He's breathing on his own. It's kind of remarkable, really. The internal damage was significant. He's doing well."

"Is he awake? Can I talk with him?"

"No. He's not. The doctor expects him to regain consciousness at any time. He's going to be in a bit of pain when he does. This isn't a bad thing. It's the body's way of telling itself to pause."

He nodded. He wanted to tell Pete he was sorry. Regretting every move, putting them at Coyote Wash and Pete in a hospital bed.

"Can I see him?"

"Yes. For a few minutes."

The nurse walked around the counter and led Parker to a glass-fronted room. Through the window, he got his first glimpse of Pete in the Intensive Care Unit bed. Wires, monitors, and screens scrolled and documented every breath, beat, and muscle contraction.

She opened the door for him. "Don't be too long, okay?"

Parker nodded and drew a deep breath before parking on a chair near Pete's bed.

"Hey, Pete." His voice cracked when he spoke to his deputy.

"I wanted to stop and tell you—tell you I'm sorry for what happened out there. I should have never put us—put you—in that position."

Parker looked for any sign Pete had heard him. The beeps and blips on the monitors remained constant.

"Pete, I'll make it up to you. I don't know how, but I will. I need you to rest and pull through this. I know you can. I need you to. Pete—I'm sorry."

Parker lowered his head. It should have been him here in this bed. Not Pete. For a moment, when he looked up, he swore it was McMillan on the bed in front of him. He closed his eyes, remembering Mac wasn't as lucky—if what happened to Pete could be considered, by any measure, luck.

Parker patted Pete's hand as he rose from the chair. "I'll check in on you soon. We need you back."

Pete's wife was sleeping when he put a fresh cup of coffee on the side table next to her. He elected for a cup from the nurses' station instead of the watered-down vending machine coffee.

She stirred when he stepped back, opening her eyes slowly, then with a start when she remembered where she was.

Parker knelt in front of her. "Everything's fine, Janet. I wanted to check in on you and Pete. The nurses are telling me he's doing good."

"I expected him to wake up by now—after they weaned him off the ventilator."

"Could be any time, they said. He's resting and getting stronger. Can I bring you anything?"

"No. I—I didn't mean to nod. I have a friend coming to sit with me."

"Do you need me to stay?"

"No, no. I'll be fine. We'll be fine." She said with a hint of hope more than certainty.

Parker made a note to have a deputy assigned to the ICU to watch over Pete and Janet. Red Dawn tried once...

As Parker made it to his SUV, his cell chirped with an incoming text message from Miguel. "Tracked down River. He's going to meet with Billie this morning around ten at the coalition offices. They're going over the schedule and how much he's going to charge for the deliveries."

Parker tapped in a text in reply, thanking Miguel and letting him know if he overheard any talk about the shipments or what happened at the Red Mountain Airfield.

A thumbs-up emoji flashed back in return. Parker had to smile. The boy was becoming more acclimated to life in the U.S. by the day.

Pulling out of the hospital parking lot, Parker wondered about the dead kid in the airplane. What did he see that Red Dawn couldn't risk him talking about? When would his parents start to miss him?

He wasn't far from the FBI offices, and a glance at his watch confirmed it was likely he could reach Lynne before she got trapped in a day of meetings and administrative quicksand. And it was early enough, he would avoid the surly gatekeeper who kept Lynne's schedule on track.

He found Lynne in the hall struggling to balance six inches of files under one arm and a coffee from the cafeteria in her free hand.

"Hey, let me get those for you." Parker took the files and pressed their edges together.

"You're up early. You don't look like you got much sleep—how's Pete? Any news?"

"I just came from the hospital. He's stable. Long ways to go, but he's breathing on his own and the doctors seem optimistic."

Lynne's face softened. "I'm glad to hear. I was worried."

"We were worried."

"I was worried about you, too."

"I'm fine."

"You've said that before, Nathan—and you were most definitely not fine."

He shrugged. "I'm better than Pete. I'm working on my own shit, Lynne. I know what I'm up against with this. I'm not going down that road again."

She narrowed her eyes at him. "I hope not."

Parker knew she kept the hurt buried as much as he did. She held the destruction of their relationship just under the surface, where it could pop up when they had a thorny interaction. Less, lately. He'd like to hope time heals.

Parker laid the stack of files on her desk and used the chance to change the conversation.

"What do you hear about Agent Thompson?"

She crossed her arms and shook her head.

"The D.C. office is sending a hotshot to take over the investigation. Which is fine by me. We don't have the time or resources. And it's not something I want to get in the middle of. However it turns out, careers are going up in flames."

"And Agent Thompson's welfare—"

"Goes without saying."

A pink rush appeared on her neck with the realization she'd put her career over the hostage rescue of a fellow FBI agent.

She cleared her throat. "D.C. says Thompson violated several bureau policies when it came to the task force. Placing team members undercover was never authorized. The deputy director wasn't aware she was chasing Red Dawn."

"She was going rogue?"

"At least for some of what she was doing. What was she trying to pull? I mean, I know she was going for a big score—noticed by the top brass. But she was already getting attention. I can't put my finger on what she was hoping for."

"No further communication from Red Dawn? I haven't gotten anything?"

She shook her head.

"I don't have much hope the outcome will be different than what you found at the airfield," she said as she sat behind her desk and sorted the files.

"Speaking of—I have a line on an ID of the pilot found in the Cessna.

Looks like an ASU student. He and his buddies ran party trips to Cabo and spring break hot spots."

Parker kept the intel he got from Joaquin Pimentel to himself for now. It was too difficult to explain where he got it from and what he gave up to earn the Cartel boss's good graces.

Lynne stiffened. "ASU students?"

"Yeah, why?"

Lynne scooted her chair closer and tapped on her keyboard. The screen bloomed to life, and she entered a string of letters and numbers. "Here. What do you see?"

She swiveled the monitor toward him.

Parker bent and scanned the series of photographs on the screen.

"These from the warehouse where Thompson was supposed to be?"

She nodded.

Two of the photographs were images of refuse scattered about the vacant warehouse floor. The close-up image of the pile revealed a letter from the Arizona State University registrar's office. The letter was addressed to Blake Visman with a Fountain Hills address.

"We might have identified our dead pilot," Parker said.

Chapter Thirty-Four

Driving back to his office at the Maricopa County Sheriff's Office, Parker felt the ground shift for the first time since this investigation began. The possible identification of the young man killed in the airplane at Red Mountain was the connection to Red Dawn.

They were careful to not leave any identification with the dead man, but must have left it in the warehouse when they rushed Agent Thompson out of the building before the FBI team stormed the place. It also meant there was a chance the FBI agent was among the living.

He left a voicemail message for Billie warning her of the connection between Red Dawn and the college flight club. Don't make any arrangements with the group, he cautioned.

When he arrived at the major crimes offices, Barry was on the phone behind his desk. He was jotting down notes from his call. Linda was also there, and instead of taking Pete's desk, she parked at an empty cubicle halfway across the room. She spotted Parker when he arrived and rose from her chair when he motioned her over.

Barry hung up and joined Parker as he entered his office.

"Get some rest?" Parker asked.

"Some. I keep going over everything. I should have done something—anything. I left my partner to bleed out. I froze."

"Barry, sit. Listen."

Parker motioned for Linda to stay out for a moment.

"I was at the hospital this morning. Pete's doing better. The docs think he'll wake up anytime now."

"I know. I must have missed you by a minute. Janet told me you came to see him."

"Listen, because of what we did out there, he has a chance to pull through this. It's natural to second-guess every single second of what happened. No matter how many times you replay it in your mind, nothing is going to change."

"If I—"

"I'm gonna stop you right there. I've been down the 'What If' road, Barry, and it leads to a miserable place." He removed the card from his shirt pocket, the one from Eleanor, his former therapist, and handed it to Barry.

"I started seeing her after I hit rock bottom—she helped me realize what I was feeling—the guilt, and wishing I'd done something to change the outcome was never going to fix anything. It was only going to guarantee one more victim—me. Barry, you've been around enough to know the department is going to mandate you go to a counselor. Eleanor's a good one. I'm going to make an appointment for me. You should, too. If you need time off—"

"I don't need time off. I need to find out who pulled the trigger on my partner," Barry said.

"Fine, but don't let a need for payback blind you. This investigation is getting more complicated by the minute."

Parker gestured Linda inside. She gave Barry a subtle rub on his shoulder as she sat next to him.

"I met with Lynne at the FBI this morning. They have no word on the whereabouts or condition of their missing FBI Agent. Seems they are bringing in someone to head up the investigation. With their task force compromised, they'll be sidelined until they manage to clear each of them. You know how fast the feds are with their beloved red tape."

"Thompson will be gone by then," Linda said.

"Likely."

"Are they sitting and waiting for another contact with Red Dawn?" Barry asked.

"Lynne couldn't tell me. They've cut her out of the loop, too, is my take. They want to limit the negative exposure something like this could generate. Everyone is covering their ass right now.

"But we do have a thread to chase down. The kid we found in the airplane. We may have an ID. Blake Visman, a student at ASU. We're not certain, but it is something we need to chase down."

"The airplane he was killed in—it's registered to Kingston Visman. I have a Fountain Hills address," Barry said.

"Good work. It'll put us a little closer to confirming his ID. We'll need a little more before we make a positive identification. The usual. We'll see what we can get from the medical examiner. Then we'll make a run at the next of kin."

"I ran the tail identification numbers on the FAA website—from the Apache Wells airport, too."

"All of them? There must have been a dozen planes out there," Parker said.

"Seventeen. I have the registration and owner's information. A couple of them stand out." Barry handed a report to Parker.

The registered owners didn't click with Parker, but Barry had circled three of them. "What's with these?"

"Those three are snowbirds. See the addresses, Chicago, Milwaukee, and Detroit. Yet the planes showed evidence of recent use."

"Okay, if they are snowbirds, they could be here on their annual summer relocation."

"Except they aren't. I contacted two of the three, and they haven't made their way out here yet. The planes are usually stored in Scottsdale."

"Huh. Someone's using them."

"The two I spoke with said their kids were allowed to use them, but they were supposed to tell them."

Parker mulled it over for a moment. "Any chance one of these kids is named River?"

"How'd you know? River Patterson. Family lives in Chicago. River is attending ASU, majoring in general laziness according to dad."

"Wonder how Dad would feel if he knew Sonny Boy was arranging spring break girls gone wild type trips down south?"

"I get the sense River's parents aren't willing to take too close a look at the boy's behavior because they don't want to know what he's up to."

"The 'flight club' we found out about—the Patterson kid seems to be one of the leaders. He's offered to fly Billie's relief supplies over the border."

"She's going to see River this morning, right?" Linda asked.

"At ten," Parker said.

Parker's desk phone rang, and he recognized the number from the medical examiner's office.

"Parker here."

"Dr. White here. Just a quick call on the burial mound bodies."

"Already? I didn't know you were scheduling a post already."

"We haven't yet. As we processed the bodies, their prints hit on LiveScan. They were both in the system."

"The older couple? They have a record?"

"They were in the system because they had both received visas for travel to Mexico. Mr. And Mrs. Cortez were both green card holders, here in the U.S. legally."

"Huh, wonder why they ended up on the Red Dawn charter flight back home?'

"That's more of a you question, detective."

"Thanks, doc. Appreciate the heads up."

Seconds later, he received a text listing Raul and Maria Cortez with an address on Calle Azteca in Guadalupe. The location was once a gathering spot for new migrants who arrived to make a new life in this country. While it remained a predominantly Latino enclave, the dynamics had changed over the years, transforming the community from a vibrant multicultural neighborhood to the most gang-infested streets in the county. A hub of violence, extortion, and drug-running. At the expense of the people trapped between the system, which excluded them, and the gangs who used them.

Parker glanced at his watch. "Who's up for a trip to the Guad?"

Chapter Thirty-Five

"Y ou did this counseling stuff before?" Barry asked as they drove out to the southern suburb of Guadalupe.

"I did. It was—I think the hardest thing for me was accepting the fact I needed help and couldn't do it on my own. I made a mess of things."

Barry nodded, glanced at the card Parker'd given him, and didn't respond.

Linda stayed behind to follow up on the ID of Blake Visman with the medical examiner. They had a photo of a guy who looked like the same man, the plane's registration number, and the ASU registrar's letter. It pointed in that direction, but they'd need more concrete forensic detail to confirm the identity.

Barry stowed the card away in his jacket pocket.

"I'll call. If you do." Barry shot a side eye glance at Parker.

"Deal."

"Calle Azteca is up ahead. We were out here looking for the truck driver a few months back. Tight neighborhood, as I recall. Everyone was looking out for one another."

"Which means the phone tree is already burning up with us cruising the neighborhood. Most of these people didn't have great encounters with police in their home countries, and they have no reason to think we'd be any different."

"Check it. Two hard cases up on the corner," Barry said.

A pair of identically dressed men, both wearing brown chinos, oversized white t-shirts, and red bandanas pulled low on their foreheads, stood on what was once a front lawn. The space was dirt and dried yellow weeds; the residents, having long ago given up holding back the desert from reclaiming the land.

The two vatos watched Parker's SUV cruise past. The moment the SUV slowed, one man pulled a cell phone from his baggy pants and made a call.

"Looks like the neighborhood watch knows we're here," Parker said.

"No secrets. Wonder what's going on in that house? Something serious enough to post a couple of guys out front. This is 40s territory."

"The 40s have been pretty quiet lately. They did have a dust-up a couple months ago with the East Side Guad faction."

"There's our address up on the left. Two cars in the driveway. Shades on the front windows are down," Barry said.

"Tells me the Cortez family is with the program in the neighborhood. Don't see anything, you can't tell anything."

Parker pulled the SUV to the curb across the street. "You have the information, Linda, printed out?"

"Yeah. I hate doing this—telling people their family members aren't coming home."

"Me too, Barry. Me too."

They got out of the SUV, and one of the window shades fluttered.

"Okay, they know we're here," Parker said.

The faded yellow stucco home bore some attention. The front yard was clear of weeds and trash. Two potted cacti guarded each side of the door.

Parker knocked.

A woman in her twenties must have been waiting, because she opened up seconds after the rap on the metal door. She peered through the crack, a thin brass chain securing the door.

"Hello, I'm detective Parker, and this is detective Johns. Is this the home of Raul and Maria Cortez?"

"Something's happened to them, hasn't it?"

"May we come in and talk?"

She unlatched the chain and held the door for the detectives.

Inside, Parker found the home well-ordered, with everything in its place.

The dated furnishings were polished and dust-free. The young woman gestured them to a sofa in the living room.

Parker passed a photograph on the wall. A family portrait. The woman was huddled with an older couple—a couple Parker had seen before—buried in the desert.

"Please, sit. Tell me what's happened."

"What's your name, ma'am?" Parker asked.

"Trinity Cortez. Trini. Raul and Maria are my parents. They went home to visit family in Hermosillo. They were supposed to be home two days ago."

"In Hermosillo?" Parker glanced at Barry.

"Yes. There was a family gathering for the quincinera for their Goddaughter. Tell me, please."

"Trini, I'm so sorry to tell you, your parents have died."

Parker found it best to take a direct approach and not use words that softened or diminished the loss the next of kin would feel. They hadn't passed on or gone on to a better place. They were dead, and in most of his cases, the death was unnatural and often violent. The last part he usually kept to himself.

Trini blinked, and tears flowed. She didn't sob or cry out. After a moment, she wiped the tears with the edge of her hand. "Both of them? Was it an accident? What—what happened to them?"

"We're investigating, but we can tell you they were killed."

"Murdered? Who would kill my parents? They were a sweet older couple. Ask anyone who knew them."

"Tell me about them—your parents. When did they come here?"

She sat back and glanced around at the memorabilia that now closed around her in the living room. Reminders of what she'd lost.

"My parents came here twenty years ago—legally. They completed the process and obtained their visas and green cards, and were living here in this house for the last fifteen years."

"Did they go to Hermosillo often?"

"Once, maybe twice a year. Never been a problem."

"When was the last time you heard from them?"

"Two, no three days ago. They couldn't get on the regular flight back and found another cheaper one."

"They tell you anything about the connection? Where was it coming in at, or what time?"

She shook her head. "No, Papa didn't have the information yet. He was working it out. No, wait, I heard him say a name. It was—different."

"Different how?"

"It had a European sound to it. Quinn, or Quint, or Quentin. It was hard to tell with Papa's accent. The last name was clear—odd but clear. Ridler."

"Had you ever heard him mention the name before? Maybe on one of his trips to Hermosillo? A travel agent, or someone who worked at the airport?" Parker asked.

She shook her head. "No, never before. I don't know who my father was talking to. From the conversation, it was someone helping him arrange a new flight home."

"Did he mention the name, Blake? Blake Visman?"

She bit her lip and shook her head.

"I'm sorry for this, Trini. Can you think of anyone who would want to do harm to your parents?"

"No one. Everyone loved them. Even those gangbangers down the street respected them. If a new family came into the neighborhood, my mother would help them get settled. Nobody would wish them harm."

"I understand." Parker handed her one of his business cards and told her someone from the medical examiner's office would be contacting her. He jotted down her contact information in return. "We have people to help you make any arrangements you might need—"

"The medical examiner—from here? They were here in Phoenix when they died and not down in Mexico?"

"Yes."

"Why? Why were they killed?"

It was always the question the survivors asked. What could you tell someone to help make sense of the violence that stole loved ones away?

170

Why? There was never a good answer. And the search for "the why" could drive you insane.

"We're trying to find out."

Parker and Barry stood, and Trini remained parked on a living room chair.

"Thank you for your time. Please don't get up. We'll show ourselves out."

Parker stopped in the hallway, turned, and asked Trini, "You went to ASU?" Parker pointed to her diploma, proudly displayed in a place of honor in her parents' home.

"I did. First in my family to graduate. My parents sacrificed to allow me to go. It doesn't matter now."

"It shows how proud of you they were. Know that, Trini."

Chapter Thirty-Six

Parker turned up the air once inside the SUV. The breeze hit the sweat on his brow and he had a chill, but it wasn't from the blast of tepid air shooting from the vent. The college connection. He believed Trini when she said she didn't know who Blake Visman was. But he wasn't the only student to be part of the flight club. Her parents might have been lured into trusting someone who played up the school angle. If they were as proud of her as she said they were, he could envision them falling for an offer for a ride home.

Barry turned to him. "I've seen that look before. What are you chewing on? It was the diploma, wasn't it?"

"Right you are, detective. It's a common thread between the Cortez family and the dead pilot. I don't know why they'd seek them out. What would the club, or Red Dawn, get from killing off an innocent couple?"

"Man, that's some twisted action. Force them to mule product over the border? It was only the two of them, and it was in one of their own planes, so I don't get the economics of it—and these cartels operate on the bottom line."

Parker pulled the SUV into drive, made a U-turn in the street, and headed back out the way they'd come in. Three men dressed in the same chinos and T-shirts came out into the street and blocked their path.

"What do these speed bumps want?" Barry said.

Parker pulled his weapon from his holster and laid it across his lap with the muzzle pointing to the door panel. He read their body language, and they didn't look tense or nervous. Most importantly, they were empty-handed and not trying to hide their movements.

He rolled his window down.

"Gentlemen? What's up?" Parker said.

One of the gangbangers lifted his sunglasses and revealed young eyes. "Is it true? Mr. And Mrs. Cortez? They were killed?"

"How'd you come by this information?"

"Trinity. She called my mom. It's true, then?"

Parker noted concern etched into the young man's face. In the moment, he didn't come off as a street thug.

"I'm afraid so."

"What happened? They were supposed to be on their way home."

"We're trying to put it together now. You hear anything about trouble-making travel arrangements home?"

"Trinity said they'd missed their flight. Didn't make sense to me because Mr. Cortez was always early—like for everything. Trinity used to say her father wouldn't be late to his own funeral. I guess she was right. They were really murdered? No accident?"

"I really can't say any more about it," Parker said.

The street thug's persona morphed back into stone-cold. "We'll find out who did it."

"These people are dangerous."

"So are we. They come in here and hurt my people—they will feel what that's like ten times over."

Parker recognized the cycle of violence on the street. It never ended. It fed on the pain and suffering, building strength, swallowing lives, and crushing dreams.

"Let Trinity grieve her parents in peace. She doesn't need more weighing down on her."

A flicker crossed the man's face. Uncertainty.

"The best thing you can do for Trinity and her family is to be here to support her. Not out on some quest for revenge," Parker said, his own obsession to find his partner's killer only recently in his rearview mirror.

"We'll do what we have to," the gangbanger said.

"They only thing you have to do is to make sure she's okay," he said as he shot a thumb toward the Cortez home.

The thug donned his sunglasses once more and stepped away from Parker's SUV.

As Parker pulled away, he caught the young man heading toward the Cortez home, and Trinity met him on the front porch with an embrace.

"Think they know about Red Dawn?" Barry asked.

"I don't think so. The gangs like the 40s keep to their few square blocks of turf here in the Guad."

"Let's hope it stays that way. They don't know what they're up against."

"You have Visman's address in Fountain Hills? We need to reach them before they find out their son was murdered. The television stations are bound to pick up the radio traffic responding to the airport."

"Yeah, I have it here." Barry tapped the address into the onboard computer terminal in the SUV. "Take the 101, then east on Shea."

Fountain Hills was an upscale enclave east of Scottsdale and home to movie stars, musicians, and self-styled influencers. Parker drove past the five-hundred-sixty-foot fountain that shot skyward every fifteen minutes. The display was once the tallest fountain in the world, and it struck Parker as a display of wealth and entitlement. We have water while the rest of the valley had to borrow the vital substance from the Colorado River.

The Visman address was near the rear of the community, where large parcels backed up against the McDowell Mountains. The residence wasn't visible from the main road and was sealed off with a tall black iron gate—the kind you couldn't see through. The Vismans were concerned about keeping everyone out of their exclusive compound. Parker couldn't help but notice the gates, fences, and cameras weren't able to shield the family from the pain they were about to experience.

Parker pulled to the gate, lowered his window, and pressed a button on a call box mounted near the driveway.

"Yes? Are you with the caterer? You're hours early. Come back at the agreed-upon time." A harried voice sounded over the speaker. A woman. Impatience bled through the call box.

"Detective Parker, Maricopa County Sheriff's Office. We need to speak with Mr. and Mrs. Visman."

"What's this about?"

"I'd rather speak in person. Is this Mrs. Visman?"

"Is this about the complaint the Wilsons filed with the HOA? They have the nerve to call the police?"

"No ma'am. This is about your son."

"Oh, my God, what did Blake do now?"

"I'd like to talk with you directly, Mrs. Visman."

She huffed, and the gate buzzed before slowly sliding back on a hidden track in the driveway. "Fine, but I don't have all day to deal with my son's issues. He's an adult now."

Parker exchanged a look with Barry.

"This is going to be interesting," Barry said in a low voice.

Parker shifted the SUV into drive and pulled through the gate. A low green hedge lined both sides of the blacktop roadway. Beyond them was a manicured desert landscape with several species of cactus and Sonoran vegetation. The dirt in which they were planted was smoothed and raked like a Japanese Zen garden.

A three-story mansion loomed ahead. The front-facing windows glinted in the sunlight. And the dark rock structure gave off a castle vibe. Parker pulled the SUV near the garage where a pair of matching dark blue Maserati sport sedans waited.

"His and Hers?" Parker said.

"Damn. Those are Gran Turismo Modena and go for about two hundred K—each."

"They aren't clipping coupons. What do the Vismans do?"

"Got me. The plane's registered owner is Kingston Visman."

The two detectives parked and strode up the grey slate steps to a massive dark wood double door.

Before they rang the bell, a younger woman opened the door for them. She was dressed in a dark-toned pantsuit. She held a clipboard under her arm.

"Mrs. Visman will be with you shortly. She's asked you to wait in the library. Please come with me."

Parker and Johns followed the woman's brisk pace to a space off the main entrance lined with bookshelves with dark mahogany hues. A few awards were interspersed on the shelves.

"There's more books here than I had in my city library growing up."

Parker scanned the titles. Some he recognized—old classics, philosophy, hard literature. First editions. This was a collector, not a reader. There wasn't a pile of books sitting on the floor near a worn club chair. This was a showroom for someone who wanted to project sophistication—or make up for a hidden failing.

"Bet they don't even read them," Barry said as he glanced at the packed shelves. "Check this out," he said, pointing at one award on display. A crystal plaque proclaiming Kingston Visman as landscape architect of the year by some association."

"A gardener?" Parker said.

"These aren't your mow-and-blow gardeners. Visman is the guy you call to design the grounds, fountains, hardscape, and pathways—you know, like you see on college campuses, or high-end business parks?"

"I guess he's doing okay."

Parker felt the energy change as an older woman swept into the room. He pegged her in her sixties with long platinum grey hair and hard green eyes.

"Now, tell me what this is about," she said, standing a few feet inside the door.

"Mrs. Visman?"

"Yes, Victoria Visman. You said my son, Blake, has gotten into some trouble."

"I'm afraid so. Is your husband, Kingston, here?"

Her expression hardened at the mention of his name. "What do you want from him?"

She was used to people trying to grab the brass ring the Visman family held. The missus was fiercely protective of what they had collected over the years.

"It's important we speak to both you and your husband, together. It's about Blake."

In Parker's experience, he'd found everyone handled receiving the news a loved one or close friend had died differently. Some fell to pieces, shattered over the loss. Others tried to play it off as nothing more than a nasty breakup. Mrs. Visman was one of those who considered the death an imposition, or complication, making their lives difficult. It was about them, and the dead person was a problem to be dealt with. If this was the nurturing relationship Blake grew up with, no wonder he was an entitled rich kid flying off to party it up with college girls.

Mrs. Visman huffed. "Fine." She pulled a cell phone from her linen slacks and called her husband. Parker had to wonder about a lifestyle where you needed to telephone your spouse in your own home. It seemed cold, distant, and impersonal.

"There are two police officers here to speak with us," she said into the phone.

After a pause, she continued. "It's about Blake—yes, I know you said you were done covering up his mistakes. They say it's important. Should I call Roger?"

She quit the call and slipped the phone back in her pocket. "He'll be here shortly. He says I should wait to see what Blake has gotten himself involved in before I bother our attorney with it."

A minute later, Kingston Visman strode into the library. Six-three, the same shade of gray hair as his wife. Visman was dressed in a tan suit, pale yellow shirt with no tie. His idea of informal business attire for working at home, Parker wondered?

"Well, get on with it. What's the boy done now?" he said in a deep, gravelly voice.

"Mr. and Mrs. Visman, I'm sorry to inform you Blake has died."

Mrs. Visman's hand covered her mouth, the shock of the news silencing her.

The boy's father stood impassively near her, never reaching over to touch his wife.

"What happened?" he said.

"We're early in the investigation, but your son was killed, murdered at the Red Mountain Airfield earlier today."

"Not likely. Blake had been restricted from using my plane."

"Why was that?" Parker asked.

"That's none of your business."

"What is my business is your son was involved in trafficking contraband and people over the border using that airplane of yours."

"Nonsense. Do you have evidence to prove any of this?"

There it was, Parker thought. Visman was more concerned about the smuggling allegations, the use of his plane, and the ramifications of asset forfeiture—when the property of the accused is seized by the government. He wasn't asking how his son died, who was responsible, or if the boy suffered.

"It appears Blake was involved with a group of his college friends and they would fly over the border to party with co-eds. He's not the first one to have been murdered after one of these trips."

"I told him those-those flings would be a problem," Mrs. Visman said.

"Did he ever talk about what, or who, he was bringing back on these flights?" Parker asked.

"Not really. I mean, he may have mentioned the trips, but I didn't pick up on any names of who was going along with him."

"But the trips back home. Any discussion of who else might have been with him?"

She shook her head. "He did mention some of his friends were picking up extra business by bringing things down south—like medicine and clothing to the refugee camps down there." Her nose crinkled at the thought of her son dealing with the squalid camps.

The same connection Billie made to ferry supplies down to Hermosillo.

"Mr. Visman, you restricted Blake from using the family plane. Can I ask what happened?"

"I use my plane for business. I needed it for a trip to Sedona, and he'd taken it on one of his larks over the border. I confronted him about it when he landed—he thought he'd slip in unnoticed before I needed the plane. But I found him with two college-aged girls and two older men. The men were…odd. I mean, they wore cheap suits and clearly not here for spring break."

"Those men, can you describe them?"

"Not really. Both were Hispanic, mid-thirties, and never said a word as they picked up their duffle bags and left. There was a car waiting for them. The duffle bags struck me as strange—what kind of businessman packs for a trip using a green canvas duffle?"

Parker knew what kind of men did. Hired killers. These were the men the Sinaloa Cartel leader told him about. Red Dawn was smuggling hired guns over the border. The real question is, what were they doing here?"

Chapter Thirty-Seven

After leaving the Vismans with instructions on when and where they could claim their son's body after the medical examiner finished their work, Parker and Johns were escorted to the front door by the house staffer who'd greeted them earlier.

"It's a shame about Blake," she said in a voice quiet enough to avoid being heard by Mrs. Visman.

"Did you know him well?"

She blushed. "Yes. I knew these Spring break adventures would turn into trouble. I never thought it would get him killed."

"He talk to you about them?"

"Once in a while. Just last week, Blake said he and his friends were onto a new gig. One that would make them a ton of cash. He was kind of quiet about it. Only said a guy approached him in Cabo last month with a proposition."

"He tell you anything about it?"

"It was clear this guy wanted Blake and his friends to fly people over without a lot of questions. I told him not to get involved, but he said it was a lot of money. And I think he got off on the thrill of doing it. It was like he needed the money." She glanced around at the surroundings.

"Mention the name of the guys who approached him in Cabo?"

"Something weird...like Rietman, Ridler, Ridman. He only mentioned him before this last trip. He was supposed to meet him and talk about plans for something more."

"More than?"

She shrugged.

Parker thanked her as she opened the front door. He caught a glint of sadness as she ducked back inside.

As they headed for the SUV, Parker asked, "What did you make of it?"

Barry Johns donned his sunglasses and said, "You mean an example of the deterioration of the family unit in America? Or the cost of living the dream?"

Parker grinned. "Thanks, Professor, but I was actually going for what the housekeeper was telling us. Young Blake was up to his neck in the smuggling business with a guy named Ridler. We've heard that name before."

"We have. Trinity in the Guad told us the name her father mentioned when making the arrangements to come back over the border."

"Right. Why would Ridler make arrangements with Blake Visman to bring over Trinity's parents and then murder them?"

"It's not like the Cortezes were undocumented and trying to sneak in over the border. They had legitimate travel visas. The only reason Ridler would have them killed was to keep them from telling anyone what they saw on the trip," Barry said.

"Those two traveling salesman types Kingston Visman saw?"

"Or whatever they had in those duffel bags."

The sun slid behind the White Tank Mountains to the west, and the sky morphed into the red and purple hues popular on postcards of the Valley of the Sun.

Billie Carson's place off Cave Creek was on the way back home, if Parker chose the longest route there. But to get to her place, they'd have to drive past Coyote Wash—the spot where they'd fallen under attack and Pete Tully nearly died.

Both of them knew it, and neither of them said anything as they drew close to the spot. The white wooden marker memorializing the place where Parker's partner, McMillan, bled out came into view.

Parker found his hands gripping the wheel so tight his knuckles turned white. This place trapped incredible pain. It held a dark power.

Parker slammed on the brakes and slid in the loose, chipped gravel and asphalt.

Johns braced himself against the dash. "What is it?"

Parker stared at the memorial for a moment.

"Boss?"

Parker opened his door and walked around the front of the SUV to the cross. In the dark of night, the last time they were out here, he couldn't see it. They found Agent Metzger's phone a few feet from the marker. Now, in the sunset's light, Parker caught the reflection. After a half-dozen cautious steps off the shoulder where the cross stood, the object became clear. At the base of the wooden cross was a grey box-shaped object. It was a body camera, an older version of the ones issued to Maricopa County deputies. This model he and McMillan wore that night—the night when his friend was murdered by Esteban Castaneda.

McMillan's body camera wasn't found the night he died. Castaneda stole it to prevent anyone from capturing the killing on video. These old models didn't upload to the cloud; they held the images in their memory. Parker knew there wouldn't be anything on the body cam because of the large caliber bullet hole in the casing.

The body cam itself was a message. A message from Castaneda.

Barry had joined him near the marker, and Parker slipped the body cam into an evidence bag Barry held.

"You think this is his—McMillan's?"

Parker used a plastic evidence bag up to pick up the obsolete recording device. "Be easy enough to run the serial number. But I don't think that's the point. Castaneda wants me to know he's involved."

"How could he play any part in this? He's in Supermax in Colorado, and he's persona non grata with every criminal organization in Mexico," Barry said.

"This is his handiwork." Parker lifted the evidence bag once more. "I thought the feds found this when he got caught last year. He was keeping it as some sick souvenir. Billie's kid mentioned it. If the feds had this—how did it get out here? What's he trying to tell me?"

"He's telling you the feds are in on this. The task force is compromised, and he wants to make you think you're on your own. He couldn't be more wrong. His big mistake was going after us out here."

Parker felt his spirits lift for a moment. Barry Johns had a big heart and was fiercely loyal to those around him. The problem was Castaneda knew it too.

He couldn't risk more people around him being drawn into this vortex of violence that seemed to circle him. Parker recognized the patterns before, and ignoring the pain never worked.

"What say we drop by and see how Pete's doing before we call it a day?"

Barry nodded before he responded. "I'd like that. Being out there where it happened—that—that was hard. I keep seeing it happen again and again. Does it get to you, or do you get used to it?"

"You never get used to it. It becomes part of you. It's up to you if it breaks you or makes you stronger. Barry, I know you. I know what you're about. What you—what we—are going through right now—we need to come out on top. Too many people depend on us to have it any other way."

Parker pulled into the Osborn Medical Center and they weaved their way through the waiting room, into the ICU, and Pete's wife, Janet, wasn't at her post in the corner chair.

He strode to the ICU station, turned, and noticed the room where Pete had been was empty. There were discarded IV tubes on the floor, monitor wires hung limp, no longer needed.

He was too late...

Chapter Thirty-Eight

Parker felt a lump in his throat. The clouds of a panic attack swirled around him. He had to keep it together for Barry. What happened? Pete was stable when he checked on him a scant few hours ago. Instinctively, Parker knew any number of sudden events could have occurred. Uncontrolled hemorrhage, infection, stroke, cardiac arrest—one of them would be listed on the official death certificate, but in his gut, it should be Red Dawn, or Castaneda. They were the cause of death.

A roving ICU nurse noticed Parker and Johns standing at the counter. She was about to speak when Parker spotted Janet Tully sweep into the ICU room her husband had last occupied.

"Janet." Parker's voice was strained. He was barely keeping it together.

She turned and, with tear-streaked, puffy eyes, looked back at him. That was all it took. Parker started crying. He found Janet, wrapping her in a hug.

"What happened?" he whispered.

"Pete's heart stopped. They think it was a complication from the anesthesia."

Parker felt her shudder in his arms.

"Is he…"

"They got him going again. Moved him to a cardiac unit where they can monitor him. I don't know if…"

"Does your daughter know?"

She bobbed her head. "I just told her. She's on the way."

"When did it happen. I-I thought he was…"

184

"About an hour ago."

"I'm so sorry, Janet."

"She put a hand on his chest and gently pushed away. "I came back up here to get my book. How silly was that? I was worried about a damn book."

She wiped the tears away with the back of her hand.

"He loved his job—working with you and Barry. It was everything to him. Now, I don't know what tomorrow brings."

Parker was about to say he was sorry again when Linda appeared through the waiting room door, holding two cups of coffee.

"There you are," she said while handing off one cup to Janet.

"I found it," Janet held the book in her hand.

Linda rubbed her back softly. "Janet called me."

"What can we do for you?" Barry asked.

"I don't think there's anything to do. Pete is where he needs to be. I need to start making calls—but it can wait until morning." Her phone vibrated in her purse. She dug it out, glanced at it, and placed it back in the handbag. "My daughter's downstairs."

"I'll go with you," Linda said.

"You don't need to."

"I'll be with you." Linda didn't pose a question.

Janet hugged Linda. "Thank you." She started for the elevator.

"I'll be right there," Linda said. Then, turning to Parker. "How are you doing?"

"I don't know, to be honest. Angry, shocked, or somewhere in between. I thought I got to him in time."

"You being here wouldn't have changed anything. Nathan, this is not the time to second-guess what happened out there. None of this is your fault."

He started to tell her Pete was only out there because he brought him there, but Linda stopped him before the words tumbled from his lips.

"No. Both of you. Listen. What happened to Pete is awful. It was not your fault. Neither of you are responsible for it. That rests with the man who pulled the trigger. If you want to help Pete, keep looking for him. Now I'm staying with Janet. I've called the department's chaplain, and they're sending someone out too."

She got on her toes and planted a kiss on Parker's cheek. "I'll see you later. Call me when you have a chance."

Linda hugged Barry and then joined Janet at the elevator. Linda pressed the down button because Janet had forgotten to, while lost in her own thoughts of what was and what might never be again.

When the two women disappeared behind the elevator doors, Barry slumped against the counter. "I can't believe we almost lost him."

"Again. I thought he was out of the woods," Parker said. "If you need to step away from this for a while, I totally understand. We've been through—you've been through a lot. He was your partner, and no one will—"

"Stop. Yeah, this is tough to process, but right now I want to find the people responsible for it."

"I get it. I need you to promise me one thing."

"What's that?"

"You see me going off the rails, you pull me in check. I'll do the same for you."

"Deal." They shook hands on the pact to watch one another.

Parker didn't think Barry should be alone, so he invited him over to spend the night at his place. Barry didn't want to admit it at first, but agreed to stop over at Parker's for a while.

On the way out of the hospital, Janet huddled with another much younger woman. The daughter. Linda stood a few feet back from them while they consoled one another. Parker waved Linda over and told her he and Barry were going to be at their place tonight. He said they'd head out in the morning, and they might be gone most of the day.

"What? Are you sure it's a good idea?" she asked.

"No. But I need to keep moving forward on this, or I think I'll drown." Parker said while Barry joined Janet.

"That's why you need to step away—for now."

"I can't; Pete deserves—"

"Pete deserves to know you're doing the right thing."

"Make sure you get some rest. When the chaplain shows up, it might be a chance to slip away and let them take over."

"We'll see. Now that her daughter is here, Janet has some support. She's overwhelmed. I'll stick close by if she needs help."

"You're a good woman, Linda Hunt."

"Make sure you don't forget it, Nathan Parker."

She kissed him and returned to Janet and her daughter.

Parker pulled out his cell phone and tapped in a speed dial number.

"I need a favor."

After a quick phone conversation, Parker hung up.

Barry joined his boss, and his shoulders sagged. His eyes were red.

"I've never met Pete's daughter before. I didn't want it to be like this."

Barry looked surprised when Parker told him to pack a go bag.

"What's going on?" he asked.

"I need to pay a visit to an old friend. You're coming with."

Chapter Thirty-Nine

Parker and Barry arrived at the Scottsdale airport at first light.

"Must be the one," Barry pointed to a lone Lear Jet with an FBI logo emblazoned near the sleek white jet's nose.

Lynne waited at the base of the air-stairs in a light blue suit. She was on the phone when Parker and Barry joined her.

"It's set. Prison staff are pulling Castaneda out of his cell, searching it, and tossing him in a holding cell until we get there."

"Thank you, Lynne. And we appreciate the ride, too."

"You don't have to go. We can handle Castaneda. You know he's going to try to get in your head."

Parker shifted his carry-on bag. "We have to go. It's personal. Castaneda sent me a message, and like I told you on the phone, he's telling me Red Dawn has someone on the inside with enough clout to pull McMillan's body cam out of the evidence room."

"Are you certain it was his?" Lynne said.

He recognized what she was doing. Slowing him down, making him think and rethink every decision.

He grinned at her. "Thanks, Lynne. I'm good here. We have the techs looking at it, and we should get confirmation by the time we hit Colorado."

A slight blush crept up her neck. "Am I that transparent?"

"I've known you a long time, Lynne."

"Remind me not to play poker with you."

A woman in a dark blue flight suit poked her head through the door at the top of the airstrip. "We're done with pre-fight and ready any time you are, Agent Finch."

"Last chance. Want to leave the past in the past?" Lynne said.

"If it were only that easy," Parker said as he climbed the stairs into the small jet's cabin.

Four rows of heavy upholstered seats filled the cabin. The seats looked more like oversized club chairs.

"The feds do it up right," Barry said, stowing his small carry-on bag on the floor in one of the aisles.

"Definitely didn't come from our motor pool."

"Buckle up, next stop ADX," the woman in the jumpsuit said as she stepped into the cockpit and slunk into the left-hand captain's chair."

"We're not landing in Denver or Colorado Springs?" Parker asked Lynne as she settled into a seat across the aisle from him.

"Denver is a hundred miles north. Besides, ADX has its own runway, so we can make prisoner transports with as few stops as possible."

"Con-Air is a real thing?" Parker asked.

"The Marshals Service runs JPATS, the Justice Prisoner and Alien Transportation System, for high security transports throughout the system. Almost half of the two hundred thousand moves a year are by air. And it's nothing like the movie."

The engines wound up, and the whine heightened. The front hatch was closed and secured, and cut out most of the sound, keeping it to a steady rumble.

Over a speaker, the pilot announced they had clearance, and the jet began moving forward along a taxiway to the Scottsdale airport's runway.

The taxi was faster than Parker was used to in a commercial airliner. This pilot wasn't wasting any time getting them into the air.

The Lear Jet turned, lined up with the runway, and Parker felt himself being pushed back into his seat, and the jet shot down the runway. The nose pulled up hard about halfway down the strip and made a hard bank to the right. Parker looked out the window and all he could see were the tops of houses, the freeway, and the desert—far too close for comfort.

He caught a smile on Lynne's face. "Kerry is a former Navy pilot. Used to land on carriers at sea in the dark."

"Maybe she should go back and do that," he said.

The jet leveled out and sailed over the McDowell range. A phone in Lynne's armchair rang. She drew it from its resting place in the arm and listened.

After replacing the phone, Lynne said they'd be on the ground in an hour and ten minutes.

Parker settled in for the quick flight and pulled a file from his bag. The file hadn't been touched in over a year and contained the last interview and incident reports concerning Esteban Castaneda.

Castaneda, in his prime, was a ruthless criminal kingpin. The Los Muertos were pure mercenaries. Castaneda would sell their services to whoever could meet his price. What started as smuggling, human trafficking, and assassination wasn't enough for Castaneda. He wanted more. He sought respect from the cartels, who looked at him and his collection of thugs as a tool used so they didn't have to get their hands dirty.

He made a play to overthrow the Sinaloa and Juarez Cartels to take over the territory and become the most powerful criminal organization in Mexico.

Parker stopped the plot, and Castaneda's greed was his undoing. The last interview with Castaneda was after his cartel takeover failed, and he was on the hit list of nearly every cartel, street gang, and hired gun in the hemisphere. Still, the man was unbroken and promised Parker he'd take away everyone he cared about. He tried to make good on his threat with a failed bombing attempt at his arraignment.

Parker had to wonder if Pete Tully was on Castaneda's ledger sheet? Could he have any pull with Red Dawn to target those in Parker's orbit? It seemed unlikely. Castaneda was locked deep in the bowels of the highest security federal prison in the country.

Within a month of his arrival, he was stabbed by two inmates who were supposed to be in protective custody. They turned out to be sleepers—waiting for an order to take out anyone the Sinaloa Cartel pointed at—in this case, at Castaneda.

The attack almost killed him, and since then, he'd been locked away in the most secure portion of the prison. He didn't even come out of his cell for meals or a shower. Everything was self-contained in his unit, one typically reserved for the most violent, staff-assaultive inmates.

Parker was jolted as the jet's wheels hit the runway in Colorado. The landing was hard and abrupt, and the reverse engine thrusters pulled him away from the seat. He imagined this is what it felt like to land on an aircraft carrier.

The jet taxied to a waiting Humvee near one of the hangars lining the small airfield. Through the window, Parker saw two 737 jets, one of which was loading prisoners for a move to another facility in the federal system.

As the engine wound down, the cockpit door opened.

"Got us here ahead of schedule, Agent Finch. You want me to fuel up and wait for a return trip?"

"That's the plan. Unless Parker here irks me and I reserve a cell for him here."

"I'm on my best behavior," Parker said.

"That's what worries me."

They stole down the air stairs, and a correctional officer waited by the Humvee.

It was a brisk walk from the jet to the vehicle in the chill Colorado morning.

"Agent Finch, I'm supposed to take you to the Watch Commander to get processed in."

"Was Castaneda's cell searched?"

"It was ma'am."

"Find anything?"

"Let's say some folks found themselves on Admin. Leave this morning. The Watch Commander will brief you."

"Does Castaneda know we're coming?" Parker asked.

"We didn't tell him. These guys always have a way of knowing what's happening. We lock them down tight, but they manage."

They hopped into the Humvee, and the correctional officer drove them to a pedestrian sally port and told them the Watch Commander would meet them.

After a series of gates, doors, and body scans for contraband, they were allowed in the Supermax administration building with an escort. The Watch Commander met them in the hallway and gestured for them to follow.

Fifty-plus years old, with grey in his temples, the Lieutenant walked them to central control.

"You must be Agent Finch. Lieutenant Webb. This the detective you mentioned?"

"Detective Parker, and this is Detective Johns," Lynne said.

Parker put his hand out, and Webb made no move to shake it.

"You want to tell me why my inmate's in contact with you?"

Parker stiffened. "Castaneda? He's not. Last communication we had was at his video arraignment."

"He says different."

"I've learned not to believe anything he says. If he's telling you we've been in contact, that's a lie. How was this supposed to have happened? I don't imagine he gets many visitors or phone privileges."

The Lieutenant pressed a button on an intercom unit and looked to a camera on the wall. The door buzzed open.

"When Agent Finch called, we pulled Castaneda out and put him in a holding cell. Searched his cell as a matter of course. Found a cell phone hidden in his mattress."

That explained how Castaneda contacted Red Dawn and used the Coyote Wash location, knowing it would put Parker off balance.

"How'd he get a cell phone in here?" Parker asked as they continued down a corridor.

"He said you gave it to him."

Parker laughed, and the Lieutenant didn't respond in kind.

"And how exactly was I supposed to have done that?"

"I don't know. What I do know is we confiscated a cell phone from an inmate in H Unit."

"H Unit?" Lynne asked.

"Our special security unit for high-risk inmates. He was under special administrative measures restricting his contact with staff and the outside world. How he got a cell phone is a particular problem. Since he's had zero visitors, it means I have to look at my staff."

"It's not the first time he's manipulated and compromised staff."

The Lieutenant stopped and turned to Parker. "Castaneda said something strange when we confronted him about the cell phone."

"What's that?"

"Detective Parker got my message."

Chapter Forty

A series of linked underground tunnels connected the housing units to the prison's main administrative area. The Lieutenant repeated the process of buzzing through a series of doors monitored by cameras until they reached the cellblock. Lime green paint, steel, and glass surfaces marked the small pod of cells.

What struck Parker was the absolute silence in the unit. He'd been in other prisons where the din was constant, with inmates shouting back and forth, or cursing out the correctional officers on the tier.

The Lieutenant led them to a room with a glass panel separating them from the day room in the cell block. A small sign posted on the glass warned that visitor communication would be monitored and recorded. Each pod had their own visiting room, but to Parker's eye, this one was unused.

The Lieutenant signaled to one of the unit staff, and a moment later, Castaneda appeared bracketed by a pair of correctional officers. The officers wore stab-resistant vests, and Castaneda was in belly chains and shackles around his ankles.

Last time Parker was in the same room with Castaneda, he was a muscled, robust man who used his physical presence to intimidate his gang members. The man in front of him now was emaciated. Thin, frail, and he shuffled with a halting gait. The stabbing was worse than Parker knew.

Castaneda broke into a grin when he spotted Parker behind the glass.

The officers guided their charge onto a steel stool on their side of the glass. There wasn't a telephone because these inmates would try to use it as a weapon. Instead, a microphone at the base of the glass served the purpose.

It caught a heavy wheeze coming from Castaneda.

The Lieutenant turned a knob on his side of the glass and said, "Castaneda, you have visitors."

He shook his head. "Parker. Parker alone."

"You don't make decisions," the watch commander said.

Castaneda started to stand. "Take me back to the house."

"Sit down." Parker tipped his head to the door, turned down the microphone on his side. Then to the lieutenant, "Are you recording this?"

A nod in return.

"All right, people, let's give our happy couple some privacy," the lieutenant said.

Lynne's forehead creased. She didn't enjoy being left out. Barry Johns stood his ground and stared at the man who had a role in shooting his partner.

"Barry. I've got this. Give me a minute."

The detective's shoulders tensed, and it looked like Johns wanted to reach through the glass and strangle Castaneda.

"Barry."

The junior detective turned on his heel and stepped from the room. Once the door closed, Parker turned to the glass and turned the microphone back on.

"You got my message—I had to be sure you knew it was from me. I thought your old partner's body camera was a nice touch."

"What do you want from me?"

Castaneda stretched his neck from side to side. "You see what they did to me in here? Lost part of a lung, my spleen, about two feet of intestine."

"They should have tried harder."

"Detective, please. The point of my message was twofold. By getting you out to Coyote Wash, you'd know it came from me. We have history there, don't we? Secondly, the body camera was locked away in a federal evidence room somewhere. What does that tell you?"

"Someone's dirty in the chain of evidence."

"Yes, but so much more. I told them you needed to see the body camera.

The fact they could get it and bring it to you on a silver platter should concern you."

"Who are you communicating with?" Parker asked.

"Why you, of course. That's what the cell phone they found in my cell will tell them. They'll dig in soon and discover it's fake. Any number they call from that phone will display Parker on the screen. Enough to make them suspicious of you for a while."

Parker started to get up. "I'm done with this—with you."

"All right. All right. Can't blame me for having a little fun at your expense. I'm talking with a man named Ridler."

"Red Dawn."

Castaneda nodded with a crooked grin. "You've made the connection, good. Ridler has people in the FBI and—"

"And here. You got the cell phone from them. What do they want with you?"

"You see the door over there?" Castaneda glanced over his shoulder to a thick steel door with black printed letters, spelling out 'Range 13.' "There are only four cells in there where they keep the highest risk convicts. El Chapo Guzman is in one of those cells."

Parker tried to read Castaneda's expression for the connection between Red Dawn and El Chapo Guzman, the once formidable head of the Sinaloa Cartel. The cartels were losing territory and power to Red Dawn. What would Castaneda stand to gain from working with Ridler?

"No, detective. I'm not working for Red Dawn. As you know, the Sinaloa cartel isn't happy with me either. The cell phone came from one of Guzman's people. They are desperate in the fight against this new threat. They believe the 'enemy of my enemy' bit and I should join their cause."

"What's in it for you?"

"Guzman's not going to be in here forever. One federal judge gets their pockets lined and he's a free man. Don't you love the American justice system?"

You want to believe the Sinaloa cartel will forgive you for trying to start a war between the cartels down there?"

"If you remember correctly, I warned the Sinaloa leaders what was to come. They owe me."

"I'm sure they also recall the arms deal to mass weapons against them. They did send a couple of sleepers to stab you. I'm not sure how you figure they owe you. So, I'm here, got your message. Now what?"

"The cartel is getting desperate. Red Dawn poses a threat that could wipe them off the map. They are joining forces with former enemies. You're in a position to stop them. Red Dawn is going to make a move on someone influential—perhaps a political leader."

Parker put the pieces together. Red Dawn conscription of the cartel's muscle. The private planes arranged to fly small groups of people over the border. Those two "businessmen" with their duffle bags seen at the Red Mountain airfield—they were coming into the country to take out a politician.

"Who? Who is Red Dawn targeting?"

He shrugged. "There are so many to choose from. They won't let you get in the way. You saw what they did at Coyote Wash. I thought they were going to take you out—so imagine my surprise when you show up here. I knew they were going to take someone off the board. I counted on your resourcefulness."

Parker felt the heat rise in his throat.

Castaneda gave Red Dawn the location—a location Parker couldn't ignore. His self-incriminations were confirmed. He put Pete Tully there. If he'd been more careful. If Parker hadn't fallen for the trap, Pete wouldn't be clinging to life in the hospital. The man on the other side of the thick glass might not have pulled the trigger, but Parker held him equally responsible.

Changing the angle of the conversation, Parker asked, "Why would Red Dawn want to take out an influential figure here in this country?"

"You have to ask yourself, what do they want? Who is in their way?"

"They'd have trouble getting to any target. The FBI is onto them."

"Ah, the FBI. The same FBI who removed the body camera from evidence? The same FBI with Red Dawn influence in their task force? You need to ask your little blonde agent friend about her involvement. I mean, wasn't she the point on finding the missing FBI agent? How'd that turn out?" Castaneda said, then started to laugh.

Lynne? He couldn't be serious. Lynne wouldn't have anything to do with Red Dawn or the botched search for Agent Thompson. Lynne was about her career, but she wouldn't go to those ends. The fact Castaneda knew Lynne was heading up the search was troubling of itself.

Castaneda didn't wait for Parker to refute the allegations he'd made. "Ask yourself, who knew the task force was coming? Who knew where the missing agent was being held? What else does she know?"

Chapter Forty-One

Castaneda refused to respond to any further questions. He stood, signaling to his minders who escorted him from the dayroom.

The door behind him flew open, with Lynne leading the charge. "That bastard. How dare he make accusations?"

Parker pinched his nose to fight off a headache.

"It's like him to make claims and sprinkle in a little truth in the mix—trying to make us question everything."

"Truth? You think what he said has any thread of truth?" Her blue eyes flashed—the sharp look he'd seen when she was well and truly pissed.

"He's telling the truth about the task force being compromised. We also know someone pulled McMillan's body camera from evidence and got it out to Coyote Wash."

"There must be a paper trail on who removed the camera from the evidence lockup. I'll track it down. If there's a leak, we'll find it."

"Lynne, Castaneda said you knew more about this? I have to ask. Do you?"

"Nathan, you can't trust him. He's trying to drive a wedge between us." She was having trouble looking at Parker.

"What aren't you saying?"

"I knew Agent Thompson wasn't at the warehouse location. She called and told me."

"Lynne, what the hell. You didn't think you needed to tell me?"

"I couldn't. Thompson knew her team was compromised, and she wasn't sure who she could trust—"

"We already knew. That's why she did her act with me in front of her team to throw them off."

Lynne huffed. "Are you going to let me finish?"

Parker put up his hands in mock surrender.

"I was going to say, she said she didn't know who she could trust on her team. There had been a small series of leaks in recent weeks. Nothing threatening the operational security of the team. A reporter finds out about a meet-up with an informant, and pages from a confidential briefing are missing. Contacts in Mexico vanish—which wasn't unusual where the cartels were concerned, but Thompson said these were cartel contacts who suddenly fell off the radar."

"She think it was Red Dawn? Sounds like someone was probing around the task force operations."

"It was her take. That's why she went dark. She's trying to put it together—who's behind Red Dawn."

"And she's doing it by herself?"

"Pretty much," Lynne said.

"She ever mention a name? Quentin Ridler?"

"No. Not that I recall. She hadn't gotten much beyond who pulled the resources together at the street level—like Jack Talent. Which you know from the files on the USB drive."

Barry waited by the visiting room door and wasn't able to hide his emotions after watching the Castaneda interview on the monitor outside.

"Barry, what's your take on this?" Parker had come to trust the big man's insight on people. It was one of the many skills the junior detective had honed. He knew how to read people. Often, he was ignored while conversations happened around him. His size could be intimidating, but more often, he was thought of as a big, dumb jock, and people talked openly in front of him. Parker learned early on Barry Johns was one of the smartest men he'd ever encountered on the job. Never underestimate the man.

Johns looked from Parker to Lynne and back again. "Agent Thompson has been chasing Red Dawn for months. She's only been able to uncover the low-level street connections who gather the local muscle. The task force arrives here out of the blue, and three of her agents are murdered—one thrown from a plane and another, Metzger, is bait to lure us out to a remote location. Red Dawn told us they had Thompson. Now we know they don't and never did have her. My take? Agent Thompson is up to her neck in this. She's the leak."

"That's highly unlikely, Barry," Lynne said.

"It seems likely to me. Her task force begins to make progress on finding out who's behind Red Dawn and what they are doing here in the Phoenix area. Then her team is picked off, one by one. We were told, by a guy on her team, she'd been kidnapped. Then we jump through the hoops to find her, including following Metzger's cell phone signal. My partner was nearly murdered because of it. Because of her." Barry was eerily controlled and calm during his delivery. His glare never moved from Lynne. It was more intimidating than if he were throwing chairs around the room.

"Lynne, when did Agent Thompson tell you she was on the run? It was before the warehouse raid, which means the meet-up out at Coyote Wash didn't have to happen. Pete shouldn't be in the hospital," Parker said.

"You can't think she had anything to do with what happened out there."

"I know I want to talk to her."

"It won't happen. I don't know where she's hiding out."

"How do you contact her?"

"She set up a message system. Online. It's a phony hotel reservation webpage."

"How does it work?"

"I go one and enter a review on the hotel's page. Then she calls. Different number every time. A burner cell, I'd imagine, so they can't track her."

"Leave a review. I want to talk to her."

"I don't know, Nathan. She's trusting me to keep her safe. She's running for her life."

"Dammit, Lynne. We all are. Don't you see? Three dead federal agents, a college kid who flew down for a spring break, and an old couple who had nothing to do with any of this. They're dead. Not to mention what happened to Pete. And Thompson goes on the run because she's scared?

Give me a break."

The watch commander had remained in the background while they argued. Parker caught his expression change.

"What is it, Lieutenant?" Parker asked.

"The name you mentioned. It's come up a couple of times from our investigations unit."

"Ridler? Your people have contact with him?" Parker asked.

"No. Not him. Thompson. This Thompson's a woman, right?"

Lynne stiffened. "What are you suggesting, lieutenant?"

"I'm not suggesting a thing, Agent Finch. What I'm saying is our investigations team flagged a woman we identified as an agent with a sister agency—Thompson—after repeated visits to this unit. Four times in the last two months."

"She met with Castaneda?"

"Every time."

"There had to be a reason for her to interview him," Lynne said. Her tone wasn't convincing.

"Federal investigators interview our inmates regularly. But they don't conduct interviews in the cellblock day room where everyone can see them. We don't have audio recording there either."

"There's no good reason for an agent to conduct an interview there," Barry said.

"Sure there is," the watch commander said. "There's no glass barrier between them, and like I said, the conversation isn't recorded."

"Contraband? Like the cell phone?" Parker asked.

"Wait a minute," Lynne said.

"We strip-searched Castaneda after each visit. He brought nothing back to his cell."

Parker thought for a moment. "You have the cell phone?"

The lieutenant nodded.

"Recall if it was sticky?"

"Sticky? Really, detective? You have any idea where most of the contraband in here gets hidden at one time or another? Up someone's keister. Sticky wouldn't be out of the ordinary."

"You have video of their last visit?"

"Yeah, but like I said, we don't have audio."

"Can we see it?"

The watch commander agreed and led them back through the underground tunnel to the main administrative area of the prison. When they reached his office, a monitor was queued up with the dayroom video.

"I asked the unit, and this is the last visit recorded in the unit logbook. Agent Thompson arrived at 0930 hours." The date stamp on the video read the date, three weeks ago, and five minutes before the visit was to have begun.

When they settled around the monitor, the lieutenant hit play, and the frames ticked by.

"There's Thompson," Parker said. The FBI agent perched on a stool at a steel dayroom table and placed a fat file folder on the surface.

Moments later, Castaneda was escorted to the table. Officers stood near the table until Thompson gestured them away with a flick of the back of her hand.

The two officers glanced at one another, shrugged, then retreated from the frame.

The meeting between the criminal and the FBI agent lasted about twenty minutes. Thompson was doing most of the talking, with Castaneda chiming in occasionally to respond. Thompson's back was to the camera, only Castaneda's face was in the frame.

"I wish we had audio," Lynne said. "There's not enough for our lip readers to pull anything from."

"They're being careful," Barry said.

"She's showing documents from a file. Any guess as to what they are?" Parker asked.

Lynne shook her head.

Twenty minutes after the session began. Castaneda got up from the table, and a correctional officer escorted him from the dayroom.

Thompson swept the documents back into her file and stood.

"This doesn't show us anything," Lynne said.

"Wait for it," Parker said.

Thompson placed the file folder on the chair, and one document slipped out onto the dayroom floor. She bent to gather it up with her right hand. Her left hand cupped a cell phone. She pressed the cell phone to the bottom of the table as she retrieved the fallen papers.

"You catch that?" Parker said. "Rewind it and show it again."

The video footage swept backwards, then ran again, capturing the FBI agent planting a cell phone in the Supermax prison dayroom.

Chapter Forty-Two

Lynne was silent during the flight back from Colorado. Parker read her mood, betrayed, lied to, taken advantage of—he'd seen them before. Except this time, he wasn't the cause of them.

When they landed in Scottsdale, Lynne flicked off her seatbelt and prepared to bolt from the plane.

"Hang on, Lynne. Barry, could you give us a sec?"

Barry nodded and stepped from the cabin, ducking through the door.

"Nathan, I don't need your I told you so right now."

"Good, because that's not what I was gonna say."

She turned in the club chair to face Parker. Her expression read she was angry at herself for being duped by Thompson.

"We need to—"

"Don't tell me what I need to do. This is my responsibility. The bureau has to contain this. If Thompson is compromised and implicated in the death of her task force members, all manner of hell will rain down from the D.C. office."

"What I'm saying is, I'm here to help, Lynne. I know how this will unfold—armchair quarterbacks will descend and pick apart anything related to the task force. Thompson pushed the boundaries to make sure she was autonomous and didn't report to anyone on the task force's operations. I'll tell them—the weenies from Washington—what I got from her. If anything, they need to look at their own house to find out how a task force could operate with little to no oversight."

She softened a little, but he could feel the weight of the bureaucratic mess awaiting her.

"Thank you, Nathan. I appreciate it. If I had some role in allowing her to get away with this…"

"You can't go there. The video shows she was deep in this three weeks ago, well before she showed up on our doorstep."

"You might be right. But after that. Pete. If I hadn't let her pull the wool over my eyes, Pete…"

"Lynne, you weren't out there. You didn't pull the trigger. With Thompson's help, Castaneda let Red Dawn know where and how to hurt me. Castaneda always promised to go after anyone close to me. Thompson knew you are close to me, too. Might be why she tried to use it against us. I'm sorry, Lynne."

Lynne's eyes welled, which made her more angry.

"Dammit. Why couldn't I see what she was doing? I can't believe I let myself get used like that."

"She was a convincing liar. I bought into her bullshit too. The fact she came to us with two dead undercover operators was hard to overlook. You know we need to rip her place apart before the feds come calling. You think we'll find anything there? Her task force guy, the marshal—Paul Compton. He found her hotel room empty, and that was the first time we got news she'd been taken."

"It's a place to start. I know the team was ordered to stand down. They will be shipping out today."

"Which is exactly what Red Dawn wanted," Parker said.

"How many of the task force were compromised, other than Thompson?" Lynne asked.

"I don't know. We know Rivers, Carter, and Metzger weren't. They were eliminated."

"I might be able to pull the task force personnel files—officially, it will be to assist the team before they ship out. Maybe I can find if any of them are a little off—especially in the last three weeks when she started pulling this together."

"You think any of them might have gotten a hint about what Red Dawn was after? I mean, Thompson was good at hiding what she was up to, but there might've been something they overheard, or saw that should tell us if Castaneda was right about Red Dawn going after a political figure in this country."

"I'm trying to wrap my head around what's in it for Red Dawn? Making a move to take out an influential person—a politician? Why?"

"Politicians make hard-line policy decisions on border issues all the time. It's like a political party litmus test," she said.

"Which one would pose a threat to Red Dawn? Anybody come to mind making noise about border security, or tamping down the cartel violence in Mexico?"

Lynne threw her hands up. "Narrows it down to half the members of congress, two state senators, three governors, and a dog catcher. It's such a high-profile issue, everyone is trying to score political points from it."

Parker had to agree on her last point. Immigration had become a third rail, and the positions were becoming more and more polarized. Candidates running for office either supported shutting the border down with walls, fences, and armed forces, or advocated for open borders with asylum for anyone who asked. The middle ground was no-man's-land. Compromise was a sign of weakness.

They both left the plane and joined Barry on the tarmac. Barry waved Parker over and pocketed his cell phone.

"Linda has something on the dead couple we found at Red Mountain."

"The Cortez's? Trini's parents?"

"Yeah. Turns out, they've been arrested," Barry said.

"The old couple has a record? Trini sure didn't mention their prior criminal record."

Barry smirked. "This one is more recent. Raul and Maria Cortez were arrested less than an hour ago."

"What? Where?"

"Linda has them in a holding cell in Chandler. Seems the local police didn't know what to do with them, so Linda said we'd take them off their hands."

"What did Chandler PD get them for?"

"This's where it gets interesting. Officer pulled over a late-model Toyota they were driving for an unsafe lane change. Routine stuff. Ran the plates and they didn't belong to the Toyota. The driver used the visa and driver's license for Raul Cortez. Officer was good and ran the license number, and it kicked back to a Raul Cortez, about forty years older than the driver. A male passenger had no ID, and a young woman in the back seat handed over a phony Maria Cortes ID."

"The IDs tracked back to our dead couple?"

"To their address in the Guad, too. Someone used their IDs and had the time to make the fakes."

Parker recalled the witness account of the two men leaving the airport. Where did they pick up the third member of their little joyriding party?

"Chandler PD have any idea where they were heading?"

Barry raised his open hands.

"Let's go see what Linda managed to find. Which substation is she at?"

"Desert Breeze, just off of Chandler Boulevard."

"Not far from the Guad. Gotta wonder if there's any connection?"

Chapter Forty-Three

The Chandler substation anchored the south end of a park, which was really little more than an open dirt patch where the city tried to reclaim the land from the desert. The police department substation building blended into the subdivision with the tan brick and stucco exterior.

Parker and Johns made their way to the back of the building. Once through the public-facing areas, the tone changed. Fewer framed photos of officers greeting the public with smiles—and more police policy advisements to turn on their body cam, use of force reporting requirements, and blood-borne pathogen exposure protocols.

Parker spotted Linda in the hallway ahead, chatting with another female officer, a sergeant, based on the blue chevrons on her uniform sleeve. Linda waved when she spotted him.

"Nathan, this is Sergeant Lindo. She was telling about what her officers found when they impounded the vehicle our Cortez people were driving."

"Sergeant," Parker said with a nod.

Despite her five-five stature, the Sergeant carried an authority about her. Looking up at Parker, she said, "Better if I show you."

The sergeant led them to a locked metal door leading out into an enclosed garage. It was oppressively hot inside, with the heat radiating off the metal door. It was large enough for two cars and looked like the space was supposed to serve as a loading dock.

"Your guys were driving this Toyota beater. Registration didn't match. The car belongs to a snowbird couple from Chicago. They didn't know it had been taken."

The car's trunk was open, and a folding table had been erected next to it. Parker noticed the contents of the trunk were neatly placed on the table. Seven semi-automatic rifles, three Uzi machine pistols, four Sig-Sauer 9mm handguns, flash-bang grenades, and twenty boxes of ammunition.

"Damn. This was in the car?"

The sergeant nodded. "In those olive-green duffels under the table."

Parker leaned over and checked out the utility bags, and they matched the items Kingston Visman saw when he spotted the two "businessmen" leaving the Red Mountain airfield.

"I take it our snowbirds in Chicago didn't know about this little weapons cache?"

"They did not. The handguns have the serial numbers removed. We haven't run the other guns in the system yet. Detective Hunt tells me you guys can handle it."

Linda flicked a glance in Parker's direction to make sure she hadn't overstepped.

"We can," he said. "Linda, you get photos of this?"

"Um…not yet."

"We got video as we unlocked the vehicle. I can share them with you," Sergeant Lindo said.

"Perfect. You mind if I have our CSI team come in and box this up? I'll call for a flatbed to take the vehicle too."

"I'd appreciate it, detective. We don't have the space or manpower to handle something like this, especially with the budget cuts coming down."

"You too, huh?"

"I've been told to prepare to leave my patrol units vacant."

"It's everywhere—do more with less," Parker said. "Where you have our fake Cortez family stashed?"

Sergeant Lindo nodded back into the building and the chill of the air-conditioning was a welcome relief after the sweltering garage. As she led them to the holding area, she said the trio hadn't said a word. Though she thought the girl looked like the one most likely to break.

"Any ID?" Parker asked.

"Negative. Nothing on LiveScan when we ran the prints." The sergeant opened an office and removed a file folder from a desk. "Here's who we have."

She handed the file to Parker. A series of booking photos of the trio. The topmost photo was a Hispanic man, in his thirties, short-cropped brown hair, in a wrinkled, but tailored suit."

"He's the driver—the one who handed my officer the Raul Cortez ID."

The next photo was the second man, similar looking, but shorter, with slicked-back hair. Tattoos were visible on his neck.

The last photos were of the woman taken into custody. Her face gave away the fear the other two were hiding. But, Parker recognized her.

"Barry check this out?"

Parker handed the photo to him.

"What's she doing with these guys?"

"You know her?" Linda said.

"This is Trinity Cortez, Barry and I did a next of kin notification—what a few hours ago—Raul and Maria were her parents."

"How'd she get hooked up with these two?" Barry said.

"Sergeant, you got a place where we can talk to her without the other two knowing what's going on?" Parker said.

Sergeant Lindo left the detectives in her office and told them to wait here.

A minute later, the Sergeant came back with Trinity in handcuffs. She led the prisoner into the room and closed the door. It was tight with three detectives, the sergeant, and Trinity.

"Trini, remember me, Detective Parker?"

"Yes. I remember. I talk to you and I'm dead."

"Those two don't know you're in here with us," Sergeant Lindo said. "I made a big deal out of getting you to medical because you had cramps. Believe me, men don't want to know anything about that."

"You seen those two before?" Parker said.

She shook her head. "No, Never. About twenty minutes after you and Detective Johns left, they were there. They had the keys—my parents' keys and let themselves in. I don't think they knew I was going to be there."

"What did they say when they found you?"

"The little one put a gun to my head, and his partner told him to wait. They—they were going to kill me, but they wanted something first."

"What?" Parker asked?

"They needed a place to lay low for a day or two. Then they had a job to do. The tall one said they were waiting for someone to call." Her eyes widened. "It was him, the name you mentioned, Ridden, Rideaman, something."

"Ridler, Quentin Ridler?"

"Yes, I'm sure of it." The short one got mad when the other guy mentioned him by name.

"What were you out doing with these guys?"

"My parents had a savings account. They want me to withdraw everything—their life savings."

"That's why you had the phony Maria Cortez identification?"

She nodded. "I told them it wouldn't work. The people at the bank know my parents. The short one—he said—he said my mother begged before he shot her. He wanted to do the same to me. They argued about the money they could get using me."

"I'm sorry, Trini," Linda said.

Parker paused. The two gunmen were arguing. One wanted a quick payoff. Did it mean they weren't sure about their target? Or their cause? It gave Parker a way in.

"When they were arguing with each other, were you able to tell what they were fighting about?"

She shook her head slowly. "Not really. I mean, I was too scared to listen much."

"Anything you can tell us? Where were you going after the bank? Who they might have mentioned?"

She squinted and bit her lower lip. "I know they were going to meet with someone like them—another killer. They had some history, and the tall one didn't like the man they were going to see. He said something about killing him after they were finished." Her eyes brightened. "The car—the car only had a quarter of a tank of gas. The tall one said it was more than enough to get them where they needed to go and back."

Killers converging within a short drive from the Guad. The gathering didn't give Parker a warm and fuzzy feeling.

Chapter Forty-Four

Linda drove Trini home and agreed to search through the place to see if the two gunmen left anything that might hint at what they were doing here and who they were going to meet.

"We should take a run at these two guys, Parker said."

"Be my guest. They haven't said a word since we booked them," Sergeant Lindo said.

"Detective Johns has a way with guys like this. They magically open up to him. He's like our very own Dr. Phil."

Barry frowned and sighed. "That's laying it on a bit thick. I simply have a way of talking to people…"

"Who you wanna start with?" the sergeant said.

"Trini said the short one was the angry, anxious one. I think that's where we push first," Barry said.

"How you want to do this? We don't have the fancy one-way mirrors and stuff you guys might be used to."

"Is there a place I can pull the other guy out for a minute?" Parker said.

"Yeah, we have an attorney interview room."

"Perfect."

Parker was the first to enter the holding cells. "Hey, Cortez, you got a phone call. Some attorney sent by the Mexican consulate," Parker said.

The two gunmen exchanged silent glances across the walkway between their holding cells.

Parker put handcuffs on the taller man through the cell bars.

"Who'd you say is calling?" the man said.

"I didn't say. I don't know. Sounded like a bureaucrat to me. Said his name was Ridler."

The man stiffened at the name. He recognized the name and didn't expect to hear it from Parker.

Parker took the tall gunman by the elbow and escorted him from the holding cells while the shorter man seethed behind his cage.

Detective Johns passed Parker in the doorway and approached the holding cage with the remaining gunman.

"My name's Detective Johns, and it seems like you're the last man standing. The girl bailed out—someone paid her bond, and your buddy there, well, the powers that be in the Mexican consulate are making noises about diplomatic immunity or some such. Leaves you on the hook by your lonesome."

The man pushed away from the cage bars and muttered something to himself in Spanish.

"What was that? Doesn't matter anyway. With what we found in the car, you're looking at life in a federal prison on gun charges. Not to mention kidnapping, and what you did to the old couple."

"I'll be out of here within the hour."

"You sure?"

"I'll bet your life on it."

"Where were you guys supposed to go after you made the girl cash out her parents' bank account?"

The gunman raised his chin in defiance and remained silent.

Parker entered the room again. "The Mexican consulate claimed that guy. Confirms his diplomatic immunity. They're on their way to pick him up."

"I told you, Negrito," the gunman said from his holding cell.

"What about this guy? Barry said?"

"Him?" Parker jutted his chin toward the smug man in the cage. "Said they didn't care. We could do what we want."

"Wait. They are taking Salcido and leaving me?" The gunman pressed against the front of the cage, and his anger bled through.

"The guy, this Ridler dude, wasn't interested in you. Said you were something stuck to his shoe. No one is coming for you."

The gunman shook the cage and spat a string of swear words in Spanish, a few of which Parker recognized because he'd heard them slung at him before.

Parker shook his head and left the room, leaving Barry with the short, angry man.

"Sorry to hear it didn't work out for you," Barry said.

"I want to call someone,"

"Sorry, no phone calls."

"I have a right to a phone call."

"No, you don't."

The man pressed against the cage and tried to force the lock open.

"Sorry, with the weapons you had in the car, the feds are going to come and claim you are a terrorist and take you to some black site. That's the way it goes sometimes."

"What if I tell you about Salcido?" About what he did to the FBI man at the airport?"

Barry held back his reaction. "What about him?"

"Salcido killed him. Shot him in the face."

"Why would he do that?"

"Because the man knew too much about what we were doing. He was going to snitch us to some task force."

"What task force?"

"Some bitch FBI lady was getting up in our business—or the people who hired us, really."

"Who hired you?"

"The guy your friend mentioned, Ridler. He's the one who paid us. We used to do work for the Zetas. Ridler and his people started putting pressure on Los Zetas and the other cartels. Made us a better offer."

"What are you doing here, in Phoenix?"

"It's where the job is. Got hooked up with the kid and his little plane down near Hermosillo. Ridler used him before, he said. When we landed, he knew what was coming. The old people. Salcido and me were going to use their identities—they had to go."

216

"The kid knew what you were going to do with them?"

"It's how things are done. He had to know. He started to—how do you people say, squirrely, and Salcido took care of him in the plane."

"And the old couple, the Cortez's?"

A shrug. "What happened, happened."

Parker felt his chest tighten with the man's response. No remorse, no guilt for killing the old couple.

"What were you and Salcido supposed to do here?"

"What we always do. Take care of problems."

"What problem?"

Another shrug. "I might remember more if I get a little fresh air."

"The Mexican consulate got your buddy the fresh air. Guess they didn't think you were worth the effort. And I guess the problem you guys were sent to take care of walks away."

The man's face hardened. "You don't know who you're toying with, pendejo."

"Oh, I think I have a good idea. A couple of washed-up cartel thugs for hire got caught, end of story."

"If Salcido's out, he'll finish the job and I'll get my share."

"Maybe. What makes you think he'll get the job done? I mean, he's already gotten caught once."

"If they came for him, it means they want it done. It will happen."

"Who's they? Ridler?"

"The people he represents. I don't care what they call themselves."

"Red Dawn?"

A shrug again, but recognition behind his eyes.

"The feds will be on Salcido the minute he walks out of here. I don't think he'll be in any position to make a move on anyone."

A smirk appeared. "What makes you think we're the only ones in town?"

The smirk disappeared when Parker brought Salcido back into the holding cells.

"Guess I was mistaken about the phone call," Parker said. "Could have sworn he said it was from the consulate. Hung up by the time we got there."

The short man glared at his partner. Unspoken accusations and a sudden realization he'd been played.

"Pendejo," the shorter man said.

When Parker locked his prisoner back in the holding cell, the man rubbed his wrists from where they were chaffed by the handcuffs. He glanced at his partner."

"Los Zetas, huh?" Barry said. "Wonder if they'll take you back after you screwed the pooch on this one?"

"What have you done? You stupid fool?"

The shorter man shrank into the corner of his holding cell.

Parker and Barry backed out of the room and closed the door behind them. The sounds of a loud argument in Spanish vibrated through the thick door.

"Good work, Barry."

"Thanks, except these two weren't the only ones in play, and we don't know who they were after yet."

"I think we do," Sergeant Lindo said, handing a Public Safety Notice to Parker.

The notices shared information between law enforcement agencies when events, protests, or high-profile appearances by celebrities or political figures were announced. Adjoining police departments could prepare for mutual aid requests for crowd control, or enforcement action if needed.

Parker scanned the notice from Lindo. An announcement about a political fundraising event. Parker handed it to Barry.

"Holy crap. Ward Connell, Xenon Wills, and McCarthy Perrson. They are coming here?"

"Okay, want to break it down for me? Who are they other than people whose parents couldn't come up with a respectable first name?" Parker said.

"Seriously, you've never heard of them?"

"That makes two of us," Sergeant Lindo said.

"These three are the CEO's of Fortune 50 companies. What they have in common is they are heavily into cryptocurrency."

"Crypto? Like bitcoin or whatever?"

"Except on a massive scale—like twice the GDP of the U.S."

"It's still make-believe monopoly money, right?"

"The market cap on these currencies is around three and a half trillion dollars. These three want to replace government treasuries with crypto."

"Why would these guys draw attention from Red Dawn? What's in it for them?" Parker asked.

"It's not what I would have expected. I thought we'd be looking for a militia rally, or hardline anti-immigration stump speech. But if Red Dawn could gain control over any of these three cryptocurrency chains, they'd control vast sectors of the economy."

"Where's the tie to the cartel push south of the border? If Red Dawn is moving on one of these guys, why did they need to take over cartel territory?" Parker asked.

"I, I don't know," Barry said.

"Let me see the notice again," Parker said.

Barry handed it back, and Parker studied the names and details about the event in Fountain Hills in two days. A slight chill hit his neck when he read the location. It turned to ice when he spotted the event sponsor, Kingston Visman, the father of the dead pilot. The ice cracked when the foundation chairman was listed as Quentin Ridler.

Chapter Forty-Five

Parker waited for the crime scene team to arrive and inventory the contents of the gunman's car and Barry arranged transportation for the two Los Zetas hitmen to county lockup. The two ex-Los Zetas hitmen needed separate transportation and housing because they threatened to kill one another.

Once the evidence team arrived, Parker wanted to make sure they used extra care processing the handguns in the duffel bag because he was certain one of them was the murder weapon used against the Cortez couple and FBI Agent Metzger.

A text flashed on his phone from Billie. "Need to check something with you. Can you come by the office?"

Billie meant the Immigrant Coalition office off of Indian School Road. Parker figured cross valley traffic at this hour would make the drive forty minutes at least. Parker was worn thin. And the realization Ridler was involved in the foundation event in Fountain Hills made his brain race.

A quick text reply to Billie asked what she needed and if could it wait until morning.

"I guess." Came her reply. "Don't want to be a bother. I'll take care of it."

What "it" was gave Parker an antsy feeling. Billie wasn't one to ask for help. Maybe she was the one feeling antsy after her last attempt to deliver supplies down south was met by an FBI tactical team.

He couldn't see a way to drop what he was doing to go look at whatever Billie was up to. Not with a fresh link to Ridler in front of him.

He pulled out his cell and shot off a quick text to Miguel. He asked if he could drop in and make sure Billie wasn't twisting herself into knots over a plan to get medical supplies to Hermosillo.

"Hey, boss, got transport arranged for our two traveling gunmen," Barry said.

"You get anything more from them? Especially about Ridler and the Fountain Hills event. Everything points to these guys heading there."

"Nothing. Although my vocabulary for Spanish swear words is getting richer."

"I don't like the possibility Ridler might be here to kick off the same takeover style violence he's been carrying on down south," Parker said.

"Why would he risk coming up here for this fundraising event? Seems off brand for a—I was going to say Cartel Boss—but that doesn't really seem to fit either. Ridler's more of a multi-national terrorist."

"What do we really know about this guy? Those two hired guns got anxious when his name came up. Definitely some fear about letting the boss down. All we know is what Espi and Lynne could pick up. We need to do our own recon on this guy. Who's had contact with him?" Barry said.

"And alive to talk about it? Those two gunmen we packed off to county, but I don't think they're up to spilling their guts about him. Agent Thompson, but she's in the wind."

"Jack Talent? He was getting his orders from somewhere. Thompson's files on the USB drive called him out in their org structure."

Barry leaned against the SUV. "I don't know, I mean, you've met the man. Is he the kind of guy you'd trust to run your business?"

"I get it. Talent is kind of a muscle head whack job, but even if he's a flake, he got his orders from somewhere. Might have been Ridler."

"Hard to believe the head of this global terrorist organization would waste his time with someone like Talent. Had to be an underling managing that connection. I mean, I would if I were running the business of taking over the world. I wouldn't have time to deal with that waste of space."

When Parker heard Barry describe Ridler and the business of taking over the world, an idea fell into place. Taking over the world? Red Dawn had effectively pushed out Cartel, taken their manufacturing and distribution centers, and conscripted their hired muscle. But what had they done with it? They didn't seem to make their own attempt to smuggle meth, cocaine, or fentanyl into the country. It seemed like a great deal of effort, and what did he have to show for it?

Parker glanced at his watch. It had been a long day, but it wasn't late.

"We're at least on this side of the valley, let's go ask Kingston Visman to let us know why the man who had a hand in his son's death is a backer for his foundation shindig."

* * *

The gate was open when Parker piloted the SUV up the private drive. His first instinct was suspicion until a line of upscale sedans, town cars, and sports cars. The detectives were going to crash an event at the Visman estate.

They found a place to park off to the far end of the garage, where it looked like the older, less desirable vehicles were exiled.

A knock at the door was quickly answered by the same young woman who escorted them out when the detectives last visited. She wore dark pants and a tailored white blouse, balancing a silver tray of light hors d'oeuvres.

Parker noticed the woman's eyes were red and puffy.

He leaned in and whispered, "What's going on here tonight?"

"A memorial service for their son, Blake. The family invited a few friends."

Parker glanced over her shoulder into the open living space. At least fifty people milled about. Most were holding plates of snacks and a glass of wine. The mood wasn't somber. The conversation level was elevated, and to his ear, it sounded upbeat.

"A memorial?" Parker jutted his jaw toward the party crowd.

The young woman nodded. "Most of them didn't know Blake. They came because they want to stay in Mr. Visman's good graces."

"Speaking of? Where can we find Mr. Visman?"

"The library."

As she stepped away to return to her rounds, Barry grabbed a crab puff in each hand, emptying her tray.

Parker shook his head at the junior detective.

"What? You've been dragging me all over the county. This is the first chance I've had to eat." Barry shoved a crab puff in his mouth.

"I'll leave you to forage. See if you can learn anything about the foundation and the upcoming event. I think I heard someone mention Wagyu beef sliders over there."

"Ooh, Wagyu. Want me to grab one for you?" Barry slid off into the crowd before Parker could respond.

Parker made his way to the library, the ornate room where he met Mr. Visman before. Two club chairs were placed in the room, which Parker didn't remember from his last visit. Mr. and Mrs. Visman perched in the chairs, and to his eye, the couple were holding court, taking a moment to recognize the attendees in this semi-private setting.

Couples were vying for attention from the powerbrokers. Parker overhead a few hollow pronouncements of sorrow and regret. Most of these people were going through the motions, making the required appearance and little more. Parker spied a younger woman, pretty, her dark hair pulled back with a simple clip. Her black dress was immaculate, and she sat by herself on a small padded bench along the wall. She dabbed her eyes with a tissue. Blake meant something to this one.

Parker started to the young woman, when Mrs. Visman spotted Parker. Her expression stiffened. Parker noticed her elbowing her husband's arm as he was speaking with an older gentleman.

Kingston glanced up, and he seemed to ignore the man speaking to him while he pondered what the detective was doing in his home—the patriarch was sure lowly law enforcement types weren't on the guest list.

Kingston rose, said something to the older gent, and cut a path around the mourners to the doorway where Parker stood.

"You have news, Detective?" Kingston asked, rolling back on his heels.

"Not so much news as more questions."

"I'm afraid you've come at a bad time. We're in the middle of a memorial for my son."

The man's face was void of expression. No emotion bled through a corporate exterior.

"I'm sorry to drop by unannounced. And again, I'm sorry for your loss."

"Yes, yes, this will have to wait. We're quite busy with our guests."

"Are these guests related to your foundation's upcoming event?"

Finally, an expression clouded the man's eyes for a moment. Something was hidden there.

"What business is that of yours?"

Parker unfolded the event poster from his jacket. "A trio of heavyweights coming to your foundation should promise a boatload of donations."

"My foundation helps bring clean drinking water to communities across North America. You'd think we wouldn't have thousands of people without access to the single most basic element of life in this country. Yet, in many ways, we are no better off than a third-world country."

"And your event—it's a fundraising effort to—what, build wells or something?"

"Wells, irrigation systems, water storage, infrastructure projects to replace old lead pipes…"

"How long have you, or the foundation, been working on this?"

"The foundation is only two years old. We've had a couple of minor projects, agricultural irrigation to make use of the scarce water available to some farmers, and three new wells. Two on the Papago Reservation and one down in Mexico, near Hermosillo."

"Hermosillo?" The city in central Mexico kept coming up in this investigation.

"The city's water system was antiquated and wasn't able to keep up with the demand of the growing population. There are vast camps of refugees—I guess you'd call them—living in squalid conditions on the edge of town with no access to fresh water. When the city's pump and filtration station failed six months ago, well, it was dire.

"The foundation drilled new wells and repaired the pumping station. Just in time, too. People were sick from drinking whatever water they could find."

"I've seen the camps in Hermosillo."

"Then you know what I'm talking about. I can't understand why the city let the pumping station go like they did. It seemed like it was on purpose."

"The levels of corruption in local governments isn't unusual. Bribes, mordita, is a way of doing business. I hope the new Mexican government helps change the culture—they seem to believe they can."

Visman nodded. "Quite so. That's where our featured guests come in. These billionaires are willing to throw their weight into the foundation's initiatives. Imagine what we can accomplish with their clout behind the projects."

"Where does Quentin Ridler fit it?"

Parker waited for a reaction from Visman after dropping the name. Nothing. Not a flicker.

"Ridler is another investor, leads the foundation's fundraising—not to the degree of our big three. But he's one of the first to invest in our projects. He was the primary source of funding for the Hermosillo initiative. Ridler leads a venture capital machine, buying up and investing in projects worldwide. It doesn't come without a cost, though."

"Cost? What do you mean?"

Visman glanced around and lowered his voice to keep anyone from hearing. "Visman was the primary funding source for the Hermosillo project, until we could secure the remaining cash from Connell, Wells, and Perrson. There was some jostling and jealousy about project branding—you know the usual stuff. But what happened down there was tragic."

"Tragic how?" Parker was taffy-pulling the story from the man. Piece by piece.

"Ridler funded the project because he believed in what we were trying to do. His daughter was some kind of civil engineering student and worked on the Hermosillo project. From all accounts she was brilliant. Something happened. She disappeared. Rumors about criminal elements and ransom. She never returned.

Chapter Forty-Six

"What do you mean, never returned? The man's daughter went missing?"

"Ridler never gave up hope. He poured thousands and thousands of dollars into the search for her. Nothing. Only rumors—you know how those go, either she ran off in some romantic encounter gone wrong, or drug smugglers sold her into white slavery."

"I can only imagine how devastating that was for him and the family," Parker said.

"Apparently, it was only the two of them. Her mother died some years ago from cancer. His daughter disappearing like she did sent him reeling."

"Does he hold you or the foundation responsible for what happened to her? She was working on your project."

Visman lifted a glass of Cabernet from a passing waiter. After a sip. "It would be natural to blame everyone and everything around her—which included the foundation. After some time passed, I think he saw things more clearly and has been slowly coming back. This event was largely his idea."

Parker's neck muscles tightened. Setting up an event where everyone associated with his daughter's disappearance gathered in one place didn't sit well with him. Add the convergence of former contract killers heading to the location spelled disaster.

"Any reason to think Ridler might have something else in mind? Like taking revenge on those he blamed for losing his daughter? If he held the foundation responsible, getting everyone in one place would be pretty tempting."

"Don't be ridiculous. He's already invested in two of our projects. Why would he do that if he was out for revenge, as you say?"

"I have to cover the bases."

"Excuse me, Mr. Visman, you're needed in the living room. Brian Shea and Timothy Pinton have arrived, sir." A young man dressed in a slick, tailored suit whispered.

Visman smiled. "Detective, Marcus here will take care of you. I have some donors to greet."

Visman ambled off through the library crowd, stopping to accept words of comfort and condolence, and if Parker was right, a fat donation check or two.

"Marcus, did you know Blake?"

The man tried to keep tight-lipped and simply said, "I did."

"How did Blake fit in with the foundation and the work Mr. Visman has going on?"

"He wasn't involved in his father's efforts. He was too young to appreciate Mr. Visman's vision. Frankly, if it didn't wear a bikini, Blake wasn't interested in it."

"I understand one of the foundation's investors, Ridler lost a daughter— about Blake's age. Did they know one another?"

"I think they might have met. I believe I heard some discussion about taking her on one of his trips to Cabo. Mr. Visman didn't think it was wise—getting involved with the girl."

"Why was that?"

Marcus glanced over his shoulder, clocking where Mr. Visman had gone. "I don't want to speak ill of the dead—especially at his own memorial service, but Blake was a wild one. Parties, girls, a bit of drug use mixed in. Combined with an American Express Black Card, well…I think Mr. Visman was afraid Blake's lifestyle would affect his business relationship with Mr. Ridler."

"Why do you think Blake was killed? I mean, you seem to have your finger on the pulse of what's happening around here."

Marcus responded to the ego stroking and puffed his thin chest out. "If it were me, I'd be looking at a girl. Someone caught him messing around with the wrong girl. Jealousy. Wouldn't shock me one bit if it had something to do with the 'brat pack' he hung around with. All money with no responsibility. Always someone around to clean up after them."

"Like you?"

He shrugged. "I did my part keeping Blake out of trouble, or jail—for what good it turned out. Hey, I've got to go keep leg-hangers off Mr. Visman. For what it's worth, I hope you find out who got to Blake—no matter who it is."

The assistant weaved through the crowd and deftly cut off a handful of "mourners" who wanted one-on-one time with the man.

The young mourner whom he'd spied at the outer ring of the crowd had disappeared.

Barry headed his way with two small plates piled with smoked meats, cheese, spring rolls, and sliced ribeye. Barry shoved a plate at Parker.

"Boss, you got to try the Jamon Iberico."

Parker took the plate carefully, to not topple the heaping portions.

"The what?"

"The Jamon—the ham. It's out of this world."

"Ham. Why didn't you just say that?"

"Because at two grand a leg, this stuff is almost impossible to find here in the states."

Parker nibbled a tentative bite from a thin slice of the Jamon. "It's ham."

"I swear. You and Pete. Neither of you have a single thread of refinement between you. I take it back, even Pete would like this."

"He should be here," Parker said.

"No news from the hospital and I'm taking it as a good sign. He wouldn't like dealing with these A-listers, but he'd do some damage in this kitchen."

"Yeah, he probably would have camped out by the buffet table while he questioned the guests. Speaking of, did you get anything from these donors?"

"Kinda strange, really. Ninety percent of them didn't know the kid."

"Yet they're here at his memorial service."

"Because it's a chance to get rare face time with the Vismans. Everyone is excited about the foundation gala and hopes for a glimpse of one of the guests of honor tonight." Barry shoved another slice of Jamon in his mouth. "Or it could be for the ham."

Parker scanned the crowd, and for a memorial service, it struck him as odd. Not only from the heightened vibe among the attendees, but there was no pronouncement of Blake's passing, no religious rites, or whatever the family's preference was on that point. No photos of the dearly departed for the mourners to reflect upon. There was nothing to mark this as a devotional gathering for Blake Visman. Perhaps the ultra-rich grieved in their own way, though that hadn't been Parker's experience.

He popped a small spring roll in and chewed. "These are pretty decent. Have to ask what brand of frozen egg rolls they use. Thanks, Barry, I didn't know I was hungry."

Barry smiled at the frozen food comment. "I promised Linda I'd take care of you."

Parker chuckled. "I'm perfectly capable of taking care of myself."

"Linda predicted you'd say that. Yet here I am."

Parker appreciated Barry looking out for him, because truth be told, he would have waited until he got home and tossed a frozen burrito in the microwave. In defense, it was a good frozen burrito.

"Anyone mention Ridler?" Parker asked, followed by tucking away the last spring roll on his plate.

"Only one. The guy over there." Barry pointed out an older man with long, dark hair braided down his back. A heavy turquoise bracelet hung from his left wrist as he spoke with someone.

"Henry Lonepine. The chairman of a tribe where Visman came in and reinvented their drinking water systems. Sounds like it was a major undertaking. People were moving off the reservation because it wasn't habitable. Visman changed that. They've even opened a casino on tribal land, and it's churning a good profit. Only possible because of Visman's work. Ridler was the money. He bankrolled the entire thing. The casino enabled them to pay Ridler back with interest."

"Checks with what I got from Visman. Ridler backed a few of the foundation's projects. Rider's daughter disappeared while she was working on one of their projects in Hermosillo."

"Huh. Now I get it. Something Lonepine said. He made a comment about Visman—'Sins of the Father.' I thought he was talking about what happened to Blake. I think he meant Ridler. When Lonepine paid the last loan installment, Ridler was angry. Lonepine didn't know why. He made comments about never doing business with Visman again, and the foundation would be sorry they took something away from him. You think he meant his daughter? They took away his daughter?"

"They being Visman and the foundation."

"He's holding Visman personally responsible for her disappearance," Barry said.

"But now he's back supporting the foundation, according to the event announcement. I think Ridler is using the event to gather the people he blames under one roof. We stopped these two sicarios from getting here to Fountain Hills."

"If Ridler is as connected as we think—with Red Dawn and all—he won't have rested his entire plan on a pair of half-assed hitmen," Barry said.

"No, he won't. There were trips over the border we know about—maybe some slipped under our radar. Ridler will have a backup plan in place."

Chapter Forty-Seven

Parker dropped Barry off at the office so he could pick up his car, and they agreed to meet up at seven-thirty to dive in on Ridler and his missing daughter. Parker's gut told him the man had ample fuel for a takedown of Visman and his entire foundation. Or the sour feeling could be from the extra spring roll he'd inhaled as he and Barry left the Visman estate.

The festivities were winding down, Mrs. Visman disappeared upstairs, and Kingston was glad-handing the late crowd, trolling for donations. Parker made a mental note to look into the foundation itself. Something sounds too good, then it probably is.

A quick call to Linda as he drove, and he filled her in on Visman, the Ridler connection, and the missing daughter.

"Did you remember to eat something?" she asked.

Parker told her about Barry shoving food at him at the memorial service. Leon just got home, and Linda was going to spend some time with him. "He's going through something, and I can't quite put my finger on it. Could be a result of getting taken by Los Muertos. She meant the young men who were conscripted to work in a tech company, many of whom died in the back of a cargo container. Leon was one of the lucky ones, but the young man had witnessed events an eighteen-year-old shouldn't ever see.

"Let me know if I can help—or Miguel—you know how those two can connect."

"I will. See you in the morning."

"Love you."

"Love you, too."

Parker was surprised how easy it was to say it. He'd been in a few relationships, some good, others doomed, and Linda was the first time he'd felt comfortable. Comfortable as in thinking about a future together.

When he pulled into his driveway, Miguel was getting out of his Camry.

"Late night?" Parker asked as he rubbed his sore back.

Miguel locked his car, hefted his backpack, and headed to the walkway. "Billie's bugging again."

"Bugging? Did you say bugging?"

The boy's face fell slack. "Did I say it wrong?"

Parker grinned. "No, no, that's fine if you're in the nineteen-eighties."

Miguel shook his head. "Well, she was. This whole business of getting supplies down to Hermosillo has her worried."

"I hope she's given up on using an air taxi service run by those college kids."

Miguel's dark brown eyes caught Parker's.

"Tell me she's not."

"She can't drive them down like she used to. There's too many roadblocks, and even though they aren't cartel thieves. Privateers, and street gangs are filling that hole. It's almost worse."

They walked up the brick path where Parker fished his keys from his pocket. He dropped them, and as he bent to gather them up, a throaty exhaust sounded at the corner. A tire skidded around the corner to the right, and a lifted F-250 truck tore around the corner.

Parker felt it seconds before the driver's window lowered. He pulled Miguel to the ground and pinned him to the door behind his body as automatic weapon fire echoed in the street. Bullets stitched the door above them.

The slugs worked their way toward them as the truck moved down the block. Parker shielded Miguel and felt something sharp burn his shoulder.

The shots stopped, and the truck tires chirped as the big blue beast sped away. Parker turned his head to catch the rear end of the truck as it turned. The driver's window was open, and he spotted the driver's profile. White.

Stringy dark hair and dark sunglasses even in the twilight. He filed away the last three numbers on the license plate. It was a partial, but better than nothing.

"Miguel, you okay?"

"Yeah, what was tha—Dad, you're bleeding."

Parker rotated his left shoulder and felt a pinch.

"Let's get inside."

Parker retrieved the dropped keys, which probably saved them both, and his hand shook as he unlocked his front door.

He closed the door and locked it, even though the center of the door was pockmarked with bullet holes.

"You sure you're okay?" Parker asked again.

"Yeah, yeah. Let me look at your shoulder."

"In a minute." Parker pulled his cell phone and dialed 911. He told the dispatcher there'd been shots fired at his residence. He needed a supervisor, a CSI team, and, after Miguel insisted, he asked for EMTs, but not code three. All Mrs. Perkins across the street needed to see was a street full of red blinking lights and emergency vehicles.

His next call was to Linda. "You know how we said we both needed a quiet evening?"

After he explained what had happened, he could hear the worry in her voice.

"We're both fine."

"I'm coming over."

"There's no need. Everything's fine."

"Dammit, Nathan. Everything is not fine. Leon and I are coming. You're going to pack some things for a few days and you're staying with me."

"Why, Linda, did you ask me to live with you?"

"Well, you were never going to get around to it. We'll be there in twenty minutes. Pack your fancy pajamas." She clicked off, and Parker had to smile.

He had asked Linda to move in with him about a year ago. She wasn't ready then. He knew it had more to do with the last time Linda lived with anyone other than Leon. Her ex-husband was abusive, violent, and left her with uncertainty when it came to bringing someone close. Parker knew she trusted him, but this was delicate.

A knock at the door, and Barry came in, a key in his hand that Parker remembered hiding under a fake rock out front.

"I caught the radio call. You guys okay?"

"Yeah," Parker said.

"No, he's not. Show him your shoulder, Dad," Miguel said.

Barry tossed the key on the kitchen table. "You need to up your home security game after this. A fake rock ain't gonna do it anymore."

Parker shrugged off his shirt and probed the hole in the fabric. There was a two-inch red blotch around the tear, but not anything he felt was life-threatening.

A knock on the door followed by "Fire Department."

Barry opened the door and gestured them in. Two paramedics from the Avondale Fire Department. Station 174 was less than two miles away on Dysart Road.

The paramedics lugged medical bags, oxygen bottles, and put them on the floor near Parker.

"Nathan, been doing some home improvement?" One paramedic said while he used a pair of scissors to open Parker's t-shirt to expose the wound.

"Hey, Scotty. Yeah, I thought the place could use a little freshening up."

"More ventilation, based on the door."

"You guys didn't notice a lifted blue pickup on your way here by any chance?"

"Dude, it's Litchfield Park near the 10. They're everywhere."

Miguel scooted closer. "Is he gonna be okay?"

Scotty glanced up quickly while he worked. "Hi, Miguel. He's gonna be fine. Looks like some concrete, maybe a small fragment, lodged up in here. I'm irrigating the wound now to see if we can flush some of it out. Wanna see?"

Miguel circled around and watched as Scotty squeezed a plastic bottle with a long, curved nozzle into the wound. Bits of debris and little blood flowed down into a gauze pad, the paramedic held under the small gash.

CHAPTER FORTY-SEVEN

"Cool," Miguel said.

"Cool? I'm glad I can entertain you," Parker said.

"Nathan. You said you were okay," Linda's voice called from the front door.

"I am."

"That's not what this looks like." She rushed over and got on her knees in front of him, taking him by the chin, tipping his face up. "This is not okay, not at all."

"Dr. Do-Right here is going to slap a Band-Aid on it and I'll be fine."

Linda glanced up and noticed it was Scotty.

"What's the story, Scott?"

"Looks like some foreign matter, I think it's concrete from the front porch, lodged itself in his shoulder. Probably when a bullet hit the surface. There is a small bullet fragment I can see lodged in there. I mean small, like a pencil lead. We'll pack him up and let the emergency room doctor remove it."

"Like hell. Can't you just take it out?" Parker asked.

"You've been around long enough to know what we're supposed to do with cases like this. When I'm working at the free clinic at the Immigrant Coalition, people ask me to take care of all kinds of things—things I'm not allowed to do."

"It's just a scratch."

"More than a scratch, less than a gouge."

"I'm not going to the emergency room for this."

"Look, Nathan. The fragment, as small as it is, needs to be removed. I don't have the equipment here to take an image to see if it's lodged up against anything important—ligaments, blood vessels. I want someone to remove it, clean the area, and patch this back up so you don't develop any infection. You shouldn't have any problems if you take care of this."

"He'll go," Linda said.

"Yeah, he'll go," Miguel echoed.

"Fine. But I'm not going by ambulance."

"Promise me you'll go, and I'll call ahead and let them know you're en route. It'll help you avoid the waiting room."

"All right. Where, Western Regional?"

"Nah, I'd avoid there tonight. They're packed after a side show got a little out of hand down in Goodyear. Abrazos West Medical Center, on McDowell, is the best bet. They're a trauma center, too."

"I don't need a trauma center."

"I'm saying they have the personnel to handle this the right way."

Scotty taped a thick layer of gauze over the wound and gathered his used equipment, tape, gauze pads, and trash, tossing them into a red biohazard bag.

"I'll call them and let the ER know you're coming."

"Thanks, Scotty."

Linda walked him to the door, and Parker could tell by her expression she was worried and wanted to make sure he wasn't hiding anything.

After the paramedics left, a crime scene unit van pulled to the curb. Old Mrs. Perkins was in for a treat today.

Linda told Parker to stay put, and she was going to pack a few things for him. She told Miguel to do the same.

They disappeared down the hall, and the reality of what happened sunk in. This attack was personal. It threatened Miguel, violated his home. The anger swelled.

Ridler was behind this drive-by. Parker tensed, and it sent a twinge through his injured shoulder. A reminder Rider was next to feel the pain.

Chapter Forty-Eight

Barry agreed to stay behind and close the place back up after the CSI team finished their work. It shouldn't take long. There weren't any fingerprints to pull, blood spatter to analyze, or weapons to process.

There would be lots of photographs, diagrams, and on the way out the door, Parker pointed out a half dozen brass shell casings in the street needing to be photographed, bagged, and tagged.

Linda, Miguel, and Leon piled into her Jeep Wagoneer. A couple of suitcases were tossed in the back.

The anger was simmering below the surface by the time they finished at the emergency room. As Parker thought, it was a quick in and out. The physician's assistant on duty plucked the small lead fragment from the wound on his shoulder, irrigated it, and sealed it with a glue that burned worse than the injury itself.

Parker left the hospital with a prescription for an antibiotic and a small bullet fragment in a specimen jar.

"Where to?" Linda asked.

"If they found me, they can find you, too. You probably shouldn't go home tonight."

"Where do you have in mind? Barry's place, Billie's?"

"I was thinking about a hotel for the night, then we can think short term while this sorts out."

"A hotel? Can we order room service?" Miguel said.

"Yeah, room service would be cool," Leon said.

"It's late for room service. Besides, didn't you both already eat tonight?" Parker said.

"I could eat," Miguel said.

"You two can always eat."

Parker found a hotel off the 10. It was next to a cancer treatment center where families of patients stayed, close to their loved ones undergoing treatment. He'd stayed there a couple of times in the past, when his home was under renovation, and once when Lynne needed space. What she really meant was she needed time to get her things out while he wasn't around.

The hotel lobby was quiet, and Parker had no trouble getting two adjoining rooms.

Once settled in, the boys in one room, and he and Linda in the other, he made a phone call for pizza delivery. Miguel and Leon devoured a pie on their own and quietly watched a movie on one of the hotel's streaming channels.

Parker couldn't settle. He kept replaying the drive-by. The sound of the truck, the window rolling down seconds before a stubby black gun barrel poked through the window. He let his mind wander to the dark what-ifs. What if he hadn't pulled Miguel to the ground? What if the gunman was a better shot? What if the shooter stopped and got out of his car to finish the job?

He tried to chase the what-ifs away, only to be replaced by more questions. Did the gunman follow him home? Why didn't he notice that behemoth of a truck? Why didn't he take the shooter down? He'd drawn his weapon but couldn't move without exposing Miguel.

"Nathan?"

He didn't hear Linda, so she tried again. "Nathan?"

"Huh, yeah, sorry."

"What can I do?" She rubbed his uninjured shoulder, standing behind him.

He shrugged, which shot a twinge through his shoulder, mostly the glue pulling against the wound.

"In the morning, we need to get the boys settled. Then we need to do a deep dive on Ridler. There's a connection between his missing daughter and Blake Visman—enough to think he might be going after Kingston Visman and the foundation this weekend—"

"I meant for you. What can I do for you? The past couple of days have been a shitshow, and you've been pulled into the middle of it. You're carrying a lot and you have us to share the load—me, Barry, Lynne, and even the boys. You're not alone in this mess. Just because you feel responsible doesn't mean you are."

"Where did you pick up that last piece of advice?"

"Counseling. After my ex-husband put me in the hospital for the last time."

He turned to her. "Jesus, Linda. I knew it got bad between you two. I didn't know how bad."

She turned and made sure Miguel and Leon weren't lurking near. "Twice. He hurt me twice, bad enough where I needed to get to the hospital. The first time was a dislocated shoulder when he pulled me and pinned my arm behind my back, pressed my face into the wall, and yelled at me for forgetting to pick up his beer at the store. I didn't forget it. I deliberately didn't buy it because I was tired of him drinking all the time."

"I'm sorry, I didn't know."

"The last time he broke my cheekbone." Linda rubbed a small, faint scar below her left eye. "We were arguing about something, and he clocked me with a beer bottle. For the longest time, I thought I was responsible for what he did. I wasn't good enough, too argumentative, or it was my fault. He told me it was, and I began to believe it."

"That's screwed up. Why didn't you ever mention this before?"

"The shame of it. It's in the past, and bringing it up never feels good, you know?"

Parker nodded. "I get it."

"It wasn't until we split and he got some jail time for domestic violence that I got into counseling. I was the one feeling guilty for him beating me. His family didn't help. Always blaming me for what he'd done. Anyways, I finally learned just because I felt responsible, it didn't mean I was. It helped me see things more clearly."

Parker nodded. He got up and gently wrapped his arms around her from behind. She wiped away a stray tear that had escaped while she recounted her past.

He rested his chin on her shoulder and kissed her neck. "Linda, I'm sorry. I had no idea—"

"Because I didn't want you to think of me in that way—as a victim, a battered and broken woman."

"You're the strongest woman I know."

She held onto his hands, clutching her waist, holding her tighter. "Don't you forget it, mister." Linda turned to face him and kissed him. A deep, long one. "You still love me? Even with my baggage?"

"More than ever. We can compare baggage anytime you want."

"We should get some rest. Got a busy day ahead," she said.

"If rest is want you want…"

She smirked. "The boys are in the next room."

"I'll order them another pizza."

She shook her head. "You're impossible."

"So you keep telling me."

Chapter Forty-Nine

Parker succumbed to exhaustion a little before three am. Holding Linda kept some of the nightmares away. Not all of them. Every time a truck with a loud exhaust passed on the interstate, he'd shoot awake, remembering the lifted blue truck.

At six, Parker woke, kissed Linda on the back of her neck, which elicited a slight purr.

He showered, dressed, and woke the boys, who complained about the early wake-up call. He told them if they got it together, they could decide where to go for breakfast, as he spied the empty pizza boxes. Miguel, Parker saw, didn't outwardly show any aftereffects from the shooting. He knew the boy had experienced worse in his short life, but the cumulative trauma was going to take a toll at some point. The kid needed a break.

"I need to go out to my place and pick up some things," Linda said as she peeked into the adjoining room."

"At least you packed me an overnight bag. You didn't have a chance. When you go, we need to make sure you have a uniformed escort as a show of force. Our gunman might be less likely to try anything if a patrol unit is parked out front."

Miguel and Leon slowly began to emerge from under the covers.

"Is there any coffee?" Miguel said.

"Sure is. At Starbucks, right down the street. Get moving."

"Aww, man…"

It turned out to be a local mom-and-pop donut shop, and that was fine with Miguel.

Linda caught Parker eyeing an apple fritter the size of a dinner plate. "You'll have to run five miles to offset the calories, you know?"

"Hey, give me a break. I was shot last night."

"Barely. How about a bran muffin instead?"

"How old do you think I am?"

Before she could respond, Parker's cell buzzed with an incoming test message.

"It's Barry."

"He got an early start," She said.

"He got a hit on the partial plate from the truck last night. He's sitting on it now. At that biker bar out in Surprise."

"That fits. One of Jack Talent's misfits," she said.

"Could you drop me back at the house. I need to grab my SUV. It's not going to be blocked off with emergency vehicles and crime scene tape anymore."

They piled back into Linda's Jeep, the boys munching on their donuts and Parker holding a white paper bag with a sad bran muffin.

Linda dropped him at the house, and as he thought, the street was empty now. His SUV was gone. Probably towed away with a couple of bullet holes in the back window. The tattered front door, pockmarked with bullet holes, sent the anger boiling up again. He needed a place to vent his rage.

Parker made sure the house was locked up, got in his Jeep, and headed out to meet Barry at the biker bar, The Kickstand.

He spotted Barry's SUV parked across the street from the bar, and he pulled in behind it.

Parker climbed in the passenger side and tossed a white paper bag to the younger detective. "Here, I got you something."

Barry unrolled the bag and peeked inside. "Is this a bran muffin from Kilroy's? It's still warm." He tore off a chunk and popped it in his mouth with a satisfying groan.

Parker shook his head. "You're an old man, Detective Johns."

"Speaking of, how you feeling this morning? Miguel?"

"We're good. We camped out at a hotel last night. I couldn't take a chance this guy or one of his friends wouldn't take a shot at Linda's place."

Parker pointed at the lifted blue Ford truck in the bar parking lot. It was the only thing parked at the bar. "We get a registered owner?"

Barry slid a printout across to him. The Arizona Motor Vehicle Department records listed Warren Block as the truck's owner. The name didn't spark anything for Parker, but the photo did. He was the driver he'd spotted in profile last night. Greasy log hair and flattened nose. He also remembered him from the night he and Barry found Jack Talent at the bar. Block was the bartender.

"How do you want to do this?" Barry said.

"He's not making any effort to hide out. Coming to work like nothing's happened."

"Not thinking this guy or his crew are Mensa members. Should we call for backup now, before we make an approach? We know the guy is armed."

"Yep. Let's do this by the numbers. I'll call it in."

Parker used his cell phone to avoid radio traffic. Biker gangs in the valley were known to monitor radio traffic on police frequencies.

"Now we wait," Parker said.

A pair of motorcycles pulled into the lot and backed into spots near the front door.

"These two are starting early." Barry jutted his jaw at the two leather-clad motorcycle jockeys. They both wore vests with Chain Slayer logos on the back. One strode for the front door while the other ambled over to the blue pickup truck.

As the first one entered, the other man pulled a switchblade from his belt, the blade glinting in the morning light. He plunged the knife in the sidewall of both tires on the driver's side.

"What do you make of that?" Barry said.

The biker folded his blade, tucked it away, then pulled a black handgun from beneath his vest.

"This doesn't look good. We got to follow him in. Looks like Warren Block is in trouble," Parker said.

Barry and Parker ran across the street, and from the front steps, they heard glass breaking and shouting inside.

The first Maricopa County backup unit rolled into the parking lot. Parker waved to the deputy to identify themselves, and they were going in.

Parker pulled his weapon and slipped through the door without drawing attention from the bikers, who focused on Block. They had him face down on the floor in front of the bar. One had a boot on the bartender's back. And the other held a fist full of the man's hair.

Barry entered behind Parker and shifted to the left while Parker sidestepped to the right for a better angle on them.

"Hey. What's a guy gotta do to get a drink around here?" Parker yelled.

The biker closest to the downed bartender kicked Block in the ribs. "We're closed. Get—"

The biker's eyes widened after he turned to see who it was.

He started a hand toward his belt, and Barry said, "Don't do it. Hands on the bar. Now."

Parker stepped toward them. "You. Let go of him and hit the bar like your buddy."

Both bikers were facing the bar, with their hands open and on the bar top. Block wasn't moving from his spot on the floor. Parker saw the man's chest expand—they hadn't kicked the life out of him, yet.

"Barry, you got those two covered?"

"Sure do."

Parker bent and cuffed Block, leaving him on the floor. Two uniformed deputies entered and moved in to restrain the bikers.

Block began to stir while the two Chain Slayers were led out of the bar. One of the bikers turned to look over his shoulder at the injured bartender. "Remember what I told you. Don't forget who you work for."

Parker helped Block up to a seated position, leaning against the bar.

"What did you do to earn an early morning chat with your friends?"

"Just a misunderstanding."

"I'm sure it was. What's not a misunderstanding is you took a shot at me last night."

Block's jaw tightened. The bartender tried to look stoic, but the slight tremor at the corner of his mouth gave it away.

"I don't—don't know what you're talking about."

"I know your two pals weren't planning on killing you. They slashed the tires on your truck so you couldn't leave after they were done 'talking.'"

"Oh, man. You know how much that's gonna cost?"

"I think that's the last thing you should be worrying about right now. Let's rewind to last night. Why the drive-by at my place?"

Block started shaking his head, and Parker put up a hand. "Don't even go there. You were there. I saw you and that big blue compensation for shortcomings you drive."

"Compen-what?"

"Block, I'll make this simple for you. I know you didn't up and decide to take a shot at me last night. Who put you up to it?"

"I need to talk to my attorney."

"You can do it from booking after we get you tucked in a nice, comfy jail cell."

"Call him now."

"That's not how this works. You call him from county lockup," Parker said.

"I think you'll want to talk to him."

"I don't make deals with attorneys."

Barry moved behind the bar and moved a couple of empty bottles. "Hey, lookie here." Barry used a bar napkin to pick up a Mac-10 machine pistol.

The stubby black barrel matched the quick glance Parker got before he dove for cover on his front porch.

"That ain't mine," Block said.

"Should be easy enough to prove one way or another," Parker said.

"Call my lawyer."

"He won't be able to help you out of this mess. Felon in possession of a firearm is the least of your worries. Who put you up to shooting up my place?"

Block was getting edgy and rocking against the bar. "Dude. I can't. I'm no rat. Call my attorney—Larry Sutton."

Parker stiffened at the name—the same attorney who connected him with the cartel boss, Joaquin Pimentel.

Chapter Fifty

It wasn't the first time one of Sutton's clients had gone after Parker. He had Barry take custody of the weapon and Warren Block.

"Sit on him until I have a little chat with Sutton," Parker said.

"Hey, boss—you don't believe this tool is the shooter from Coyote Wash, do you?"

"I'm not leaning that way. The type of weapon doesn't line up, and Block can't quit shaking long enough to hold a sight picture with a sniper rifle. I think he's coming down off something. Maybe a little meth to give him the balls to take a shot at me last night."

"I'll get him medically cleared before booking."

Linda entered the bar as Barry was leading Block out.

"This the one? This the little coward responsible for last night?"

"I ain't no cow—"

"Listen to me, you little turd. I've dealt with men like you who get off on trying to hurt others. I ought to slap some sense into you. Though I'd be wasting my time because nothing's going to get through that. Thick. Head."

The last three words were punctuated with a fingertip to the man's forehead.

"You can't talk to me like that. Tell her she can't do that."

"I'm not getting in the line of fire."

Linda cast a heavy side eye at Parker.

"Barry, you best get your prisoner out of here."

"I was going to get him medically cleared anyway…"

"Barry."

"On my way, boss."

After Barry left them alone inside the bar. Parker leaned against a table until his hand came away with a sticky residue.

"Who was that directed at?" he asked.

Linda took a deep breath. "Him, men in general."

"The in general part include me?"

"Take it as a warning shot across your bow, mister."

"Noted."

"It was kind of cathartic though..."

"How about we take this self-therapy session on the road? Remember Larry Sutton, the attorney?"

"Yeah," she said with hesitation. "The one who's connected to the mob."

"Our shooter invoked his name."

"Like you say, it three times and the demon appears?"

"Something like that. This low-budget meth head doesn't have the bandwidth or the bankroll to keep Sutton on retainer. We need to go ask him how that works."

* * *

Parker didn't wait for the law office receptionist to call Sutton and find out if he was available. Instead, Parker walked around the slight receptionist when she popped up from her station.

"You can't disturb Mr. Sutton. He's with a client," she called out as Parker swept past.

Parker shoved the conference room door open, and he and Linda strode in. Sutton was taken aback at the sudden interruption.

"What is this?"

The client was more shocked, and the color drained from Kingston Visman's face.

"Mr. Visman, thanks for the swell party last night," Parker said.

Sutton furrowed his brow and looked to Kingston.

"Detective, this is highly irregular," Sutton said.

"What's irregular is one of your clients taking a shot at me after I left the home of another client of yours."

"What? What are you saying? Someone tried to shoot you?" the attorney said.

"On my way back from talking to this guy." Parker slapped Visman on the back. So, which one of you arranged a hit on me?"

"Parker, really," Visman said in a weak voice, staring to recover from the shock of seeing him in Sutton's office.

"I ask you questions about the foundation, the upcoming event, and Quentin Ridler, and the next thing I know, I'm diving for cover in my front yard. You send someone after me?"

"Don't say a word, Kingston," Sutton said, finally standing from his chair, buttoning his two-thousand-dollar suit jacket. Parker recognized it as the attorney donning his armor, preparing for battle.

"You here to handle estate issues now that your sole heir is dead?" Parker picked up a file from the desk, and the label sent a jolt up the back of his skull. He tossed it back down on the worktable. Must be a shame to lose your son like that. I can't get over how well you are taking it."

"What are you talking about, detective? Have you gone mad? I'm calling your superiors," Visman said.

"Fine…you do you. But when you call, make sure you tell them you arranged for your kid's disappearance."

The man's face lost another shade. He was nearly white now.

"I don't know what—"

"Kingston, I'll handle this. If the detective wants to conduct an interrogation, we'll treat it like one. Now, detective, what evidence do you have my client had anything to do with Blake's tragic murder?"

"Who said anything about Blake? I'm talking about his stepdaughter, Kira. Kira Thompson, who happens to be an FBI agent."

Sutton fell back in his chair as if he were shot.

"Kingston? No, wait, don't say anything. Detective, I need a word with my client."

Parker shrugged. "We'll be right outside."

Parker and Linda stepped outside and closed the door. Sutton's extravagant office furnishings also meant the hallway was cut off from the conference room. They couldn't overhear anything going on behind the thick door.

"Agent Thompson is Visman's daughter?"

"I just put it together. He's not here about his estate. He's filing for divorce. That file listed his wife's maiden name—Thompson."

"A common last name, Nathan. Could be a coincidence."

"I thought it was too, but remember the USB drive Thompson gave us? She has a list of people she 'cleared' from involvement in the Red Dawn action."

"Yeah, I sort of remember. I don't recall seeing any mention of Kingston Visman in any of the files, though."

"What was mentioned was the Visman foundation. The organization was supposedly cleared of any connection to the criminal activity going on in Mexico. Cleared by Agent Thompson, herself."

"If she's his daughter—or step-daughter—she shouldn't have been investigating her family's connection to anything. That's against any ethical rule you can imagine."

"Why would she get involved in any case where the family's foundation was in question? Was it to give us a list of organizations and people who were 'cleared' so we wouldn't go looking where she didn't want us to?" Parker said.

The conference room door opened, and Sutton gestured them in with a quick twitch of his hand. Parker and Linda shared a look between themselves. Parker had seen the attorney knee deep in cartel activity, cleaning up the legal aftermath of drug wars, and this was the most anxious he'd seen the attorney.

"Let me tell you how this is going to go," Sutton said.

"We're listening," Parker said.

Sutton stood behind his client in what was supposed to look like a show of support, but indeed, to Parker's eye, it came off like the attorney was hiding behind the man. Unsure. Tentative. Very unlike the lawyer, who was well-acquainted with the shadier side of the legal profession.

"In exchange for immunity—"

"You know I'm not the one to make any promises about what will and won't be prosecuted," Parker said.

"Understood. I'll leave it to you to deliver the offer."

Parker rolled his hand, begging the attorney to get on with it.

"My client is willing to tell you what he knows about the disappearance of the FBI Agent in exchange for immunity when it comes to the foundation's activities and any act or omission by Mr. Visman in relation to his role in the foundation."

"Why would I care about the foundation? What? We talking embezzlement, or some tax dodge? Not on my radar," Parker said. "But what I am interested about is why would you kidnap your own daughter."

Parker didn't have to wait for the reaction.

"I-I had no other choice."

Chapter Fifty-One

"What do you mean you didn't have a choice?" Parker asked.

Sutton cleared his throat. "I think before we go any deeper, we need to have that immunity agreement."

"I told you I can't promise anything."

"Then you best get someone here who can. My client has said enough." Then, with a side eye toward Kingston Visman, "More than enough."

Parker pulled out his cell phone and noticed there was no signal. He glanced to the credenza, and the back box Sutton used before was displaying a red light on the front of the device. The attorney was serious about his client's privacy. But there was more than simply attorney-client privilege going on here. Sutton used the cell phone jammer when Parker talked to the attorney about cartel activity. Who did he think might be listening?"

Parker held up his phone and gestured to the black box. Sutton shook his head.

"Does this concern your southern client? Are they involved?"

"Detective, you know I can't talk about any of my clients. But I will tell you our interests in this matter are somewhat aligned. If you need to make a call, I suggest you use the satellite phone in my vehicle. It's in my space in the garage. I believe you know where." Sutton slid a key fob across the table.

Parker knew exactly where the lawyer parked his Bentley.

He motioned for Linda to follow him, and when they got to the lobby, he asked her to stay and make sure Visman didn't leave.

"Okay," she said. "What are you thinking here?"

He leaned in. "Sutton gave me notice Visman and the cartel are in bed together. I need to make a call—a call you don't need to overhear. It's not exactly protocol, and I don't want this to blow back on you. Besides, I need you here to make certain Visman doesn't try to give us the slip. He's about to break, and I want to make sure no one else pressures him to do otherwise."

"No one else, as in?"

"Red Dawn, Ridler, the Chain Slayers..."

"The same ones who may have called the shots on you and Miguel last night?"

"It's possible. Lock the door behind me."

He waited outside until Linda threw the deadbolt on the door and closed the blinds. From appearances, it looked like the law office was shut for an extended lunch hour.

Parker remembered where Sutton kept his high-end car because the lawyer had taken him there before to use the satellite video connected in the car's spacious back seat. A connection to the head of the Sinaloa Cartel, Joaquin Pimentel.

The raised button on the key fob unlocked the Bentley and, like last time, Parker slid into the leather backseat. Not an uncomfortable office for a shady attorney to conduct business.

From memory, he found the power switch on the armrest. The screen between the driver's seat and the plush mobile office slid on a hidden track, exposing a video monitor from a compartment in the bulkhead behind the driver's seat.

The monitor bloomed to life, and lists of frequently called numbers displayed on the screen. There were no identifying names or initials to tell him which number belonged to the cartel boss. The most frequently called number was one with a 662-area code.

Parker used his cell phone, and a quick search told him the area code was for Hermosillo, Mexico. That had to be the number for Joaquin Pimentel.

He cleared his throat and pressed the connect button.

The screen showed the call connecting, and then the monitor flashed.

Joaquin Pimentel leaned forward and didn't look pleased to see the detective.

"What have you done with Sutton?"

Parker knew what the cartel boss really meant was. Did his attorney roll over and become a snitch for the government? One wrong word and the counselor to the mob would be a dead man. One less sleazy attorney was not totally a bad thing, but, in truth, Sutton had helped Parker out of a jam here and there. Granted, it was usually a mutual benefit, but there it was.

"Sutton thought I needed a private word with you."

"This have anything to do with the subject of our last conversation?"

"Red Dawn? Maybe. I'm hoping you can tell me. There's a man up here. He has a foundation that supposedly does work to bring drinking water to communities in need. It sounds all good and high-minded—"

"But you think it's too good to be true."

"Color me suspicious. There seems to be a ton of money flowing in and the projects the foundation claims to have done—well even if they pay top dollar and line these water pipes with gold, it doesn't add up."

"It's difficult to do business here. There is an expectation certain palms be greased, as you would say. It's a way of life here—it's a way of doing business here."

"One of the water projects was in Hermosillo a while back. I gather something happened."

"I remember something about a water project outside of town. It went poorly. Didn't finish the build."

"I understand people got hurt—a girl may have died there. You know anything?"

"What are you saying, detective? Are you accusing me of involvement in her death?"

"I don't know much about her or how she died. But what I do know is she is the connection to Red Dawn."

"She was Ridler's daughter..."

"You knew?"

"Not until now. Red Dawn has been plowing through cartel territory, as you know. Ridler's only communication to us—any of us—was we were going to pay for some loss he suffered. We believed he was talking about a business loss."

"How did the girl die?"

"I have no knowledge of the event. What I can tell you is the misguided water project was stopped."

"The water. Why would you stop a project like that?"

"I don't expect you to understand, detective. Here in the desert, water is a precious commodity. He who controls it wields great power. I control it."

"People pay you to get the water they need to survive?"

"It would have no value it if it was given away."

"What happened to her—the girl?"

"Who knows? The people who dealt with it—they are animals. This was the only time we used Los Zetas' muscle. We couldn't have people in Hermosillo connect this to Sinaloa. Now they work for the highest bidder like mercenaries."

"You contracted it out to another cartel? Why would they agree to help you?"

"They needed to discourage one of the foundation's projects in Nuevo Leon. They were more than willing to help with our problem."

Los Zetas again. Parker's mind snapped to the pair captured by the Chandler P.D. The hitmen who held Trinity hostage were headed for the foundation's fundraiser. The puzzle pieces became harder to piece together. If the Sinaloa cartel paid them to get rid of the foundation's project in Hermosillo, why would Ridler use them to take out Kingston Visman and the foundation at their Fountain Hills event?

He wouldn't.

Pimentel ended with a warning. "Detective. This does not concern you. I offer this because you have been honest with me in the past. Stay away from this. Distance yourself from the foundation, Red Dawn, all of it."

Chapter Fifty-Two

P arker ended the call with the Sinaloa cartel boss, and he was left with more unanswered questions. The warning to distance himself from the investigation was troubling. Was he getting too close to uncovering a cartel connection? He already been threatened by biker bartender Block with a meth-impaired drive-by. Block was connected with the Chain Slayers, who were bankrolled by Red Dawn. Ridler controlled Red Dawn. Ridler's daughter was completely off the grid—missing or dead, perhaps at the hands of a cartel assassin. He knew hundreds of cartel victims had disappeared. Thousands of square miles of vast, empty desert. Mass graves were not an uncommon discovery.

The two Los Zetas hitmen weren't going to spill anything. In a way, he had to respect their loyalty—even if it was to whoever paid them. Ridler, from the way the men reacted in the holding cell. It's the one thing that made sense. Ridler was out for blood—revenge against everyone he held responsible for his daughter.

The man was consumed—obsessed with revenge. Parker understood where Ridler was coming from.

Did he trust the cartel leader's accounting of the events? Not completely. There was little Pimentel didn't control. If there were bodies dropped somewhere, he'd know who. He'd know exactly where.

He rapped a knuckle on the glass door, and Linda unlocked the office and let him in.

"Visman pop his head out of the conference room?"

"Only once to use the restroom. The guy is spooked."

"Can't say I blame him."

"You learn anything?" Linda asked.

"Less than I hoped. But I did uncover a strange connection. Those two Los Zetas hitmen Barry and I talked to in Chandler—they might have been in on the attack against the foundation where Ridler's daughter went missing."

"Why would they come up here to disrupt a fundraising event? Am I missing something, Nathan?"

"I don't think you are. Those two cartel hitmen are guns for hire. I don't think they are working with a strong moral compass, if you get my drift. But sending them here to burn down the foundation doesn't make sense— if—Red Dawn sent them. But if I've been wrong all along and Red Dawn didn't send these flights over…"

"That's what we've been working with, isn't it? It's been Red Dawn burning through the cartels and sending a team of assassins up her for some catastrophic event, right?"

"Where did we get the intel?" he asked.

"The first we heard of it was from the FBI."

"From Agent Thompson. What if she intentionally misled us?"

"Mislead? Why? How?" Linda's forehead crinkled.

"The two hitmen were hired to do a job—get rid of the foundation and their project in Sinaloa country."

"I'm following so far."

"What if they are finishing the job? What if they came here to finish off the foundation—not by Red Dawn, but by the cartel?"

"Visman and his donors, I get, but why would Ridler come here? He has to know the cartels think of him as public enemy number one," Linda said.

Parker paced the lobby. The receptionist kept track of him over her glasses. She looked worried. Parker caught her expression when he turned.

"Excuse me, Miss. How long have you worked here? For Mr. Sutton?"

"Three—three months."

"Long enough to know what he really does?"

"As a lawyer? I don't know. Really. All I do is answer the phone and keep his calendar straight."

"What doesn't his calendar show for day after tomorrow? Something in Fountain Hills?"

"How did you? I can't say."

Parker smiled, and the receptionist knew she'd given too much information away." Please don't say anything to Mr. Sutton. I really need this job."

Parker motioned for Linda to follow him back to the conference room. He tossed the Bentley key fob to Sutton.

"Were you able to get what you needed?" Sutton said.

Visman looked worse in the short time that had elapsed. Gray pallor to his skin, a sheen of sweat on his brow, and he'd unbuttoned his dress shirt.

"Mr. Visman, I think you have a big problem coming your way."

"That's where I believe my client has something to offer. He's gone to great personal risk, and before we get into details, we need an understanding of an immunity deal."

"I told you, I can't make those promises," Parker said.

"I know, and while you stepped away, I made a call of my own."

Parker glanced to the credenza where the cell phone jamming device rested. The bottom no longer glowed. Sutton had turned it off.

The conference phone on the table buzzed, and the receptionist's voice came over the line. "Mr. Sutton, an Agent Finch from the FBI is here to see you. She said you were expecting her."

"Yes, please show her on back, would you?" Sutton said.

Seconds later, the receptionist opened the door, and Lynne strode in along with another woman Parker hadn't met. She carried herself in a stiff, formal manner, dark red hair gathered with a simple black clip. The woman's face bore no evidence of smile lines—ever. Lynne raised an eyebrow when she caught Parker's expression.

"Agent Finch, please have a seat, and we can begin."

"This is Assistant U.S. Attorney Mary Alice Schmaus, Organized Crime. As luck would have it, she was in the office when you called."

"Miss Schmaus."

The woman glared in response.

CHAPTER FIFTY-TWO

Lynne sat opposite Sutton while Parker and Linda leaned against the credenza.

"Your call mentioned testimony in exchange for immunity," Lynne said.

"Yes, my client is prepared to speak to you about what he knows in exchange for immunity. He has knowledge—"

The U.S. Attorney put up her hand. "Hold on. What is your client asking immunity from, and against whom will he be providing testimony?"

"Mr. Sutton leads a foundation operating projects in several countries."

"I don't care if he serves the Pope breakfast in bed. What has he done requiring immunity?" Mary Alice swept her hair off her shoulder.

"As we'll explain, there may be acts or failure to act in his corporate position—"

"Corporate? I don't give a damn about corporate charters or conflicts of interest of his board members. What has your client done requiring immunity from criminal prosecution?"

Parker cleared his throat. "Perhaps you might want to begin with Visman's involvement in the disappearance of FBI Agent Kira Thompson."

Lynne tried to hide her surprise and rolled her shoulders back—something Parker remembered from when she would take a pause before lashing out at him in the dying days of their relationship.

"He knows something about her abduction?" Lynne said.

"He does," Sutton said while his client refused eye contact with the two women opposite him at the table.

"What was your client's role in taking the FBI agent?" U.S. Attorney Schmaus said.

"Active participation."

"Why shouldn't I arrest him now and sweat it out of him? He doesn't look like he'd stand up to much interrogation," Lynne said. "But most importantly, is she alive?"

Parker caught Sutton's subtle glance and nod. He wanted Parker to break the attorney-client confidence. Sutton couldn't say it, but Parker could.

"Lynne, Agent Thompson is fine. Visman's not going harm his own daughter.

Chapter Fifty-Three

"Well, stepdaughter actually. Thompson is his wife's maiden name. Kira is from his wife's first marriage. But I think he cares about Kira, or he wouldn't have arranged such an elaborate disappearing act for her. Isn't that right, Kingston?"

"She's your stepdaughter? Is this true?" Lynne said.

"My client is prepared to confirm—"

"I need to hear this from him." Lynne pointed an accusing finger at Visman."

Kingston peered up from under his brow. "Yes, Kira is my daughter—stepdaughter."

"Did you forcibly abduct her?"

"I'll ask my client to refrain from answering, Agent Finch."

Lynne threw her hands up. "Then what the hell are we doing here?"

"My client is prepared to tell you about the criminal organization known as Red Dawn, the structure, the funding behind it, and about Quentin Ridler's role in the organization."

Mary Alice withdrew a small digital recorder from her satchel and placed it on the table between them. "Now we're getting somewhere. This is Assistant U.S. Attorney Mary Alice Schmaus. Also in the room are FBI Assistant Special Agent in Charge Lynne Finch, Kingston Visman, represented by attorney Larry Sutton. Are we ready to begin, Mr. Visman?"

He bobbed his head in a slight nod. "Audibly for the record, Mr. Visman."

"Yes. I'm ready to tell you about Red Dawn and Quentin Ridler."

Mary Alice looked over at Parker and Linda and tilted her head toward the door. Their services were no longer needed. Lynne tightened her jaw and nodded.

As they walked to the conference room door,

Lynne stood and formally whispered a thank you to Parker with a firm handshake. "Thank you, Detective, we have it from here."

Parker closed the conference room door, and when they were in the hallway, Linda leaned in and asked, "What was that about? Thank you, Detective?"

Parker opened his hand to show her the note Lynne had passed when they shook hands.

Parker unfolded the paper. "Call Espi. Red Dawn and Ridler on the move. Must find Thompson before they do."

Parker waved goodbye to the receptionist and they strode to their SUV, thankfully tucked into a shaded space in the garage not far from the Bentley.

Parker started the engine and turned the air on high. They both aimed the vent away until the SUV's air conditioning coughed out a stale ozone-flavored belch.

The attorney's Bentley struck Parker as an ostentatious symbol of Sutton's self-worth. God and a handful of criminal organizations knew where the money came from. The money.

"We need to get back to the office and work up a warrant affidavit for Visman and the foundation."

"Makes sense, and we might make a case for a warrant—if we get the right judge to sign off. You think the U.S. Attorney will think kindly of us poaching on her turf? I mean, he's in there talking about immunity."

"I think she's going in another direction anyway—Red Dawn's financials. I'm interested in the Foundation."

"You want me to call Barry and have him get started? He's a genius with warrant requests, and he should already be there after booking Block, the bartender from The Kickstand."

"Tell him to stand by. I want to brief Captain Morris, too. I think we're onto something here. Did you notice the cell phone jammer in Sutton's office? It was on when we left to make my call. It was off when we came back."

"Why would he shut it off? He's always been paranoid about who's listening in. Having us drop our phones in Faraday bags and all. But you're right. He didn't this time. What changed?"

"What changed is he was performing. He wanted the jammer off so the Sinaloa cartel could hear what he was saying—and where Visman was sending the feds—away from their interests."

"It was about Red Dawn and Ridler," she said.

"And nothing pointing back to Pimentel and the Sinaloa Cartel."

* * *

The Major Crimes Unit was quiet in the mid-morning. Barry was propped at his desk, tapping away on his keyboard. Parker spotted the NIBN website up on Barry's screen and the brown cardboard evidence box, which held the MAC-10 used by Warren Block.

Parker's mind snapped to his front porch for a flash with bullets slamming into the door above his and Miguel's heads. Thankfully, between the meth addled gunman and a hard-to-control weapon, they both came through relatively unscathed.

Barry nodded hello and gestured Parker and Linda over. "Got a hit on the Mac-10."

Parker took a position over Barry's shoulder to view the monitor.

Barry tapped the screen. "The weapon was part of a gun bust at the border last year."

"How is it showing up here if it was confiscated?"

"I made a few calls. The Border Patrol made the bust. They turned the weapons over to Homeland. Homeland said the confiscated firearms were destroyed."

"Yet here it is. They have any explanation for how a weapon they claim was melted down magically appears here?"

"The guy I spoke with kept going on about 'the records show' and the destruction was handled by a third-party contractor."

"How many other weapons were in that bust?"

"He couldn't tell me. I doubt this one simply fell off the truck on the way to the smelting pot."

"He tell you who the contractor was?"

"No. He said he'd run it down and give me a call."

"Yeah, I can bet he'll get right on it. When you have a second, join Linda and me in the office. We have some threads to pull."

Linda noticed Parker twinge when he shrugged off his jacket.

"You need to have that looked at again?"

"No, it's fine. It pulled a little—the glue."

Linda looked as if she didn't believe him, cocking her head to one side.

"No, really. I'm okay."

Barry entered, and Parker began.

"Let's divide the workload here. We have less than twenty-four hours before the foundation's big event, and it's lining up to be something other than a charity fundraiser."

Parker filled Barry in on the details—the foundation, Ridler's missing daughter, and Kingston Visman's connection to the missing FBI agent, Kira Thompson.

"This is a twisted little affair, isn't it? Now Visman is rolling over on Ridler? What doesn't he have to offer other than the guy was a money man for his water projects?" Barry said.

"That's a good question, and Lynne and the U.S. Attorney booted us out before we could find out more. I'll circle back to Lynne and see if she's able to share anything to help us pull this together. They are laser-focused on Ridler and Red Dawn, Lynne is convinced they are coming for Thompson.

"Linda, I need you to dig into anything you can find out about Ridler's missing daughter. When she disappeared, who did she hang with, any details you can find on the search."

"On it."

"Barry, take a run at Ridler. What do we really know about the guy? What's his connection to the foundation? He's a public guy, and it doesn't seem likely he's some anti-Batman who runs a terrorist organization in his spare time. You know what I'm getting at?"

"I know what you're saying. A wealthy venture capital group doesn't risk its investments with a multi-national organized crime syndicate. Want me to run him down?"

"He's supposed to be on the move. I'll reach out to Espinoza, who has some intel on his recent activity. See if his office has any statement to offer and drop the Red Dawn connection on them and see how they respond."

"What about the missing FBI agent, Thompson?" Linda asked.

"Kingston Visman is holding back. He's using it as his hold card. Lynne and the U.S. Attorney might not be able to pry it from him. Unless—"

"Unless what?"

"We need to find out what Victoria Visman knows about her daughter."

Chapter Fifty-Four

Parker left a message with Espi. Whoever answered the call didn't identify themselves or comment on when Espinoza would be available. Even after identifying himself to the caller, Parker got dead air, followed by a terse, "I'll tell him you called."

Parker had called Espi's personal cell phone. He'd left it behind in the office—the background noise was enough for Parker to discern that much. It meant Espi was out on an undercover job. The note Lynn slipped to him was about Red Dawn and Ridler on the move. He hoped Espi was careful on this one. There was a history of bodies being dropped when they crossed the organization.

While he waited for a call back from Espinoza, Parker left Barry and Linda to their tasks, and he decided to take a run at Mrs. Victoria Visman while the feds detained her husband.

While the missing FBI agent was Kingston's stepdaughter, she was Victoria's flesh and blood—her last surviving child after the murder of Blake. She's been in lockstep with her husband. Maybe if she knew he was at the attorney's office making a deal with the feds, she might change her mind.

Parker knocked on the door, and the young woman he'd met previously, the one who knew Blake, motioned him in.

There was a flurry of activity in the area ahead of Parker. Teams of people dressed in catering uniforms were setting up buffet tables, crisp white linen runners, and small scripted signs for what would appear on those tables at tomorrow's event.

"Mr. Visman isn't here, detective," she said.

"I'm aware. I'm actually here to speak with Mrs. Visman."

"Oh, okay. Certainly, I can take you to her. If you'd wait here for a moment, I need to let her know you're here. She's in the middle of a yoga lesson."

"Fine. Oh, before you go—did you ever meet Mrs. Visman's daughter?

"Kira? Of course. Whenever she was in town. She lived on the east coast, I believe."

Parker nodded. "Yes, that's what I understand. When is the last time you saw her here?"

"I don't want trouble. Mrs. Visman doesn't need trouble either."

"Just trying to see if I can draw a connection between Kira and Blake."

"You think something could happen to her?" The young girl's eyes widened. Shock.

"I hope not. When's the last you saw her?"

"She's been here popping in and out. Foundation business, I imagine. With the event tomorrow."

"Yeah, you're probably right, thanks. Please let Mrs. Visman know I'm here.

The girl turned on her heel and strode off to let her boss know the detective was here.

Parker found it unusual Kira's job as an FBI agent wasn't common knowledge among the household staff. No mention of her tracking down a criminal organization like Red Dawn, and the girl didn't seem aware Kira had vanished.

Secrets. More secrets in a family built on them. The funny thing about secrets, once you unravel one, the rest come crashing down. Parker was on the brink of sending the entire Visman facade to rubble.

The young woman returned and told Parker Mrs. Visman would be with him shortly. She would meet him in the library.

The library again—the Visman throne room, Parker thought.

He looked at the collections on the shelves rather than park in one of the low club chairs. One shelf was a carefully curated collection of family photos. Parker's eye drew to three silver frames in the center of the display. Blake and his older sister Kira in one. They couldn't have been in high school yet. Two others were individual shots featuring each of the kids with Victoria. Happy times long past.

"Detective? Should we wait for my husband?" Victoria strode into the room wearing tight workout clothes. Black leggings and a teal crop top, which revealed a toned core.

"No. I came to speak with you, actually?"

"Do I need to call our attorney?"

"Larry Sutton? No, he's busy with Kingston right now."

Victoria stopped dabbing at her neck with a towel.

"I wanted to talk to you about Kira, your daughter."

"She's not here."

"Can you tell me where she is?"

"Why should I? Are you going to try and blame her for something now?"

"Mrs. Visman, I find it odd none of your staff here at the house seem to know what your daughter does for a living."

"It's none of their business."

"Really? I'd be pretty proud of my daughter if she were leading a national organized crime task force."

She handed the sweaty towel to a staff member who offered her a glass of something tall, iced, and clear. Nothing for him.

"What are you saying, detective?"

"Where's your daughter, Mrs. Visman?"

"She's working."

"Mrs. Visman, at this moment, your husband is meeting with the U.S. Attorney to explain why he shouldn't be arrested for staging her abduction. Do you have any idea how much has gone into the search for her? One of my detectives was shot and is in the ICU because we went looking for her. Now. Where. Is. She?"

The last words were harsh, and Parker stepped closer to her with each syllable.

"I—I can't say. It's for the best."

"The best? The best for who? Don't tell that to my detective who's in a hospital bed tied down with tubes and wires. Who's missing part of his lung because he went looking of your daughter."

"I-I'm sorry, but Kira is all I have left."

"Do you have any idea of the shitstorm you and your husband have created behind hiding your daughter?" Parker closed on Victoria Visman and noticed the tremor in her hand.

"I met her—your daughter. She didn't seem the type to cut and run in the face of adversity. What have you and Kingston done?"

She turned away.

"What we had to do."

Parker followed her gaze to the bookshelf behind him—the one crowded with photos.

"You think you're protecting Kira? You don't want to have her end up like Blake."

"She's all I have." A tear streaked down her cheek.

Parker sensed a crack in the woman's stonewalled front.

"Ridler is on his way here."

"I'm aware. It's even more important he can't get to her."

"If you're afraid of him, why are you letting him attend your foundation event?"

She chewed on a thumbnail. "It was supposed to be over."

"Over? What was?"

"That man's vendetta. He lost a daughter, and we sacrificed a son. It was supposed to be even." Her voice trembled as she let it out.

Sacrificed. The word struck Parker like a hot poker. Not lost a son, sacrificed.

"Are you saying you let Ridler kill your son?"

"He told us it would be over. The score would be even. A child for a child."

Chapter Fifty-Five

Parker was stunned at the admission. What kind of parent would give their child in a twisted exchange with a killer?

Victoria collapsed in one of the club chairs and wept into another towel.

Ridler lost his daughter and wanted something of equal value. Blake Visman was put up on the sacrificial altar. Parker couldn't imagine any parent willingly killing their son.

"Ridler killed your son. You let him do it? Tell me why? How could you let him take your own flesh and blood?" Parker asked.

"We didn't have an alternative. He was coming for one of our kids. If we didn't choose, then he'd take them both."

"You and Kingston chose Blake? You chose him? How could you?"

"Kingston said Blake was the right choice. He'd caused us so much pain with his behavior. The legal troubles both here and on his frivolous excursions in Mexico. Kira was self-sufficient and successful. It made sense."

The Vismans chose to kill their son because he was more trouble than he was worth.

"You knew it was going to happen when Blake left on his flight to Mexico, didn't you?"

She nodded and cried into her towel.

They arranged for their son's death and held a memorial service in this room, accepting donations while they pretended to grieve.

Unable to mask the disgust in his voice, Parker asked, "If the score was settled, why is Ridler coming here tomorrow?"

"Now he wants Kira. Said Blake wasn't enough to balance the scales."

"Where is she, Victoria?"

She shook her head. "No. I won't lose her, too."

Parker knew she wouldn't give up her daughter. She was shutting down. Could he arrest her for obstruction? Maybe, but it wasn't enough to make up for what she and her husband had done.

Parker turned to the bookshelf, ran a finger down the row to a photo of a young Blake with Victoria. Both wore smiles and were gazing at something Victoria pointed at in the distance.

He plucked the frame from the shelf, held it to Victoria, and tossed it in her lap. "I hope you see that every night when you try to sleep."

Parker strode out of the library to Victoria's sobbing. He shoved open the front door and inhaled a deep cleansing breath of outside air. God only knows what spores infested the place to convince them Blake was little more than a line on a balance sheet.

Parker started his SUV and sat while the air conditioner caught up, and noticed his white-knuckle grip on the steering wheel. He pulled his hands from the wheel and opened his palms to get the blood flowing once more.

He pulled out his cell phone and hit a speed dial button.

Miguel answered. "Hey, Dad, what's up?"

"Hey, buddy. Just wanted to hear your voice for a second? What's you up to?"

"I'm at the coalition offices. Everything okay? You sound weird?"

"I'm—I'm fine. What you and Billie got going on today?"

In a lower voice, "I'm kinda glad you called. Billie's spun up about getting a supply shipment down to Hermosillo. You remember the guy I told you about, River?"

"Yeah, I do. We both told her it wasn't a good idea."

"She's dead set it's gonna happen."

"Where is she now?"

"She's here but getting ready to head out to meet River to help load up."

"Dammit. Put her on the phone, would you, buddy?"

Parker heard some background conversation. He could make out the words spoken, but Miguel's tone was pleading, and Billie was short and clipped. He'd seen it before when she dug her heels in.

Miguel came back on the line. "She says she doesn't have time."

"Where's she meeting River? You know which airport he's using?"

"Yeah, a small one where his parents keep their airplane stored. Oh, wait. Billie just left."

"Remember the name? The name of the airport?"

"Red something. Red Mountain? I think it's in the east valley. Want me to follow her?"

"No. Miguel. Please stay where you are. I'm not far. This River kid, you know what he looks like?"

"Entitled White skater kid."

"That should help. Now promise me you'll stay put and I'll call you as soon as I stop Billie from doing something she'll regret."

"I can't sit here and wait for news," Miguel said.

"I'll tell you what would help. Using your connections with the Immigrant Coalition, only ones you can trust, can you ask down there if they know of any people disappearing? Not the usual undocumented, but people who had legit visas. We're probably talking pairs, or single individuals who come down there and vanish when they tried to come back home. Can you do that?"

"Yeah, I think so. Like the old couple from the Guad? The Cortez's."

"Yes, exactly. How—"

"I heard you and Linda talking."

"All right. Yes, like the couple from the Guad. See if your contacts know about similar disappearances." Parker also made a mental note to watch what he and Linda talked about in the late hours while Miguel was tucked away in his room with homework. "You have the photo of those kids from the university? The one with Blake Visman and River Patterson?"

"Yeah, want me to send it to you?"

Parker agreed and begged Miguel to stay put while he tracked down Billie. He promised to call Miguel when he made sure Billie was okay.

From the Visman compound in Fountain Hills, it was less than twenty minutes to the Red Mountain airstrip. The small private facility didn't show any evidence of the carnage inflicted by the two Los Zetas assassins less than a day ago.

The single-engine Cessna Blake Visman bled out in was too large to be towed to an impound lot. Instead, the aircraft was tucked alongside one hangar with a temporary chain-link fence erected around the plane.

Parker knew the evidence that could be removed: seats, carpeting, cargo liners, and electronics were taken and secured by the crime scene technicians.

Parker tucked his SUV in the hangar's shade near Visman's plane. He didn't spot Billie's huge F-250 pickup truck, but she could have pulled into any of the hangars to unload. Or she might have already stashed the medical supplies on Patterson's plane and left with him to make sure they got to Hermosillo.

A security man in a golf cart zipped toward him, and Parker recognized him from yesterday. The man's shoulders released as he pulled to a stop.

"Hi, detective. Saw someone pull up next to the plane. Your people made it clear it was off limits to any civilians who came wandering by.

"Thanks for that."

"You need something from the plane? I can help you move the fence."

"No. Thanks." Parker noted the plump security guard looked relieved he didn't need to get out of his air-conditioned golf cart.

"You know where River Patterson keeps a plane here? One of Blake Visman's pals," Parker said.

"Oh, him. Yeah, I know the little shit. Last hanger on the right. He's there now. What you got on him?"

"Have an opinion about the kid, I gather?"

"Him and the rest of their little circus. Blake, too, rest his soul. Entitled trust fund kids. River's probably the worst of them—the attitude on that one."

The flutter of a small engine caught their attention from down the flight line. A light blue Cessna taxied from a hangar.

CHAPTER FIFTY-FIVE

"That's him. River."

"We gotta stop him from taking off," Parker said.

"It ain't like we got an air traffic controller in a tower around here."

Parker hopped back into his SUV and shot down toward the aircraft as it crept from the pad in front of the hangar. Parker skidded to a stop in front of the slow-moving plane. It was more dramatic than he intended—it wasn't as if River was O.J. Simpson on a crowded California freeway.

The plane's engine cycled down, and the pilot's door flew open. Parker recognized the kid from the photo Miguel sent. Tall, dark hair, and a smug attitude, he sensed from a distance.

"Hey man! What the hell you think you're doing? Move that pile of shit outta my way," River said over the engine noise.

Parker pulled his badge from his belt.

"You have no right to stop me like this is some DUI checkpoint."

"You been drinking, Mr. Patterson?"

Parker glanced in the hanger, and tucked along the back wall was Billie's blue pickup truck.

"Billie in there with you, River?"

"Nobody here, just me."

Parker stepped from his SUV and peered around River into the plane's small cockpit.

No, Billie, but there was a young blonde in the right-hand seat. Parker gestured for her to get out with a thumb.

"That's her truck back there. Where'd she go?"

"What business is that of yours, cop?" A defiant chin with a slight beard when the sunlight hit it just right.

"You've got Billie's supplies in your plane, so where is she?"

"I don't have to tell you—"

"Listen here, you little piss ant. Your little school flight club has been used to smuggle cartel hitmen over the border. Two of your people are dead."

"Blake? That didn't have anything to do with—"

"Oh, come on. Don't give me that. You know he was murdered by the people he brought over, like the guy who dropped off people at Yavapai

Dunes. You can't trust these people."

The blonde crept around the nose of the plane after the propeller had stopped turning.

"Blake's dead? Murdered? You never said anything about murder, River. I am so out." The blonde stomped off, leaving River alone.

"Sorry I ruined your hookup plans. Now, where's Billie? I'm not asking again." Parker dangled a pair of handcuffs.

"She's left with the first plane. There was too much cargo for one flight. She went ahead."

"To Hermosillo?"

"No. Some private strip near Ocotillo."

Parker remembered the reference from Pimentel. Red Dawn was using the airfield, and Billie was heading right into their arms.

Chapter Fifty-Six

"How long ago? When did the plane leave?" Parker asked.

River shrugged. "I dunno, maybe thirty minutes."

"Can you reach them? Radio?"

"Yeah, I guess. Why?"

"Just do it."

"Fine." River climbed into the pilot's seat once more and gripped the microphone. "Rebel Leader to Rebel Six, over?"

Parker could help but think River and his buddies watched too many Star Wars movies, and it gave him a queasy feeling Billie's life depended on them.

River repeated his call. No response from his teammate.

"Why don't they call back?"

"Might be out of radio range. These are pretty short range, especially when you're on the ground."

"How long was the flight supposed to take?"

River glanced at his watch. "They should be there in five, maybe ten minutes."

"How can you reach them and tell them not to land? You can't let them land."

River's phony surfer dude vibe was wearing on Parker. When River said, "Whatever, man," Parker snatched him by the collar and pulled him from the cockpit.

"Can you warn them?"

"No man, I can't. Chill."

Parker released River with a shove. He looked in the space behind the front where a pile and passenger might sit. The rear seats had been removed, and the space was jammed with cardboard boxes sporting labels denoting bandages, gauze, personal protective equipment, and sterile saline solution. Medical supplies, as Billie claimed.

Unless she tried to smuggle something else like she did before. Parker reached in and tugged the closest box to him. He tore open the tape and bags of simple saline solution. His eye caught a smaller cardboard box with a slightly different color tape—more the glossy sheen on the tape than anything else. Parker placed it on the pilot's seat while he opened it.

Stacks of banded cash filled the container. Parker guessed at least ten grand, maybe more. Billie? What were you up to?

"What do you know about this?" Parker asked River.

"Nothing."

The kid was quick to respond, and Parker noticed a twitch under River's right eye. He wouldn't have been a good poker player.

"Wanna try again, River? I can take you in for trying to smuggle cash out of the country." Parker didn't know what the relevant federal statutes were, but the FBI task force tried to confiscate Billie's shipment before.

"Hey, hey, Billie said it was cool. It's like her money. She can do what she wants with it, can't she?"

"Depends on where it was going. She mention who was going to pick this up on the other end?"

"That's her business, not mine. I know she called someone before she left with Kenny."

"You catch who she was talking with?"

"Nah, some woman. That's what it sounded like."

"She say why she needed to go down there—on this trip?"

"I know Billie didn't plan on going down there. She seemed kinda butthurt she had to. Her flying down meant we had to reshuffle the cargo because of the weight limits. It's why we needed to use a second plane. Billie wanted the cash to come down after her—like she had to make sure whoever was gonna get it was there."

Parker pulled back from the cockpit door and pondered the possibilities.

Who was Billie paying off? This wasn't money intended for her network down south. She could get funding to them by more legitimate means. This reeked of desperation. The Coalition had stockpiled supplies in Hermosillo and other smaller towns. Why the rush to get this to— "The airfield? They ever use it before?"

"No. That was a new one to me. Billie gave us the directions and location. I usually don't like to fly in blind, but she said she'd make it worth it. Figured she could based on what she had laid down in that box."

A woman. Who was Billie working with on the other end of this connection? Thompson? Was it possible the FBI agent had been working in tandem with Red Dawn all along? Parker mulled the idea around. She could have tipped off the organization about her task force objectives and sold out her team. It was possible.

He glanced at his watch. "What were they supposed to do when they landed?"

River shrugged. "The usual, I suppose. Unload, pick up anything coming this way, and hightail it back. Don't spend too much time down there on these runs."

"How do you know if they get there?"

"Kenny usually calls while he's getting his fuel topped off."

"So he's got a phone?" Parker was feeling the anger well up within as he tried to extract information from this pothead.

"Well, yeah. But he keeps it off while he's in the air."

"Call him. Call him, now."

"Chill, man. Don't get it twisted up. I'll send him a text. Call, whatever, you think I'm that old?"

Parker watched as River snagged his phone from the cockpit and opened a messaging app. "Hit me up when you land." River pressed send. "They're happy, now?"

Immediately, a ping sounded on River's phone. "Landed and unloading. You ready to bring in the second load?"

Parker nudged River. "Ask him who's there? Who's taking the supplies?"

River tapped out the message and sent it.

A response popped on the screen. "I dunno. Billie's talking with some woman. Got some dudes with her. Strapped."

"Tell Kenny to describe the woman Billie's talking to."

River tapped in the question, and Kenny came back with, "Dude, I saw her first. Go find your own on Bumble or where-ev."

River didn't wait for Parker to respond. "Dude, what does she look like. Might be sus."

Kenny got the message. "Five-seven. Dark hair—long. Might be Mexican."

Parker thought it was Thompson until the last piece. Thompson wasn't even tanned; there was no way she could be taken for Mexican. Who was this woman Billie was dealing with in the middle of the desert?

A chill ran up Parker's spine. The only woman he knew matching the description and running around north Mexico with an armed posse was Carmen Delgado, the on-and-off-again girlfriend of Pimentel, the Sinaloa Cartel boss.

Chapter Fifty-Seven

"Get Billie on the phone, now," Parker said, grabbing River by the elbow.

Carmen was an opportunistic snake. Once the Public Information Officer for the Maricopa County Sheriff, Carmen cozied up with Los Muertos gang forces and framed Parker for a murder of a suspect. She fled to Mexico and was last known to be in league with Pimentel.

Billie had received a message from Carmen after she ordered the hit on Esteban Castaneda in prison. The cartel has a long reach. He wasn't aware Billie was in their grip—until now.

River's cell phone rang.

"Put it on speaker," Parker said.

"River, when you landin'?" Billie's voice came over the connection.

"I haven't left yet."

"I have people waiting for what's you bringin'."

"Billie, tell me that's not Carmen Delgado," Parker said.

"Nathan? What's goin' on?"

"Billie, what are you doing? Get back on that plane and get back here. Whatever you have going on with Delgado, don't."

"What with the mess down here, I can't risk my medical supplies gettin' jacked. Carmen's in a position to make sure they go where they need to go."

"You can't trust her, Billie. You know that."

"Which is why I need River to get down here."

"He's not coming, and you already got caught once trying to send cash out of the country."

279

"I can do what I want with it. 'Sides, it's the cost of doin' business down here. You know how it works."

"Billie, listen carefully. Who picked the place where you're meeting her? The airfield? Whose idea was it?"

"Carmen said it was off the grid and wouldn't get no attention. A friend of hers turned her onto it."

"This friend, have a name?"

"I din't ask."

"Billie, listen and trust me. The airfield is connected with Red Dawn. If she brought you there, she's connected with them. Billie, you gotta get out of there."

A rustle on the line, Parker heard what sounded like two men shouting in the background. The tone came off as angry and urgent. Then the pop of semiautomatic gunfire.

"Billie! What's going on?"

"Dammit all, they come in and start shooting at my people. They just come here to pick up the supplies."

"Can you hide? Run away?"

"They's chasing 'em away. Not trying to kill 'em. Oh, no. They took Kenny. Pushing him back to his plane."

"Don't try to stop them, Billie."

"It's my fault the boy's here."

"No, it's not. They wanted a quick payoff. These people are the same ones responsible for killing the old couple from the Guad. And the federal agents shot Pete Tully."

"I gotta make them stop."

"Billie, no," Parker said to a dead connection.

Parker slammed a fist against the metal side of the hanger, and River pocketed his phone.

River kicked at a loose chunk of asphalt with the toe of his Converse high-top. "They're gonna make Kenny fly them here, aren't they? Then they'll do what they did to Blake? They are, aren't they? They're gonna kill him."

Parker knew the kid was right. Kenny was most likely dead on arrival.

"Any idea where they'd have him fly into? Back here?" Parker asked.

"The last couple of trips, the people we brought over made the decision in the air. We'd plan on landing at Glendale or Sky Harbor, because that's the rule—you fly over the border, you drop in on a designated airport and clear customs."

Parker mulled it over, and River's description matched what Jack Talent had admitted. Red Dawn would make a change mid-flight. They also eliminate any witnesses to the flight after landing. If Billie tried to stop them, she'd be dealt with, too. He hoped she kept her wits about her. She'd survived on her own, and she was going to need those instincts now.

"Don't these planes have transponders or something?" Parker remembered Espi mentioning the pilots had turned off their transponders on these flights. Their planes were visible on radar, but by the time air traffic control figured out where they were heading, they were on the ground.

Parker chased River away, and the kid wasn't happy leaving without his box of cash. It took Parker fifteen minutes to load the supplies from the small plane and stuff it in the back of his SUV. The box of cash was stashed on the floor of the front passenger seat.

What was Billie hoping to buy with that much money? Mordida, or bribes, were common to grease the wheels, especially where government officials were concerned. This payoff seemed different. What was she buying and from whom? The assassins coming up from down south were connected with Red Dawn. Ridler's people were bent on taking down Kingston Visman and the foundation that claimed his daughter.

Parker recalled the note Lynne slipped to him when confronting Kingston Visman. Espi hadn't returned his call, but the note claimed Ridler was on the move. He'd bet Kenny was the taxi service bringing the crime boss over the border.

Where he would land was the question.

Chapter Fifty-Eight

Parker took a chance Espi was checking his voicemail and left him a message about the pirated aircraft in Ocotillo and the possibility Ridler could be on board.

He turned on the air in his SUV and called Billie's cell. She didn't answer, which meant she was hiding from Ridler's people, or they already had her, which left him with a hollow feeling.

Glancing down at the box of cash, banded and packed tightly in the cardboard box, he spied a tiny edge of white sticking up between two of the bundles.

Parker hefted the box onto the seat next to him and pulled the flaps open. He dug a finger against the side and pried up a bundle, revealing a folded sheet of paper.

The white paper was the corner of a document. A handwritten note scrawled on the upper corner. Parker recognized Billie's angular script.

"Half now—half on delivery."

What was Billie buying from Carmen? It wasn't goodwill. Even after Carmen's attempt to take over Los Muertos, she played for power wherever she could find it. Last Parker heard, she was cozying up with Sinaloa boss, Pimentel.

Was Billie dealing with the cartel? And what were they going to deliver?

He didn't need this in the middle of trying to figure out what happened to Agent Thompson and how far Ridler would go as payback for his daughter.

The first shot pinged off the SUV's hood. Rapid fire from the left as a gunman walked his direction with a rifle slung low down by his hip. He was thirty yards or more away and fired shot after shot, adjusting his aim as the bullets hit the vehicle, the hangar, or the asphalt.

The shots hit the front fender, the radiator, then the windshield. Closer with each trigger pull.

The SUV engine died, and white streams of steam wafted from the pierced radiator.

Another rifle blast triggered the airbag, slamming the safety device into Parker's face and chest, pinning him to the seat.

Trapped.

A flash from the muzzle and the driver's window shattered. The gunman was close, and Parker had his weapon drawn, turned in his seat to line up an awkward shot, but had trouble focusing with glass and blood trickling in his right eye.

He caught movement as the gunman raised his rifle.

A high-pitched whine distracted the gunman for a split second. Before he had the chance to turn his rifle on the source of the noise, the security guard ran over the gunman from behind and pinned him under the golf cart.

Parker forced the door open and brushed the airbag accelerant off his face.

The gunman flailed under the golf cart, but the weight of the machine and the security guard who remained in the electric cart, the downed gun thug wasn't going anywhere.

Parker pulled the rifle away as the gunman tried to reach it, his broken fingers not able to pull the butt of the weapon toward him.

"Thanks for the assist," Parker said. "You can probably put this in reverse now."

"Oh, okay."

The golf cart sounded a beep-beep as it backed down from the gunman's back. The assailant moaned as the cart moved. Parker thought a couple of busted ribs would slow him down.

He quickly handcuffed the man and tugged a wallet secured with a chain to the gunman's belt from a back pocket.

The driver's license was for Anthony Hawkins. The name didn't ring a bell with Parker. The address in the far south reaches of Buckeye, one he recognized as a filthy nest where the Chain Slayers bedded down.

"So Anthony, what brings you out here?" Parker asked.

"The bounty is mine."

"Bounty? What are you talking about? What bounty?"

"The one on your head, Parker. Ten grand."

Parker got down on one knee, and what was on the man's face wasn't anger or even greed. It was letting a payday slip away. He'd failed at his chance to cash in on the detective's killing.

"Who posted the bounty?"

A moan filled the space between them as the man tried to move. "It don't matter. We're gonna keep coming until it's done."

"That's what Warren Block was trying to collect?" Parker said. The Chain Slayers bartender who shot up his home.

"Yeah, except he didn't wait his turn. I had the green light, not him."

"He jumped your chance at the bounty? That's why a couple of Chain Slayers worked him over."

"It belongs to me."

"I don't think you'll be collecting."

"It ain't over yet." He spat a wad of phlegm toward Parker.

"Who were you planning to collect from, if you were successful?"

Parker saw the fight evaporate from the biker as the realization he wasn't going to collect.

"Talent. Talent said he had it set up from someone down south."

"He mention who? The name Ridler ever come up?"

"Nah, never heard who. That was Talent's deal."

Jack Talent, the militia leader he and Barry met at The Kickstand. Parker asked the security man to call for an ambulance, while he needed to call dispatch for a unit to the airfield to take custody of Hawkins.

Parker trotted back to his SUV and fished his cell phone from the floorboard. The screen had a diagonal crack, but the display showed a connection to the network.

He reached the dispatcher and got a uniformed deputy heading in his direction. Then he tapped in Billie's number from the call log.

After four rings, Billie answered.

"Nathan? They done took Kenny and left."

"Billie, are you all right?"

"No. I'm not all right. I'm darned pissed off, thanks for asking."

"You're okay, though? Nobody's there after you?"

A sigh. "No, they saw me and coulda taken me out. But instead, they's just shoved Kenny back in the plane. Then two of them gets in with him and fly off."

"They say anything you could pick up about where they were heading?"

"They dint say where they were landing the plane, or what they were doing with Kenny. But I did hear somethin' about taking out someone at Fountain Hills."

"The foundation event," Parker said.

"Gotta be."

"Billie, you got a way to find somewhere safe?"

"I reached out to Armando, and he's got someone coming to grab me and these supplies. Looks like we'll be able to deliver them."

"The guys who came there didn't take the stuff?" The hair on the back of Parker's neck tingled.

"Nah, Carmen and whoever came in shootin' done left it alone. Which struck me kinda odd. Everyone left in two big vans and coulda taken all of it. But they didn't. I've never seen the cartel pass up a chance to steal something so they could sell it back."

"Neither have I, Billie."

A car horn sounded in the background.

"Looks like my ride's here. Thanks for callin' to check up on me. I appreciate that—not too many people woulda."

"Yeah, yeah. You have more people who care about you than you imagine."

"Maybe they shouldn't. Thanks, Nathan. I gotta run and get these supplies loaded and tucked away before someone does walk off with them."

Parker disconnected the call, relieved Billie was okay after her encounter with the plane hijackers. Something she said—actually, it was more than one thing she said, stuck in Parker's mind.

The first was the shooters kept Billie's people away while they commandeered the airplane and pilot. They didn't kill them, or Billie, and didn't steal the valuable commodity for resale on the black market.

Carmen's alliances were typically murky. Los Muertos one day and the Sinaloa cartel the next. At the root of it, it was always what was best for Carmen. The airstrip attack was very uncartel-like activity. What if it wasn't the cartel taking the plane, forcing Kenny the pilot to fly them over the border to Fountain Hills?

If it wasn't the cartel, it meant Quentin Ridler was on his way to face off with Kingston Visman. What was Carmen Delgado's part in it?

Chapter Fifty-Nine

The uniformed deputy arrived and took custody of the injured would-be bounty hunter. He waited for the paramedics to check him over, load him in the ambulance, and the deputy followed to the hospital. Hawkins would get cleared for booking and housed in the county lockup, hopefully in a cell next to Jack Talent.

Parker turned and headed to his SUV and pulled to a stop. He wasn't driving this home. Not with the shattered windshield, exploded airbag, and bullet holes in the front end

His phone picked that moment to give up the ghost.

He sighed and waved the security man over.

"You have a phone I can borrow?"

Another Maricopa County patrol unit pulled into the airpark. Linda hopped from the passenger seat and jogged to him.

She put a hand to his brow and brushed away a small shard of glass from the shattered windshield.

"Nathan…"

She didn't wait for him to say anything before hugging him and didn't care who was there to see it.

"I'm fine, Linda."

"What? Didn't you call? You should have told me you were hurt." She slapped his chest lightly with her palm.

He held up his broken cell phone. "I was trying to get to a phone. How did you end up out here?"

"I heard the dispatch call for a unit and a medical response after an officer-involved shooting."

"It really wasn't—"

Three more Maricopa County units pulled into the airpark.

"After what happened to Pete, then the shooting at your place. We couldn't take a chance."

"The shooter got the worst of it. He has ties to the biker gang, Barry and I rousted when we found the connection to Red Dawn and the local soldier-for-hire scene. Except—except something about the connection isn't fitting together for me."

"How's that? We got the intel from Agent Thompson before she disappeared. It's what turned us onto Jack Talent, right?"

"Exactly. What if it was misdirection? Thompson's people handed me the flash drive before she vanished. The Red Dawn connection to Talent and his band of misfit toys came from the file. I trusted the source. What if Thompson purposely misled us?"

"What? Why would she? What's the payoff for her?"

"Honestly, I don't know. It revolves around Kingston Visman and Quentin Ridler. Of that much, I'm sure."

"Speaking of Ridler—the daughter, Catherine—I dug up some of the reports and notes around her disappearance. She was apparently quite the party girl. You know, rich daddy, the club scene. She liked to duck out from her security team all the time."

"The girl had bodyguards?" Parker asked.

"She did. Her father was aware of her inclinations."

"What was a party girl like her doing in Hermosillo? Was she working on Visman's water project, or was that a lie too?"

"I was starting to dig into it when you called dispatch. You want me to let these other units get back to doing actual police work?"

Parker paused for a moment. There were more than a few puzzle pieces that didn't fit together, and the picture was going to be violently revealed at the foundation's event at the Visman compound.

"I think we might need them."

Linda furrowed her brow. "Are you okay?"

He nodded and motioned for her to come with him to the cluster of arriving backup units.

"Can you call for a crime scene team to come and load my unit on a flatbed? The beast is evidence and undrivable now."

Linda made the call while Parker met with the three deputies. After a short briefing, the deputies got in their SUVs and headed out of the airpark.

"Send them back out to their patrol sectors?"

He shook his head. "They're headed to the Visman compound in Fountain Hills. Everything is coming to a head there. We might need the additional presence there."

He pointed at her phone. "Could you call Barry? Put it on speaker. I need to get both of you up to speed on what I've run into. Maybe we can figure out what the foundation event is really trying to do when Kingston Visman and Ridler face off later today."

"If Ridler blames Visman for his daughter—"

The call rang through, and Barry picked up.

"Everything good? The boss okay?"

"I'm fine, Barry."

"Good to hear. When I heard the report about an officer-involved shooting, I thought—I have found some interesting things on Quentin Ridler," Barry said, changing the course of the conversation.

"I think he's on his way here as we speak," Parker said. "Billie's in Hermosillo, and the plane she used to get relief supplies down there was hijacked, and a couple of guys forced the pilot to fly them back north. She overheard them mention Fountain Hills."

"The foundation fundraiser?" Linda asked.

"Sounds like it," Parker said.

"Huh. Ridler is an investment guy. I mean like uber nerdy. He hardly seems like the arch-villain capable of running an evil empire. There are interviews in business journals going back a few years and the guy is about leveraging assets, buying out competitors, and even a hostile takeover—in the business world. There's nothing linking him to a criminal organization. There is a regular mention of his family. Apparently, he lost his wife recently and has been slightly less visible. Fell completely off radar after his daughter went missing."

"That tracks."

"I found some information he put out after she disappeared. Organized search teams, a reward notice, posters. He put together an effort to find his missing daughter."

Linda filled Barry in on the girl's partying lifestyle and how she liked to evade her father's security teams.

"Fits with what I found. The posters weren't the usual 'have you seen this girl' type thing. They said she was 'spirited' and 'curious.'"

"I haven't found anything about her that screams social activist, or someone who would roll up her designer sleeves and dig water lines in impoverished communities," Linda said.

"Which means she was there for other reasons," Parker said.

He paused for a moment.

"Hey, Barry. You have one of Ridler's posters you can send to Linda's phone? A photo of the girl?"

"Sure, hang on a sec." Parker and Linda heard him tap on a keyboard in the background. "Okay. Should be coming at you."

Linda's phone sounded with a frog croaking ringtone.

"Professional, detective."

She blushed as she pulled the text image up on her screen.

Parker leaned into the small screen. That face. He'd seen her. She was at the Visman residence during Blake's memorial. The girl who sat alone.

Chapter Sixty

"Barry, drop everything and meet Linda and me at the Visman estate. Linda tucked the phone on her belt clip.

"You mean the Ridler girl had a thing going with Blake Visman? The kid who was killed in his plane?" she said.

"The same. I saw a photo of the two of them in the Visman library when I spoke to Mrs. Visman. The girl was there at the house the night of the memorial service."

"Ridler's daughter isn't dead?"

"No, and the cartel didn't take her. This got weird."

"Hey, the package Barry sent—did it include a photo of Quentin Ridler?"

"Let me check," Linda said, snagging the phone and scrolling through the attachments Barry forwarded to them.

She stopped at one image and handed the phone to Parker. "Looks like a press release of some kind."

"Last year. In Geneva at some conference. I thought maybe I'd get a flash of recognition. Maybe remembering an encounter with the guy. I got nothing. Looks like a corporate bean-counter, doesn't he?"

The image on the phone captured a man in a business suit. His thinning hair was clipped short to hide the receding hairline. While most of the man was hidden behind a podium, he was smallish and unassuming.

"Says Ridler's firm is considered one of the most aggressive corporate takeover groups in the world," Linda said, peering over his shoulder at the phone.

"Maybe he applied the same approach, looking for his daughter. Say,

291

could you forward that photo to Billie? I'd like confirmation if he's the guy she spotted getting on the plane in Hermosillo."

"I don't have her number," Linda said, scrolling through her contact information.

He glanced at his busted cell phone with Billie's phone number locked away inside. "Miguel would have it."

Linda hit the speed dial button she had set aside for Miguel, who picked up on the first ring.

"Hey, Linda, what's up?"

"Hey buddy, Linda's gonna send you a photo. My phone's broken, so could you get it to Billie?"

"Broken? Again?"

"Yeah, long story. I need to know if Billie recognizes this guy. She claimed he got on the plane in Hermosillo."

"She called me and told me what happened. The plane getting jacked and all. I've been here getting connections made to distribute some of the most needed supplies out to the camps on the edge of the city. We've been having our supplies looted and stolen in the last couple of months. Whatever Billie did, she's chased off those bandits."

Parker feared Billie's liaison with Carmen Delgado lay at the center of it. Whatever Carmen had done, it wasn't out of some charitable notion. The woman was only interested in power and control. What was she getting out of allowing the medical supplies to reach those who needed them most?

"Miguel, if you talk with your connections down there, please tell them to be careful. This has the makings of a trap, and those supplies could be the bait."

"They are being careful. Okay, have Linda send me the photo. I'll stay on to make sure it comes through."

Linda swiped the screen carefully so she wouldn't disconnect the call and pulled up the photo once more. She sent it off, accompanied by a whooshing sound effect.

A few seconds later. Miguel cleared his throat. "Coming through. Yeah, got it."

"Good—let me know if Billie says—"

"This guy? Who is he supposed to be? I've seen him before. Hang on."

Parker and Linda heard Miguel's chair scrape back and then the metallic tinkle of him parting the window blinds.

"This guy? Who is he?"

"It's a man named Ridler. He's the one behind the Red Dawn killings. You've seen him before?"

"Yeah, and I'm looking at him right now. He pulled up in front of the Coalition offices. Him and two other guys."

"Ridler? He's there?"

"Just got out of the car. The two big guys with him act like bodyguards or something. He's looking this way."

"Miguel, get out of there. Go out the back and don't let them see you."

"What does he want here? I've got the front door locked anyways."

"Miguel, listen to me. Ridler is obsessed with his daughter's disappearance. Anyone who he believes had something to do with it is dead. I don't know what he thinks the coalition had to do with it, but we don't want to find out. Get out now and—"

A crash sounded in the background. Broken glass. Parker envisioned the front plate-glass window shattering. Another noise in the background— more broken glass, smaller this time, followed by a whoosh.

"Fire. They're burning the place!" Miguel said.

"Get out now."

They heard Miguel's footsteps as he ran across the office space to the back door.

"It's jammed. It won't open. They've—they've blocked it."

Miguel began to cough.

"It's getting hard to see."

"Miguel, push hard. With everything you've got."

Parker's gut twisted in knots. Miguel was trapped in a burning building, and he was powerless to do anything.

"Miguel, keep trying."

Coughing sounded over the speaker.

More breaking glass and background noise.
Then nothing.
Miguel wasn't responding.
The connection died.

Chapter Sixty-One

Linda snatched the phone from Parker and dialed 911. She gave dispatch the address and told them a man was trapped inside toward the rear of the building.

She tugged on Parker's arm enough it shook him out of his shock and twisted it to anger. He felt the rage bubble within. Ridler firebombed the Immigrant Coalition offices with Miguel trapped inside. What had Miguel done to deserve that fate? After everything the boy had survived on his solo trek from El Salvador, he'd get burned to death like the first body Parker found in the desert.

That first body. Parker snapped upright in his seat as Linda raced the SUV toward the coalition offices.

"Son of a bitch! Ridler."

"The fire department is probably there already. They'll find him."

"No. Ridler. I've seen him before. I know who he is."

"What are you talking about?"

"The first bodies we found out on the crossroads outside of Quartzite? Remember?"

"I wasn't on the callout. That was you, Pete, and Barry.

"Pete called it. The two scoutmasters. He said he didn't believe them—said something was off about them. Dryden. He's Ridler. I'm sure of it. Dryden is a little older than in the photo, has a beard, and his hair's a little longer. But it's him."

"You think so? What was he doing out there with a bunch of kids?"

"The kids part, I'm not so sure. Could have been a smokescreen to cover what he was doing out there?"

"Which was what exactly?"

"The bodies. He wanted to see if they belonged to his daughter. He must have followed the trail up here and had reason to think she might have been along for the ride."

"Then he didn't kill them, those first two you found?"

"I'm thinking he didn't—Red Dawn didn't."

"What are you saying? We've been chasing ghosts this whole time?" Linda said.

Linda accelerated into the intersection, turning west on Indian School Road.

"Something like that—whoa," Parker said as the column of thick black smoke boiled up from the strip mall housing the Immigrant Coalition.

A half dozen fire engines lined the road, red lights flashing. A pair of Maricopa County deputies were directing traffic away from the location.

Linda hit the button and let loose a chirp of the siren. A deputy waved her around the cars stuck in traffic. She had to park on the street because the three-inch fire hoses snaked across the road to the engine crews who doused the building.

The entire building was engulfed. The businesses on either side of the coalition offices had closed during the pandemic and never reopened, but the check-cashing business at the end of the squat brown strip mall had resumed operation. The flames shooting from the establishment's windows marked the end of predatory secured paycheck loans in the community.

Parker made his way to a firefighter wearing a white helmet, marking him as a command-level officer.

"Did you find the man inside those offices?" Parker pointed to the coalition spaces in the center of the building.

"We haven't been able to gain entrance. The building's unstable. It's about to come down. We're protecting exposures to adjacent structures now. What makes you think there was anyone inside?" The firefighter's nametag read, Battalion Chief, Whitehead.

"Chief, he called me. When the place was firebombed—he called me."

"I'm not sending anyone in there. There's nothing to be done. If there was anyone inside—I'm sorry.

Parker felt his knees wobble. Linda put an arm around his shoulder, steadying him. She felt him tremble.

An ambulance had parked at the far end of the complex. The doors to the rear compartment were ajar. A paramedic stepped down from the back, but Parker didn't have a clear view inside.

"Chief, what's going on there?" Parker pointed to the ambulance.

"We caught some kid hanging around. Probably had something to do with starting this. The arson investigators want a word with him. We have him on ice until they can wrap up their interviews. Another undocumented—"

Parker didn't wait for the Chief to finish. He ran to the ambulance, pulled the door open, and there he was, Miguel, sitting up on a gurney with bandaged hands.

Miguel's face relaxed when he spotted Parker. "Dad..."

Across from Miguel, an arson investigator perched on a stool.

"You can wait out there, pal. I'm not done with him, yet," the pot-bellied investigator said.

"Yeah, you are," Parker stepped into the back of the ambulance and sat next to Miguel. He spotted bandages on both of the boy's hands. "Are you okay?"

"No, he's not okay. He was getting around to telling me how he happened to be in an office building when it burned. He ain't no office worker."

"What are you trying to say? Because he's young, he can't possibly be employed?"

"Look at him. Does he look like a business type? Or should he be out picking strawberries on the 303? And he's sitting there with burns on his hands and soot from the fire on his clothes. I—"

"What rock did you crawl out from this morning? Because he has brown skin, you assume he's undocumented? You think he's somehow less than you?"

"I'm saying—"

"No. I'm done listening to anything you're saying. I'm taking my son.

You got anything to say about it, talk to my attorney. Miguel was on the phone with me when the place was firebombed by members of a criminal organization called Red Dawn."

"I ain't heard of them."

"Don't care if you have or not."

Linda cleared her throat. "I was on the phone with him, too. We heard the breaking glass from what must have been a Molotov cocktail tossed through the plate glass out front."

"We caught him out back. Looking like he was trying to bust inside to loot the place before the fire spread by breaking open the window. Guess he didn't count on the business blocking the exit door with a garbage dumpster."

Parker looked at Miguel's hands. "You escaped through the bathroom window?"

"Yeah. The back door. I couldn't open it."

"Let's get you home."

"He ain't going anywhere until I say so." The arson investigator puffed up his already rotund form.

"You think you can stop me?"

Parker saw Miguel's driver's license tucked on his clipboard. Parker reached and snatched it up.

"Probably fake. I need ICE to come and check his status."

"Is that so?" Parker fished out his own ID and held the two side by side. Notice the same address? He's my son."

"Because you say it don't make it so."

"What the hell is wrong with you?"

"I'm damn tired of people who don't belong here ruining it for us good folks."

"You meant to say white folks, right?"

The investigator popped up from his chair and chest bumped Parker.

"People like you make me sick. Colluding with these mud people."

Parker's fist shot out and connected with the portly racist's nose. It wasn't hard enough to break it, but it pushed the man back from Parker's space back onto his stool.

The man held his hands over his nose. "I'll have your ass for this. Assaulting a fireman is a felony."

"You're no fireman. Come on, Miguel."

Parker helped the boy up from the gurney and steadied him as he stepped from the vehicle.

A Black paramedic held the door open for them. "Man, I've wanted to do that for a long time."

Parker nodded.

Linda huddled over Miguel. "Are you all right? Do we need to get you to the hospital?"

Miguel shook his head. "No. I'll be okay. I want to get out of here."

He glanced at the flames devouring the Immigrant Coalition offices. "Billie's going to be mad. Everything we had was there, and now it's gone."

"You guys built it up once before; you can do it again," Parker said. He put his arm around the boy, too. Parker and Linda on either side of Miguel.

"Besides, I might need a job at the Coalition now."

"Don't worry about it, I got it on video," Linda said. "That little ray of racist sunshine isn't going to do a thing."

Parker smiled.

Miguel stopped, looked at Parker. "That man—"

"You don't need to give him a second thought."

Parker said.

"Not that pendejo. The man who burned down the offices. Ridler. He had a woman with him."

"A woman?" Parker's mind flashed to Carmen Delgado, but Billie made it sound like she was in Hermosillo.

"I think—I think it was the woman FBI Agent. The one supposed to be missing."

Chapter Sixty-Two

"Agent Thompson? Are you sure?"

"I think so, yes. I mean, I never saw her in person before. But the Marshal, who came to the house the night she disappeared. He showed you a photo of the FBI task force team. She was in it—the photo."

"At the coalition offices? Was she—did it look like she was being held against her will?"

Miguel shook his head. "Just the opposite. It looked like she was running the show. She was bossing the other man—Ridler—around."

Parker nodded toward the SUV.

Linda got behind the wheel.

"Hey, where's yours? How come Linda's driving?"

Parker didn't make eye contact with Miguel in the rear-view mirror. "Long story."

"Linda, what is he not telling me?"

She grinned.

Parker turned in the seat and faced Miguel. "Everything's fine—now. It ties back to the man you saw with Agent Thompson—Ridler. It's connected."

"What did he have against Billie and the coalition?"

"I don't know if it's him, or Agent Thompson, or the woman Billie met in Hermosillo. Her name the woman was—her name is Carmen. Carmen—"

"Delgado?"

"How do you know her name?"

Miguel's eyes widened. There was more tone in Parker's voice than he intended.

"I'm sorry, buddy. I don't mean it to sound like that. Carmen goes back a ways—before I met you. She used to be with the sheriff's department, broke bad, and ended up running south over the border to avoid arrest for drug trafficking, among other things."

Parker didn't want to tell him the woman nearly ended his life, trapping him on the other side of the border. She was playing the cartel against Los Muertos and always seemed to land wherever the power shifted.

Carmen's involvement left Parker on edge.

"I've heard Billie mention her. As recent as yesterday. I didn't catch all of it, but enough to know Carmen was making Billie pay to make sure the relief supplies got where we needed them. It's not unusual—paying bribes of one sort or another happens. There was more to it, though."

"I know Billie met with her today in Hermosillo. Whatever exchange they had planned went belly up. Someone hijacked the plane. Billie's safe and got her people to meet her. Carmen's skipped out and didn't get paid."

"The thing is, we didn't have to pay her. We already had the route cleared a couple of days ago. Whatever Billie was paying for had nothing to do with the relief supplies. What is she keeping from me? I'm supposed to be her partner in this. Doesn't she trust me anymore?"

Parker could see Miguel's eyes downcast. His shoulders slumped. Parker knew it was more than about Billie and what she kept from him. Billie never revealed her cards.

What ate at Miguel, Parker knew, was the treatment he received by the arson investigator. The kid had seen it before and had certainly been profiled and tossed off as invisible at best and targeted for misplaced hate and blame solely for the color of his skin. That's a cumulative trauma, and God only knew how much he could carry on his shoulders.

"Billie's keeping secrets from me, too, and I get worried when she does. She kept the secret about having a kid—Armando—remember? She had her reasons, I get it. But she could have trusted us."

"I don't think she's got another kid out there this time. There's something about the way she was talking with Carmen. There's something—something like Billie was paying her—like she was being blackmailed."

"That would be in Carmen's wheelhouse."

"I don't know what Billie is trying to hide."

Linda pulled into the parking garage at the sheriff's office. Parker hadn't even thought about where they were headed, and he noticed the furrowed brow on Linda. The drive-by shooting, the firebombing attack at the offices where Billie and Miguel worked.

"I told Leon to meet us here—in your office. I'd feel better with the boys here while we do what we have to do in Fountain Hills."

Parker nodded. She was way ahead of him.

"Good thinking. Barry should be waiting for us, and he's been working on finding out who Ridler is and what's his play with this Red Dawn business. Miguel and Leon can camp in my office."

"I can help," Miguel said as he unstrapped his seat belt.

"You can help—the both of you. I need to make sure nothing happens to you. I can't focus on what we have to do up in Fountain Hills, if I'm worried about you."

"I'm not a little kid anymore."

"I know, but you're my son, and I get to worry about you."

Miguel's lip quivered.

Linda opened her door, and the desert heat swept inside. "Could we have Leon and Miguel do a little informal research? Kind of off the books?"

Parker stepped from the passenger seat, and he was stiff from crashing his SUV into the airport hangar. "What are you thinking?" He knew the boys couldn't be officially involved in the investigation. Having them decrypt the USB drive Agent Thompson gave him was enough of a stretch. The drive. They were concerned about the drive and triggering any tracking code hidden in the device.

"There might be something we need you and Leon to handle. You two are way more tech-savvy than me. Is there a way to use the USB drive you guys looked at to set off every alarm bell and warning she had installed in it?" Parker asked.

"I thought that's what we were trying to avoid," Miguel said.

"It was then, but I think we need Agent Thompson's attention now."

Chapter Sixty-Three

Leon was waiting in Parker's outer office, talking with Barry. They were both looking at the computer screen.

"Barry, Linda, my office. Let's map out our plan and what we'll need for Fountain Hills."

Parker huddled with the two boys for a moment. They both listened to him intently, nodding along as he spoke.

"Can you do it?" he asked them.

Leon was the first to pipe up. "Yeah. It's possible, but we were careful not to trigger any of the code that would backtrace or trip an alarm. We want to do it now?" His brow furrowed.

"But not until I tell you. Got it?"

"Yeah, yeah. It's going to get attention from whoever's watching this thing."

"That's the idea."

"Oh, okay. Where do you want us to work?"

"How about my office after we leave?"

The boys both nodded.

Parker joined Linda and Barry in his office. After Linda got Barry up to date on Quentin Ridler, and Parker revealed Ridler might have been on the scene of the first body drop under the name of Dryden, the tall detective smirked.

"Huh, fits with what I found on Ridler. Which is basically a blank slate until less than a year, year-and-a-half ago. The name first popped up in the Asian financial markets when Ridler began buying up foreign debt held by

Chinese and Indian governments. Some of the debt was in Mexico, Central America, and here in the U.S. What's interesting is most of the recent action is American debt. Ridler's acquisitions focused in on one company?"

"Let me guess? Visman's water projects."

"The same. The timing fits with what we know about his daughter going missing. Not long after, Ridler buys up over ten million in debt in Visman's business."

"Why would he take on Visman's debt?" Linda asked.

"He does, and he can call it due at any time. Visman doesn't have the pocket change lying around to fight a takeover."

"It would bankrupt him," Linda said.

Parker paced behind his desk.

"It's great leverage if he knows his daughter is alive. Maybe force Visman to broker a deal."

It hit him as he thought out loud.

"That's exactly what he's doing. He's forcing an exchange. His daughter for Visman's stepdaughter."

"But, Ridler's daughter wasn't kidnapped. She ran off with Blake Visman," Linda said.

Barry shifted forward in his chair. "When did Ridler know? I mean, he went all scorched Earth on the cartel, thinking they were behind her disappearance."

Parker started putting the pieces together. Barry was right. Ridler went at the cartel for abducting his daughter. It was the kind of action Pimentel's people had developed a reputation for carrying out—snatch and grab of rich tourists.

In reality, Blake Visman had flown down to meet her.

It should have been easy to establish the fact she hadn't been abducted but had run off with her boyfriend. Why couldn't Ridler, with his resources, uncover that simple fact?

Agent Thompson. She was with Ridler at the Immigrant Coalition offices, and Miguel's observations put her directing the assault. She was influencing Ridler—telling him the Sinaloa Cartel was responsible for his daughter's disappearance. It wouldn't be too much to believe she convinced Ridler the coalition played a role in stealing her away from Hermosillo and spread the lies to force Ridler to move against the cartel. It was actually kind of brilliant.

"We need to get to Fountain Hills. Ridler knows he's been played."

Linda and Barry set out to the open office to gather their gear for the encounter. What does one wear to a formal fundraising event where both parties wanted to kill one another?

Leon poked his head above the monitor, and a worried look spread over his face. When Barry pulled a shotgun from a weapons locker, the boy stiffened.

"Mom? Is everything okay"

Linda came to him and rubbed his shoulder. We're taking precautions. They won't be focused on us, they'll be after each other. Ridler and Visman each have something the other wants."

"The two women? The one Miguel saw at the offices—the kidnapped daughter?" Leon said.

"Looks like it. Except—there was no kidnapping, was there?" Miguel said.

Linda tilted her head and furrowed her brow. "No. But, how did you—"

Leon tapped the monitor. "The number. The number."

The monitor was filled with lines of letters, numbers, and symbols.

"What are we looking at?" Parker said as he stepped in with a ballistic vest in hand.

"That's what I'm asking, too."

"The number." Leon huffed and tapped a line on the monitor. There. It's a phone number."

"I'll take your word for it," Parker said.

"You don't remember the number?"

Parker shrugged in response.

"This phone number gets an alert triggered by accessing the USB drive. The listening device? This was where the signal would go. And the geolocation data."

"Whoever had the phone could listen and track where we were when the drive was operational?"

Leon nodded. "But the number. It's one we used."

"One of ours?" Barry asked as he stacked his ballistic vest on a nearby desk.

"We used that number to track Agent Metzger out to Coyote Wash," Leon said.

Whoever used the phone manipulated Parker, Johns, and Tully to lure them out to the remote location. It was a setup, and it was more elaborate than Parker thought.

"The phone belonged to the task force member who claimed to have been in a relationship with Thompson," Parker said.

"The Marshal's Service guy, Compton," Linda said.

"Right. Good recall."

Parker pulled his cell phone out and tapped a speed dial button.

"Agent Finch, please?"

He noticed Linda stiffen slightly.

"Yes, Delores, it's Nathan. It's urgent."

Parker pulled the phone to his chest for a moment and closed his eyes. He didn't need to hear the litany of excuses why Lynne shouldn't take his call.

"Delores. Delores. Tell Lynne to find one of the task force members on Agent Thompson's team. Compton. Deputy Marshal Compton. He's compromised."

Parker disconnected the call and tossed the phone on the desk, harder than he intended.

"Will Lynnette get the message?" Linda said.

"I don't know. We can't wait to find out. Let's get moving."

Barry and Linda gathered their vests and handheld radios with fresh batteries from the charging rack.

Parker leaned to Miguel and Leon.

"Great work. When I text you, Miguel, can you guys make that thing light up with everything it's worth?"

"Oh yeah," Miguel said. "Want to give them something special to listen to?"

Parker grinned. "That's my boy. Make it memorable for them."

"Count on it."

Chapter Sixty-Four

Parker and Linda piled in one SUV. Barry followed with two deputies, the Watch Commander freed up from the department's tactical team.

Linda had fallen silent.

"Nervous? That's okay, you know? If you aren't, I'd worry."

"No. I mean, yeah, I've never been on an operation like this. I'm anxious about what we're walking into."

Parker sped up the steep incline from the valley floor toward Fountain Hills.

"I sense a 'but' coming," he said.

"You have Lynne on speed dial."

That was the reason for the stern look back at the office.

"Yeah. We work a lot of cases together."

"Is that what you're working?"

His hands gripped the wheel.

"What? You think Lynne and I are—you notice how she hasn't rushed to call me back?"

"Do you want her to call you back?"

He twisted in the seat to face her. "Where is this coming from, Linda?"

She fell silent once more.

Parker felt a surge of guilt mixed with anger. What had he done, or what did Linda think he'd done? He didn't have time to deal with this.

"Dammit, Lynne. I don't need this right now. We need to focus on this takedown."

"Linda."

"What?"

"You said, Lynne. I'm Linda, remember?"

Parker gripped the wheel tighter. His knuckles turned bone white.

"What the hell brought this on, Linda?"

"Do you want to be with me?"

"Of course I do. What would make you ask?"

"I need to be sure of where we're going—"

"I asked you to move in with me, remember? The offer is on the table, you know?"

"I know I'm the one who put that aside before."

"Before? Like in you might change your mind, now?"

She shrugged.

"Linda, what's going on?"

She took a deep breath. "I think—I think I'm pregnant."

Parker slammed on the brakes and swerved the SUV to the shoulder of the roadway.

"You're what? Really?"

"I took a test this morning. So maybe."

Parker grinned. "How do you feel about it?"

"I-I don't know. I'm so confused. I'm thirty-five years old. I'm considered a geriatric pregnancy."

Parker chuckled.

"That's not funny, mister."

"It is a little. I'm going to be a father?"

"Does it scare you?"

"No, yes, maybe a little. I never thought it would happen."

"Because you didn't want it?"

"No. I never thought I would be lucky to find someone like you to raise a child with."

Barry trotted up to the driver's window and tapped on the glass. Parker lowered it, and Barry tried to make sense of the red-eyed Linda and grinning Parker.

"What's up? We have intel on the exchange?"

"I'm gonna be a dad."

Barry leaned into the window, ducking his head to see Linda. She looked at him and nodded.

"Well, damn that was quick work. Never even saw the SUV swerve on the way up here."

"I think it's been longer than that." Parker turned to Linda. "How far along are you?"

"Couple of weeks."

"Congrats," Barry said. He glanced up the hill toward the Fountain Hills community.

A dark helicopter swooped in low over the hilltops, coming in from the south.

"We have a welcoming committee. Any bet it's Ridler?"

Barry ran back to his SUV, and Parker put his vehicle in gear and pulled back out onto the road.

"I'm gonna be a dad." He grinned.

"You're not upset? This is going to change everything, you know?"

"Sure is. You okay with this? With me?" he asked, as he reached out for her hand.

She nodded. "I was worried you wouldn't want anything to do with it, or me."

He squeezed her hand softly. That bastard of an ex-husband must have really done a number on her. To make a woman feel afraid—vulnerable—and dependent on his approval and control. Parker would love to get his hands on the creep.

"We're getting close to the compound. I want that vest on you, and you're staying with the SUV."

"I can do my job," she said.

"No doubt. And your job will be to manage communications between dispatch, FBI's HRT, and seal our perimeter."

"FBI? You think Delores will pass on your message?"

"She got grudge-holding down to a science, but loyal to her boss. Lynne will get the message, even if it's something like, 'That no good detective called again.' I feel certain we'll have a response once she gets the message about the meetup and compromised task force member."

"That's a lot to hang your hat on."

"You might be right."

The gate at the Visman compound was open, and high-end cars lined the side of the road. Two young men in red vests scurried from car to car, handing a valet receipt to the occupants. To a person, everyone stepping from a Range Rover, Bentley, or Jaguar seemed decked out in their black-tie social best.

Parker pulled to a stop at the far end of the drive, with Barry on his tail. One of the red-vested valets trotted to Parker's door and was about to tuck a yellow valet ticket under the wiper when he spotted the ballistic vests with the bright yellow MCSO patch on the front.

"We're gonna self-park," Parker said.

"Barry, you're with me. You two," Parker pointed at the two deputies, "Go around back. If anyone asks, we're here for additional security. Linda, keep a channel open to dispatch in the event things turn ugly. You're going to be in position to monitor the entrance. Let us know if Ridler, Agent Thompson, or anyone who looks like a cartel hitter shows up."

She nodded.

"You think the cartel has a hand to play in this?" Barry asked.

"They might. Pimentel and the Cartel are hurting from Red Dawn pushing the cartel out of their usual territory. It wouldn't be beyond them to exact a little revenge."

"Would explain those two cartel hitters we found in Chandler. They weren't working for Ridler. They were waiting for him," Barry said.

Parker replayed the conversation with the cartel assassin over in his mind. Something didn't match what the man said when he put it up against Pimentel's statement. The Sinaloa Cartel boss hadn't mentioned cross-border attacks. It had been defensive actions, blending cartels against a common enemy in Mexico. Sending hit squads north didn't fit with the cartel's reluctance to make enemies on this side of the border.

Powerful enemies could threaten their grip on the cartel's economic engine—trafficking drugs and people.

"You see anyone who looks shady, let us know," Parker said.

They agreed on a radio channel, and Parker inserted his earpiece and checked the radio was secure on his load-bearing tactical vest.

"Let's go crash a party."

Chapter Sixty-Five

Parker and Barry strode through the open front door into a full-scale formal cocktail party. Blake's memorial service was merely a dry run for the important task of extracting donations from the rich and powerful in Arizona. Waitstaff in crisp black uniforms passed through the crowd with trays of hors d'oeuvres. One came near the detectives, and Parker couldn't figure out what was on the serving tray.

Barry leaned in. "Whatever happened to old-fashioned pigs in a blanket?"

One of the society matrons nearby overheard Barry's comment and scowled.

Parker nodded out across the open living area to the windows in the back. At the edge of an enormous expanse of green lawn, a black helicopter sat parked, with one man tending to the aircraft. Lawn in this part of the desert was a display of wealth and power. A few miles away in the Guad, people could barely afford water.

If Ridler arrived by helicopter, he was already inside the building.

He tipped his head down the hall to the library where Mr. and Mrs. Visman held court at the son's memorial service.

The large wooden double doors were closed. The two massive men who stood blocking the entry reinforced the message no one was getting in.

They both wore black sports coats over black shirts to provide a menacing vibe. The bulge at their right hip told they weren't about to put up with anyone who tried to get past them.

"The guy on the right just clocked us. We don't exactly fit in," Barry said.

"I think it was you asking for pigs in a blanket. I mean, really—read the room."

"They are a classic."

Parker pulled his cell out and tapped out a text.

"Let's see if Miguel and Leon can give us the distraction we're looking for," Parker said.

Parker hit send, and within seconds, the library doors flew open and another pair of musclebound hulks pushed through. There was the unmistakable sound of loud K-pop music coming from cell phones in the library and in the living room.

The two door guardians had orders from someone inside and ran after the other bodyguards to the back of the residence.

"Leon got creative."

Parker keyed his microphone. "Be advised, we have activity in the rear of the home. Four armed men heading that way."

"Ten-four," was the reply from one deputy near the building's rear exit.

Parker and Barry trotted to the library door and peeked inside.

Kingston Visman sat in his chair, but the one opposite him was empty.

"What is the meaning of this, Detective? This is a private affair."

"Where's Ridler?" Parker asked.

"He isn't here yet." The man's Adam's apple bounced as he spoke. He was definitely spooked.

"Isn't his helicopter out back?"

"I don't know what you're talking about."

"Where's Mrs. Visman?"

The man swallowed hard. His eyes shot to the left.

Parker pulled his weapon from the holster at his hip and held it in a low, ready position. Barry did the same but faced the door to cover anyone coming in behind them.

The K-pop music blared from beyond the door.

Parker edged closer with one hand on the doorknob and the other gripping his Glock.

He pressed the door open, and a wide-eyed Victoria Visman stared back at him. Restrained to a chair with zip ties and a scarf stuffed in her mouth, the woman's glance kept shifting to another door.

Parker kept the muzzle of his weapon trained on the threat on the far side of the door. As he approached Victoria Visman, he yanked the scarf from her mouth.

"Ridler?"

"No. No. It was a woman. She was going to hurt me. Please let me go."

"We will, Mrs. Visman. Right now, I need you to stay right here."

"Untie me!"

Parker wanted to stuff the scarf back in the woman's mouth.

"Quiet! You want her coming back in here? I'm going to cut you loose, but I want you and Mr. Visman to lock yourselves in the library. Can you do that?"

She nodded.

Parker used his free hand and pulled a folding knife from a pocket in his load-bearing vest. Flicking it open, he stepped behind her and sliced the bindings.

She started to scurry to the library, and Parker held her quivering arm.

"The woman who tied you up. Describe her," he said.

"Dark hair, tall, and spoke with a heavy accent—Spanish. With a great big gun."

Parker shook his head. "Go. Lock yourself in."

While not a great description, Parker felt it in his gut. Carmen Delgado was here. What was she doing? Carmen was with Billie in Hermosillo. Did Billie know that snake was headed to Fountain Hills?

Parker keyed his microphone. "Carmen Delgado is here—armed."

He trained his weapon at the door Carmen used. As gently as possible, Parker lifted the lever and, rather than the closet or hallway, the door opened directly into the living room.

The open space teemed with party donors. Parker estimated fifty black-tie frocked couples in the room. There was a podium and microphone at one end of the room, waiting for Kingston Visman to address them and collect their checks. At the rate they were putting away the appetizers and prosecco, Visman better hurry.

Parker's eye caught one man standing at the rear of the room. Slim back suit. Close-cropped hair and no beard. Ken Dryden had cleaned up since the crossroads.

Dryden, or Ridler as he was known to Visman's crowd, didn't seem interested in the party atmosphere, and he certainly wasn't here to make a donation.

Ridler stiffened when he spotted Parker in his black and yellow vest.

The man turned his head away and stepped away from the wall into the crowd.

"Eyes on Ridler. Living room, black suit."

"Everyone's wearing a black suit," Barry responded.

"He's heading your way, Barry, toward the front entrance."

Parker drew a few dismissive glances as he waded into the crowd. A woman in a sequined gown tried to pass him her empty glass.

Ridler was ten feet ahead of him, waving his way through the crowd. Ridler stepped up from the sunken living room to the foyer.

"Barry, see him?"

"Got it."

Barry emerged from the right at the far end of the foyer. Parker weaved through the crowd toward Ridler when motion to his left caught his attention.

Carmen Delgado spotted Ridler as she stepped from the crowd to his left. His expression, Parker judged, was one of recognition, but there was a wariness hidden below the surface.

Carmen hooked Ridler by the arm and pulled him close to her. I would have seemed intimate except for the small black handgun she held against his side with her free hand.

She propelled Ridler to the front door after whispering in his ear. Carmen was here to do what the cartel hitmen failed to finish.

"Linda, they're coming your way. Do not engage."

Barry and Parker fell in behind them without Carmen acknowledging their presence, some twenty feet behind.

Carmen and her unwilling companion stepped through the heavy front door. The moment it closed behind them, Parker and Barry hurried to the entrance.

Before he reached for the door, two gunshots rang out in quick succession.

Parker shoved the door aside.

Linda lay sprawled on the ground near the SUV.

Chapter Sixty-Six

"Oh, God," Parker rushed to Linda.

A moan rose from the left. Carmen was down.

"I'll get Delgado," Barry said.

Parker rushed to Linda and looked for the gunshot wound. She stirred beneath him.

"I-I think I got her," Linda said as she tried to catch her breath.

"You did. Where were you hit? Are you okay?"

"She flopped a hand to her chest. It's hard to breathe."

Parker ran a hand over the plate carrier for the ballistic vest, and his fingertip caught on a small hole. He tore the Velcro tabs off the side of the vest and lifted the protective layer.

"It didn't go through. The plates stopped it."

"It doesn't feel like it." The breath was coming easier now. She rubbed the spot on the upper right side of her chest.

Parker helped her to a sitting position, leaning against the SUV.

She spied Barry cuffing Carmen across the courtyard.

"Is she?"

"She's alive."

"It happened fast. She and Ridler came out, and once she spotted me, she raised her arm and shot. She must have already had the gun in her hand. I couldn't see it, until..."

"She did. She was holding it against Ridler when she forced him outside."

"I should have used cover behind the SUV—"

"Enough for now. You did the right thing. Did you see where Ridler

318

went?"

Linda pointed around the corner of the home. "When she spun around on me, he split around back."

Parker keyed the radio and directed the deputies at the rear of the residence to secure the helicopter. Ridler had unfinished business here, and Kingston Visman was inside.

"Can you get up?"

She extended her arm, and Parker helped her up. He couldn't help but hug her when she got to her feet. "Are you okay?"

"I'm fine. Shaken up a bit, but I'm good."

"Hey, boss, I called in for an ambulance and another uniformed deputy to take this one to the hospital for medical clearance before booking."

"Is she—she gonna be okay?" Linda asked.

"Yeah, you winged her. Left shoulder."

Carmen's eyes flashed at Parker when Barry rolled her over.

"It's been a while, Carmen."

"You're a pig."

"Nice to know you remember me. It was a risk coming back here over the border. You know you have warrants out up here—from us and the feds. Was Ridler worth getting caught?"

Anger radiated from the woman whom Barry helped to her feet. She glared at Parker. The last time he saw that look, she was the sheriff's office public information officer, accusing him of murder. It wasn't until much later he discovered the truth. Carmen was working with Esteban Castaneda to set him up.

Parker paused as the puzzle piece fell into place. Carmen's actions had felt off. She was connected with the Sinaloa Cartel and was Joaquin Pimentel's off-and-on girlfriend. Though listening to the cartel boss, she was not in favor at the moment. Was she working to get back into the cartel boss's good graces? Carmen was always working an angle. A flash came to Parker. She was working one again.

"You knew the Cartel didn't take Ridler's daughter."

"What does it matter?"

"It matters because you convinced Ridler the cartel was responsible. You knew he would spare no expense and use his private army to dismantle the cartel's operations and network. He would do anything to find his daughter, but you knew the cartel didn't take her."

A smirk graced her lips. "What Joaquin has is rightfully mine. Ridler was a pawn."

"He weakened the cartel. But you don't have the power to take control."

"Don't be sure, you've underestimated me before."

Parker wasn't sure how much was bluff or if there was a thread of truth running through the river of lies.

"What I do know is you wanted Ridler out of the way before he realized his vendetta against the cartel was your manipulation."

Carmen sat silently and huffed.

"Barry, you got this? Linda, are you up to shutting down Visman's party?"
She nodded.

"By policy, we should bench you after the shoot. But, I'm deeming this as an ongoing incident with the lives of dozens of citizens at risk."

"I understand. I'll put in my time with professional standards and ATO after this is done."

Parker led them back inside the home, where the two gunshots must have been muffled enough to keep the festive atmosphere going.

The two musclebound thugs were back in front of the library door again.

Parker realized they weren't Visman's people, but Ridler's men. Both had a mercenary feel to them. Big, tough, and the scars to prove they'd seen it before.

The two mercs turned as Parker and Linda approached.

"You're Ridler's people, right. Tell your boss we need a minute."

"He's busy. Doesn't want to be disturbed."

Check. They'd confirmed they were Ridler's security, and he was in the room with Visman.

"Listen, it's over for your boss. He's backed himself into a corner. If you do have any shred of loyalty to the guy, go find the two Sinaloa Cartel hitters who are hiding in the crowd."

Parker played on the image Billie had painted at the airstrip outside Hermosillo. Carmen put two people on the flight north. She must have arrived separately.

The two gunmen looked at one another, and Parked sensed a crack in their resistance.

"Find them, remember there are people here who have no dog in this fight. No collateral damage," Parker said.

One thug elbowed the other, and they stalked away from their post toward the living room.

"You think there are cartel hitmen hidden in the room?" Linda asked.

Parker shrugged. "It's possible. But if they were here, they would have been working against Carmen. She might have already neutralized them."

"You think she's capable of that?" she asked as she rubbed the spot on her chest where Carmen's bullet hit. "Never mind."

Parker pushed the door open and entered.

Kingston Visman leaned uncomfortably in one chair, with Ridler opposite him. Victoria Visman slouched in a small club chair, exhausted from her ordeal.

"Gentlemen, I hate to interrupt your meeting."

"Detective, he has my daughter," Ridler said. "We are negotiating an exchange—of sorts."

Parker spotted the small semi-automatic pistol on the end stand within reach of Ridler's right hand. Negotiations were about to become complicated.

Chapter Sixty-Seven

Parker kept his weapon trained on Ridler while Barry swept in from behind and removed the firearm from the table.

"Let's put these negotiations on an equal footing," Parker said.

"These people stole my only child and kept her from me," Ridler said.

"Christine wasn't taken. She wanted away from you. Overbearing, controlling, you treated her like a possession," Kingston Visman said.

"You were responsible for taking her. Your son lured her away."

"And now he's dead!"

"That was not my doing."

"I don't believe you."

"What you believe doesn't change the fact my son is dead."

Victoria Visman whimpered in the club chair behind her husband. She displayed more emotion here than Parker noted at Blake's memorial service.

"I believe Ridler is telling you the truth," Parker said. "Two Sinaloa Cartel hitters were responsible for Blake's death."

"The Cartel? No. That can't be. It was him and his Red Dawn fanatics." Visman pointed a stiff finger at Ridler.

"The cartel believed you and Ridler were conspiring to move against them. So they needed to act."

"Why would they think I would have anything to do with him?"

"It wouldn't take too much convincing. The money trail. His daughter working at your project in Hermosillo. And he's bought up most of your debt."

"That's impossible. The cartel can't believe I'd—you—you bought up the foundation's debt?"

Ridler nodded. "I now hold a shareholder proxy giving me a majority stake in the organization."

Visman turned white.

"Give me my daughter," Ridler said.

Visman leaned back in his chair. Parker could sense a shift happening.

"I have conditions."

"You aren't in a position to demand anything."

"You have my stepdaughter, Kira. A one-for-one exchange."

"I don't have any control over your stepdaughter. She's free to do as she wishes. She's a full-grown FBI agent and can do as she wishes."

Parker cleared his throat. "Speaking of Agent Thompson. Care to explain why the two of you burned the Immigrant Coalition offices?"

"That organization helped steal my daughter and take her away."

Parker shook his head. "They had no part in it. But I think I know where you got the idea they did—Carmen Delgado. Am I right?"

Ridler stiffened. Even though the woman had pulled a gun on him minutes ago, Ridler was only now seeing the depths of Carmen's betrayal. Parker saw the man's posture slump with uncertainty.

"She also told you the cartel was responsible for abducting your daughter, right?"

Ridler's jaw gaped with the realization everything he'd done—everything he sacrificed for, killed for—was based on a lie.

"Why? What reason would she have to deceive me?" The tone was pleading and weak. There was confusion behind his eyes.

"It wasn't only her, was it? Agent Thompson confirmed the story the Cartel was behind the kidnapping, too. That makes sense now. You were being played, and they counted on you attacking the cartel and weakening their organization."

"To what end?"

"Carmen wants the cartel."

"Where is she? My daughter?" Visman asked.

Parker tapped his earpiece. "She's here."

323

"Here? She's supposed to be in Tucson."

Lynne Finch and an HRT member dressed in black tactical gear with an MP5 rifle slung across his chest entered the library.

"Glad you could make it, Lynne," Parker said.

Linda watched with an artfully concealed side eye.

"Got your message—it got delayed in transit."

Parker knew Delores must not have bothered to pass on the message right away.

"Better late than never."

"We've got Agent Kira Thompson in custody along with two known cartel gunmen. They had enough firepower to take down this building and everyone in it. They were a half mile out."

Another HRT member escorted Christine Ridler into the library. Quentin Ridler relaxed at the sight of his daughter.

"Chrissy, are you hurt?"

"How can you even ask me that? Blake is dead. Because you want control over everything, including me."

"That wasn't me."

"It is because of you. If you weren't consumed with power, taking over organizations you want to crush, none of this would have happened."

"The cartel did this, not me?"

"You were ready to hear it. Once you thought it was the cartel, you couldn't wait to take over their territory."

"You can't believe that. I was looking for you. No one was going to get in my way."

Christine blinked. "You only want me back under your control."

Parker turned to the young woman. "Where did you get the idea that your father wasn't actually looking for you, but was more interested in stealing you back and punishing anyone who helped you?"

She blinked twice.

"It was Carmen Delgado, wasn't it?"

"She said I needed to hide from him. Promised me Blake and I would be safe up north."

"She lied. Carmen set up the hit on Blake. Carmen set up most of this to strip power away from the cartel. She knew your father would tear through Mexico until he found you. She even lured him up here with threats you were killed. Isn't that right, Ridler?"

He nodded. "That's when we met for the first time on the crossroad. Carmen told me I'd find my daughter there. When I saw those remains, the ones they tossed from the airplane. I thought I lost her forever."

"I think it's time we break up this family reunion," Parker said.

HRT and responding sheriff's deputies took Ridler into custody.

Parker knew the case for obstruction was thin on Kingston Visman, but he didn't balk when Lynne directed her team to put him in cuffs.

When the dust cleared and the potential donors evaporated along with their checkbooks, only Victoria Visman and Christine Ridler remained behind. Victoria's glare at the young woman was enough to force Christine to leave the room. Victoria blamed her for Blake's death.

Lynne and the feds left, and Barry was coordinating transportation for Visman, Ridler, Carmen, Thompson, and the two cartel hitters. "I need a bus, but I gotta keep these guys separated. Carmen's already threatened Ridler."

When Linda and Parker were alone in front of the home, he glanced back at the mansion, which now felt shallow and artificial.

"Think Victoria's going to sell the place?"

"I think she'll have to. If the foundation was in debt and the projects are done, she won't have a choice. Why, thinking about making a bid?"

"Please. I couldn't afford the electric bill in this place. Although, I might have to start looking for a bigger place." His eyes flicked down to her flat belly.

She blushed.

"Let's check you out and make sure everything is okay."

She nodded, and they headed for the SUV.

Parker felt the need for one more look back at the house. In a window on the second floor. Christine Ridler looked out. The young woman looked small, lost, and unsure.

"Think she'll be okay?" Linda asked.

"I don't know. She's got a lot of betrayal to swallow. Her life just got complicated.

"She's not the only one."

Chapter Sixty-Eight

Ridler and Visman immediately lawyered up when they hit the interrogation room. Visman looked discouraged when Larry Sutton refused to represent him. Parker wasn't surprised. After all, the cartel's attorney wouldn't represent the man they had sent hit squads to take out.

Parker was also certain Sutton would let Pimentel know how Carmen had worked against him.

Speaking of Carmen Delgado, she didn't look comfortable in the interrogation room of the department she had once served. The former public information officer, the conduit to the news media, now took a turn on the other side of the table, shoulder in a sling and her free hand cuffed to a stainless-steel eye bolt on the edge of the table.

Parker entered and sat in a chair opposite her. He didn't say anything.

Her dark hair cascaded over her shoulder and partially covered her face. But from what Parker could see from her tight jaw, the pulse in her neck, and rapid breathing, Carmen was fuming.

"You'll never see me in a courtroom, you know that, don't you, detective?"

"I think my odds are pretty good. Better than yours, I'd imagine."

"You've bet against me before and lost."

Parker read her Miranda rights from a laminated card.

"You waive your right to an attorney? Wanna talk?"

She shrugged. "Sure. It won't matter."

"What made you set this in motion? Get Ridler to take on the Sinaloa Cartel?"

"Joaquin is weak. More interested in making peace deals with Los Zetas and Juarez than taking what rightfully belongs to him. Ridler was a means to an end. Obsessive, driven, and filthy rich. Take something that belongs to him—like his daughter—there's nothing he wouldn't do to get his possession back. That's what Christine was to him. A thing. A possession."

"You got him to believe the cartel nabbed her?"

She shrugged. That was the simple part. Getting the FBI agent to turn on her family was a little more challenging. No love lost with stepdaddy. But when I got her to believe her brother, Blake, was flying cartel players over here and Kingston was paying for it, well, let's say she saw the light."

"And a way to put your hands on Kingston's money. I mean, Ridler must have promised her a piece of the action."

She nodded.

"You never thought Joaquin would wise up to what you were doing? You set up the boss of the Sinaloa Cartel to lose everything. You had to know he'd find out."

Carmen shrugged. "He'd never expect a woman to outsmart him. By the time he figured it out, it would be too late." She paused and straightened as much as she could. "Have you figured it out, Detective?"

Not much to figure out if you ask me. You went against the cartel and lost."

"Did I?"

She laughed and rattled her cuffs. "Esteban sends you his best. He says, we'll be seeing you soon."

She laughed again, and a chill ran down Parker's spine. Even though Castaneda was locked away in a Colorado Supermax prison, and Carmen was looking at years behind bars, the threat made him wince, which was exactly what Castaneda wanted.

Parker stood and turned to leave.

"Ask your friend Billie what she bought from me in Hermosillo. In exchange for letting her supplies through."

Another sinister laugh.

Parker left and closed the interrogation room door harder than he needed.

In the next room, soon-to-be ex-FBI agent Kira Thompson was being questioned by Lynne and another agent from the DC Field Office.

Parker entered. "Mind if I sit in?"

The DC man's eyes shifted to Lynne along with a shrug.

Lynne nodded and continued with her line of questioning.

"You're telling me Red Dawn never existed?"

"It didn't then. It does now. Red Dawn spawned from the paid mercenaries Ridler bought to search for his daughter. At first, it was search and rescue. As he became more desperate, the private military contractors met more resistance and started fighting back. And winning. The legends and stories started to spread. They started to believe their own press."

"And became a criminal organization?" Lynne said.

"Something the Sinaloa Cartel feared."

"When did you first contact Ridler?"

"We needed him to keep pushing at the cartels, taking their territory and resources. I met with him south of Hermosillo and fed him fake intel about sightings of his daughter."

"You knew the cartel wasn't behind the girl's disappearance."

"Of course. We knew she'd developed a relationship with Blake Visman. We had an eye on her as a high-visibility American citizen in the area. Blake would regularly fly down over the border on his bro-ventures. He got caught with some underage girls and enough fentanyl to spend a decade in a Mexican prison.

We came to his rescue and got him released with a promise he'd resume his cross-border trips and take Christine north."

Parker had a bad feeling forming in his gut. Thompson was too casual and flippant as she recounted her interactions with Ridler and the origin of Red Dawn as a criminal organization.

"When did you begin to falsify your reports to the bureau?" Lynne asked.

Instead of the denial, Parker expected to hear, Thompson admitted deceiving her DC handlers.

"After Ridler's private army made progress pushing back cartel strongholds, it occurred to me Red Dawn was doing what decades of our foreign policy couldn't do. We needed to support them, not rip it apart. My reports painted it as the usual cartel violence. Red Dawn was a new cartel making their place in the Mexican drug machine."

"But your task force team members figured out what you were doing. Carter, Rivers, and Metzger. They confronted you about the free pass you were giving to Red Dawn."

"I think this is the point where our immunity agreement ends," Thompson said.

Parker's guess had been right. Thompson managed an immunity agreement for her misdeeds, but it didn't cover the murder of federal agents.

"Lynne, what are you giving her in exchange for this?"

"It's important, Nathan. We need to know how deep this corruption goes. Who on the task force was involved in this?"

"You didn't answer the question, Lynne."

Lynne's leg bounced under the table. A sign she was anxious and afraid. She wasn't often afraid. Something bigger was going on here.

"The bureau wants this shut down quickly. In exchange for immunity for activities related to Red Dawn's activity in Mexico, Thompson agrees to fully debrief—"

"And she gets a free pass? She created a criminal organization. We don't know how many lives were lost in the process."

"Her activity related to Red Dawn in Mexico is off limits."

It struck Parker as strange Lynne emphasized "in Mexico" in her response. Her blue eyes never left Parker as she spoke.

Thompson wore a smug expression on the other side of the interview room.

Parker glanced at a text message on his cell phone.

"You about done with her?" Parker asked.

Lynne glanced to the man from the DC office, who nodded.

The FBI agents stood and gathered their files. Thompson also stood and prepared to leave.

"Thompson, you're not going anywhere," Parker said.

"What are you saying?" You heard them. I have immunity."

"Not for the arson at the immigrant coalition offices, and not for the attempted murder of Pete Tully. Ballistics came back on a shell you missed out there in the dark. Has your print on it."

"Agent Finch, order him to stand down and honor our immunity deal."

"I've found Nathan doesn't listen to my orders. Besides, our immunity deal related to criminal activity in Mexico. The two events he's talking about occurred domestically."

"But—"

Lynne nodded to Parker as they left the room. He stopped around the table and cuffed Thompson.

"You can't do this. You know who my father is?"

"Your stepfather, actually. The same man who you tried to financially ruin? That man?"

She sulked, but didn't pull away from Parker.

"Ex-cops don't have it easy in prison. I don't envy you the protective custody housing in your future. Maybe you and Carmen Delgado can share a cell."

Parker felt her stiffen as he escorted her out of the interrogation room.

Chapter Sixty-Nine

"It's a big day today," Linda said.

"Everything's big," he said, eyeing her slightly swollen belly."

Linda tossed a couch pillow at him.

"That's not what I meant, smart ass. Pete coming home is a big day."

Parker returned the pillow to the couch, out of her reach.

"He did great in rehab. He worked hard to recover motor function in his arm. That nerve damage was more than a little worrisome. The lung function is as good as it's going to get."

"He handled not being able to return to the department better than I thought he would." Linda said.

"Yeah, I expected Pete to be angry, or push back to try and prove he could do the job. He seemed to accept his medical retirement. When we started talking about it, I didn't think he'd settle into retirement mode."

"I think Janet might have had something to do with his acceptance."

"Bet you're right. We should get going if we're going to be there on time."

Parker helped Linda up. She wasn't that big yet. He looked at her and smiled.

"What?"

"You're beautiful."

"I bet you say that to all the chicks you knock up."

"Apparently," he said as he stepped in for a hug.

Parker felt something he hadn't known in months, years, really. Contentment. For as long as he could remember, there were always demons chasing after him, hiding in the shadows, ready to disrupt his life. McMillan's murder, almost losing Miguel to Los Muertos, Pete's shooting—it took a toll.

In the six months since arresting Thompson for the attempt on Pete's life, Parker felt a shift in his perspective. Bringing a new life into the world would do that. But he and Barry started attending a PTSD survivors' group of law enforcement types, all of whom experienced on-the-job trauma of one sort or another. The group thing wasn't something Parker warmed up to right away.

But he found there was a power in that group. A power he could draw upon when those nightmares appeared. He had recurring visits from the demons in his past, but they were less frequent and didn't hold the weight over him they once did.

"Miguel and Leon will meet us at Pete and Janet's," Linda said.

Those boys have been through so much," Parker said.

"Is Miguel still having nightmares about being trapped in the coalition offices?"

Parker nodded. "Flashbacks, yeah. It's going to take a while before he feels comfortable inside enclosed spaces. He sleeps on the couch sometimes. Says his room starts to close in on him."

"Maybe it'll be good for Miguel and Leon to get out around people," Linda said.

"Nice of them to invite them. Billie's going to be there, too. She was a little put off by the formal invite to Pete's, but he insisted she be there. Said he had something he was going to announce, and we needed to be there."

"That's dramatic," she said.

"Speaking of drama, try not to snap at anyone for trying to rub your belly."

"It's assault. Ask me first. It's just weird."

He laughed. "You're right. And you're barely showing."

"You always say the nicest things."

"I'm going to be in a car with you-it's self-preservation."

She backhanded him. "Let's get."

* * *

Twenty minutes later, they arrived at Pete and Janet's. Janet answered the door and greeted them with a big smile. She beamed at Linda. When it looked like Janet was going in for a tummy rub, Linda begged off to the bathroom.

"How's she doing?" Janet asked.

"Great—I think. We have another appointment with her doctor next week."

"You know if it's a boy or a girl?"

"No. We decided to go with the surprise."

"Come, come—Pete's on the patio."

"How's *he* doing?"

"It was a long road, but my Petey is good. Happy, and I'm glad to have him home."

Parker slipped an arm around her. "I bet you are, and we miss him."

"Hold that thought."

Parker craned his head around and noticed the smirk on her face.

They found Pete holding court in the backyard. He and Janet created a comfortable oasis with shade structures, misters, and native desert landscaping.

Miguel, Leon, Barry, Espi, and Billie were seated in chairs around a fire pit. It was too early for a fire, and it was going to be too warm for one. Miguel was comfortable with the lack of flames from the fire pit. It'd been a slow recovery for him as well. The feeling of being trapped in a burning building would be with the kid for a while.

"Good to see you home, Pete." Parker gave him a pat on the good shoulder.

"I know I've said it before. Thanks to you and Barry for what you did that night."

Parker nodded, and Barry lifted an amber beer bottle at Pete.

"You'd have done the same," Barry said.

"Maybe not after you hear what I've got to say."

Linda joined the rest of them on the patio.

"If it's not the little mother," Pete said.

"Do you want to go back in the hospital?" she said.

334

Parker motioned Linda to an empty chair next to him.

"Is it true the District Attorney isn't going to prosecute anyone for the death of the old couple—the Cortez family? That's a damn shame."

"Or the deaths of the three task force members. There isn't enough evidence to say who killed them. The two Los Zeta's killers admitted offing Blake Visman after he dropped them off. The confession from one of the hitters won't be enough to get a conviction. They've clammed up tight."

Parker caught Billie staring down at her beer bottle where a nervous finger had peeled the label from the glass.

"We got Thompson on the arson at the coalition headquarters. I know she's good for winging you. I wish we had found something out there at Coyote Wash to take to a DA. "

"What's this big announcement that got us out here. I'm hungry," Barry said.

"You have a tapeworm," Pete said.

Parker leaned to Linda. "I miss this."

"All right. Here it is. I've applied for my private investigator's license."

"You what?" Barry said.

"I'm gonna be a PI."

"You just medically retired, Pete," Parker said.

"I checked with personnel and as long as I'm not a peace officer, which they said I can't be, I'm good."

"A PI? As in a gumshoe?" Barry said again.

"I have a little left in the tank. The firm I'm gonna be working with will have me on desk duty—no field stuff—at least for now."

"Or ever," Janet said.

"What investigation firm you going to be working with?" Parker asked.

"It's an attorney."

"What attorney? Tell me it's not Larry Sutton."

"He's gonna pay me a lot."

"You know what he's about—"

"And he told me I'm not going to be involved in anything shady. Nothing smacking of his criminal defense work. He's starting a skip trace and missing persons deal. The whole bit with Ridler's daughter going missing must have struck a nerve."

"I don't trust that guy completely."

Or at all, Parker thought. There was a shady angle in this new endeavor, and he hoped Pete wasn't signing up as a fall guy.

"Be careful, Pete."

"I'm goin' in with my eyes open."

He shifted to Barry. "Since you're hungry, go start the grill."

"About damn time. If I heard the doctors have you on some healthy diet, it wouldn't be the worst news."

Billie's cell phone chirped, and she got up and strolled away from the fire pit.

"Miguel, what's eating at Billie?" Parker asked.

"I dunno. She's been like this since she came back from Hermosillo."

"Problems with the operation down there?"

"Not that I know of," Miguel said.

Parker's mind conjured up an image of Billie and Carmen in deep conversation at the airport near Hermosillo. Parker had an idea what had her torn.

Chapter Seventy

Parker followed Billie inside, where she leaned against the kitchen counter.

"What's got you out of sorts, Billie?"

"I'm good."

"No, you aren't. What's eating at you? Even Miguel's noticed."

She flicked her eyes up at Parker.

"I don't know where to go with the Coalition. We got no offices, people don't got nowhere to go. I'm stuck."

"I get that. There's more to it, isn't there? This has to do with whatever you and Carmen agreed to down in Hermosillo."

Parker knew he struck a nerve when Billie couldn't make eye contact.

"Are you in trouble, Billie?"

"No. Yeah. Maybe. Hell, I don't even know."

"What did you and Carmen talk about down there?"

"I made a deal with her."

"For what?"

"For proof of who shot Pete Tully."

"What are you saying? "

"Carmen gave me the rifle used out there. Said Thompson's prints were on it on account of her takin' the shot. The shot Carmen told her to take."

Billie fell silent.

"If it comes out at trial, Thompson's going to ask how you got your hands on this evidence? It's not exactly on the up and up," Parker said.

"She won't. I just got this text." She handed her phone to Parker.

337

"The matter has been handled. JP"

"What's handled, Billie?"

Parker had a bad feeling about what Billie had gotten into.

"Thompson's not going to testify."

"Is Pimentel putting a hit on her for the Red Dawn trouble she created?"

"No. Just the opposite. He's going to leave her alone as long as she takes a plea deal and never testifies."

"Billie, what did you promise Pimentel? This is deep water."

"He wants the coalition. The cartel will run the coalition. They'll decide who makes a crossin' and when they happen."

"Billie, you can't let them take that from you."

"I don't have no choice. I let them run with it, and they'll allow the medical supplies to come in. I don't, and everyone down there who's helped me and Armando and Miguel is toast. They done sent me pictures of my place. They're already here."

"Does Miguel know?"

"No, he don't. I'm in a real cross here."

"There was more to the meetup with Carmen down there, wasn't there?" Parker asked.

She nodded. "Carmen was anglin' to push Joaquin out of power. Red Dawn knew where the cartel was soft and them mercenaries would go after the labs and storage facilities. When I met with her at the airport, she was scared. Joaquin found out she'd played him. She needed a way out of the country without him findin' out."

"You smuggled her over the border?"

She bobbed her head. "Then she done what she did in Fountain Hills. Nathan, I swear to God, I didn't know she'd go there. What she did to Linda—I'm to blame."

"Not even a little. Carmen's entire scheme was unraveling, and she needed to get Ridler before he turned it against her."

Billie scuffed the kitchen tile with the toe of her worn Converse sneaker.

"She said somethin' when she handed me this." Billie held a plastic baggie with a brass rifle shell inside. "Carmen said this would be enough to put

Thompson away."

Parker took the baggie from Billie. Carmen always played a game where she was several moves ahead.

"Don't do anything yet. I might have a way out. I need you to do something…"

Chapter Seventy-One

Three days later, Parker made an unscheduled visit to Larry Sutton's office and caught the man getting out of his Bentley in the garage. "We need to talk, Counselor."

"Detective, what's burdening your soul?"

Parker pointed to the Bentley. "Your office."

The attorney shrugged and headed back to the car, using his key fob to unlock the doors.

They both slid into the rear compartment.

"I need to speak to your boss. Get him on the video."

"I don't know if I can.

"Just do it, Sutton."

"Red Dawn pushed him out of his estate in Hermosillo. Killed dozens of his people. He's on the run."

"Try it."

Sutton shrugged. He turned on the satellite connection. A few seconds elapsed, and a grainy feed popped up on the screen.

It wasn't Joaquin Pimentel. It was a cell phone video featuring Esteban Castaneda from deep within the Supermax prison.

"You look surprised to see me, detective."

"Not really. I figured Carmen was running the operations out here in your name. It had the same stink as Los Muertos," Parker said.

Sutton butted in. "What's happened to Joaquin?"

The attorney was more than worried about billable hours here. He didn't want to be connected with Esteban and Los Muertos.

"There's been a change in leadership. You'll work for me now."

"The hell I will," Sutton said.

"I want Carmen released immediately," Castaneda said.

"Not happening," Parker said.

"Then Carmen will testify your friend Billie Carson is in possession of the weapon used against your detective. Think about it. One or the other. Someone's going to prison for the shooting. You know you want Agent Thompson to go down for what she did."

Parker fished a small plastic baggie from his pocket.

"You mean this evidence? The spent shell casing? Thompson's prints aren't on it."

Parker pulled up the forensic report with DNA and prints that didn't match the former FBI agent.

Castaneda stared into his small phone screen.

"You're faking it. You couldn't risk blowing up the case against Thompson. She shot your detective."

"No, she didn't."

The cellphone flickered dark for a moment while Castaneda moved to the back of his cell.

"I know Carmen took the shot."

"You have no proof, and Thompson will walk."

"She ain't walking. We have her dead to rights on arson and attempted murder for the coalition bombing. She's history, even if the feds can't nail her for killing her own team. As far as Carmen goes—she gave Billie the rifle she claimed Thompson used. Thompson's DNA won't be on it will they? But Carmen's will."

"I will end you," he said with spittle, landing on the cell phone screen.

"Doubtful. You know I heard there are Sinaloa members loyal to Joaquin out there—in fact, you'll be housed next to one in about ten minutes. I called the prison…"

"You bastard!"

The metallic clank of the cell door opened, and a correctional officer with a Lexan shield rushed in and pinned Castaneda to the back wall of the cell.

Three more correctional officers filled the screen.

"I may have told them you had a weapon."

The cell phone connection ended.

Sutton shut down the video feed.

"What are you going to do without your southern client?" Parker asked.

"Breathe without looking over my shoulder. I've been looking for a way out for a long time. I should thank you, Detective."

"Thank me by not drawing Pete Tully into your shit. He's a good man, and I think he'll make a good PI. You screw him and you'll wish you were sharing a cell with Castaneda."

"Maybe I should have him start with cases dealing with threats from police officers."

Parker opened the door, stepped from the vehicle, looked back inside, and said. "If Pimentel does reach out, don't take the call."

Waiting in his SUV, Billie nervously nibbled on a thumbnail. She stiffened when Parker got back behind the wheel.

"Is it done?"

"It was Castaneda—the connection between him and Carmen—Coyote Wash—all of it. It was too much."

"What about Joaquin? The coalition?"

"Carmen never had a chance to pass the deal onto him. It wasn't his idea. The text —that wasn't Joaquin. It was Castaneda. He was trying to get to you and the coalition. It's over."

"Over—over? Like, I don't have to give up the coalition?"

"All yours."

"If the cartel is out of the play—it means Red Dawn is left in charge. People down there tell me they're settin' up camp in the cartel's place. Lots of guns coming in. I don't like what they're tellin' me."

"Only one reason they'd be bringing that much firepower into their new territory—they aren't done yet. Maybe Ridler wasn't running it, but he gave birth to it. Gave it a place to breed. He'll carry that stain with him—sins of the father."

He started the SUV, glanced at the rifle in the back seat. "Come on, Billie, let's get this booked into evidence the right way."

As he adjusted the seatbelt. It rubbed on a small jewelry box in his pocket, one containing his mother's engagement ring.

Acknowledgments

Sins of the Father is a work of fiction. However, the opening chapters of the book were heavily drawn from actual crimes which took place while I was working in the prison system. A pair of drug dealers strangled and tossed a San Juan Capistrano man from a plane into the ocean hoping to evade capture. I remember how the family of the dead man felt in the years after his death while the legal battles dragged on. The killers were convicted, but the toll it took on everyone involved was devastating. I employed some creative license and rather than the ocean, our first victim is dropped in the desert, not to hide it, but to make a statement. I experienced another crime phenomenon back then—those who crossed a drug dealer or gang shot caller were dealt with harshly. A surprising number ended up murdered and their bodies burned in the Southern California desert. Combined, these crimes provided a foundation for Sins of the Father.

Writing is a solitary endeavor, but can't be completed alone. I'm forever grateful to my editor Shawn Reilly Simmons at Level Best Books. Shawn is an amazing human and I absolutely love working with her. She's helped bring this series to life and I'm proud to call her my friend. Kudos to Verena Rose and Deb Well at Level Best for keeping the wheels moving.

The book community is incredible, and I appreciate the support of independent bookstores like the Raven Award winning Face in a Book (Tina Ferguson and Janis Herbert) and Book Passage (Kathy Petrocelli and Luisa Smith) They make a bookstore feel like home. Mystery Writers of America, International Thriller Writers, and Sisters in Crime are an amazing support network and if you're in this world, go find your people there.

Sometimes it's words of encouragement, or a kick in the butt that came when they were most needed. J.T. Ellison, Wendall Thomas, Karen Dionne,

Lou Berney, Baron Birtcher, Matt Coyle, Reed Farrel Coleman, Pam Stack, and Bruce Robert Coffin. I thank you for your support. A special shout out to my two a.m. ThrillerFest road crew.

Thanks to my kids, Jessica, and to Michael—I love you guys.

I wasn't always alone at the keyboard, and I owe Emma and Bryn the Corgis extra treats for all the plot points they helped me work through on countless walks. The book would have been done a month earlier if not for their constant demands.

A special thank you to Ann-Marie L'Etoile for tolerating my nonsense over the years. You let me disappear behind my keyboard and still love me when I come up for air. Love you back.

And finally, thanks to you, dear reader. It's only possible because of you.

About the Author

James L'Etoile uses his twenty-nine years behind bars as an influence in his award-winning novels, short stories, and screenplays. He is a former associate warden in a maximum-security prison, a hostage negotiator, and director of California's state parole system. His novels have been shortlisted or awarded the Lefty, Anthony, Silver Falchion, and the Public Safety Writers Award. *Sins of the Father* and *River of Lies* are his most recent novels. Look for *Illusion of Truth* coming soon. You can find out more at www.jamesletoile.com

AUTHOR WEBSITE:
https://www.jamesletoile.com

SOCIAL MEDIA HANDLES:
https://www.facebook.com/authorjamesletoile
https://www.twitter.com/jamesletoile
https://www.instagram.com/authorjamesletoile
https://www.goodreads.com/author/show/7076886.James_L_Etoile
https://www.threads.com/authorjamesletoile

Also by James L'Etoile

River of Lies

Served Cold

Face of Greed

Devil Within

Dead Drop

Black Label

Bury the Past

At What Cost

Little River

www.ingramcontent.com/pod-product-compliance
Lightning Source LLC
Chambersburg PA
CBHW021454110726
47899CB00001BA/159